DISENCHANTED

BOOK ONE IN THE DISENCHANTED SERIES

ARIELLE SNOW

ISBN 979-8-9896994-0-7 (paperback edition)
ISBN 979-8-9896994-1-4 (hardback edition)
ISBN 979-8-9896994-2-1 (E-book)

Book Cover by GetCovers
Print book formatted by Jen Houser at Painted Wings Publishing
Page edges by Painted Wings Publishing
Ebook formatted by Heather Creeden at CreedReads
Edited by Heather Creeden, CreedReads; Dawn Yacovetta; Emily Lawrence, Lawrence Editing

1rst edition 2024

To my loving family (who had no idea I was even writing a book), you make my life enchanting every single day. To my loyal pets who always kept me company while I wrote, no matter what time of day or night it was. And to the readers who still believe in magic.

CONTENT WARNINGS/TRIGGERS

Please be advised that while much of this story takes place in a fairytale realm, *Disenchanted* is an adult fantasy fiction novel, and there are a few darker elements to be aware of that some readers may find distressing. This includes murder, attempted sexual assault, blood, violence, some nightmare imagery, some sexual content, and strong language.

BOOK ONE IN THE DISENCHANTED SERIES

DISENCHANTED

ARIELLE SNOW

FROZEN SEA
WHISPERING WOODS
FROSTMEADOW
RAVEN VALLEY
WILLOWBROOK
MYSTIC VILLAGE
DARK HARBOR ISLE
MYSTIC GROVE
EMPIRE ISLES
SHADOW RIDGE
SIREN FALLS
HIDDEN HOLLOW
MISTY SEA
NEVERLAND LAGOON
IVORY SEA
RAINBOW REEF
CASTLEBERRY
CLOUDBAY CANYON
EMERALD FOREST
WOODMIST
FOXWICK
FABLE ISLES
EVERGREEN ISLES

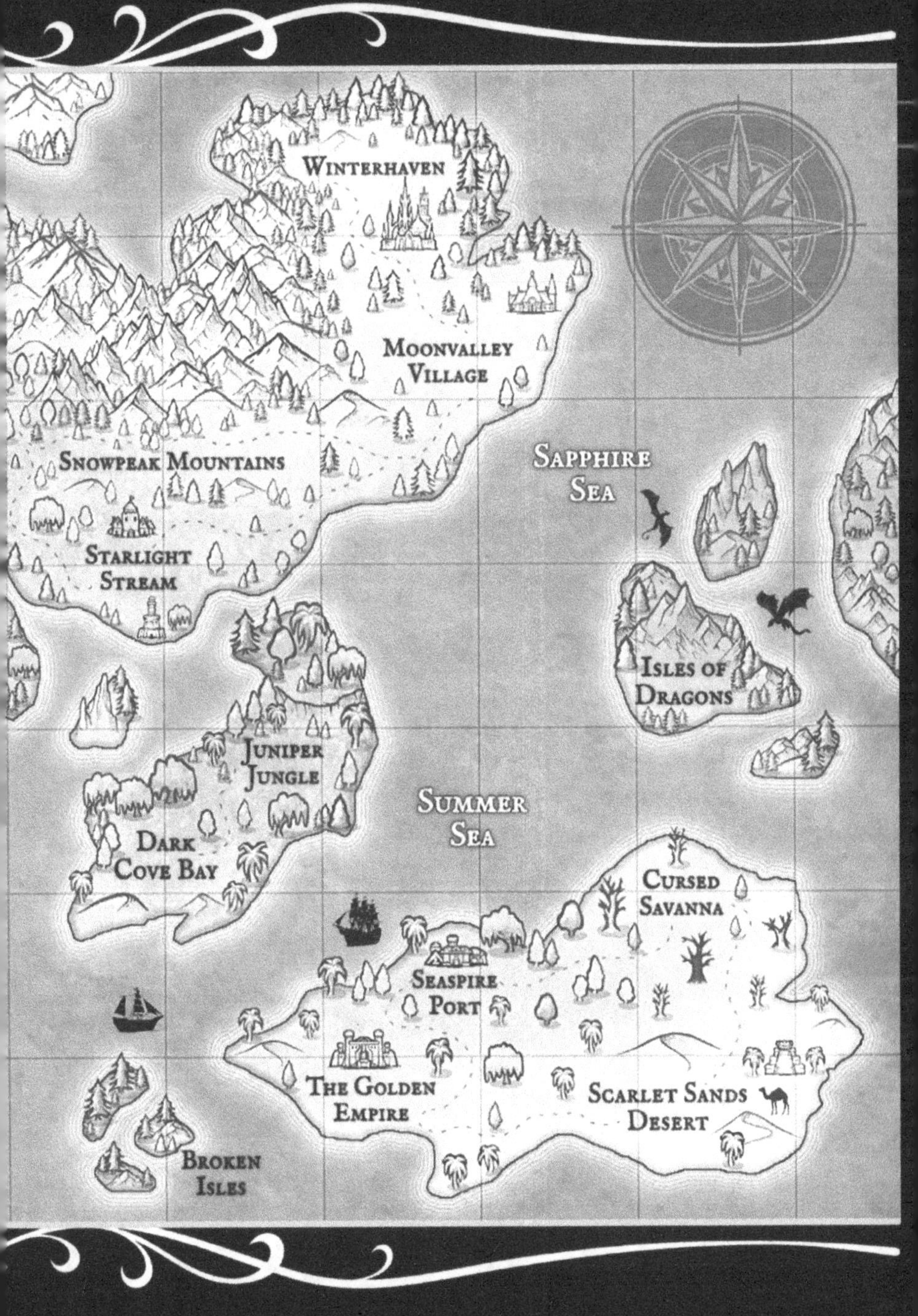

WINTERHAVEN
MOONVALLEY VILLAGE
SAPPHIRE SEA
SNOWPEAK MOUNTAINS
STARLIGHT STREAM
ISLES OF DRAGONS
JUNIPER JUNGLE
SUMMER SEA
DARK COVE BAY
CURSED SAVANNA
SEASPIRE PORT
THE GOLDEN EMPIRE
SCARLET SANDS DESERT
BROKEN ISLES

PROLOGUE

Since the dawn of our childhoods, remarkable stories of legends and fantasies have been etched into our very essence. These tales came to life every night when the sun dipped down to make way for lilac-brushed skies, and the fireflies would wake to dance outside our bedroom windows. Tales with words so masterfully woven, they pieced together parts of our soul that were still undiscovered.

We didn't know it back then—the power of it all. We only knew how it felt to tightly cling to our last remaining bits of sensibility before surrendering ourselves over to sleep and the way it felt to rest in the safe embrace of our parents as they whispered of fantastical worlds filled with imagination, love, and adventure.

As we drifted between states of consciousness, visions of noble princes and beautiful princesses swirled through our dreams. We were transported to mesmerizing lands full of magic. These places presented us with enchanting escapes from our own realities where anything and everything could happen, and we were free to be anything we wanted to be.

These were the stories that helped shape us. They made us believe that we had the power to proclaim our own destinies. They reminded us to always take leaps of faith and to believe that good would always prevail over evil. Most of all, they fooled us into always having hope that everything would work out in the end.

As we grew up, we gradually let go of these childish notions. Our imaginations grew dimmer underneath the harsh light of the real world. It's easier to believe in the wildly impossible when you're young...when the burden of time and experience hasn't yet had a chance to erode the spirit.

But have you ever just stopped to wonder how these stories came to be? They must have originated from somewhere. Generations upon generations have shared these tales, passing them down for hundreds of years. They've stood the test of time, altered perspectives, offered glimpses of life lessons, and represented a solid moral compass.

But what if...somewhere down the line...the narratives got twisted? There's bound to be a margin of error embedded in a period consisting of centuries, right? What if essential details, or even characters, had been left out or forgotten altogether? What if the stories we were always told weren't the ones that actually happened? What if...we've been wrong all along? Would knowing the truth even matter? It isn't like it would alter our lives now.

After all, real life isn't a fairytale.

CHAPTER ONE

The impact of my fury stung my hands as I shoved the gaudy glass-paned door out of the way. It rattled violently in return as it bounced on its hinges, colliding with the brick wall behind it before reluctantly falling back into place.

Nearly stumbling off the sidewalk as a rush of people stormed by, I stole a quick glance down at my palms to ensure they weren't bleeding. My head was pounding, and I wasn't sure if it was from the ear-splitting music, the flashing blacklights, or...

"Gwen, wait up!" The noise roared back to life around me as Jacob emerged from the crowded building, fumbling with the newly defective door.

"Leave me alone, Jacob." My voice betrayed me with a regrettable tremble as I began to march away in a show of defiance.

"Gwen! Come on, would you just stop?" he yelled after me, ignoring the sea of blurry, baffled looks from the spectators as we raced by.

His pleas faded slightly under the sound of my heels clacking against the pavement. My feet were killing me, but not enough to slow me down. I was more than eager to get back to my little apartment, lock the world outside, and put this night behind me.

"Gwen!" His voice rang out again as he shuffled behind me obediently, and I couldn't contain the eye roll that it induced. Why couldn't he just take a hint and go away already?

"Come on, baby," he pleaded, twisting his fingers around my wrist as he spun me around to face him. "Why are you acting like this?"

"Let go of me!" I jerked my arm away. The gesture was so careless, so sudden; it left him no time to mask his shock.

"If you would just stop and talk to me like an adult—" His thick brows furrowed together as a mix of anger and confusion darkened his round features.

"Like an adult?" I sputtered back. "You've really got some nerve, Jacob Jenson. You haven't bothered acting like an adult the entire time I've known you."

His petulant brown eyes flinched as though I'd deeply wounded him. But I knew Jacob, and I knew that fractured look was fleeting…just as I knew I would inevitably be forced to shoulder the responsibility he would refuse to take in this dispute.

"Come on, Gwen, don't say things you will regret later. You've got everything all wrong. I've told you over and over again that nothing was going on with Holly, and I meant it." He pulled me in close again, more cautiously this time. "Nothing happened tonight or will ever happen again."

The amber glow from the streetlights fluttered across his boyish face, revealing a hint of sincerity. I considered yielding for half a second before I felt my jaw clench in protest. Jacob always did this. He always disregarded my outrage when I had a valid reason for being upset. And over the last couple of years, he'd given me plenty of valid reasons. I had no intention of letting him off the hook so easily this time.

"Then explain to me why Holly showed up here tonight. I walked away for two seconds, Jacob. Two seconds. That's all it took. And she was hanging all over you!" I'd seen the way Holly had her arms tightly wound around his body...much like a snake who was about to crush the bones of an unsuspecting meal just before devouring it whole.

If it had just been that, I probably would have been able to let it go. But I'd also seen the sickening way Jacob's eyes lifted when he realized she was beside him and the smug smile that lingered on his face as he leaned down to embrace her like a close friend. Mentally recounting the events felt like pouring fuel on a wildfire. I was livid, and everyone within a five-mile radius of this city street knew it.

"You've got to be kidding me, Gwen!" Jacob huffed in disbelief as he ran his hands through his short sandy hair in exasperation. "I did not invite her out here tonight. I can't help that she showed up."

I pulled my cardigan closer to my chest as a chilly burst of late October air made me wince. The leaves from the city park across the street took flight, scattering specks of brilliant autumn hues all around us. If only there were a gust strong enough to blow me away from this conversation.

"I just..." I paused, allowing a moment to collect myself. "I can't do this right now. Or right here. I think I need some time away from you for a little while...to cool off. I don't want to think about it anymore tonight."

What was I saying right now? I only stopped to consider my words after they had been laid out between us.

I waited for Jacob's opposition, but he simply sighed as he stuffed his hands into the pockets of his jeans and nodded reluctantly. "If that's what you want."

I stared up silently at his solemn expression as an internal battle raged. What *did* I want? I wasn't even exactly sure of that myself.

"But I can't let you walk the streets alone, Gwen," he proclaimed. "You're drunk."

"I am not drunk!" I fiercely stammered, brushing the long, dark locks of windblown hair away from my eyes. "I only had enough time for two drinks before your ex showed up and started flinging herself at you."

Maybe I was being a bit dramatic, but it was my birthday after all. That, and for argument's sake, I might have slightly lied about the number of alcoholic beverages I had consumed.

"Why don't we just go back?" Jacob pulled out his phone from his pocket, and a photo of us smiling on his lock screen flashed across my peripheral. "It's only ten o'clock. You've still got two hours of birthday left."

I hadn't even wanted to go out tonight in the first place. I wanted to stay home and order a pizza, but Jacob insisted this would be a more exciting way to celebrate. He was wrong.

"And I'd prefer not to spend them watching Holly visually assault you."

"How would you rather spend them then?" Jacob's dimpled, sly smile alluded to what he always wanted.

His sheer audacity was enough to make me contemplate his murder, but there were simply too many witnesses out here to harp on that thought for too long. "Are you fucking kidding me, Jacob?" I was not in the mood for him right now...in any form.

"You're so tense, babe. I'd hate to let your birthday go to waste." He brushed his hands against my shoulders before reaching up to tuck another piece of my unruly hair back into place. The suggestion in his eyes was enough to tell me that he cared nothing about the entire war of words that had just spilled out here between us in the middle of the sidewalk. "You know I could make you feel better."

It was exactly what I should have expected from him, and somehow, the fact of knowing that only made me angrier.

"You're unbelievable. Really fucking unbelievable," I scoffed, rolling my eyes as I turned away sharply and headed straight for my building.

"All right, fine," Jacob conceded from somewhere behind me. "But you're still not walking alone." The scorned echo of his footsteps trailed behind me diligently.

"Back already, Gwen?" My roommate's voice called out from the kitchen.

I clicked the lock of the door more aggressively than necessary, hoping it would deter Jacob from having any delusional thoughts of knocking and trying to worm his way inside.

"Hey, Bree. How was work?" I muttered, plopping down at the little kitchen table across from her.

She took a sip of her tea as she studied me carefully. "Bad night?"

"You could say that." I cradled my face in my hands, recounting all the grisly details to my best friend.

"Yikes, I'm sorry, hon. That sounds rough." Bree winced in response as she combed her fingers through her silky raven hair, inadvertently shuffling the layered pieces to perfectly frame her caramel-colored face.

"This wasn't exactly how I pictured my birthday going," I whined, feeling a little more sober now.

"I'd be upset, too." She nodded in solidarity. "I'm sorry that your night was ruined."

"Well, to be fair, it was ruined when I found out we were going to a bar and then, once again, when you said you weren't coming."

A wary smile crept across her face. "You told me not to come, remember? But if I knew it was going to be so eventful, I would have asked for the night off."

Bree was a waitress at a popular little restaurant called Nightingales down the street from our apartment. She'd been picking up extra hours over the past few months to save up some money, and it didn't feel right to ask her to trade that in solely to drag her to the bar with me. She wasn't the type of person who frequented those kinds of places, something I could relate to since I had never been either...until I'd started dating Jacob anyway.

"And you know I don't have to tell you how I feel about Jacob." She picked up her mug and attempted to conceal her smirk as she took a sip.

I shot a cynical look in her direction. "I think you've made yourself quite clear on how you feel about that." I sighed in defeat. "Truth be told, I'm starting to think I should have taken your advice."

"You'll learn one day."

"I don't even know if we're still together. I mean, I guess we are. He followed me home...and he seemed fine, but I told him I needed some space to think."

"Do you *want* to be together?" She eyed me suspiciously.

That was the million-dollar question. And the answer often varied depending on the day. Today was not a good day. "Some days yes, some days no." I shrugged at the admission. "Don't get me wrong, I love him. I do. It just feels like there's always something going on, and it tends to complicate things."

Jacob and I had certainly had our fair share of arguments over the span of our relationship. Mainly ones surrounding his lack of commitment and his incessant need to surround himself with people who shared that problematic trait. I didn't ask for much besides loyalty, but even that had proved to be a line I'd drawn too shallow in the sand.

One that had been blurred from being stepped on too often until it was finally washed away completely by rising tides.

"Well, I hate to say it, but you knew that before you got involved. You just wouldn't listen to reason." Bree wasn't afraid to call me out on anything. I think that's why we got along so well. It was one of her most endearing qualities, despite how much it got under my skin at this exact moment.

"Can you stop being right about everything now?" I sulked.

"I'm sorry, Gwen, but sometimes you have to enforce tough love. I've tried to tolerate him for your sake. I've tried to see the good in him, but I just don't think there's much there to find."

"Jesus, Bree. He's not the devil."

She nearly spat out her drink as she coughed down a laugh. "That's debatable. I know it sounds harsh. I know you have feelings for him. And maybe, deep down...way deep down, he has some good qualities. But you and I both know the way he is. You know he strings girls along. He's always done it. He did it with Holly, and I'm scared he's doing it to you."

"But Holly—"

Bree lifted her hand, not allowing me any sort of opportunity to voice my excuses. "Yes, she's a horrible human being. But can you honestly blame her for everything? Can you honestly say that Jacob isn't at fault here at all? Do you really trust him not to cheat on you again with her?"

The consequential tone in her voice wasn't lost on me. "Remember when I asked you to stop being right?" I moaned.

I'd leaned on Bree in the past, perhaps a bit too heavily, to rant about Jacob and his betrayals more times than I could count. But I'd told her about all the good times too, like the thoughtful ways he would surprise me out of the blue with fancy dinner dates and flowers...or when he took me ice skating in the city last year for Christmas because I'd mentioned in passing it was something I had always wanted to do. To the best of his abilities, I knew Jacob honestly tried to make me happy. Despite his regrettable indiscretions in the past, I didn't doubt that he loved me. Underneath it all, I knew Jacob had a good heart. It's what kept me tethered to him.

Bree, on the other hand, wasn't so quick to forgive. As far as she was concerned, the bad things he'd done significantly outweighed all of the good ones.

She set down her mug, pushed up the sleeves of her oversized sweatshirt, and gently took my hands from across the table. The apologetic look she wore made me worry about what was coming next.

"You haven't been happy for a while. Not truly. You've been with him for over two years, and things haven't gotten any better. He's still sneaking around. He's making you feel like the crazy one for questioning his loyalty when he has none to begin with, Gwen. What exactly is it that you are even trying to hold onto?"

I couldn't stop the sting from forming behind my eyes or the drops that escaped immediately after.

"I don't know," I quietly admitted. Except...if I let him go, I have *no one*. I have *nothing*. I shook away the intrusive thought. "I do love him."

"I know, but I don't want to see you get hurt anymore." She gave my hands a slight squeeze. "You're practically my sister, and I care about you. It shouldn't be this hard all the time."

I swiped at the corner of my eyes. "I guess I just always thought I'd be settled down by now. I keep getting older, and I'm not where I expected myself to be, you know?" My voice cracked at the admission. It was at this moment I realized I'd been dreading October 23rd all month long. I used to look forward to my birthday and to what the future held. Now though...now I was beginning to wonder if there was anything left to look forward to.

"I'm twenty-eight. I thought I'd be married by now, maybe even have a kid or two. But here I am, sitting at the kitchen table, complaining to you about these juvenile things like my boyfriend's ex-girlfriend crashing my birthday at a bar I didn't even want to be at."

Bree's dark brown eyes were soft and sympathetic. "You can't find and commit to someone who's actually worth committing to while you're still holding out hope for someone who isn't. You deserve to have all of the things you want, Gwen. You just need to let go of the things that no longer serve you first."

I knew that she was only trying to help. Bree would never intentionally hurt me. Nevertheless, her sharp words cut through my chest like tiny daggers.

"Why can't I just be like you and have my shit together?" I forced a smile, attempting to shift the conversation away from the despairing state of my relationship.

Her responding laugh broke through the heaviness in the air. "We all go about life at different paces." Bree leaned back in her chair and pressed the mug to her lips again, allowing me a silent sigh of relief in the newfound space. "And trust me, I've certainly had my share of bad boyfriends...like you wouldn't even believe," she huffed in amusement, rolling her eyes as she seemed to reminisce. "So, don't compare yourself to me or anyone else."

"What am I going to do when you leave?" I glanced around the room at all the stacked cardboard boxes. Bree was getting married in a couple of weeks and had already moved half of her belongings to her fiancé's house.

"I'm going to miss you too, Gwen." She smiled.

"You're lucky, Bree. Ryan is such a good guy. He's straight fairytale, prince charming material."

Bree snorted in amusement. "Well, I don't know about all of that."

"Please. The guy worships the ground you walk on. It's basically every girl's dream come true."

Bree pressed her lips together and lifted the mug back to her mouth to conceal her affirming smirk. She knew there was no point in even trying to deny it.

"Seriously though, I'm happy for you both, but I'd be lying if I said I wasn't a little sad too. I'm going to miss this. I'm going to miss you." I frowned at the thought.

Bree had moved to Raleigh a few years ago, just before I graduated. I had never been the type of person who had a lot of friends or made them easily, so when she approached me at the coffee shop one rainy afternoon, upset and asking for directions, I was surprised to find how effortlessly we had connected.

We kept in touch after that and started spending more time together over the summer. I'd shown her around and introduced her to a few of my old classmates, which is how she met Ryan. Months later, when she could no longer afford the rent for her first apartment, I invited her to stay with me for as long as she needed.

"As happy as I am to marry Ryan, I'm a little scared too. It's a strange feeling—knowing everything is about to change. And I doubt Ryan will be so eager to sit up with me until three a.m., binge-watching Christmas movies and eating extremely unhealthy amounts of pizza rolls."

"A favorite pastime, I must admit."

"The best." She chuckled.

"You know you can still come over anytime to watch Christmas movies and eat pizza rolls, even if it's in July. Just promise me that if it's at three a.m. and I'm asleep, you'll cook the food before you wake me up."

"Deal," she declared.

I forced out an unsteady laugh, trying not to dwell on how lonely the house already felt. "Oh!" Bree shouted as she lurched forward, nearly splattering her tea across the cream-colored wall behind her. "I almost forgot to tell you what I found out. You know how Ashton has been planning the bachelorette party?"

Ugh, Ashton. "Yep," I muttered, hoping the confirmation didn't sound as distasteful as it felt in my mouth.

It wasn't that I hadn't tried to give Ashton a chance; I had. She was just the type of person who thought that the world owed her something, and she didn't even try to pretend otherwise. Ashton had a way of looking at you—through you—that made you feel like the most inadequate person in existence.

I tried my best to steer clear of her...of course, it had been harder to do lately with Bree's upcoming nuptials. She'd shown up at our apartment not even twenty-four hours after Ryan had proposed to Bree with a binder full of outlandish plans and ideas. At the time, Bree was too flabbergasted to contest her input. From that day forward, Ashton had taken the reins and rode off into the sunset when it came to planning the wedding. Her pure entitlement to Bree's big day had only increased my initial aversion.

"Well, she was trying to keep it a secret, but I kind of overheard some fundamental details." A disturbing grin spread across her face.

"So, where's it going to be?" Knowing Ashton, somewhere overpriced and way too fancy for Bree's taste.

"The Renaissance Faire!" Bree could barely get the words out as she burst into laughter.

"What in the actual hell?" I blurted out.

"I know!" she squealed. "I didn't even know they had those things around here."

"I have so many questions. First of all, why would she think that would be a good place to have a bachelorette party? Is she aware of what a Renaissance Faire even is? And does she know there will be horse poop on the same ground that her precious feet will have to walk on? Dear God, what is happening?" My voice trailed off as I envisioned the inevitable train wreck.

Bree ignored my jabs. "I have no clue; I'm just glad I found out beforehand so I can work on my surprised face. How's this?" She mustered up a horrified expression.

"Yeah, you'll need to work on that some more."

"Oh my gosh, Gwen!" She grabbed both sides of her face dramatically and slumped down onto the table. "Why did I leave her in charge of this?"

I didn't bother saying that Ashton would have taken charge whether Bree allowed it or not. Bree already knew that.

"Look, she's clearly trying to throw you off the trail," I reassured. "Don't worry, we'll end up at a male strip club like every other normal Bachelorette party does."

"No way. Uh-uh, I told her absolutely no strip clubs," Bree asserted.

"Well, this is completely your fault then."

She suppressed another laugh as she took in my unfavorable expression. "It'll be interesting at any rate."

"Bree, is it too late to make up an excuse as to why I can't go? I think I feel a head cold coming on...it's definitely contagious. I wouldn't want to get the horses sick."

"Oh no, don't you even try pulling that one...I need you there for emotional support. You are going whether you like it or not, Gwendolyn Winters."

CHAPTER TWO

Clink Clink Clink

Ashton cleared her throat as she tapped her blood-red fingernails against the rim of her wineglass.

She waited until all our eyes were settled on her before she spoke again. "Ladies, I just want to say a few things before we get to where we're going today." Her shrill voice assaulted my ears even more than the dinnerware she'd been banging on.

We were all stuffed inside the limousine, headed to the top-secret bachelorette party location. Bree had been trying all day to act like she didn't know that location was, in fact, a traveling Renaissance Faire.

We'd researched it later that night when she had first told me about it, and it sounded even more dreadful than I'd previously imagined.

"Step back in time to experience a thrill like no other." Bree had read from the flashy website. "Visit our artisan marketplace, feast like royalty, and enjoy our theatrical entertainment where you can become a part of the show!"

"Dear God. Does it get any better?" I'd asked helplessly.

Bree had simply laughed at my anguish as she stretched out across her bed and continued reading from her laptop, "For our thrill seekers, we offer horseback riding, jousting shows, fortune-telling, and axe throwing!"

"Axe throwing!"

"That sounds hazardous," she'd said in between giggles.

"You know you're my best friend."

"Yes, and I fully understand that's the only reason you're going along with this," she'd replied with a sunny smile.

Ashton informed us before we left this morning not to worry about what we wore. I suppose that was because the horses wouldn't care.

"Bree, today we celebrate you. It is such an honor to be a part of your journey, and I know all these beautiful ladies in here feel the same way!" Ashton chuckled and looked around the car for approval. I forced a faint smile when her focus shifted to me.

Her long chestnut hair bounced flawlessly around her face as she gleamed at us from behind her fake eyelashes. Why anyone would need to wear fake eyelashes to a Renaissance Faire was beyond me.

"Here-here!" exclaimed Ashton's overly enthusiastic lackey, Heather, as she raised her glass in the air.

"Thank you, Ashton." Bree smiled sweetly.

For reasons unknown, Bree genuinely liked her. I suppose that was a good thing, considering Ashton was Ryan's sister, and she would have to endure her forever.

"We want you to know how extremely thrilled we are for you and Ryan. I am over the moon for my baby brother. He deserves all the happiness you've given him, and I can't tell you how excited I am to have you join our family." She swiped a hand across her face as though she were wiping a tear away before clasping her dry fingers together in her lap.

She always had a flair for being dramatic.

"That means more to me than you know." Bree gleamed at her future sister-in-law. "I can't wait to officially be a part of your family."

Ashton leaned across the car to embrace her with a smile plastered across her face that lacked any honest emotion. I averted my gaze from the cringe-inducing performance, only to accidentally lock eyes with Heather, who was genuinely on the verge of tears.

"I'm just so glad we were all able to get together today. I've got a lot of surprises up my sleeve!" Ashton cheerfully interjected.

Bree threw me a worried glance. She still hadn't perfected a convincing surprise face for when Ashton dropped the Renaissance bomb.

"Also, I know you all probably thought it was a little strange that I asked you not to get dressed up for the party, but trust me when I say there's a good reason for that!"

"So, when are you going to tell us?" The girl with the short, dirty blonde hair sitting across from me had only just met Ashton today, and I could already tell she wasn't impressed.

"Paige, is it?" Ashton asked, her fabricated smile still locked in place.

"I'm Sarah. That's Paige." She pointed to the girl sitting beside her.

Paige and Sarah were sisters who worked with Bree at Nightingales. I'd only met them a couple of times in passing before when I'd gone into the restaurant. In Ashton's defense, they did look very similar.

"Right, I'm sorry. I've just got so much on the brain!" Ashton threw her hands up as she forced out a high-pitched laugh.

"Yep." Sarah's tone was as indifferent as the expression she carried.

"Well, the reason I told you not to worry about it is because I've got all your outfits right here!" She pointed to several dress bags discreetly hanging up at the back of the car.

"What?" I sputtered.

"Yes, ladies! It's all taken care of. When we get there, you'll each get your own outfit. Heather and I will be helping each of you with your hair and makeup."

"Whoa-whoa-whoa. Wait a damn minute..." Sarah started.

"Now, I know that's a big surprise, but I promise it'll be totally fun and worth it!" Ashton interrupted.

Sarah's angular face crinkled in frustration, and she leaned up in her seat as though she were contemplating jumping across the car on top of Ashton. "I just don't know how I feel about having a makeover sprung on me like this," she said sharply.

"It'll be fine, Sarah," Paige whispered. "Just let it go."

I got the feeling Paige had to frequently calm Sarah down.

Bree leaned over and lowered her voice to a whisper. "Hey guys, I'm sorry. I know Ashton can come off a little harsh until you get to know her."

Bree's future sister-in-law was far too involved in her own conversation to even notice the exchange.

"I hope we aren't around her long enough for that," Sarah quipped, narrowing her eyes at Ashton as she laughed loudly with Heather. I couldn't help but fight off a slight smile. It was strangely validating to have an ally who was equally agitated by her theatrical antics.

"She's not so bad." Paige sounded like she was trying to convince herself.

"I'm just glad we're all here together. I don't want anything to ruin anyone's day," Bree smiled, but her words were strained. I could tell the sudden tension was making her uncomfortable.

"Nothing will ruin anyone's day," I reassured her. "That's something you don't have to worry about. Ashton's right, today we are celebrating you." I shot a quick glance at Sarah, who reluctantly nodded in agreement.

"Okay, girls." Ashton raised her voice, drawing the attention back to her. "I'm going to ask that as soon as we get out of the car, we quickly make our way into the welcome center. They've reserved a space for us to get ready."

As the car came to a stop, Paige squinted past the buildings and the trees to the colorful tents set up in the distance. "What's going on back there?"

"No need to worry about that yet. You'll find out soon enough!" Ashton replied as she opened the door.

"This is some ominous-sounding shit," Sarah said as she grumpily climbed out of the car.

"You have no idea," I muttered.

Once we had made it inside, Ashton dragged out all her costume bags. I was dreading the atrocities in there that awaited us. However, I was also a little eager to see Sarah's reaction.

"Before I unveil the outfits, I want to say that I considered all the usual bachelorette themes for Bree's party, but I felt like none of those truly fit her..." she began her tangent.

After her lips stopped moving, Ashton unzipped the largest bag and pulled out an exceptionally beautiful white dress donned with delicate lace flowers that flowed from the waistline to the floor. Tiny sequins sewn throughout the lace sparkled like diamonds as the fluorescent overhead light reflected against them. The off-shoulder sleeves mirrored the lace of the train and flared out near the hands. The medieval-inspired design was perfectly feminine and perfectly Bree.

"Oh my goodness," Bree whispered as she reached out to touch it.

"Isn't it beautiful!" Ashton squealed.

"It's the most beautiful dress I've ever seen," Bree exclaimed, ignoring the stream of tears that were now flowing freely down her face. "How did you...where did it..."

"Let's not dwell on all the details." Ashton smiled. "Here, go with Heather. She'll help you get changed."

As Ashton turned to unzip another bag, Heather and Bree disappeared into the dressing room.

"A bit extravagant for a Renaissance Faire," I whispered casually to myself.

Regret immediately set in as I heard Ashton gasp. She rushed over to me in a panic and pulled me into a quiet corner of the room away from everyone before I could fully process it.

"How'd you know?" She searched my face with eyes so wide I momentarily worried they might detach from her body.

My mind raced as I searched for a semi-reasonable excuse. "I, uh, saw the flyer the other day and figured it out when we saw the tents."

"Does Bree know?"

"No, I don't think so," I lied.

After her eyes rescinded back to their proper place, Ashton drew in a breath of relief. "Well, since the cat is out of the bag. I have a little something special planned. Some bridal photoshoots and such." She shrugged curiously and averted her gaze as she grabbed another dress bag.

I examined her skeptically, sensing something else was hidden behind her dodgy mannerisms. "You didn't just get that dress for a photo shoot, did you?"

Ashton bit her lip and sighed, visibly trying to decide how much information she was willing to divulge. "When Ryan told me he and Bree were going to get married at the courthouse, I just couldn't understand why anyone would want to do that. And then he told me she didn't even have a white dress to get married in!" Ashton's whispers grew faster and louder as she tried to explain herself.

It was true, Bree didn't have a "proper" wedding dress. I'd offered more than once to help her get one, but every time the topic came up, Bree would politely decline and insist she would wear something that she already owned. She just couldn't justify spending a lot of money on something that would only be worn once.

"Gwen, I just couldn't bear the thought of her not having something special for her special day." Ashton's body seemed to ease as the weight of her secret lifted away from her.

The confession took me by surprise, almost as much as the way she'd briefly allowed her social mask to fall as she spoke to me candidly. "That was actually very nice of you, Ashton," I finally admitted.

"You don't think she will be upset, do you?"

I shook my head. "No, I don't think so. In fact, I think it will mean the world to her."

"Good, I didn't want to overstep, but I couldn't let her go down the aisle in some store-brand maxi dress!"

"The horror."

"Exactly! And so, when I saw it, I instantly thought of her. It just screamed Bree!" She threw her hands up for added demonstration.

I couldn't argue with her there. If I had to pick a wedding dress for Bree, it would be next to impossible to find anything that topped the one Ashton had brought with her today. "It really does. It's a beautiful dress."

"Ahem," Heather's voice cut through the noise as we all turned our heads to face her.

Bree stood across the room, looking otherworldly as she waited for a collective reaction. Her smile stretched as far as it could manage, and her copper-toned cheeks were glowing even brighter than the glittering dress.

She could barely contain her enthusiasm as our eyes went wide. Heather positioned a tiny tiara on her head and shuffled Bree's dark, loose curls around it. Bree had always been painfully beautiful, but seeing her like this, like she was some sort of mythical goddess who stepped down from the heavens to grace us with her presence, it was almost too much to comprehend.

"Bree, holy shit!" Sarah exclaimed. "You look gorgeous!"

"So stunning," Paige chimed in.

"Ashton, I can't believe you got this for me." Bree approached her for a hug.

"When I saw it, I just had to get it for you. I was hoping you'd love it as much as I did, but if you don't, please tell me. I promise I won't be offended."

"No...no! I love it." Bree looked down at the dress as she twirled. "It's absolutely perfect."

"I was thinking we could take some bridal pictures of you wearing it today," Ashton suggested. "And if you decide that you still like it, you can wear it when you marry my brother. Because every girl deserves to feel like a princess on her wedding day!"

"I certainly feel like a princess." She dabbed a tissue to her eyes. "More so than I could have ever imagined."

"Whew! Okay! Enough with these waterworks! At this rate, we are all going to ruin our makeup!" Ashton laughed as she grabbed a tissue from Heather, who was waiting on standby. "Let's get everyone else ready so we can get these pictures done!"

As the other girls found their dress bags and disappeared, I took hold of Bree's hands and pulled her to the side.

"I think I was wrong about Ashton," I admitted.

Bree chuckled. "I can't believe she did this. I know I said I didn't want a real wedding dress, but this one is..."

"It was made for you." I nodded. "You look absolutely beautiful, and Ryan is going to lose his ever-loving mind when he sees you. Hell, he will probably pass out."

"I can only hope so!" She laughed. "But he better say 'I do' first!"

After making my way into the changing room, I took a deep breath before pulling my own dress out. It was more elegant than anything I'd ever owned. The flowy, floor-length gown was covered with sparkling flower embellishments. It was light blue—my favorite color. I wondered if Ashton knew that or if it was just a lucky guess.

A knock sounded at the door and Heather popped her head into the room before giving me time to adequately respond.

"It's just me," she chirped. "Do you some need help?"

"Sure."

She waited for me to pull the garment over my head before stepping to my side and tugging up the zipper. I leaned down to straighten out the bottom of the dress before turning to face the mirror. The color accentuated my sky-blue eyes, making them appear even icier than usual.

I unleashed my hair from the high ponytail I'd pulled it into earlier, allowing the unruly chocolate brown waves to cascade down past my shoulders.

"Do you want me to help you with your hair? We could do a side braid. It would be gorgeous with the one-shoulder design."

"Uh...sure." I complied, still filing my fingers through the residual tangles. "Thanks, Heather."

She smiled in return and went to work, twisting the strands and letting a few wispy pieces fall around my face.

"Gwen?" she said timidly when she was nearly finished. "I was really sorry to hear about you and Jacob."

The mention of Jacob's name made my heart skip a beat. My eyes flickered up to meet hers in the mirror. "Sorry? What'd you hear?"

"That you'd broken up."

"Oh…" My breath caught in my throat as the blunt tone of her words hit their mark. "Well. I wouldn't say that we broke up, technically…" I stammered, unsure of the direction I wanted to take this conversation. "We just had a fight."

"He told Holly that you broke up with him."

"He what?" I had nearly forgotten that Heather and Holly ran in the same crowd sometimes.

She tied off the bottom of the braid. "When he came back to the bar that night."

"He went back?"

"Yeah. He didn't stay very long, though."

"Did Holly leave with him?" The question was nearly inaudible over the profanities that were soaring through my mind. My cheeks were growing hotter by the second, and I knew the rage that was boiling inside was evident all over my face.

"Oh God no. Holly is over him. You don't have to worry about that."

"Great. Thank you, Heather. That makes me feel a lot better." The sarcasm dripped like venom, stinging my mouth as I uttered the words.

"How's that?" She gestured back toward the mirror before draping the braid over the front of my shoulder.

I barely even looked at it. It could have been a unicorn horn for all I cared. "That looks nice." I forced a hard smile back at her reflection. Her revelation was still too fresh for me to focus on anything else right now.

"I'm going to go see if Ashton needs any more help. Then we should be ready to hit the festival!"

"Sounds great," I lied.

Heather let the door fall shut behind her, and I found myself facing the mirror once again, thinking about Jacob and how much time I'd have to serve if I ran over him with my car. The conversation from that night replayed in my head, urging me to contemplate my next move. I'd said I needed space to cool off, but Jacob took that statement and ran with it...all the way back to the bar to tell Holly. Out of all the things he could have done, why did he pick the one that he knew would infuriate me the most?

He hadn't even tried to call me these past few days, but that wasn't entirely out of character for him following a big fight. Regardless, there was no good reason for him to tell Holly our personal business, and no amount of consideration would convince me otherwise. All I knew was our relationship was starting to feel more like a chess game these days, and I was more of a Scrabble girl myself.

I needed some clarity. I needed to know what my next move should be. But to determine that, I first needed to know where his head was. But that would have to wait. This wasn't my day, and it sure as hell wasn't Jacob's day. This was Bree's day, and I couldn't allow myself to be upset about this right now.

I straightened out my dress once more before taking a deep breath and walking back out to meet everyone.

"Before we go, I have something I want to give each of you." Bree picked up her oversized purse and pulled out several tiny gift bags with our names written neatly on them. She handed them all out, one by one. Mine was last.

"This one is special," she said softly as she handed it over and waited eagerly for me to open it.

I reached down and pulled out a small white box with a necklace strapped inside.

"Oh, it's so pretty, Bree," I said as I held up the shiny silver crescent moon before letting my eyes fall to the hypnotic sapphire jewel that dangled in the center.

"I've had this forever; it was my favorite necklace."

I lifted my gaze to her wistful face. "Why are you giving it to me?"

Bree's eyes grew misty. "Because...it brought me good luck. I know that sounds a bit crazy, but I truly believe it did. My dad gave it to me when I was a little girl." She smiled as she reached out to cup the tiny moon in her hand. "He used to say it was a reminder that, even on the darkest nights, there's always still a little bit of light."

I clenched the chain in my hand and tried to hand it back to her. "Bree, I can't take this. It's too important to you."

Bree had never talked much about her parents, but I knew her father had passed away several years ago. She moved away from home shortly after that. Her mother, from what I gathered, had never been in her life. I didn't pry too much, considering my own parental issues weren't in short supply. I knew all too well the sting of those questions and was careful not to inflict that pain on others.

"Gwen. Please. I know you're going through a bit of a dark time. If there's any chance it'll bring you some light, I want you to have it."

"Bree..."

"Please."

"Thank you, Bree." I sighed in defeat as I hooked it around my neck. "I suppose I'll take all the good luck I can get."

"That's the spirit." She smiled graciously.

"Okay, girls, we are going to make our way over by the lake for a few pictures before we hit the festival," Ashton ordered.

By now, everyone was in on the Renaissance Faire plan and surprisingly seemed excited about it. We all lined up beside Bree in front of a photographer who was waiting for us outside. All our dresses were outfitted in different shades of blues and purples, Bree's wedding colors. We struck all the typical bridesmaid poses in front of the large flower garden outside the welcome center.

"All right, ladies, you're doing a great job. Now I'd like to have you go over there and do a few more poses by the gazebo," the photographer instructed after several minutes before pointing to a location behind us.

As we turned, a wave of instrumental music began to play. In the midst of all the commotion, I noticed Ashton's unusual expression. I followed her focus to the gazebo and saw Ryan waiting with an enormous smile extended across his face. He was wearing a suit and tie, and he was surrounded by several other similarly dressed men.

Bree nearly doubled over when she realized he was there and began to weep. Ryan rushed over from the gazebo and picked her up in a tight embrace.

"Bree, I don't want to wait another day to marry you," he exclaimed as he gently placed her back down in front of him.

Bree looked back at Ashton, instantly understanding that this had been the plan all along.

"Like I said, every girl deserves to feel like a princess on her wedding day." She smiled.

Between gasps of tears and laughter, Bree vigorously wiped her eyes as she tried to compose herself. "I just can't believe this."

Ryan lifted her face to meet his and wiped her tears away before planting a kiss on her lips.

"So, what do you say?" he asked. "Will you make me the happiest man in the world and marry me right here, right now?"

Bree nodded as she threw her arms around him. "I love you so much."

CHAPTER THREE

The wedding was exquisite. Standing in front of the gazebo, under the canopy of a dozen oak trees draped in Spanish moss, Bree and Ryan tearfully exchanged their wedding vows. We stood alongside her in our apparent bridesmaid's dresses as Ryan's groomsmen stood across from us. I wondered if they, too, had been blindsided by the pop-up wedding. A decent number of guests had shown up, mainly Ryan's large family. Obviously, this event had been in the works for quite some time.

After Ryan and Bree were pronounced husband and wife, we all migrated toward the woods, strolling down a well-beaten path that led to the realm of the Renaissance Faire.

"I still can't believe that just actually happened," I said to Sarah as we trudged through the thickest part of the forest.

The cheers and chants from the colorful tents up ahead grew louder with each new step.

"And you didn't know anything about it?" Sarah seemed just as astonished as I was about the whole ordeal.

"I had absolutely no idea."

"You know that Ashton might not be as dense as I thought she was," Sarah admitted with a laugh.

"I suppose we must give credit where credit is due," I agreed.

We passed by the first tent, and I nearly screamed when a flamboyant man dressed in full Renaissance attire came barreling out after us. "Hello, weary travelers! Welcome to the Sherwood Renaissance Faire!"

Sarah already had her fists balled up in response to the jump scare, "Dude, what the hell was that about? You can't just be charging out of tents and shouting at unsuspecting people!"

He laughed jovially, ignoring her violent stance. "My sincerest apologies, madam!" He bowed and tipped his feathered hat. "What brings ye fair maidens my way on this lovely fall day?"

"We have just attended a beautiful wedding!" Ashton beamed as she caught up to us.

"Ahhh, how marvelous!" He clapped his hands and spun around. "What a joyous occasion indeed! Come grab some spirits, and let us celebrate the nuptials!"

A few hours and a few drinks later, Bree and Ryan had left to go on the honeymoon he had secretly booked. As night settled in over the festival, slowly draining the color from the neon sunset, the temperatures began to dip. Not even the alcohol running through my veins was enough to shield me from periodically shivering underneath the crisp autumn air.

I'd danced until my feet hurt with the other girls and even a couple of the groomsmen. As I sat down at the table to rest for a moment, I remembered that I hadn't thought much about Jacob since Heather had informed me I was newly single. Thoughts of him began to consume me all at once. Should I call him? Would he call me? Should I act like we were still together? Should I ask him why he went back to the club? God. Why was this always so difficult?

"Gwen!" His voice rattled through my brain.

"Psstt! Gwen!" I heard again. I looked around suspiciously, halfway beginning to wonder if I was losing my mind.

Then, there he was. Wading through the herds of decked-out Renaissance dancers, a casually dressed Jacob was making his way over to me.

"Jacob? What are you doing here?" I asked, confused as he pulled out the seat beside me.

"I could ask you the same." He looked around, locking his eyes on a group of drunk, dancing knights.

"It's a long story. I sort of ended up being a bridesmaid at Bree's surprise wedding today—"

"I'm just messing with you." Jacob chuckled at his own response as he scooted his chair closer to mine. "Heather told me."

"You talked to Heather?" I guess I shouldn't be surprised.

"Yeah, and she told me that you said we weren't broken up. Gwen, I thought that's what you meant when you said you wanted space. That's why I haven't called you. It's killed me not to, but I didn't want to push my luck." He placed his hand on top of mine, and I found myself fighting the urge to pull away.

"That's not what I meant, Jacob. I was just so mad at you that night. And then you didn't call. I mean, it's not the first time, but I had to be told by Heather that we weren't in a relationship and that you went back to the bar after you followed me home."

"It was on my way back home. And I only went back in to tell them what happened and that I was leaving."

I felt my brows draw together as I contemplated that confession. "You told them I was upset about Holly and that I broke up with you?"

"Well, I thought that was what happened." He shrugged as if it were no big deal.

My jaw went rigid at the sight of his indifference. I could feel the venom rising to my lips again, threatening to unleash a slew of words I knew I would inevitably regret. I swallowed it back down, desperately trying to convince myself not to make a scene right now, no matter how many people might be too inebriated to remember it later.

"So, what is it that we are doing here, Jacob?" I finally asked.

"Gwen, I love you. You know that. I don't want to be without you."

"You say those things, but I don't know if you know what they mean. You don't exactly act accordingly."

Jacob weaved his husky fingers in between mine as he carefully deliberated what to say next. "Baby, I know I've fucked up. I have done some bad things in the past, and I've apologized for them all. I've taken accountability." He sighed heavily and tightened his grasp as he waited for me to meet his gaze. "But you can't hold them over my head forever. We'll never be able to move past it that way."

"I don't want to keep getting hurt," I whispered.

Jacob looked at me as though he were seeing me for the first time...as if he didn't realize he had ever truly caused me any pain. "I don't want to hurt you, Gwen. That's the last thing I'd ever want to do."

"But you have. You do. And I don't know if you can stop...I can't keep—"

"Give me another chance," Jacob blurted recklessly, cutting off my train of thought. "I'll show you I can be the person you deserve."

His golden-brown eyes burned into me, melting away all traces of the animosity I'd been so damned determined to hang onto. Despite everything, Jacob knew me. He knew me better than I'd like to admit, and because of that, he knew precisely what to do to get around my defenses. The walls I'd spent far too many years trying to build up to keep people out were ones he was all too familiar with climbing by now. I wasn't entirely sure yet if that was something I appreciated or something that I hated.

"I know we've had our moments, but you're the one for me, Gwen. No one else compares to you. I've known that since the moment I met you."

"What are you saying, exactly?"

"Gwendolyn Winters, I've never felt this way about anyone else. You drive me downright insane, but you make me the happiest I've ever been. You make me want to be better. I didn't plan on doing this here, or now, or like this at all...I don't even have a ring yet, and I don't know the right words to say, but I know I want to spend my life with you."

"Are you..." I fought to find my breath. We'd never discussed marriage in the two years that we had been together, not with serious intentions anyway. That's not to say I didn't frequently think about it. "Are you proposing, Jacob?"

"Yes. I am." Jacob's smile radiated, blazing through every trepidation I initially thought I had when we started this conversation. "Will you marry me, Gwen?"

I searched his face frantically, too stunned to find the words. I'd imagined this moment before a hundred different times, but the shock of it actually happening was exceptionally disorienting. *Jacob just asked me to marry him.* I had to repeat the sentence in my head a few times for it to resonate as true. He was right here, kneeling in front of me, and he looked happy enough to burst.

"Gwen?" The corners of his lips sank slightly as he stared at me. "Did you hear me?" The panicked whisper broke me out of whatever deep-rooted trance had taken hold. Oh God, I hadn't answered him yet. I hadn't even moved.

"Yes," I answered, nodding as his dimpled smile reappeared.

"You will?" His voice cracked in response.

"Yes, I'll marry you!" I laughed, noticing the way his features twisted in disbelief just before he jumped up, placed his hands on both sides of my face, and kissed me feverishly.

"Jacob!" I laughed, pulling back slightly from the public display.

"I'm sorry, baby, I couldn't control myself. I'm just so damn happy. And I damn sure didn't think you were going to say yes." His cheeks flushed red at the admission. "I love you so much, babe."

"I love you too." I beamed, throwing my arms around his shoulders.

He wrapped his around my waist in return and dipped his head down to brush his lips against my ear. "It's getting kind of late. What do you say we leave this nerd fest and go back to the house to celebrate?"

I laughed, rolling my eyes at his underlying request. "Sure," I consented. "Bree's been gone for a while anyway. Let me just go find a few people and tell them that we're leaving. I'll meet you right back here."

"Sounds good, babe. I think I'll go grab a plate of food to carry with us. Do you want anything?"

I shook my head, grimacing as he narrowed his gaze on a man at a nearby table who was ravenously tearing into a turkey leg.

***

Jacob was nowhere to be found after I'd made my rounds to tell everyone goodbye. He wasn't waiting for me at the table or standing at any of the food tents. I quickly scanned the blurry faces in the dancing crowd, half wondering if he'd been dragged into all the commotion. That was when my thoughts were interrupted.

"Hello, child," a raspy voice rang out from behind me.

The startle caused me to flinch as I turned to take in the small elderly woman standing nearby. Her face was shockingly frail, held together by wrinkled tan skin that had been deeply weathered by time. What stood out the most, though, were her vibrant green eyes and the haunting gaze that lingered there as she lowered it to where my hand still clutched my chest.

I settled at the realization, allowing it to fall back to my side. "I'm sorry," I apologized. "You caught me a little off guard."

A crooked smile spread across her gaunt face, exposing a missing tooth. "Sorry to frighten you, child. My name is Madam Cosmina." Her fragile frame wobbled as she approached. "Would you care to have your fortune read?"

"No, thank you. I'm in a bit of a hurry." I took a step away from her to resume my search for Jacob.

She reached for my arm, gently turning me to face her once again. Her bright green eyes glistened with what I could only describe as anticipation as she stared up at me. The scraggly gray hair that escaped from underneath her dark headscarf hung near her waist, and the beads that adorned the braided strands clattered together in discordance as she moved closer.

"In such a hurry to deny your future, my dear? Please...allow me to enlighten you. I think you'll like what I have to say." She pulled open the burgundy curtain of her tent and smiled as she gestured toward the empty table waiting inside.

"Okay, fine," I reluctantly agreed. "Quickly please, though. I need to find someone and get back home."

"Yes, child. Of course." The curtain fell closed behind us, ushering in a rapid darkness. The old woman guided me to the center of the tent and pulled out a wooden chair.

Dozens of flickering candles were stationed inside, and it was hard to dismiss the eerily way the glow of the flames danced around our shadows on the walls.

"Such a beautiful day for a wedding," the woman said, smiling impassively as she stood across the table from me. I shifted my focus away from her. Her gaze was unnerving, and something about it made the hair on my arms stand on edge.

"Yes. It was." I searched for the curtained door, hoping Jacob would appear so that we could leave, but I couldn't find any light filtering in through the crack.

"Oh my"—she gasped— "and what a lovely necklace. The way it glows in the candlelight..." She leaned down, reaching for it as I instinctively recoiled.

"Thank you," I muttered, shielding it with my hand.

"Well then, my child"—she cleared her throat— "let us begin." The fortune teller took her seat across from me and closed her eyes before waving her hands over the crystal ball stationed between us.

"Ahhh yes...hmmm...ohhh, I see," she mumbled incoherently.

After what seemed like an unnecessary number of noises, I moved to stand. "I'm sorry, ma'am, I really have to go."

"Do you see?" she asked suspiciously.

"See what?"

Her eyes cracked open as she held her trembling hands over the crystal ball. A spiral of lavender mist now circulated inside.

"See..." she repeated softly.

"It's foggy," I said, unamused. "That's a nice trick."

"There is no trick, child." She pursed her thin, pale lips together and glared at me as though I'd made her angry. Even in the absence of adequate light, her strange eyes sparked a sense of terror in my core. "Your future is an interesting one, indeed. It could go...so many ways." Her lids drew together once more as she began to sway and hum a sinister song to herself.

I shouldn't have agreed to come in here. This was beyond creepy. I was only trying to be polite, and now here I was, stuck in a voodoo tent, seemingly about to have a séance with some crazy lady who doesn't look to be too far from death's door herself.

I cleared my throat as I tried to rise. "Thank you for your time, but I really have to—"

"You will sit down!" She sprang up, moving faster than she ought to have, raspingly yelling as she clamped her hands down over mine. The crystal ball flickered as the fog began to rush out from under the table and spread across the floor of the tent.

"And you will look," she demanded, her cryptic glowing eyes shot me a warning, threatening me in a way that I'd never felt before.

I followed her gaze back down to the object, feeling all the air leave my lungs as I did. Inside the glass sphere, I saw myself, not a reflection and not a video, but something like it. I was running through the woods, looking behind me as though I were being chased. I was falling against the twisted trees, visibly struggling to escape from something. And I was wearing the same icy blue dress that I had on right now.

I sat frozen, unable to comprehend the vision I was seeing. Unable to react or even breathe.

"Listen well, child...and you will hear." She touched her long, bony finger to her lips. "Shhh."

"Help me! Please! Someone help me!" My screams rang out in an echo from the sphere.

"What is this? What are you doing?" I managed to whisper.

She leaned her sullen face down closer to mine, lowering her raspy voice to a volume I could barely perceive. "You are important, child. For the condition of our world does indeed lie with you."

"Who are you?" I demanded, nearly choking over the accumulating fog. I turned, searching for the door as I yelled for Jacob. Why the hell hadn't he figured out where I was by now?

The woman laughed manically, and the blood in my veins ran cold. "I told you already, child, I am Cosmina." She shoved her skinny finger toward my face. "That's not the question you should be asking, though, is it?" Her words were slow and deliberate, as though she knew much more than she was letting on. "I suppose it will all be revealed in time."

"Look, I don't know how you did...whatever that just was, but this isn't funny." I coughed again, waving the fog away from my field of vision. It cleared long enough for me to see that the crystal ball was now levitating several feet above where we sat.

"What the..."

Cosmina's head jerked back in a startling haste. An uncontainable scream erupted from my mouth as a blinding purple light shot out from the object, breaking off into dozens of tiny bolts of lightning that flashed all around us.

I watched in complete horror as Cosmina's body contorted unnaturally in front of me. Before I could react, she lurched forward onto the table and began to crawl toward me, "You will embark on a treacherous journey..." Her voice grew raspier under the weight of each word.

"Stop it!" I screamed as she painfully latched onto my hands again.

My pleas went unheard as she shouted her perilous threats over my voice. "Great evils await you on the other side. All is not what it seems to be..."

The fog was nearly unbearable. All I could see was Cosmina's erratic silhouette illuminated by the flickering violet hue of the crystal ball that floated overhead.

"Find the break in the sky..." she rattled on, as her body shook violently.

"Oh my God! Jacob!" I yelled for him again, praying he would find me and take me away from this fucking madwoman who held me down and dug her nails deeper into my hands as her disjointed warnings tumbled all around me.

"...or thy shall not perish..." she groaned as if speaking the words exerted too much of her energy. "...but by the break in the sky..."

The old woman's neck was bent so far back that it looked like it was on the verge of snapping in half.

"...the light of the snow moon..."

I clenched my eyes together as tight as I could manage. The sight of her was too gruesome to bear.

"Jacob!" I cried over and over again, trying to pull away from her predatory grip. "Someone help me!" I screamed as the fog invaded my senses. My throat was burning so much I wasn't sure how much more of this I could take.

The curtains of the tent blew open violently, and Cosmina unleashed her hold. She stood over me as I fell to the ground, watching as the ferocious purple haze whipped around us like a hurricane. I squinted through the wind and debris, catching a glimpse of the crystal ball long enough to see a fleeting image of a castle just before it plummeted to the ground and shattered into hundreds of tiny pieces all around me.

"Jacob!" I pleaded again, wild with fear.

"Foolish girl. He cannot help you," she replied impassively.

I dug my nails into the ground, desperately trying to claw my way to the door. It was only a few feet away, but the wind was too furious—too unrelenting. It stole my breath as it pushed me back down to the ground again and again.

"Make it stop! Please! Make it stop!" I gasped for air as I tried to fight against it.

"As you wish, child." Her voice was nearly inaudible against the raging roars.

Immediately, as if it were as simple as flipping off a light switch, the whirlwind ceased. I found myself lying motionless on the ground, trying to gather my wits. The silence was deafening. Slowly, I rolled over to face the old woman, but no one was there.

"Cosmina?" I called out. There was no reply.

"Where are you!" I screamed, frantically gripping the edge of the table and pulling myself to my feet.

The responding stillness sent a shudder down my spine.

My knees shook as I snatched the curtain open to leave the tent. They nearly gave out altogether when I saw for the first time what was...or rather what wasn't, on the other side. There was no festival, no tents, no people. There were no sounds of laughter or music floating in the air. There were no echoes of the horses clomping down the gravel trail. In a matter of seconds, everything that had existed outside had vanished away into the shadows of the night.

Worst of all, there was no Jacob. I stumbled out cautiously, trying to understand the gravity of what just happened. The comprehension never came. I was in the middle of nowhere, surrounded by an uneasy and immeasurable darkness.

"Cosmina?" I whispered desperately once more against the night.

CHAPTER FOUR

The early morning sun crept through the cracks of my eyes. My head was throbbing as memories of last night rushed through it incoherently...the dancing, the drinking, Jacob. I smiled as my thoughts settled on him, remembering the way he'd gazed at me as he confessed his love. He had finally asked me to marry him.

I shifted to my side, unable to get comfortable. Why was my bed so hard? It was chilly in here. I rolled onto my back again, searching for the blanket to pull up. Instead, I grabbed a handful of grass and dirt.

"What the—" I mumbled as the rest of my memories ruthlessly flooded in.

I shot up from the ground, recalling the old fortune teller who had lured me into her lair... the unexplainable things I had witnessed. My eyes darted around the tent, trying to focus underneath the dim light of day.

"No...no, no!" I began to panic. This was not happening.

I was dreaming. Clearly, I was dreaming. There was no other plausible explanation for the things that had happened. I slapped my cheeks in an effort to wake myself up. Why wasn't I waking up? This didn't feel like a dream...no, I was definitely awake. I had the stinging marks on my face to prove it.

My mind reeled, attempting to reach for any justifiable clarification. Maybe someone had slipped something into my drinks? Of course! I was suffering from severe hallucinations. Who would do such a thing, though? I thought of the groomsmen I'd danced with, how two of them had brought me drinks. They had both seemed so nice and incapable of committing such a heinous act. Either way, I was certain that was what must have happened. I only needed to wait until the side effects wore off.

I wondered if Jacob had left me here last night...if he had searched for me. Maybe he assumed I had left without him? I'd have to explain everything when I found him. We'd just reconciled, and the last thing I needed was for him to think I abandoned him here.

I needed to find someone—the old woman or another festival worker—and let them know what happened. I also needed to call Jacob...but that would be impossible to do, thanks to Ashton, who had convinced everyone to hand over their phones to her before the unexpected ceremony. A shimmer in the grass caught my eye as I frantically paced the tent. I looked down to find Bree's necklace lying near the base of the table. It must have fallen off during...whatever happened. I picked it up, quickly inspecting it to make sure it wasn't broken before clasping it around my neck again.

After working up the nerve to exit the tent, I was by no means shocked when I opened the curtained door once more to find that there was still nothing familiar waiting to greet me on the other side. Disappointed but not shocked. The towering trees that surrounded the tent blocked out much of the morning sky. It was as if a tornado had picked me up and dropped me in the middle of the woods, but I saw no sign of any damage. I reassured myself that I must still be hallucinating. As long as I was aware that I was under the influence of something, I should still be able to find help.

I strayed farther away from Cosmina's tent, searching for a building, another vendor's tent, or any other indication of life to help guide my direction. Eventually, I'd ventured far enough away that the tent had vanished from view altogether. I wasn't even sure how to get back to it anymore. Surely, I'd have to run into someone soon.

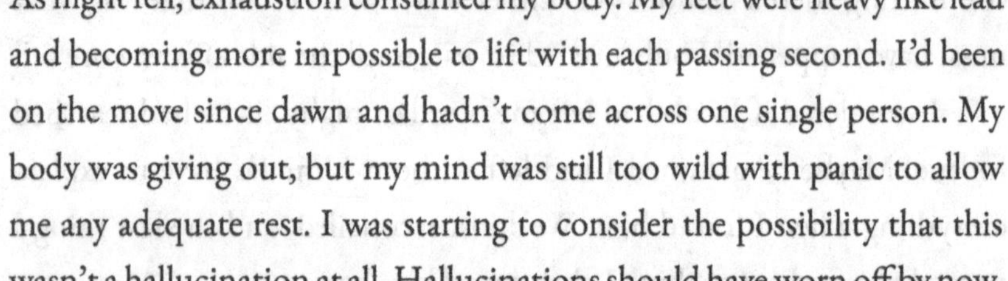

As night fell, exhaustion consumed my body. My feet were heavy like lead and becoming more impossible to lift with each passing second. I'd been on the move since dawn and hadn't come across one single person. My body was giving out, but my mind was still too wild with panic to allow me any adequate rest. I was starting to consider the possibility that this wasn't a hallucination at all. Hallucinations should have worn off by now. I pushed it aside. The most pressing concern right now was to find food and shelter. I'd have to worry about whether I was crazy or not after that.

The sky was nearly black when I stumbled across an unusual hollowed-out tree. The large limbs hung low and twisted together. In any normal circumstance, it would have looked too unsettling to approach. However, this wasn't any normal circumstance. Every instinct that I retained was on high alert, but I was far too paranoid to try to sleep out in the open on the ground. I forced my aching feet to push me up as I grabbed onto the lowest branch and pulled. It was at this moment I was thankful that I hadn't decided to wear heels yesterday.

Once I was secure against the trunk, I tried to persuade my body to relax. I had no idea what I was going to do. I had no food, no water, and no one to help me. At this rate, there was no way I would survive much longer. All I wanted to do was cry, but between being fatigued and dehydrated, even that was impossible.

"Gwen, there you are!" Jacob raced over, hugging me tightly.

"Jacob!" I latched onto him feverishly. "I swear I didn't leave you there that night. Something happened..." I began to explain.

"I know. It's okay. All that matters is you're here now. I was so scared, Gwen. We all were."

"We?" I asked.

"Me, Bree, your parents..."

"You talked to my parents?"

"Of course, I talked to them. You were missing. They were worried sick."

"But it was only a couple of days."

"What?" Jacob's troubled brown eyes narrowed as he took a slow step back. "No, Gwen..."

"No? What do you mean? How long was I gone?"

"Gwen..." he repeated my name softly, sensing the sheer panic tangled in my voice.

"How long have I been gone, Jacob?" I demanded.

"Twelve months," he hesitated to measure my response. "It's been a whole year, Gwen."

"That's not possible," I refuted.

"I thought you'd never come back to me." His words blurred together as I tried to process them.

"Twelve months?" I repeated in disbelief.

"Where were you all this time?"

"I...I don't know."

"Did you do what you were sent there to do?" he asked softly.

I shook my head in confusion. "What?"

"Did you finish it?"

"I don't...I don't understand what you're saying."

"I told you that you were special, child." The compassion faded away as his voice cracked.

"Jacob?" My heart sped instinctively.

He placed his arms around my shoulders and pulled me into another embrace. "It's all up to you now," he whispered against my ear. "You have to do what you were sent here for."

He stepped away slowly, and I watched as his warm, familiar face morphed before me into a ghostly shadow. Unnatural green eyes cut through the darkness as Cosmina's laughing, wrinkled face appeared to replace his.

"Get away from me!" I screamed as she evaporated right in front of me.

"Wake up." The request ricocheted through my head.

"Leave me alone!" I yelled, throwing my arms out in a defensive stance.

"Please, wake up!"

The sound of my body thudding onto the ground jolted me awake right before the searing pain kicked in.

"Oh my! Are you all right? I'm terribly sorry..." A melodic voice rang out. "I didn't mean to startle you!"

I groaned and opened my eyes to the sunlit silhouette of a young woman standing over me.

"What happened?" I asked, rubbing my face.

"You fell out of that tree. Why on earth were you sleeping in a tree?" she exclaimed.

"It seemed like a better idea than sleeping on the ground."

"Here, let me help you up." She extended her hand out toward me. "I'm Rowan, by the way."

I grabbed on as she helped pull me upright, bracing me against the jagged tree trunk. "I'm Gwen...thank you."

The girl kneeled in front of me, finally offering me a detailed glimpse of her features. She couldn't have been older than sixteen or seventeen years old. Her long brown hair contrasted heavily against her porcelain face as her large dark eyes studied me with distinct concern.

"I think I'm okay," I managed to mumble.

"You look utterly famished."

"I haven't eaten in a while. I think I'm lost, actually. Do you think you can help me? I'm looking for an old lady—"

"Of course!" She cut me off with an odd enthusiasm. "First things first, why don't we get you back to the village and get you something to eat."

I nodded. While I just wanted to get back home, I couldn't deny the immediate pain gnawing in the pit of my stomach at the mention of food. "That would be amazing. Thank you."

She helped me stand, looping her arm with mine as we walked until she was confident enough that I could securely balance myself.

"I can't tell you how glad I am you found me. I was beginning to think I had gone mad."

"Were you out here all night? The woods are not a safe place to be, especially right now." The threat of her words was muted by the sugary tone of her voice.

"Yes, I'm not entirely sure how I ended up out here so far away from the festival."

Rowan tilted her head in a quizzical manner. "The festival?"

"Yes, the Renaissance Faire...how far is it from here exactly?"

She chuckled nervously. "I think you may have bumped your head a little harder than I thought!"

"My head feels fine," I said, rubbing my temple instinctively.

"The village isn't too far from here; it's just over that hill." She pointed out ahead of us. "You'll feel much better after a hot meal and a warm bath."

"A bath?" I scoffed at the suggestion. "That really isn't necessary." I knew I'd been out here in the woods for a couple of days, but I didn't smell *that* bad. "I can do that when I get home. I'll need to use a phone, though. I don't have mine. My boyfriend—er, fiancé—doesn't know where I am. He's probably really worried."

"You say such strange things, Gwen." Rowan's voice danced whimsically as she giggled.

"Listen, I know you guys are supposed to play along and set the mood for this whole Renaissance thing, but please, it's not necessary. I'm just ready to get back home," I blurted.

"Where is your home? Perhaps I can help you get there once you're able to safely travel again."

"Um, thanks, but that's okay. I stay in an apartment just downtown. It's not that far away. Jacob, my fiancé, can come and pick me up."

Her doe eyes widened as she seemed to ponder. "What is an apartment?"

Clearly, this girl was devoted to staying in character. It was admirable yet slightly irritating.

"Right, I forgot, they don't exist in this time period. Remember what I said, though? You really don't have to stay in character around me." I glanced back over at her as we strolled down the leaf-strewn path. "Who are you supposed to be anyway?"

Rowan's costume was quite charming and a lot more detailed than many of the character costumes I'd seen last night. She wore a white blouse with puffy sleeves under a russet-colored corset, and her long skirt resembled a heavy winter quilt composed of stunning autumn-hued patchwork fabrics.

"I'm Rowan," she replied, noticeably confused by the question.

"Right," I laughed to myself. "I have to admit, you're a lot better at your job than those knights were. They were nowhere near as devoted to the role."

Panic fell across her face as she grabbed hold of my arm. "You saw knights? How many were there? And how close to the village were they?"

"I don't know how many, maybe a dozen or so."

"A dozen!" she shrieked.

"Yeah, maybe more. It was hard to tell; they were kind of all over the place last night. Several of them were excessively drunk and making lewd remarks to a bunch of the girls. I'd advise steering clear if you see them."

Rowan's brows pulled together. "Are you positive they were knights? The knights don't usually come this close to the village, not unless the prince orders them to."

"They were definitely knights. They were wearing the armor things and the whole nine yards. They did, however, take that off when they were dancing. Too restricting, I guess."

"Dancing knights!" Rowan relaxed her grip as she chuckled. "What a curious thing to say!"

As we approached the top of the hill Rowan had previously pointed out, I paused to take in the unexpected view of the horizon. My stomach no longer twisted from the pain of hunger. Instead, it sank straight down to my feet, taking what was left of my sanity with it.

"Rowan. Where are we?" The question was barely a whisper.

"Welcome to my village, Gwen." She smiled. "This is Woodmist."

CHAPTER FIVE

An eerie fog hovered over the quaint settlement. Nestled inside the thick emerald forest that lay before us, the buildings that comprised this town all looked similar – sandstone walls with pointy brown roofs. Winding cobblestone streets stretched across the hills, running straight through the center of the picturesque town. Woodmist looked like a page that had been pulled straight out of a children's storybook.

"And you...live here? All of the time?" I reiterated.

Rowan nodded obliviously. "There's my home over there, just beyond that stretch of cypress trees." She pointed to a tiny cottage sitting off in the distance, and I stared in silent horror as the puffs of smoke from the chimney dissipated into the dreary sky.

Perhaps I had gone mad. Or perhaps an insane magical woman really had sent me through a portal that defied time, space, and any logical explanation. I wasn't sure how to process either of those options.

I followed behind Rowan closely, unable to utter a word as we weaved through the town on uneven pebbled streets. She filled the silence with stories about the shops that we passed and pointed out the homes of the people that she knew. I couldn't comprehend anything she said. My mind was racing far too fast to pretend to pay attention. I couldn't make sense of this place, of her, of me being here, of any of it.

"Well, good morning, Rowan." A boisterous voice boomed as we passed by another small stretch of buildings.

Rowan jumped back as an immense man appeared in the threshold of one of the doors. "Oh, good morning, Mr. Adams!"

"Out shopping early today, I see. Are ye out of bread again already?"

She nodded apologetically. "Oh yes. We're all out. Nana sent me down to fetch some more."

"'Fraid it's not ready quite yet, you'll have to come back a little later, eh?" He tipped his hat to me and eyed me with discernible intrigue. "Hello, miss."

Rowan grabbed hold of my arm and began pulling me away as she yelled out, "See you later then, Mr. Adams. We must be off now!"

"Are you all right?" I asked, noticing the immediate difference in her demeanor as a prickle of danger pierced the air.

"Fine," she said from behind a faint smile. "Mr. Adams is nice. He's just...a bit nosy. If we had stayed there any longer, he would have started asking questions."

"Oh..." I glanced back, meeting his curious gaze as he stared after us.

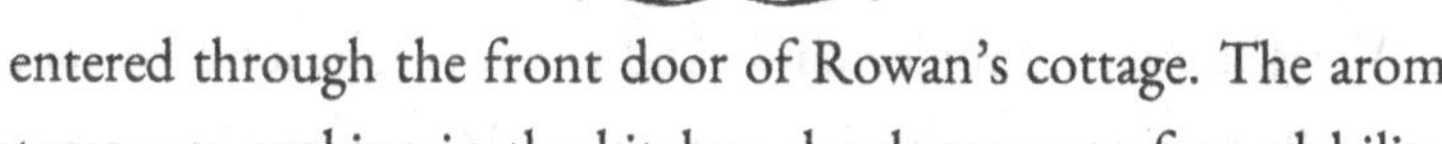

We entered through the front door of Rowan's cottage. The aroma of whatever was cooking in the kitchen shook me out of my debilitating thoughts long enough to remind me how desperately ravenous I was.

"Nana!" Rowan called out. "I'm home!"

The small cottage was warm and inviting. The wood-paneled walls were adorned with small tapestries and paintings that brought color and life into the room. A patchwork quilt similar to the skirt Rowan wore was draped over the back of a small couch sitting near the entryway where Rowan placed her shoes.

An older lady with a plump pink face entered the room. Her gray hair was pulled tightly on top of her head into a perfectly sculpted bun, and she had kind, cheerful eyes that were partially obstructed by the small-framed glasses that she wore.

"Nana, this is my friend Gwen."

"Well hello, dear." She greeted me graciously with a hug. "I don't believe I've had the pleasure of meeting you before."

"I'm not from around here—"

"Gwen is lost. I found her out on the trail," Rowan interjected.

"Rowan!" Two harsh lines took form between the woman's brows as she scowled. "What have I told you about going off into the woods?"

Rowan tilted her head back in annoyance. "I know, Nana. I'm sorry, but we really needed more firewood. There's barely enough to last us the rest of the week. I didn't get it, of course, because I found Gwen first."

"The woods are far too dangerous. You know that more than anyone." Her words were hushed. "And with all those knights stationed outside the village..." She glared daggers through the tiny spectacles, relaying other sentiments she didn't dare to voice out loud. "We can get firewood from the hunting groups when they go back. You mustn't venture out by yourself again, Rowan."

"All right, Nana. I understand. And I won't." She lowered her head before adding, "But I also wouldn't have found Gwen had I not gone out today. She needs our help getting home, and I offered her something to eat. She's not had any food for days."

"Of course, dear. I'll get you a nice hot bowl of porridge right away." She placed her arm around my shoulders and led me straight to the kitchen table.

"Thank you, Ma'am."

"Please, call me Thora." She grabbed a bowl from the cabinet and filled it generously. "So, my dear, how long did you say you were lost? And how can we help you?" She sat across from me, waiting patiently as I devoured the meal.

"She says she's from a place called The Apartment," Rowan chimed in.

I nearly spat the food back out into the bowl. Somehow, I didn't think telling a bunch of strangers the truth was the wisest idea at the moment.

"What does that mean?" she asked Rowan.

"I was hoping you would know. Gwen truly says the most amusing things!" Rowan chuckled as she pulled out a chair and sat beside me.

"I, uh, hit my head earlier," I blurted, hoping to deflect the conversation.

"Yes, quite hard, too," Rowan added.

"Poor dear. You need a good night's rest." Thora's eyes softened. "After you finish your meal, why don't you get out of those dirty clothes. Rowan can draw you a nice hot bath, and I'll wash them up for you in the meantime. You can rest here for as long as you need to."

"Thank you." I tried to smile, but the action was harder to do than it should have been. "Truly."

"It's no bother, dear," Thora assured me just before looking down and noticing my bowl was empty. "Here, let me get you some more." She stood, reaching for the dish. "Would you like some bread too? We've plenty in the oven."

After a much-needed bath, Rowan gave me one of her nightgowns to change into and showed me to the room I'd be staying in. A tiny wood-framed bed, complete with another patchwork quilt, was stationed in the middle of the room. The neon embers of recently doused flames still glowed inside the charming stone fireplace on the far wall. I made my way to the bed, unable to resist its lure after these past couple of days. The mattress was stiff, but it was certainly better than the tree I'd resorted to last night.

"Nana washed your dress earlier while you were in the bath; it's hanging out back to dry. Do try to get some rest, Gwen. It will do you a world of good."

"Thank you, Rowan. For everything. I don't really know what I'm going to do." I fought back the tears that were quickly welling up behind my eyes. "I don't know how I'm going to get home."

"Just rest. You can worry about all of the other stuff later." She blew out the candle on the nightstand and pulled the covers over me as I drifted off easily into a dreamless slumber.

"Nana, I don't know!" I heard Rowan exclaim from the other room.

I rolled over, unsure of what time it was or how long I'd been asleep.

"She seems like a nice young woman, but we don't know anything about her other than she's not from around here," I heard Thora respond softly. "Her clothes are...so peculiar. When I was washing them earlier, I noticed there was a strange fastener on the side. I've never seen anything like that before."

I sat up in the bed, tilting my head toward the door in an effort to hear them better once I realized I was the subject of the tense exchange.

"I don't think she means any harm. I couldn't just leave her out there in the forest alone. She would have died, one way or another. You know that," Rowan retorted.

"With everything that's been going on, we must be careful of who we choose to trust. I know you meant well, dear. She wouldn't have made it out of the forest by herself, that's for certain."

"I'm sure after she gets some sleep, she will feel much better tomorrow," Rowan continued. "She may even remember more, and she probably won't even want to stay for very long."

"My dear," Thora hesitated. "It's just not a risk I'm willing to take. I must keep you safe...I will do anything to keep you safe. I need you to understand that."

"What are you saying, Nana? Are you going to tell her she has to leave?"

"I can't put my finger on it, but I feel like something just isn't right," Thora confessed. "Mr. Adams even asked about her today when I went to the market, and you know how he likes to talk. I don't want people to start questioning us. It wouldn't end well."

"You've already told her she can stay for as long as she needs."

"Yes, but that was before I started thinking about the consequences it could bring. She could be a spy or something even worse. I can't risk our safety. And the prince has ordered that we report anything unusual..." Her voice trailed off.

"Nana, what did you do?" Rowan inquired, her voice rising as she did.

"I'm sorry, Rowan. I have already sent word that she's here. The guards will likely be here soon to collect her. I felt you should know—"

"Nana! How could you do that?" Rowan yelled. "You know what they will do with her! It's a death sentence!"

"Not if she is truly lost, as she says. They will surely try to help her."

"Just like they've helped all the others in the village?" Rowan shrieked.

The outburst was followed by a barrage of footsteps.

"Gwen!" Rowan roared as she busted through the door...a far cry from her former meek demeanor. Her face fell as she saw me sitting wide-eyed in the middle of the bed. I didn't have to say a word; she knew I'd already heard everything.

She wasted no time on explanations. "You've got to get out of here. Now," she warned harshly.

I nodded, scrambling to get out of the bed as Rowan turned and raced past Thora to the back door.

"Rowan! You can't leave. They'll be out there soon!" Thora exclaimed.

"They'll be out there because you brought them here!" Rowan shouted as she came back inside, holding my clothes.

I grabbed the damp dress from her, hastily jerking off the borrowed gown while she helped me get changed. She fumbled with the zipper as though she'd never seen one before.

"I am so sorry, Gwen," she apologized as I yanked it up effortlessly. "I wouldn't have brought you here if I knew this would happen." Her dark eyes were filled with rage and turmoil.

"Where can I go?" I asked.

"Out the back. A few miles through the forest, there's a creek. Follow it. Stay off the main trails. There will be knights posted all along the way, and they'll find you if you go there. And Gwen, if they find you, they will certainly kill you. I haven't the time to explain everything...you must go. Now," Rowan ordered; her voice was shaded with a dangerous urgency.

Thora's face twisted with regret as she took hold of my hands. "I'm sorry," she whispered, tightening her grip. "I have to keep her safe. If they knew we were harboring someone, they'd—"

"There's no time for this now," Rowan interjected, firing a harsh glance.

I stood, frozen in a full-blown panic as Rowan ran to the living room window. "They're almost here," she warned.

Behind the opaque glass, dozens of torches raced steadily over the hills as they entered the village.

My heartbeat thudded so violently that it blocked out the mounting thunderous yells of the soldiers who were narrowing in on us...on me. Fuck.

"What about you?"

"Don't worry about us. We'll be fine." Rowan rushed me to the back door and snatched something off the wall before pushing me outside into the chilly air.

"Rowan, no!" Thora yelled from behind her.

Rowan ignored her and tossed a red garment at me. "Take this."

"What is it?" I asked, quickly inspecting it.

"A cloak. Put it on. It will protect you...from the wolf."

"The wolf?"

"Just trust me, Gwen," Rowan pleaded.

My entire body went numb as I processed her command. "Wait, are you...holy shit." I could feel my eyes growing wider as the strange realization crept over me. "Are you Red Riding Hood?" The absurdity of what I'd said immediately set in.

Rowan and her grandmother stood dumbfounded in the doorway as if I'd just revealed a secret that I shouldn't know about.

"That's insane." I laughed nervously. "I don't even know why I said that."

"How does she know of that name?" Thora muttered to Rowan.

"I...I don't know." Rowan replied, narrowing her eyes as she analyzed my reaction.

"What is happening?" I whispered, mainly to myself.

The voices were closer now, and I could feel the ground rumbling underneath the heavy hooves of the guards' horses.

"Gwen. Please. Just go now," Rowan begged.

A forceful knock sounded at the front door as Rowan slammed the one where we stood shut in my face. I turned, not allowing myself another moment to hesitate, and raced blindly into the dark forest as fast as I could.

I ran until the voices of the soldiers faded, until the light of their torches no longer tinted the night sky orange, and until my lungs could barely gasp for another breath.

Exhausted, I finally made my way to the creek Rowan had told me about. I mean, Red Riding Hood. God, please let me still be hallucinating from someone putting something in my drink at the wedding. Was that still an option? Never before had I hoped to have been roofied so badly in all my life. What the hell other option was there? The other option was that I'd been hanging out with a fictional storybook character all day.

I carefully unclenched the cloak and held it up to see under the light of the full moon. The scarlet, crushed velvet material was soft and glistened under the iridescent beams that broke through the whispering leaves of the treetops. This was silly. This was just a cloak, not some magical fairytale element. Maybe Rowan had just believed it would protect her from random wildlife encounters. Perhaps she had a close call before. I knew better though.

I achily walked alongside the creek, wondering how long it would be until morning arrived, wondering when I'd get to the next village, and wondering what potential fictional characters awaited me there. I laughed at the thought. Rowan and Thora's bewildered looks were still seared in my mind. They clearly thought I was insane. Maybe I was. Maybe I just needed to accept that at this point.

A rustling noise behind me broke my train of thought. I picked up my pace, matching my strides with the swift current of the creek.

I wondered if Thora would tell the soldiers which way I was going. It was likely, considering she was the one who called for them and seemed hell-bent on thinking that the knowledge of my existence somehow put Rowan in danger. I just wish she would have at least waited until it was daylight to sell me out.

Another shuffle sounded in the trees behind me, louder than the one before. A surge of panic instinctively pulsed through my veins, warning me to run. And I obeyed.

The adrenaline fueled me, allowing me to push my stinging legs faster than they wanted to go. Crisp autumn leaves crushed under the sound of my footsteps...and the footsteps that were closing in behind me. Someone was chasing me. The noise echoed through my head. The soldiers had found me already. There was no way I'd be able to escape them now—not in this unforgiving and unfamiliar forest.

My foot twisted painfully underneath an exposed tree root, flinging me forward onto my hands. Before I could regain my sensibility, the footsteps surrounded me. This was it; Rowan had warned me if they caught me, they would kill me. I was surprised I lasted this long, to be honest. It wasn't as though I was ever well-versed in outrunning skilled guards. To my absolute horror, when I looked up to accept defeat, it wasn't a soldier's face that met mine.

The snarl that emitted from the mouth of the beast standing before me made my blood run cold. Larger than any wolf I'd ever seen, his silver coat stood on edge as he crouched down and bared his sharp, vicious teeth. Was I even breathing? I wasn't sure anymore. I couldn't feel my body. There was only the sound of the wild pulses that pounded through my throbbing head. I was far too terrified to move, knowing that once I did, he would pounce. I was completely helpless, and he knew it.

"Please…" I whispered breathlessly as though the wolf would show me mercy.

He snapped his feral face close to mine as I cowered down, impulsively covering my head with my hands. I had never given much thought to the manner in which I would die, but getting mauled to pieces by a monster wolf would undoubtedly be on the more painful end of the spectrum.

The wolf encircled me menacingly as though he were deciding which body part to eat first. His angry, vacant eyes glared bitterly, daring me to make another move. I realized I was still clenching Rowan's cloak. My only chance of survival right now depended on her outlandish claims that this piece of fabric could protect me, as loony as that sounded.

I took the deepest breath I could summon and flung the garment over myself. The wolf snarled and lunged forward on top of me. He pinned my body to the ground as he landed, swiping me with his heavy claws.

White-hot pain surged down my arm as I cried out instinctively. I didn't have to look down to know I was bleeding; I felt the warm gush of liquid pouring out and pooling around my shoulder. But it was not the most pressing issue at hand.

The wolf's face was mere inches away from mine. His hot, murderous breath radiated behind every growl. I dizzily yanked the cloak up over my head, not entirely sure that my heart was even still inside my chest. *Please God, no.* After a few quaking moments, I realized that he hadn't eaten me yet.

I waited, clenched my jaw tight to keep from screaming, and pulled the scarlet cloth down from my face as slowly as I could manage before meeting his gaze once more. He was still there, but the tension had shifted. He no longer growled or bared his teeth. He simply stood over me, staring silently as though he were less inclined to tear off my extremities and more curious by what he saw. There was no longer a trace of the murderous malice left on his face that had been evident several shallow heartbeats ago.

As I waited for my breath to stabilize, something strange happened. The wolf bowed his head, then took several gradual steps away from me before lowering his body to the ground. I clutched the cloak as close to my chest as humanly possible. He stayed put, quietly watching me as I slid in the opposite direction and crawled behind a fallen tree.

When I finally found the strength to stand, I draped the cloak around me and tied it around my body as tight as I could manage. I needed to put more distance between us. Keeping a cautious eye on him, I backed away slowly. Then he stood.

"No," I breathed the plea.

The vicious beast that had threatened to devour me just minutes ago whined in defiance before sitting back on the ground. His wails continued to grow as I expanded the space. It almost seemed like he was distraught at the sight of me leaving him. It made zero sense, and yet I couldn't help but feel a twinge of guilt as his cries penetrated the air.

When I could no longer see the creature, I turned to make a run for it. The wind whistled all around me, sailing through the trees as it snatched dead leaves from the branches and scattered them along the haphazard path. I raced across them clumsily as they cracked under my feet, stealing periodic glances over my shoulder to see if the wolf was trailing me. Several moments later, the noise of rapid, galloping paws closed in on me again, forcing me to stop in my tracks. I knew there was no point in trying to outrun him.

He appeared beside me and nudged his large head against my waist. I flinched at the contact, mentally noting that his expression continued to carry no threat. Despite that, I was still wary about the possibility that he'd take an unsuspecting leap at my throat when I least expected it.

He orbited me as I stood motionless. My knuckles were throbbing under the tight grip I had on Rowan's cloak as I held onto it for dear life.

"Go," I finally managed to whisper, hoping against all reasonable hope that he would obey.

He glanced up once more as though he understood before dashing ahead of me and disappearing into the shadows of the night.

A wave of relief engulfed me as I fell to my knees and choked on the breath I'd been too terrified to release. I guess Little Red Riding Hood knew what the hell she was talking about, after all.

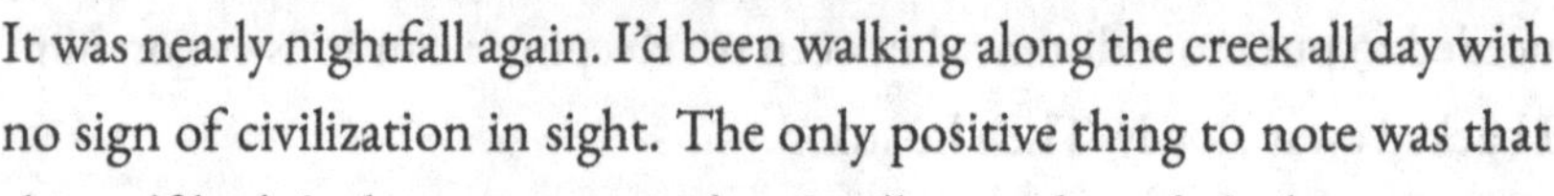

It was nearly nightfall again. I'd been walking along the creek all day with no sign of civilization in sight. The only positive thing to note was that the wolf hadn't shown up again, but I still wore the red cloak just in case he decided to make a sudden reappearance.

The back of my arm still stung like hell from the three scratches he had marked me with. A chill ran through my body as I recalled the way his wild, rabid face had looked hovering over me as I was pinned to the ground underneath his monstrous grip.

Kneeling at the creek to quench my thirst, I was starting to worry about where my next meal would come from. While Thora was my least favorite person at the moment, I would undoubtedly commit an act of violence to get another bowl of her porridge.

A faint rustle sounded nearby. I whipped my head around, half expecting to find the wolf lunging out of the bushes with his teeth bared at me.

"Well, would you look at that. What do we have here?" a gruff voice exclaimed.

I stared into the faces of the two enormous, armored guards who were already approaching me.

"Looks like we finally caught ourselves a Little Red Riding Hood."
The other sneered as he moved in closer.

"Grab her."

CHAPTER SIX

"Let me go!" I screamed as the guards clutched my arms tighter. "I've already told you I'm not Red Riding Hood!"

The dark hallway was just wide enough for the three of us to fit in, and barely gave me enough room to move as I frantically tried to escape their grasp. The flames from the lanterns that lined the desolate tunnel flickered ominously overhead against the dreary stone walls, making it impossible to see where they were taking me.

"I'm not her!" I yelled again.

"We know. She'd never let herself get caught so easily," the guard who clenched the cloak in his free hand responded.

"So why are you detaining me then?" I struggled against them.

"Trespassing on royal grounds and illegal use of sorcery." He shook Rowan's cloak aggressively in my face.

"What!" I stammered. "Sorcery? That's just my coat...you don't understand! I need to find someone. It's urgent."

"The feisty little minx has demands," the other guard scoffed.

"Excuse me?" I huffed back.

"The only thing you'll be finding, miss, is the inside of a dungeon cell."

They slowed their pace as the hallway opened up into a larger room that was lined with a scarcely illuminated wall of bars.

"Please." I resorted to begging. "I truly don't mean any harm. I'm just trying to get back home."

The guards halted abruptly in front of an open cell and forced me inside.

"Please, no!" I tried to grab onto the taller one's hand as he locked me behind the bars.

He clenched my wrists painfully from the other side. "Learn your place, filthy little wench," he spat as he glared back, tossing me off of him.

With that, they were gone. I stared after them, hoping, against all logic, they'd feel remorseful and come back. How'd I get myself in so deep? How was I ever going to get home? My eyes welled up as thoughts of Jacob flashed into my mind. I longed to see him...to touch him. I missed his dimpled smile and the sound of his laugh after he told a joke that only he found funny. I missed the way his arms felt when he'd wrap them tightly around me, and the way he'd try to console me when I was upset. God, I just missed *him*. I wondered what he was doing and if he was looking for me. Would it ever even be possible for him to find me...here? Sinking to the ground, I let the emotions take hold.

"Don't let the bastards get you down, love." A soothing voice spoke from somewhere nearby.

My head snapped up. I'd thought I was alone. "Who's there?" I glanced back toward the doorway.

"Over here," he answered.

I followed the sound to the cell beside mine and allowed my eyes to focus on the silhouette leaning with his back against the farthest wall of bars.

"I thought I was the only one here," I admitted.

The figure pushed off the wall and slowly made his way closer to my cell.

"Lucky for you, you're not." A hint of an unplaceable accent was now evident.

"Unlucky for you, it would seem."

"It's not my first time in a dungeon," he quipped.

I swiped my hand across my forehead and brushed the unkept hair out of my eyes, the tangled strands mixing with my tears as I did. "Well, it is mine."

"That is quite clear, love."

"Please stop calling me that," I commanded.

"Very well." Amusement laced his tone. "What shall I call you then?"

"Gwen."

"Do you have a last name, Gwen?"

"I do...I just don't give it to shadowy figures who linger around in castle dungeons."

"Might I remind you we are both presently lingering around in a castle dungeon?" The sprightful tone of his rhetorical question caught me by surprise. "Besides, what harm could it do you now? You're already in a great deal of peril."

I huffed at the candid remark and rolled my eyes in annoyance, even though I knew it wouldn't translate in the dark. "While that's probably a valid point, I still don't know you."

"My name is Demetri Alexander Hawkins." The figure bowed sarcastically. "Now, what's your excuse?"

"Just because you told me your whole name doesn't mean that I know you any better than I did five seconds ago. That might not even be your real name for all I know."

"You're a sassy lass." His laugh echoed through the cells, persuading the unsteady shadows on the wall to sway in response. "Is that how you ended up in here?"

"I ended up in here through no fault of my own."

"Aye, that's what they all say."

"Look, I've been through a lot of traumatic experiences these past few days. I'm really not in the mood for your snide remarks," I snapped.

The moments of silence that followed were uncomfortable, even more so than his brazenness.

I sighed in defeat. Maybe I was being too harsh on him. "They apparently think I'm some sort of sorceress."

"Are you?" he asked.

"If I were, don't you think I'd get myself out of here?"

"Perhaps. Unless here was where you wanted to be."

"Trust me. This is the last place I want to be." I rose from the floor and dusted off my dress. The silhouette stood motionless, and I could only assume he was staring at me. "What?" I asked self-consciously.

"I was merely waiting for you to impress me with some sorcery."

"Hilarious." I inched closer to him. "So, what's your story?"

"I have many."

"You could start by telling me the one about how you ended up in a dark and dingy dungeon."

"Ah, yes. That one is fairly straightforward. I robbed a royal carriage."

"Of course you did."

"Are you judging me, sorceress?"

I took a cautious step closer to the bars that separated us. "No. Who am I to judge, anyway?" I muttered. "I'm still trying to decide if I've lost my mind."

"What makes you think that you've lost your mind?" He mirrored my movement, stepping into a subtle stream of amber light shining in from the hallway. It flickered across his face, illuminating his sharp, striking features for the first time.

"Oh," I gasped; the sight of him nearly took my breath away.

He stared me down behind the tousled strands of dark hair that fell just below his arched brow, storms raging in his deep blue eyes as he analyzed my face. The corner of his mouth pulled up into a smug smirk as he took in my bewilderment. He knew he'd caught me off guard. Leaning into my state of shock, he took another slow step forward, casually bringing his hand up to stroke the edge of his dark-stubbled jaw as though he were contemplating to himself.

"I...uh..." I searched for something to say to conceal the awkward awareness that I suddenly felt.

"What is it, love?" He refused to release my gaze...a silent validation that he was completely aware of the situation at hand. "No sarcastic remarks? Are you at a loss for words?"

"Don't be ridiculous." I tore my eyes away from his.

"However will you decide then?" he continued to pry.

"Decide what?"

"If you've lost your mind, as you say."

"Oh, right." I shook the distraction out of my head, retreating a few feet from where he now stood. "I guess only time will tell. I'm just trying to take it all as it comes."

He lowered his head and laughed to himself.

"What's so funny?" I asked.

"You're determined to keep your secrets, aren't you?"

My gaze found his again. "You wouldn't believe me if I told you any of them."

"I've heard many wild and fantastical tales. You'd be surprised at what I'd believe."

I shook my head instinctively before approaching the cell door to inspect the lock that confined me to this prison. "Even so..." I turned toward him again. "I'm not sure that telling you anything would be in my best interest."

"Are you trying to intrigue me by being mysterious?" he asked, folding his arms across his chest as he leaned against the wall of bars.

"What?"

"If you are, I must admit it's working."

"No! I'm not trying to intrigue you," I stammered in disbelief. "The only thing I'm trying to do is get the hell out of here! Jesus. Intriguing you is the last damn thing on my mind."

"Did I offend you, love?"

"Yeah, you did, actually." Apparently, men who bore the burden of possessing copious amounts of audacity were a universal experience, not just one limited to Earth.

"My apologies. That was never my intent."

"Do you always just blurt out things without thinking about them first?"

His lyrical laugh swirled around me, reverberating in my bones. "Actually, I've restrained myself quite a bit."

"Fine, I'll tell you," I complied, cracking a reluctant smile at his response. "Why not? I doubt it would make things any worse. I'm... not from here."

"That doesn't sound so outlandish," he replied. "Many people aren't."

"No, that's not what I mean." A heavy sigh escaped as I contemplated sharing my whole secret with this hypnotically handsome stranger. It truly couldn't do me much harm now, considering my predicament.

"So, where are you from then?" he pressed.

"Raleigh," I muttered, cautiously raising my eyes to his face in an effort to gauge his reaction.

"Raleigh?" His voice piqued as he repeated the word. "I've never heard of that land nor seen it on any map that I can recall. How far of a journey is it?"

"A long one—if I had to guess anyway."

He smiled crookedly, shaking his head. "You still insist on speaking in riddles."

I placed my hand on one of the bars between us. I wanted to tell him everything, if anything, just to get the weight of it off my chest, but I also knew that it wasn't the wisest decision.

A strange surge of adrenaline flared through my body when he placed his hand over mine. The sudden interaction sent sparks of sensation shooting straight down my arm. I jerked my hand out from under his with far more urgency than necessary.

"Sorry, I didn't mean..." He trailed off.

"It's fine. I just didn't expect it," I sputtered, the energy dissipating just as quickly as it had arisen.

He pushed away from me, but the sudden space felt suffocating.

"Okay, I'll tell you," I resolved. "Demetri...is it? The reason you've never heard of Raleigh is because it doesn't exist...not in this world anyway."

His dark blue eyes narrowed on me as his brow arched up. A flecting rush of danger engulfed me, and I instantly regretted telling him. But it was too late to take it back now.

"So, you expect me to believe that you're from another world?"

"No, I guess I don't expect you to believe it. It's a hard thing to expect anyone to believe."

"Perhaps this is why everyone thinks you're a sorceress, love." A deliciously wicked smile crept across his face, and I wasn't quite sure how to process the way it made me feel.

"I haven't told anyone else because I know it sounds insane. I don't know why I'm even telling you. I guess I just felt like I needed to tell somebody, and you've expressed a lot of random interest..." I rambled quickly.

"If you're from another world, how'd you get here?" he interjected.

"An old fortune teller. I met her at a wedding...she tricked me." I scanned his face, trying to read the thoughts hidden behind his composed expression. "She sent me here...I don't know how...and I don't know why. Worst of all, I don't know how to get back home. I've been trying to find her ever since I got here, but as you can see, I haven't had the best of luck."

"An old fortune teller, you say?" he pondered out loud.

"Yes, with a crystal ball and everything. Her name was Cosmina. She said a lot of...crazy things." I shook my head, trying to remember. "Something about the sky breaking, and snow moons...I don't know. It didn't make any sense." Haunting images of her contorted body flashed through my brain again, eliciting a shiver down my spine.

"Interesting..." His voice trailed off as though he were withholding some valuable information.

"Demetri...do you know her? Do you know how to find her?" I eagerly grabbed his hands through the bars, trying to disregard that familiar surge of electricity flooding through my veins.

"I've had an encounter with a dark witch in the past. Perhaps it is the same woman; there's no way to know for sure, but it certainly sounds like something in the realm of her capabilities."

Tears jabbed through the corners of my eyes and raced down my cheeks as I gasped for the breath that fled with them. Through the bars, he lifted my chin to meet his mystified face.

"Don't cry, love. Isn't that what you wanted to hear?"

"I thought you would think I was crazy." I swiped away the moisture from under my eyes. "And that I'd never get back home."

"I hate to break it to you, but we are still locked in a dungeon. The chances of getting out of here and going home are still quite slim."

"No, no. It'll all be fine," I assured him. "When the guards come back, I'll tell them everything. Maybe they'll even know where I can find the witch—"

"Are you completely mad?" Anger flashed across Demetri's face.

"They can't keep us in here forever."

"Oh, trust me, they don't intend to."

"What do you mean?"

"If you haven't figured it out yet, you and I, we're sitting ducks. They don't put people in dungeons just to let them go again," he hinted.

"Are you saying..." I couldn't even finish the sentence.

Demetri met me at the wall of bars again, lowering his voice to a soft, lulling tone. "I'm saying they intend to kill us, love."

I blinked back the tears as denial set in. "No...they can't do that. We haven't done anything."

"Actually, I robbed a royal carriage, remember? And they won't take any chances on you if they think you're a sorceress."

"But if I tell them what happened, they'll know I'm not—"

He leaned down to meet my gaze, his voice more forceful now. "If you so much as utter a word about being sent here from another world by a magical portal witch, they'll kill you right where you stand before you can even think about taking a step out of that bloody cell."

"What do we do then? We can't just sit here and wait to die!" I panicked.

"Do you see another option?"

"Maybe there's a key somewhere...or maybe we can break these bars somehow..." I tugged on the poles between us in a pitiful effort to test their strength.

"I've been in here for two days. Unfortunately, there is no secret way out."

"But you said you've been in dungeons before. How'd you escape?"

The door down the hallway swung open, and echoes of angry footsteps quickly filled the room.

"Demetri..." I whispered. "What's happening?"

He leaned down closer to whisper a warning. "If you only listen to one thing I say, let it be this—don't dare to tell them any of the information that you've disclosed to me," he commanded.

"Demetri Alexander Hawkins!" the first guard yelled as he approached the cells. "By the order of Prince Phillip Barrington, you are to come with us immediately to be tried for your crimes."

The remaining guards filled in behind him, holding their swords and torches as though they were ready to go to war.

I felt like I wasn't here, like this was a nightmare I was witnessing from somewhere far away. I was frozen, unable to react, unable to save him. Everything was happening in slow motion, but I still couldn't keep up. The guard unlocked the door and pulled Demetri out of the cell into the circle of armor and torches.

"No!" I shrieked as they began marching him back down the hallway.

"Hold your tongue, wench. You'll have your turn soon enough," another guard warned as he spit in my direction.

Demetri turned back to face me. The light from the torches radiated over his stunning face, making it possible to see all of him clearly for the first time. He didn't look frightened—the way I knew I did.

"Remember what I said," he shouted, smiling at me once more before a guard jerked him back into place.

***

The floor was cold, but it was my only source of comfort now. I don't know how long I had been lying there, but it seemed like an eternity. How could they just take him like that? How could I just stand there and not even try to stop them? The unrelenting regret gnawed through every fiber of my being.

I knew what would happen now; they would kill him. And then when they were done killing him, they would come back...and they would kill me. I couldn't stop thinking about it. I couldn't stop picturing his face writhing in agony.

I had no more tears left in me to cry tonight. I was completely defeated.

CHAPTER SEVEN

When the door creaked open again, I didn't bother looking. I didn't care when the angry footsteps stopped outside of my cell. I didn't listen to the guard who ordered me to get up. I couldn't make this any worse on myself. The worst was already going to happen. I had accepted that.

The weight of my bones vaguely eased as the floor disappeared from under my body. The guards clenched my arms much tighter than necessary as they pulled me up and carried me down the hallway, verbally assaulting me the whole way for not obeying. I didn't care.

"Your Majesty, this is the other prisoner," I heard before being tossed to the marble floor.

"What's wrong with her?"

"I don't know, sire. She refuses to comply."

"Leave us," the deep voice ordered.

The noise of their footsteps faded away before disappearing altogether as the door slammed shut behind them.

The moments that followed felt heavy as I waited silently for some type of ruthless repercussion.

"Tell me, my dear, what is your name?" There was no hint of wickedness in his tone.

Grudgingly, I lifted my head to face him. He certainly looked regal in his embellished attire as he sauntered toward me in the massive throne room. I took immediate notice of the sword strapped to his belt and the bright red cape that almost concealed it as it fluttered behind him obediently.

"I am Prince Phillip Barrington. I do profoundly apologize for my men keeping you locked in the dungeon while I've been away." His voice soared through the airy room. "I am well aware of how unpleasant that experience can be." He stalked closer, zoning his gaze in on me. He was conventionally handsome...tall, and strapping with short sandy hair. He had the sort of chiseled face that could rival a Michelangelo sculpture, but there was still an entrancing youthful air about him. "I'd like to make it up to you by offering you a seat at my dining table tonight."

"You want me to...eat dinner with you?" I balked at the unexpected proposition.

"Yes, to make up for the treatment you've endured during your stay here. I do honestly feel terrible for it all."

He kneeled before me, meeting my gaze as he extended his hand in an apparent peace offering, flashing his hazel eyes to mine in a sympathetic fashion. His troubled expression reminded me a bit of Jacob when he wanted my forgiveness.

I placed my hand in his as he helped me to my feet. Declining his offer probably wouldn't grant me any favors in getting out of here.

Prince Phillip smiled kindly in return, raising my hand to his lips before lightly pressing them against my skin.

"Cecilia," he beckoned out as he gently unleashed me.

A meek young woman rushed into the room as though she'd been waiting impatiently on the other side of the door to hear her name be called. She held her head down, refusing to meet our eyes as she led me to the door.

"Wait," he called out from behind us. "You never did tell me your name."

I turned to face him at the threshold. "Gwen...Gwendolyn."

"A beautiful name." He smiled graciously. "Cecilia, please see to it that the lovely Miss Gwendolyn is ready for dinner at seven o'clock."

"Yes, Your Majesty."

She shuffled me up a striking spiral staircase and down a long-arched hallway filled with dozens of identical doors.

"We'll need to get you out of those rags, draw you a bath, and find something suitable to wear for your dinner with the prince," Cecilia said, quickly ushering me into one of the rooms.

I glanced down at the icy blue dress she'd referred to as rags and pulled at the newly tattered fabric. Days ago, it had been one of the most beautiful dresses that I'd ever owned. Not anymore. Now it was covered in blood and dirt and told unexplainable stories of survival.

"Cecilia?" I asked, hesitating as she pulled several dresses from a large wardrobe.

"Yes, Miss Gwendolyn?"

"Oh, please, no. That's not necessary. Just call me Gwen."

"Yes, Miss Gwen." Well, it was somewhat of an improvement.

"Why does he want me to have dinner with him?"

"I sense Prince Phillip feels dreadful that the guards threw you into the holding cell all night. That's no place for a fair maiden like yourself to be."

"So he says. He could just...let me go, though."

"Perhaps he will after dinner, Miss Gwen."

"Perhaps?"

"But we mustn't keep him waiting." She scurried around to help me undress. "He wouldn't like that at all!"

After my bath, Cecilia settled on a stunning, floor-length, lilac gown befitting of an actual princess. It was intricately detailed with beaded lace that shimmered like constellations in a twilight sky. The sparkles reminded me a bit of Bree's wedding gown, and I intuitively reached to grasp the pendant of her necklace.

"It's beautiful." I smiled, admiring the delicate ivy lace that bordered the neckline.

"You look lovely, Miss Gwen," Cecilia smiled for the first time as she tucked her mousy brown hair behind her ears.

She sat me down in front of a vanity and gathered my hair to the side before she began brushing it forcefully. "It's horribly tangled." She apologized several times through my wincing. Given what it had been through these last several days, I guess tangles were to be expected.

"There, that's much better," she said as she arranged the way the waves fell around my face.

"Thank you. I feel a little more like myself again," I professed. My pale, jaded reflection stared back at me in the mirror as though it were calling me a liar. Cecilia must have noticed the lack of color, too. She silently pulled a powder pad from the drawer and dotted my cheeks with dashes of pink pigment.

"And just in time. It's nearly seven now. Enjoy your dinner, Miss Gwen."

I was escorted downstairs by a large, silent guard. After he knocked on the ornate dining room doors, we were left waiting for several moments. I used that time to try not to look as out of place as I felt.

When the doors finally opened, I couldn't help but gawk at the spectacular room on the other side.

"Thank you, Maxwell. You may go." Prince Phillip said, standing before us in another embellished tunic.

The guard turned away without a word, leaving me to face the smiling prince alone.

"You look...like royalty." His ravenous eyes took me by surprise as he led me through the door.

A long wooden table occupied the center of the room. It was filled with every type of food imaginable, but my gaze didn't linger there for too long. The main attraction to behold was the elaborate stained-glass windows that stretched from the floor to the ceiling and reflected broken shards of rainbow light across the stone walls.

An iron-wrought chandelier that housed dozens of long-lit candles hung above us. The entire setting looked like something I'd only ever seen before in movies.

"Welcome to my royal dining hall. Do make yourself comfortable." Prince Phillip motioned me in front of him, guiding me to the table as he gingerly placed his hand on my lower back.

"This is incredible," I admitted unapologetically, unable to stop myself from glancing around the room in awe.

There was enough food here to feed an army – roast, chicken, sandwiches, fruits, and vegetables – it was entirely too much to absorb at first sight. Prince Phillip simply pulled my chair out and took a seat beside me.

"Who else will be joining us?" I asked, scanning the feast laid out before us.

"No one else. Why do you ask?" He studied me as a hint of amusement illuminated his expression.

"Oh, this is just a lot of food."

"Mmm, yes," he said, sounding satisfied with my answer. "Whatever we don't eat, the servants will have."

I felt my face contort. "They eat the leftovers?"

"Don't feel so bad for them." He laughed halfheartedly. "This is much better than what the villagers eat." He picked up a wine bottle and poured some into my glass.

"I suppose..." I grabbed a roll that was sitting on a nearby plate, suddenly remembering how starved I was.

Phillip shifted back in his seat, allowing me to take a few more bites before he spoke again. "Let's cut to the chase, shall we? Why don't you tell me about yourself, Lady Gwendolyn?"

I hesitated, lifting my glass to my lips before offering a response. "What would you like to know?"

"I heard something rather interesting about you." His eyes lifted playfully.

"I'm sure it wasn't true."

"Well, my dear, that's why I called you here this evening. I know stories sometimes have a tendency of getting...twisted." He smiled as he looped his finger around a wispy strand of my hair and tucked it behind my ear.

I pulled back cautiously. Something about the gleam in his eyes made my stomach crumple in knots.

"I'm not sure what exactly you've heard, Prince Phillip, but I've only been here long enough to be thrown onto the floor of your dungeon. There's been no time for engaging conversations with your men between being tossed about and being called demeaning names."

"Again, I do sincerely apologize for that. They shouldn't have treated you in such a vile manner." His eyes softened, but the tone of his words didn't convey the same sentiment. "But rest assured, my dear," he continued. "There is a reason for their presumptuousness. They are looking for someone. Someone specific. Until they find that person, they are under strict orders to take every measure, every precaution, to ensure that person doesn't slip through the cracks."

"Oh..." I took another sip of wine, letting that sink in as I tried to conceal my unsettlement.

"And while you are seemingly not that person, we must consider everyone. Because somewhere, someone does know something. Somewhere, someone has been aiding them in their unrighteous endeavors."

He ran the back of his fingers softly down my neck, and I tried not to let him see me cringe.

"I can assure you I haven't helped anyone. I don't even know who this person is that you speak of."

He stared intensely as though he were deciding whether to believe me or not. The way his brows furrowed suggested that it wasn't looking favorable.

"Did they do something to you?" I asked, hoping my artificial sympathy would convince him to reevaluate his decision.

"Yes. They did." He looked away. "They betrayed me."

"I'm sorry to hear that."

"Never you mind," he said, running his hand over his tight-lined lips. "I trust that you have no part in it."

"Thank you for believing me." I smiled back as I allowed a small sense of relief to settle in.

He carefully placed his wine glass back on the table and moved his hand to rest on my knee.

"If only all prisoners were as cooperative and benevolent as you. It would make my life so much easier."

Memories of Demetri being pulled away by the guards once again flooded my mind. They'd been doing that a lot today, despite my best efforts to block it out.

"Were you able to talk to the other person who was in the dungeon?" I asked as indifferently as I could manage.

Phillip raised his brow suspiciously. "You're acquainted with Mr. Hawkins?"

"I wouldn't say that." I cleared my throat before distracting myself with another sip of wine. "We spoke briefly while incarcerated."

He leaned back in his chair as he bit into an apple and smirked. "My dear, you don't have to worry about him anymore."

My heart sank, and I was sure it was visible on my face.

"Is he...?" I couldn't even bring myself to ask the question.

"Mr. Hawkins has been on the run for quite some time. He's been a menace to me and my kingdom for far too long. He was bound to pay for his crimes sooner or later." Phillip smiled to himself as he relished his thoughts. Thoughts I was too appalled to even contemplate.

I sat quietly, fighting back the familiar sting in my eyes.

"Nevertheless, his misfortune is nothing to sulk over." He finished off his glass. "Life goes on, does it not?"

"What are you going to do to me?" I whispered.

"Oh darling, are you worried you might suffer the same fate?" He huffed out an unnerving laugh as though he were musing over the idea.

Tears pressed at the corners of my eyes. I squeezed them closed, but several still managed to quietly escape down my cheeks as I couldn't help but wonder exactly which fate it was that Demetri had suffered.

Phillip placed his hand under my chin and gently pulled my face up to meet his. "I don't want to hurt you, pet."

"You don't?"

"No, of course not. You've done nothing to warrant that."

"So, you'll let me go?"

He leaned in closer, locking his gaze with mine. "Yes, darling, of course. But before I do, I fear I must ask you to grant me a gracious favor."

"What do you want?"

"I want your assistance. Your cooperation. I want your help to find who it is that I'm looking for."

"I don't understand." I shook my head in confusion. "I've already told you I don't know anything about it."

"Yes, but I hear that you're a woman who possesses a certain type of magic...that you can conjure spells." His eyes gleamed with anticipation as he leaned closer to me.

I fought the urge to scoff at his remark, a task that was only made possible by focusing all of my attention on a faint scar that lingered above his left eyebrow, one that I hadn't noticed until right now.

"Prince Phillip, that is absolutely not true. Your guards...they were falsely under the impression that I was several people. First Red Riding Hood, then some kind of sorceress. Your Majesty, I am neither of those things."

"So, you mean to tell me that you truly cannot help me find the person who I seek?"

"No. At least, not by magic, I'm afraid."

His disposition shifted abruptly as he rose quickly and began to pace the floor. There was something dangerous pulsing through the air, and it pushed against me, warning me to flee.

But I couldn't. I'd never make it to the door without him catching me first. Even if I did, I didn't know a way out of this place. No, fleeing was not a viable option. I'd have to try to calm him down somehow instead.

"Are you...okay?" I asked lowly, hoping he wouldn't hear the shakiness in my voice.

He silently seethed a few moments more before deciding to acknowledge me again.

"Someone is lying to me." He glared up. "And I think that it's you."

The accusation sent my fear spiraling into an unstable rage. "I am not lying to you!" I shouted defensively. "What reason would I have to do so?"

"Why would there be people under the impression that you possess a certain magic if, indeed, you do not?" he retorted.

"I don't know. That's a great question." I scowled back at him, matching the fire in his expression. "Maybe you should ask the people who lied to you about it."

"The people in my kingdom know better than to lie to me." He slammed his chair into the table. "I think that you're helping her." He stalked closer, towering over me as he placed his arms on either side of my chair to pin me in.

"I'm not helping anyone. I don't even know who you're talking about!"

He analyzed my face apprehensively as I watched the unwilling acceptance light his eyes.

"I swear it," I whispered through shallow breaths.

His face was inches from mine now. "Surely, you must know."

"I don't. Interrogating me over and over again isn't going to get you anywhere. Maybe I could help you if you would just tell me who it is you're talking about."

"I am talking about Gabriella Chamberlain." He nearly shouted her name and my body tensed in response.

"Prince Phillip, I have never heard that name before in all my life."

"What kingdom do you hail from?" he asked abruptly.

Shit. Get it together.

I drew in a quick breath. "It's a long journey from here." My heartbeat thumped wildly in my chest as he analyzed every inch of my face. "I...survived a shipwreck and ended up in Woodmist."

"How dreadful."

"Yes, it's still very hard for me to talk about." I pretended to get emotional. "I'm sorry, I don't mean to shift the subject. You were telling me about Gabriella?"

He pushed away from me, scoffing at the mention of her name like it was something contagious. "Indeed. Our little lost princess." He turned and wistfully gazed toward the large, variegated windows.

"Lost princess?" I echoed the term, fully aware that he didn't mean it as any form of endearment.

"Princess Gabriella hailed from the nearby kingdom of Willowbrook. We were betrothed before she disappeared."

"What happened to her?"

"The night before our wedding, the guards burst into my chambers late in the evening to inform me she'd run off like a thief in the night."

"Oh, I'm sorry. That must have been horrible," I muttered.

"She made a complete and utter fool of me!" he vehemently shouted, swiping several plates of food off the table as he did.

I flinched as one landed near my feet. "I'm sure no one thinks that."

"Oh, but they do." An untamed fury ignited behind his eyes. "They think I'm ignorant of their taunts, but I hear their whispers. Things no one dares to speak to my face, but I know what is said behind my back," he fumed. "I made a vow after she left to find her, no matter how long, no matter what it took. I will find her, and I will make her pay for what she's done to me."

"Prince Phillip, don't you think that's a little...extreme?"

"She made a mockery of me in my own kingdom. I've no choice but to make an example of her. My people will know I am not one to be betrayed."

"Don't you think killing a princess might cause more problems for you? There'd be retaliation. Wars even."

"I am not afraid of war," he scoffed.

"I do sympathize with your pain. It's hard sometimes to love someone who hurts us, but it seems like a lot to risk."

"Love?" He laughed dementedly as he said the word. "I never loved Gabriella. We were arranged to be married by our fathers to join our kingdoms together. If I am to be honest, her mere presence was an exacting annoyance."

I could no longer fight off the disgust that my face insisted on displaying. "So, she was purely a business transaction? And you're upset that she ran away?"

"She betrayed me, and that betrayal cost me her entire kingdom. A joining of our kingdoms would have allowed me to rule this entire hemisphere."

"I suppose, but can't you understand why she left?"

"What I understand is that she was a selfish woman. She put her needs before the needs of her kingdom."

I sat silently as he reeled in his anger, reliving the irrational memories in his head. There was clearly nothing I could say to change his mind on the matter.

"So now you see why I need help to find her...to bring her to justice for her reprehensible actions," he finally said.

"I'm sorry, I just don't see how I could help you."

Phillip walked around to the back of my chair. "Nor do I." He sighed. "If you do not possess the skills to aid me in finding her, I suppose I have no further use for you."

"You said you'd let me go," I whispered, knowing good and well he was not the kind of man to be taken at his word.

His thoughts seemed to visibly consume him as he paced to the edge of the table and back. I just wish I had some sort of inclination as to what those thoughts were. Was he considering my request or just the most violent manner in which he wanted to kill me? My shaky breaths nearly ceased altogether at the exact moment his footsteps did.

"Maybe we can work out another arrangement," he finally spoke. "If you can't help me find Gabriella, perhaps you could help me with something else entirely." His eyes grazed over my chest.

I immediately understood his intention and stood quickly, nearly turning over my chair during the commotion. But I wasn't fast enough.

"Prince Phillip!" I shrieked.

Within seconds, he was in front of me, pushing me onto the dining table before I had time to properly react. My head smashed against the plates as he greedily rushed his hands over my waist.

I screamed as I tried to push him off.

He grabbed hold of my throat, pressing me back down to the hard surface and carrying on as though he didn't hear me begging for him to stop.

Plates crashed to the floor all around us as I tried to break free, but I wasn't strong enough to fight him off as he forced his body on top of mine and pinned both of my arms together over the top of my head.

"Help!" I screamed, finally able to summon my breath once he had removed his hand from around my neck. "Someone, help me!"

He ignored my cries as he snatched my dress up over my knees and stood to fumble with his pants.

Oh, hell no. Rage ignited inside me, and I did the only thing I could think of doing. With all the strength I could muster, I delivered a swift kick straight to his groin with the heel of my foot. He emitted an unnatural groan and fell over instantly with a loud thud as his body hit the floor.

I clambered to get up and run, knocking more things off the table as I did. Phillip tried to latch onto me again as he stood, but I evaded him. Bursting through the door, I rushed down the hallway, looking for a way out...any way out. It was there that I ran right into a mob of baffled guards who seized me immediately.

"No! Let me go! Please, let me go!" I fought against them to no avail.

Phillip appeared from around the corner, looking furious and disheveled.

"How dare you, you lowly bitch!" His eyes were emblazoned with a hatred that I'd never witnessed from anyone before.

"You tried to rape me!" I shouted in response as the guards painfully gripped my arms.

"You should feel so lucky that a man of my stature would even deem a foul, spiteful woman like yourself worthy of such an honor," he spat as his livid eyes scrutinized me. "I don't want to see her face again tonight. Take her to the dungeon, she will be properly dealt with tomorrow," he commanded before he turned and limped away.

"Enjoy your last night," the guard taunted as he threw me back onto the frosty floor of the same prison cell.

CHAPTER EIGHT

It felt like several hours had passed. I never moved from the spot where I'd landed after being tossed back inside the cell like a disposable ragdoll. I'd thought about a lot of things since then but mostly about Jacob and how I'd never see him again.

The tears had long been puddled around my face on the stone floor as I ruminated about the future I'd never get to have now. I wondered if Jacob was still looking for me and how long he'd continue to do so. I wondered if he'd told my parents I was missing yet and whether Bree and Ryan were back from their honeymoon and had heard the news.

I'd never be able to get back to any of them now. What would they all conclude happened? Would they just write me off? How long would it take Jacob to just give up and move on with his life with someone new? The thoughts churned viciously in my head, providing me no sense of comfort in my last hours.

The screeching hinges of the door echoed as it opened. I lay still as I heard the sound of footsteps quickly approaching. There was no fight left in me anymore. I'd accepted my fate, the fate Demetri had already warned me of.

"Get up." The hushed nature of the voice was startling.

I rolled over, expecting to be met by a mob of vicious guards. What I found instead was a single silhouette standing at the door of my cell.

"Who—"

"No time for that, love." His words melted over me.

"Oh my God, Demetri!" I scrambled to my feet and rushed over to the door, nearly tripping over myself.

"Shh, keep quiet." He quickly inserted a key into the lock.

"I thought you were dead."

"I only said they intended to kill me. I, on the other hand, have no intention of dying tonight." He swung the door open.

I flung myself into him, locking my arms around his body as tightly as I could, as though I'd known him for much longer than I truly had.

"But how?" I breathed. Sweet, sharp hints of leather and evergreen invaded my senses as I clenched onto his black coat. He smelled intoxicating.

Demetri wrapped his arms around me in return as he attempted to help me regain my balance.

"That's a story for another time. Right now, we need to focus on getting out of here." He released his hold in exchange for my hand and silently led me out into the desolate hallway.

"When we get out of here, we'll make a break for the forest and head to the coast. There's a boat waiting for me there," he whispered before stealing a glance around the corner.

"A boat? Where will we go?" I asked.

"You there! Stop at once!" a deep voice bellowed through the corridor.

Demetri tightened his grip and pulled me along behind him as we ran through several mazes of narrow, dark hallways.

"Do you know where you're going?" I exclaimed, trembling from the sheer panic of it all.

"Shh! This way!"

"Stop this instant!" The voice chased us.

We rounded the corner and ran straight into another pair of surprised guards, scarcely dodging them as they tried to grab hold of us.

"I gotcha now!" the larger one shouted as he jerked my arm toward him.

I cried out in pain and nearly fell to my knees. Demetri released my other hand, and I was sure he'd made the quick decision to leave me there and save himself. A fist flew by my face faster than I realized where it came from, making contact with the guard's nose. The hollow snapping noise that immediately followed made my stomach twist.

"Come on," Demetri urged, catching my hand again as the bloody guard fell out cold on the floor behind us.

We took refuge down a steep flight of stairs. As we descended, the lights grew dimmer, and I nearly toppled over on top of him. "I can't see!" I whispered breathlessly.

"Don't let go of me," he commanded.

At the bottom of the staircase, we stopped momentarily to catch our breath.

"Which way did the prisoners go?" A voice roared from above.

"We lost them." Another responded.

"I hope you know a way out of here," I said as quietly as I could manage. "If Phillip catches us now, I doubt he'd grant us the privilege of waiting until morning to murder us."

"Have I failed you yet?"

"No…but I haven't known you for very long."

"I nearly forgot how feisty you were." I could almost hear the smile spread across his face as he spoke.

We soon reached a door at the bottom of the passageway. Moonlight flooded through the jagged, wooden cracks that had long been forged, teasing me with slivers of freedom from the other side. Demetri held up the set of keys that he'd broken me out of the dungeon with and quickly searched for the one that could break us out of this hellhole castle.

"Hurry," I pleaded as he jammed in the second one.

The fourth one finally worked. The door swung open, and scented waves of jasmine from the castle garden slammed into me. Demetri peered out to assess our location as I braced myself against the threshold, fighting the sudden urge to vomit.

"Are you all right?" He asked, dipping his head down to evaluate my bleak   expression. "I'm fine," I lied. My head was spinning too fast. The absolute terror I'd been subjected to over the last several days tangled with the floral rush of exhilaration was far too dizzying.

"There are guards patrolling near the main entrance," he whispered.

"How far away is the main entrance?"

"Far enough to make a run for it." He glanced back over his shoulder at me, waiting for some type of confirmation.

"Okay." I nodded, trying to contain my ferocious heartbeat.

"We'll head straight for the tree line there." He pointed. "Then, run as fast as you can until we get to the shore."

My breath was shaky and rapid as we crept against the outer wall. "Stay close. It's not much farther," he reassured. The sentence had barely left his lips before we were compromised.

"There they are!" a far-away voice called out as others began to yell in recognition. "After them!"

We bolted through the royal garden and straight toward the trees. "Faster, Gwen!" Demetri demanded as he took the lead.

I could barely feel my feet touch the ground as I kept a close pace. The guards' horses were gaining on us, the sound of their hooves drumming loudly in my ears.

"Demetri, I can't keep..." I gasped for air.

"You must!" he yelled, gripping my hand tightly as he pulled me along.

The frosty air was painful as it whipped violent bursts of gusts into my face.

I was on the verge of collapsing when he halted suddenly. "Dammit!" he yelled, rubbing his temple in distress.

"What?" I barely had the lung capacity to ask the question.

Then I saw it. Looking past the place where he stood, I realized there was nowhere left for us to run. We were trapped on the edge of a fucking cliff.

Demetri peered over the pointed ledge. I didn't have to look to know what was down there. I already heard the furious sea beating angrily against the rocks below.

"I think we lost them. I don't hear them anymore," I said when I finally caught my breath again.

"Don't let your guard down. They've nothing better to do than to keep looking, and they won't stop until they find us," he said before turning to face me with a wild and unusual expression. "I need you to trust me right now. Do you think you can do that?"

"Yes..." And I did. He'd come back to save me after all.

"We're going to jump."

"I'm sorry...what?" Clearly, I had misconstrued his words.

He threw his arm up toward the castle in defeat. "We can't go back that way. The boat won't be too far from here—"

"Demetri, I'm not jumping off a fucking cliff."

"I don't see another choice, love. It's our best chance of survival."

I glowered at him in disbelief. He could not be serious right now. "Absolutely not. Jumping off a cliff...into the ocean...in the dark doesn't exactly seem like it'd have a good survival rate. We could bust our heads open on the rocks. And if we don't do that, we'll most definitely drown...I'm not even that good of a swimmer!" I rambled off my reasons.

"Listen," he whispered as he moved a finger to his lips.

The ground underneath us tremored as the horses drew nearer, and the glowing torches racing toward us looked like a wildfire burning straight through the forest.

"We must jump," he demanded. "And we must do it now."

I shook my head as I backed away from him. "No, I'm sorry. I can't."

"They'll kill us both if they get the chance. You're scared, and that's okay, but we are running out of time." His eyes pleaded with me, and something inside me shifted at the sight.

I wasn't sure at this point exactly how many deadly scenarios I'd already been in today alone, but I knew my luck had to be running low by now. Regardless, he was right. I really fucking hated that he was right.

I took a deep breath and nodded against my better judgment. Silently, we approached the edge of the overhang just as the guards edged their way out of the tree line.

"Stop! By order of the prince!" one of them yelled out.

Demetri grabbed hold of my hand and leaped first, not allowing me a marginal chance to change my mind. As the ground disappeared from under my feet, I tumbled weightlessly against the night. It was only a few seconds, but it felt like I was frozen in time, forever floating somewhere in between the blurry depths of darkness. I closed my eyes and braced myself for the inevitable icy impact.

CHAPTER NINE

Everything went silent. The howling wind, the roar of the crashing waves, my thunderous pulse...as soon as I'd broken through the water, it had all stopped. My body throbbed as though all my bones were broken, making the struggle to swim back to the surface even more impossible.

Traces of moonlight rippled through the dark, murky sea. I struggled to reach it, but the harder I tried, the farther I sank. I knew my luck had finally run its course.

"Why'd you leave me?" Jacob asked, the heart-wrenching words cutting me to the core.

"I'm sorry. I never wanted to," I cried, reaching out to touch his face.

"We could have had it all."

"I still want that. I still want you."

"If you did, you wouldn't have left," Jacob lashed out. "It's too late, Gwen."

"I'm here now. Please Jacob, I love you."

"You've been gone too long. I've moved on." He turned to leave, ignoring my cries as he faded away into the darkness.

My eyes flew open as I leaned over, coughing violently. Water poured from my mouth as I struggled to catch my breath.

"Ah, there we are." Demetri appeared above me, dripping water onto my face from his own drenched hair.

My throat blazed with pain as I tried to speak. "What happened?"

"I knew you were still under the water...you said you couldn't swim, so I dove down until I found you."

I stared up at the stars, blinking wearily as they blurred together and came into focus again. "I thought I was going to die," I quietly confessed.

"I wasn't going to let that happen." His gaze was piercing, and it was enough to convince me that he meant it.

I stared back weakly, still unable to fully comprehend everything that had happened tonight. "Thank you for saving me," I whispered. "...twice."

"I'm sorry about that, by the way." Demetri tore his eyes away from mine long enough to call my attention elsewhere. "Your dress got hung between the rocks, and I had to intervene."

I looked down and realized I was only wearing the thin white slip and corset that Cecilia had stuffed me into earlier.

"We'll find you something else as soon as we can." He smiled reassuringly, and I could have sworn I saw his eyes rake over my ensemble.

"Believe it or not, this is a pretty modest look where I come from."

Demetri arched his brow in distinct astonishment. I wasn't sure if it was from the revelation or my indifference to the situation, but I couldn't contain the giggle that erupted, even as it set fire to my throat.

"Sorry, I didn't mean to make you feel uncomfortable," I teased.

"Trust me, love, I've seen it all. It would take a lot more than that to make me uncomfortable." He smiled deviously, and I couldn't help but laugh at the candidness of the moment.

He extended his arm to help me stand, holding me at the waist until I was stable enough not to cause an accidental injury to myself. "The ship should be a couple of miles up the shore from here. Are you able to walk that far?"

"Yes." My legs were aching more than they ever had, but I could manage a couple of miles, especially if it meant getting away from Phillip and his goons.

"As soon as we get there, you can change."

"I'm not so worried about that. I just want to get the hell away from here."

He watched as I took a few shaky steps, slowing his confident stride to match my more leisurely pace. "Regardless, the men on the boat will be worried about it, so you'll change before they get the chance to cause any trouble," he said sternly.

"While that sounds mildly entertaining, I suppose I have had enough trouble recently to last me a lifetime."

"What kind of trouble are you referring to, exactly?"

"I wouldn't want to bore you with all of the details."

"We've nothing but time, and you're no bore to me."

"Well, for one," I decisively complied, "Phillip tried to rape me tonight."

After a few silent moments, I glanced to my side to see him staring straight ahead. Even in the dark, I could tell he was furious by the way his jaw flexed and the way he held his fists clenched at his sides.

The recollection of Phillip's similar sudden shift in disposition right before he attacked washed over me like a warning. I pushed it down. Demetri wasn't Phillip, I knew that, but I still couldn't help but find myself intimidated by the change in his demeanor.

"Demetri?" I whispered.

"That fucking bastard," he spat.

"He didn't succeed," I added.

His feral, handsome face was nearly unrecognizable. "What stopped him?" he asked through gritted teeth.

"I...kicked him in the dick." I shrugged.

Every trace of fury that etched his expression subsided as he began to roar with laughter. "You what!"

"It was the only thing I could think of at the time!" I laughed at the sight of him doubled over in hysterics, utterly unable to compose himself.

"What did he do?" he finally asked when he could speak again.

"He chased me down the hallway and told the guards to take me back to the dungeon again, which is where I stayed until you came and got me out."

"For God's sake, Gwen." His eyes danced with amusement and disbelief. "You kicked the royal dick in the royal dick. You're lucky he didn't kill you right there on the spot."

"He was too busy limping to consider it."

Demetri boomed with laughter again at the thought. "It was still better than what he deserves," he finally declared.

"True. Strangely enough, before that happened, he told me a story about some lost princess that he wants to exact his revenge on. The guy is a complete nut job."

Demetri nodded knowingly. "Princess Gabriella."

"Oh, so you've heard?"

"Everyone's heard. If she's smart, she'll stay away."

"Phillip wanted me to help him find her."

His dark brows drew together in confusion. "How?"

"Everyone thinks I'm a sorceress, remember? His guards must have told him, and he wanted me to perform some voodoo spells to help him."

"And when you said you couldn't, he tried to rape you instead?" Demetri's jaw flexed again at the mention of Phillip's immoral intentions.

"Pretty much."

"Well, if that's your only trouble, you needn't worry about it anymore. He won't get close enough to try again."

A flashback of the vision I'd had of Jacob before Demetri pulled me from the water invaded my thoughts and reignited the desperate need to see him again. I knew that it wasn't real, but I couldn't shake his words or the threat of him moving on without me...especially not now. Not when I had a real chance of getting home again.

"What is it?" he asked.

I crossed my arms across my chest, shivering under the chill of the breeze against my wet clothes. "It's nothing."

Demetri paused to slip off his coat. "Did something else happen?"

I shook my head, abruptly halting my steps beside him. "No. Not with Phillip. I just...I have to figure out a way to get back home. And fast."

My eyes flashed to his as he moved to place the coat over my shoulders. I started to resist, but decided against it after realizing how much it shielded the wind.

A knowing look crept across his face, and the tension it created felt unusually palpable in the air that circulated between us.

"You have someone." He finally spoke.

"Yes," I replied, weirdly relieved that I wasn't the one who had said it.

"In your other world," he added, as he resumed our journey.

"Yes...Jacob."

"Ah," Demetri said softly.

We walked in silence for several minutes as I mulled over the jumbled thoughts and words shooting through my head. The stillness was too uncomfortable. I didn't know why I felt guilty about it, but something in my mind begged the question: Would Demetri have even come back for me if he had known?

"It's complicated," I ultimately blurted, pulling his damp coat against me as another gust of wind swept over us.

"How so?"

"It's a long story." I sighed. "We were going through a rough patch right before I was sent here. I thought that it was over. Now we're engaged. Wow, that still feels weird to say out loud..."

Demetri listened as I blabbered on, trying to make the situation sound less absurd. "...you see, I thought he was cheating..." God, I was only making it worse.

"So, you're with a man who betrayed you?" he interrupted.

Heat flashed in my cheeks. "Um, no, I mean, he has in the past, but that was a long time ago."

"And you love him?"

"Yes, very much," I replied softly.

"Your world does indeed sound strange."

I laughed uncomfortably. "My world, or me?"

"A bit of both, perhaps," he quipped, a quiet chuckle escaping his lips.

"I guess I shouldn't have dumped everything out there like that," I said, feeling somewhat regretful and exposed. "It's been a weird night."

"I asked for it."

"I guess, but..." My voice trailed off as he stopped in his tracks.

"Look out there, Gwen."

I followed his gaze out into the ocean, spotting an enormous ship stationed idly off the coast.

"We made it." Demetri turned, flashing a devastating smile that made my breath catch in my throat.

The sails billowed out with each gust of wind as broken beams of moonlight scattered around the lapping waves. Faint melodies of joyful music and laughter rang out from the top deck.

"We made it." I echoed, taking in the mesmerizing view.

Demetri took a step closer to the shoreline before he paused. "And Gwen..."

My gaze flickered back to his.

"Don't worry. You'll find your way back home," he promised just before wading into the shallow water.

CHAPTER TEN

Demetri had called for one of the men to send down a rowboat to collect us. The bitter air made my teeth clatter as we both waited knee-deep in the rolling waves.

"Where will we go?" I asked, watching as the tiny boat made its way closer.

"First, we are going to get the hell out of Castleberry. We'll worry about finding your witch after that."

I winced, gripping my arms tightly as another frosty gust crashed over us.

"Ahoy, Captain! We were startin' to wonder if something happened to you!" a voice called out as it stalled a few feet away.

"Oh, come now, surely you know me better than that, Felix!" Demetri laughed.

"What'd he call you?" I asked.

The stout little man jumped out of the boat and splashed over to us eagerly, dragging it behind him with distinct purpose. His round, bearded face was jovial and unnaturally red. He'd obviously been partaking in the festivities on deck.

"Why, hello, madam!" he exclaimed.

"Hello." I smiled, subtly trying to cover myself.

"Felix, this is Gwen. She'll be joining us on our journey for a while."

"Oh, what a pleasure!" Felix shouted. "I know the crew will be thrilled!" He chuckled.

Demetri shot me a quick apologetic look. "No, Felix. She will not be joining us in *that* way."

"Oh, my apologies, madam." Felix snatched the knitted hat off his head and held it to his chest.

"That's...okay," I responded.

"I just thought with the way you were dressed..."

Demetri lifted his hand abruptly. "That will be enough, Felix."

"Of course, terribly sorry, Captain."

"Very well, then. Let's get back to the ship. We both need a change of clothes, and the temperature is dropping quite rapidly," Demetri commanded.

"You didn't tell me you were the freaking captain," I muttered as we approached the rowboat and climbed inside.

"It didn't come up." The corner of his mouth lifted up into a smirk.

When we'd made it back to the ship, Demetri lifted me to the ladder rope and followed me up. I would have typically been concerned about his view from underneath, but I was too busy focusing every ounce of my anxiety on exactly how many men were about to see me in this medievalesque lingerie.

Finally reaching the top, I cautiously peered over the railing and took in the scene. Half of the crew was playing instruments while the other half sang and danced, and I noticed nearly all of them had a drink in hand.

"I don't want to go first." I threw a worried look down the ladder at Demetri.

"Kind of late for that, love."

"Fuck," I muttered, holding my breath as I climbed over.

The music stopped as soon as my feet hit the deck. I stared back in silence at their bewildered faces. While the men all varied when it came to color, size, and age, they all shared the same confused look as they gawked at me. Several uncomfortable seconds that felt more like eternities passed before Demetri and Felix hopped over the ledge to join me.

"Captain! What'd you bring us!" a burly man holding an accordion shouted out.

"For he's a jolly good fellow!" Another man with several wooden teeth began to chant as the others laughed and joined in.

I felt my cheeks burn red and pulled the pirate coat around me tighter as Demetri stepped in front of me to shield me from their view. "That's quite enough, Alistair." The threat that radiated was delivered by a deeper voice than the one I'd already grown accustomed to.

"Come on, Cap. You can't always keep them for yourself," the accordion man yelled again.

I felt my eyes narrow in on his gaunt, bearded face.

"Another word, Jasper, and you'll lose that loose tongue." Demetri glared.

A younger man spoke up. "It's all in good fun, Captain Hawkins."

Demetri ignored him. "This is Gwen. She is our guest for the time being. You will treat her with the utmost respect while she's on board," he commanded.

"Gwen who? Is she important or something?" another one slurred drunkenly.

Demetri approached the inebriated man, expertly snatching a sword from another pirate's belt as he did, and pointed it at the man's bobbing throat.

"Somebody get the mop," Jasper cackled in the background. "We've got a bleeder."

Jesus Christ. I'd already been through enough tonight. The last thing I wanted to see right now was somebody's tongue getting cut out of their mouth.

"That's not necessary!" I raised my voice in a panic, and all of the men fell unnaturally quiet. "My name is Gwendolyn Winters. I don't intend to inconvenience you for very long. I'm only trying to get home."

Demetri was looking back at me as though I had three heads.

A younger man finally broke the silence. "Pleased to meet you, Miss Winters."

Demetri released the man in his grasp, tossing him backward as he threw the sword to the deck. "Now, if you would all quit acting like a bunch of blubbering idiots, let's use this time wisely and get the hell out of here."

"Aye-aye, Captain Hawkins!" several of the men shouted in unison before scurrying off.

I followed him to the back of the ship and swiftly slipped inside the room he gestured me into.

"I apologize for my men," he said, shutting the heavy door behind us and drowning out the sounds of a resumed celebration.

"I kind of expected it." I motioned to my clothes.

"They aren't quite as brazen when they aren't intoxicated." He slipped off his riveted black tunic and tossed it to the floor, revealing a thin, still-wet shirt underneath that clung perfectly to his body. "Most of them, anyway."

I tore my eyes away quickly before he could catch me staring. "Is this your room?" I turned, surveying the ornate details of it all. The mahogany-paneled walls were warmly lit by two glowing lanterns stationed on the opposite side of the cabin. An intricate ivory rug with burgundy accents stretched across the wooden planked floors, and there was a navy blue armchair in the corner. In the center of the room sat a round table with three wooden chairs placed around it.

I took a step closer, taking notice of the compass and parchment maps that were messily scattered across the surface.

"Aye. Welcome to my humble abode."

"I like it." I smiled. "It's cozy."

Against the far wall stood two large bookshelves with an unmade bed positioned in the middle. "Ah, is that where you take all your conquests?"

He cocked his head as a sly smile pulled at the corner of his mouth. A startling jolt of exhilaration surged through my body as he bit his lower lip in a visible effort to hold back his thoughts.

"While I'd personally love to discuss conquests with you, I think perhaps that's an inappropriate topic to talk about with a betrothed woman."

"Oh, a man of honor, are you?"

"I'd like to think so."

"Were you so honorable when you robbed that carriage?"

He smirked sarcastically. "You met the prince. You tell me."

"I guess you have a point."

He pulled out a trunk from his closet. "There are some clothes in here for you to choose from."

"Interesting...wherever did they come from?"

"I think you know the answer to that."

I slid out of his coat, laying it across the back of one of the chairs before lifting the lid of the trunk. It was packed to the brim with colorful gowns. "Jesus, Demetri." I shuffled through the contents inside the trunk. "I don't think I even want to know what you did to get this many clothes."

"Rest assured, love, these were stolen, not earned." He winked in amusement.

I fought back a laugh. "Why'd you steal women's clothes?"

"We never know what's in the cases. We just grab them. Lucky for you. Otherwise, you'd be in those wet undergarments all night."

"Lucky me," I echoed sarcastically.

I pulled out several dresses that were clearly not made to sleep in. "Wherever this lady was going, she must not have had any intentions of going to bed."

Demetri sauntered over and removed a pile, placing them on the table before pulling out a simple, long white gown and handing it to me.

"I'll leave you to get dressed then." He turned to walk out of the room.

"Actually..." I said, completely embarrassed by what I was about to request.

He spun back to face me, arching his brow suspiciously.

"Don't give me that look," I commanded, motioning to the corset. "I need help. I don't know how to get out of this thing."

An arrogant smile spread across his face as he strode closer. "It truly is your lucky day then."

"Oh my gosh, please don't make this any more awkward than it has to be." I turned my face away in shame as he approached.

"Turn around," he commanded. I obeyed, allowing him to gather my hair together and place it over my shoulder. His breath grazed across the back of my neck, causing an unsolicited chill to trickle down my spine.

"Hold still," he leaned down to whisper against my ear, brushing by me as he slid something off the table.

I felt a tug against my waist, followed by sweet, instant relief as the sound of his blade sliced through the laces all at once.

"Demetri! You could have just undone it like a normal human being!" I shrieked, frantically trying to hold what was left of the corset up over my chest.

"Did you want to wear it again?"

"Well, no, but—"

"I didn't think so."

"You could have warned me, at least."

"It was more enjoyable for me this way." He shrugged, suppressing a smirk as I furrowed my brows at him. "I'll warn you next time."

He took his leave from the room as I changed into the nightgown. I was still in the middle of packing the other dresses back into the trunk when the door swung open again.

"Miss Gwendolyn, so sorry to intrude. I just wanted to let you know there's a private room under the deck where you can sleep if you'd like." Felix averted his eyes when he noticed my clothes, as if this gown was much more scandalous than the one he'd met me in.

"That won't be necessary," Demetri entered again immediately behind him. "Our guest will be sleeping here. In my bed."

My eyes went wide in response to the declaration.

"Of course, Captain! What a fine idea!" Felix exclaimed before hurrying back out on deck and shutting the door behind him.

I stared him down, scoffing to myself when he smiled back. "Demetri, I can't sleep in your bed…"

"You can, and you will. My bed is very comfortable."

"But where would you sleep?"

He huffed out a laugh. "That's up to you." The tone of his voice was more seductive than what was warranted in this particular situation.

The fire involuntarily rushed back to my face. "Demetri," I scolded. "I'll go below deck. It's not a problem, really."

"Like hell you will. I'll not leave you to fend for yourself around a bunch of drunken imbeciles," he declared.

"Fine..." I surveyed the room. "I'll sleep in that armchair."

"You'll take the bed," he replied sternly, crossing his arms.

"But—" I began.

"Take the bed, love. I insist."

He was clearly not going to give in. Accepting defeat, I crawled in between the sheets and watched as he moved across the room to extinguish the lights.

"You were right," I teased, pulling the heavy blanket up to my neck. "This is nice. It's way better than last night's accommodations." I forced a smile, not quite ready to relive the trauma of those events.

Demetri seemingly shared that sentiment. "Don't remind me of that wretched place." He muttered before grabbing a quilt from the foot of the bed and tossing it onto the armchair.

He wandered to the back of the room where a line of four arched windows occupied the wall. The dark curtains that hung down had hidden them from view until now. He pulled the fabric back, allowing the shimmering beams of moonlight to flood across the cabin floor.

Demetri leaned against the wall as he gazed out over the glowing, tranquil sea. "For a moment there, I almost wondered if I'd ever get to see this view again," he confessed.

"How'd you escape?" The question had been gnawing at me all night, but only now did I have enough courage to ask.

"The maid helped me." He hesitated as though he were considering whether or not he should provide further details.

"Cecilia?"

"I didn't catch her name." He pushed himself off the wall, leaving the curtains cracked open. "Barrington had just left the room after disclosing all the ways he wanted to kill me. Then the guards came in and took me somewhere else while they awaited his orders. When he finally called for them, they all left the room. That's when she came in, unlocked my chains with the set of keys I used to free you, and told me how to escape."

I watched quietly as his silver crested outline crossed the room and returned to the chair. He pulled off his shirt, letting it fall to the floor beside him. Moon rays dripped over his body, drawing attention to the way his muscles flexed and all the sculpted lines that were forged across his back.

It made me recall the first time I'd seen his silhouette...back in the dungeon cell that neither of us was meant to make it out of.

"Demetri?" I whispered.

"Yes, love?"

"Thank you...for saving me."

"You don't have to thank me."

"Yes, I do. I'd be dead without you."

"I couldn't leave you there. Not when I knew he would have killed you."

"Why?" My voice felt strained as I sought to see his face in the dim light. "Don't get me wrong, I'm glad that you didn't. But you don't even know me. Why'd you risk your life?"

"You didn't deserve that fate. No one does."

"No," I whispered. "They don't."

Demetri settled into the chair and draped the blanket over his body. "Get some sleep, love," he replied as though he sensed the unsettlement that still lingered within me. "We'll live to see another day."

CHAPTER ELEVEN

I wasn't sure how long I'd slept, but it felt like days. Despite that, it was still a struggle to convince myself to abandon the comfort of the pirate captain's bed. The mere thought of that statement sounded so ridiculous. I should be scared out of my mind…being stranded on a ship with a bunch of wayward pirates. I wasn't, though. The fact of the matter was that this was the safest I'd felt since being sent to this bizarre and unpredictable world.

I pulled myself out from under the covers, stretching as I surveyed the sunlit room. Demetri was nowhere to be found. Instead, I found a modest emerald dress laid out on the back of the chair where he'd slept. After freshening up, and feeling much less self-conscious about today's attire, I decided to join the crew out on the deck.

"Mornin', Miss Winters."

I turned, taking in the weathered face I recognized from last night. "Good morning…Alistair, right?"

His brown eyes twinkled underneath his bushy gray brows. "That's a good memory you got there, Miss Winters."

"No need for formalities. Please, call me Gwen."

"Yes, ma'am." He tipped his hat as he smiled warmly, showing off his array of wooden teeth.

I climbed the steps to the top deck and took in the view of the turquoise water that stretched out ahead of us as far as the eye could see. Vibrant rays of sunlight bounced across the waves like dancing diamonds scattered along the horizon. A breeze tousled through my hair, and I allowed myself to inhale deeply for the first time in several days, letting the sweet, salty air consume me.

"Morning, love." Demetri's voice chimed from behind me, and I melted into the smooth familiarity of it.

"Good morning." I smiled. "How'd you sleep?"

"I've slept on worse but also on better." He winced playfully as he approached, rubbing the back of his neck.

"Now I feel a little guilty because I slept great," I taunted.

"I told you my bed was comfortable." He was right. The subtle scent of evergreen on the sheets didn't hurt either.

"So, where are we off to, Captain?"

He raised his brow suggestively and leaned in closer to me. "I rather like it when you call me *'Captain.'*"

I smirked at the extra emphasis he extended on the last word. "I guess I better not do it then."

Ignoring the jest, Demetri leaned against the ship rail as he shifted his focus to somewhere off in the distance. The assertive vision of him here in his element made me momentarily question why I was ever surprised to discover he was a pirate captain.

"The good news is we're not in Castleberry territory anymore."

"Demetri ..." I responded, lowering my voice to a barely audible tone. I was unsure of how to even ask the question that I'd finally had the time to concern myself with. "What is this place?"

"This is the Ivory Sea."

"No, I mean..." I shifted my body closer until my arm grazed against his. "You're the only one here who knows my secret...about where I'm from. This world, it's so different. Yes, there are oceans and forests, but they're not the same. And there are witches and castles...and it's all just...incomprehensible." I shook my head, struggling to keep my thoughts from derailing. "I want to know more, to understand it, but I don't know where, or even how to start trying to make sense of it all."

He leaned down closer to my ear, blocking out the others from overhearing our conversation. "This world is composed of four main regions, kingdoms if you will. Each of the kingdoms has its own ruler...one of whom you've already met." His face twisted at the thought of Phillip before he managed to push through the disdain. "Then there are the outlying regions. Those are the smaller territories that surround the main kingdoms. Some of the regions lie in a close enough proximity to the main territories to be governed by the nearest leader."

"So, there's Castleberry...and what else?"

"Willowbrook is the nearest kingdom to Castleberry. Those are the two main territories on this side of the world. On the other side, there is Winterhaven, and The Golden Empire."

"Where are you from?" I inquired.

"I'm not from any of the main territories. I descend from a small region south of here known as Fable Isles. The closest ruler to my home would be Barrington, but it's fortunately far enough away to not be under his control."

"That's a relief."

"Aye. Altogether, the territories in this world make up what we call the Isles of Everwood," Demetri explained.

"The Isles of Everwood," I repeated, trying to compartmentalize all the information he was giving me.

"The name derives from an ancient, enchanted Everwood tree believed to be the first source of magic in this realm."

"So, do all of the lands here have...magic?" It felt silly to ask, even after everything that I'd witnessed.

"In a sense," he answered. "It was once limited to a very few certain lands. So much so that it was merely a myth that it ever even existed. Those who wielded it wanted to keep it that way. Over time, though, it began to trickle out and show up in places where it wasn't supposed to be."

"Why keep it a secret?"

"Because, as I'm sure you know, love, great power inevitably spawns great corruption. The wielders knew that in the wrong hands, magic could prove to be utterly destructive."

"Like with Phillip," I mused out loud.

"Aye. Imagine what he would do if he wielded such a capability. Luckily, he doesn't, but that doesn't mean he can't gain access to it in other ways."

"I guess that helps to explain how I got here at least," I crossed my arms, mulling over Demetri's words. "I just wish I knew why."

His body tensed as though he had been waiting for this turn of the conversation. "That's the next thing that I wanted to talk with you about. I'm afraid I do have a bit of bad news."

"What is it?"

"You asked earlier where we were sailing to. The answer to that question is Mystic Grove. It's one of the original lands of magic. Power runs deep there, perhaps deeper than any other place in this world. It's also where I've encountered the witch before, so it seemed like the best place to begin our search."

My heart nearly flipped over inside my chest. "Demetri, that's great! That means we actually have something to go on here."

"That's not the bad news I was referring to."

"What is it then?"

"The land is a few days' journey from where we are now, but to reach it, we must first travel through a dangerous part of the sea." He shifted uncomfortably, and the grim expression on his face told me the most important thing I needed to know—that it was a deadly endeavor. "It's called Shadow Ridge. There's a sea cave there, and it's the only direct passageway from here to Mystic Grove."

"Shadow Ridge? Is it as ominous as it sounds?"

"It can be." He glanced back down at me, letting his eyes settle on my mouth for a fleeting moment.

"Should I be concerned?"

"Tell me, love..." He whispered the words as though he were about to tell me a secret. "In your world, is there such a thing as sirens?"

"Sirens, as in mermaids?"

"Then you've heard of them."

"Of course. I never thought they really existed, but I suppose these sorts of developments shouldn't shock me anymore."

"Aye, in this world, they do exist." Demetri leaned down, propping his elbow on top of the rail as he stroked his chin in a thoughtful manner. "On top of that, Shadow Ridge is rather treacherous to navigate through."

My eyes darted back between his as I tried to piece together the parts of the story he wasn't telling me. "But you've made it through before, right?"

"Yes, once. But barely so," he admitted. "The sirens...they're volatile creatures. They kill for no reason other than sheer enjoyment, dragging as many men as possible to their death to simply lie at the bottom of the sea like some type of ghastly trophy." His face turned pale as he seemed to reminisce.

I fought to push down the nauseating feeling that was building up inside. "Hey, we've made it this far," I assured him. "Surely we can survive a cave of mermaids."

"I like your optimism. The men will need that sort of reassurance."

"Do they know yet?"

"Aye, and they're not thrilled at the idea."

"Did you tell them why?"

"Do you mean to ask: Did I tell them you're from another world, and we are going on a perilous quest to find a witch to send you home who may or may not even be in the land we are sailing to?"

"Uhh...yeah." I tried not to grimace at the blunt synopsis.

Demetri's laugh chased away the worry that edged his features moments ago. "No, I spared the details. They needn't know everything."

"Thank you." I placed my hand over his and felt his knuckles tighten underneath. "Are you sure there's no other way?"

"Not that I can tell. I've been scouring the maps, trying to find an alternate route from this side of the sea, one that wouldn't take weeks to safely travel." He sighed as he pulled his hand out from under mine to run it over his windswept hair. "Mystic Grove is shrouded in some of the most powerful magic that exists in this world. It's nearly impossible to access unless it's through certain entry points, and this location is the only one that I'm certain of that's located on this side of the world."

"We could always try searching somewhere else first," I offered.

Demetri shook his head. "It's too risky to backtrack now. Phillip has probably sent his fleet of ships this way and alerted the neighboring kingdom to be on the lookout as well. I imagine that, by now, there are probably guards stationed everywhere on this side of the coastal hemisphere from as far north as FrostMeadow down to Woodmist."

A chill raced down my spine as he uttered the familiar word. "Woodmist? I've been there before. Probably not a good idea to go back."

Demetri's face lit up with intrigue. "Did you make enemies, Winters?"

"Red Riding Hood's grandmother ratted me out to Prince Phillip's guards. Does that count?" I smiled sarcastically.

A hint of shock tinted his expression. "Are you to tell me that you met Red Riding Hood?"

"I did...do you know her?"

"No, she's a bit of a legend around here. Elusive, though. No one knows exactly who she is, and she's been on the run from Phillip for quite some time."

My eyes narrowed and flickered up to his in suspense. "What? Why?"

"He claims that she was one of the ones who helped Princess Gabriella escape. He retaliated by making some sort of deal with a magic wielder to unleash a cursed beast on the land to find her. She's somehow managed to evade his efforts all these years."

"A beast? You mean the wolf?"

"Aye, a wolf as big as a bear, they say...a merciless creature whose sights are not limited to Red Riding Hood alone. It will attack anyone who tries to leave the village, with the exception of Barrington and his guards."

Flashes of the sharp, snapping fangs inhabited my thoughts. "It's not quite as big as a bear, but it's terrifying nonetheless."

"You saw the beast?" The color drained from Demetri's face.

I lifted the sleeve of my dress, turning my arm slightly to show off my battle wounds. "Phillip's castle isn't the only near-death experience I've had since I was sent here."

"How..." Demetri stammered as he grabbed hold of my arm to inspect it closer. "How did you survive that encounter? The stories I've heard..." he trailed off, peering back up at me as though he had no idea who I even was.

"I wouldn't have, not without Row—Red Riding Hood's help."

"Lucky for you." His expression was still disturbed.

"I just hope she's okay. Things were...intense when we parted ways."

While I'd been so busy trying not to die recently, I hadn't had much time to reflect on Rowan's unselfishness, how she'd given me her only protection from the wolf – the wolf who was seemingly created to seek her out – and how she'd probably never get that protection back now that Prince Limp Dick had it in his possession.

"I wish I could find a way to thank her for everything that she did to help me."

"Perhaps one day you will."

"Not unless she, too, is randomly on a boat headed to Mystic Grove, it would seem."

He offered me a sad smile. "I'm sure she knows regardless, love."

I sighed, hoping he was right about that. "How much longer until we get there?"

"If all goes well, we should reach Shadow Ridge by tomorrow night. Perhaps a bit earlier, depending on the wind. After we pass through the sea cave, it'll take another day or two to reach Mystic Grove. I'll need to try to prepare the newer crew members for what lies ahead."

"Newer crew members?"

Demetri's eyes fell, but not before I saw the turmoil that ignited in them. "As I said, we've ventured through the area before. It was not too terribly long ago. We lost many men that day and had to recruit more once we docked."

"I'm starting to get worried," I admitted.

"No use in worrying, love. It'll only distract you."

"I don't want to be responsible for—"

He lifted his finger to my lips. "Let's not dwell on things that haven't happened yet."

I nodded. His suggestion made sense, but it wasn't so easy to drown out all these troublesome thoughts.

"What can I do to help?" I asked.

"Perhaps you can just take this time to have a look around the boat. Felix can show you around if you desire."

"How's that helpful?"

"It'll boost the morale of the crew," he quipped.

"And get me out of your face?" I added, folding my arms across my chest as I scowled.

"I'd much rather gaze upon your face, love, but misfortune favors the ill-prepared."

CHAPTER TWELVE

I spent the rest of the day touring the ship. Felix was all too happy to volunteer his time while Demetri tried to prepare the crew for what they'd soon endure. The men had been assembled in his cabin for several hours as they studied the maps and heard the tragic tales of the supernatural sea creatures we'd soon be forced to face.

"...and this is where the other half of the crew sleeps." Felix's voice invaded my intrusive thoughts. He gave extremely detailed tours, right down to each and every broom closet.

"Felix, why aren't you up there with the rest of the men?" I asked. "Shouldn't you be preparing too?"

"No need. Unfortunately, I've had firsthand experience."

"Really? Can you tell me what happened?"

"Oh, it was horrible. I surely thought we would all die out there at the rocks that day. I'd hate to relay such details to you, Miss Gwen."

"I don't mean to pry; I'm just trying to understand what we're up against."

He pulled a handkerchief from his pocket and dabbed it across his glistening forehead. "I wish we'd known before what to expect. But now that we do, I'm not so sure it helps put our minds at ease."

"Do you think it'll be easier this time?"

He quietly contemplated his words for several moments before daring to share them with me. "I wish I could say it would be, but no, my dear. I don't mean to frighten you, but we barely escaped last time. I don't know why Captain Hawkins insists on going back. He nearly died himself that day."

"He did?" My heart sank under the weight of guilt.

"Oh yes, Alistair had to dive in after him and pull him back out. It nearly killed them both."

Besides the movies I'd watched as a child, I didn't know much useful information about mermaids. And unless there was a talking crab out there to negotiate with, I doubted those movies would do us any good. "They sing, right? The sirens...they sing to lure you to them?"

Felix simply nodded in return.

"Do you think maybe there's a way to shut them out? If we couldn't hear them, it could help us get through?" I pondered out loud.

Felix sighed, his shoulders dropping in despair as he did. "It's a nice thought, but unfortunately, I just don't think there's any escaping it. Not when we're sailing straight into their lair," he replied somberly.

After Felix had taken me to the kitchen and forced me to eat a sandwich, we ended the tour back on the top deck, where it had begun hours earlier. The men were beginning to trickle out of the cabin and head below deck to their quarters for the night as the heavy orange sun hovered over the edge of the sea. Some of them wore worried faces, and I could only imagine the stories they were told after squeezing out a few glazed-over tales from Felix.

I lingered at the door of the room, waiting for the last two men to take their leave.

"This isn't what we signed up for!" a younger man standing across the table from Demetri exclaimed.

"You're leading us right to our death! And for what?" the other man chimed in.

"I understand your frustration, but we've no choice." Demetri's voice struck a stern tone. "We must prepare for the situation at hand the best we know how."

They left disheveled, glaring at me as they walked by as though they knew I was the reason for the daring endeavor. Demetri sat silently at the table, staring down as he mindlessly pinched the bridge of his nose.

It felt intrusive to witness. "Demetri?" I called out softly.

He met my eyes and flashed a quick smile as though nothing was wrong. As though he hadn't just told the entire crew that some of them would likely die tomorrow at the murderous hands of malicious mermaids. "How was the tour, love?"

I approached the table. "Felix showed me all of the broom closets."

"Splendid."

"I heard those two before they left." I motioned over my shoulder to the door and attempted to lighten the mood. "I must say I'm surprised they still have tongues after that."

Demetri almost chuckled. "Those two would be John Hayes and Daniel Wiley. They're some of the newest members, the youngest ones on board. They're none too happy with our proposed journey."

Reaching for the closest chair at the table, I took my seat across from him. "I gathered that."

"You're a sight for sore eyes," he confessed with a ghost of a smile.

"Demetri..." The sight of it made my heart drop. "Do you want to talk about it?"

"Not particularly. I've been talking all day."

"Fair enough." I nodded. "What would you like to do then?"

He rose from his chair, picked up two glasses from a small chest in the corner, and poured something dark into them before handing me one.

"Cheers." He clinked his cup against mine. "To sharing what could quite possibly be the last drinks I'll ever have with the most ravishing woman I've ever laid eyes on."

"Don't talk like that!" I shrieked.

He gulped his liquor down greedily before pouring more into his glass. "You are ravishing," he said with a dark arch of his brow. "I'll not apologize for saying so."

"You know that's not what I meant. You won't die on me. I won't allow it."

His expression shifted into one of amusement. "Is that so?"

"It is."

He tilted his glass toward me. "I'll hold you to it then."

"How else would I get home if you did?" I teased.

"I suppose you'd have to take my place as captain."

I took a sip from my glass, wincing at how strong it was. "I'm not so sure your men would take too kindly to that."

"Well, you'd be the captain, so you could just make them walk the plank."

"Is that how you solve all your problems?"

"Sometimes." He laughed, lowering his gaze to the map taking up space on the table between us.

I shook my head. "No...I don't think so. I don't see that in you," I admitted.

"I'm a pirate, Gwen." His voice fell flat, as though he were annoyed I had commended him.

After everything he'd done to help me, it was almost infuriating to hear him discredit himself. "There's more to you than that. You saved me, remember? That wasn't a very piratey thing to do."

"Special circumstance. Don't let that fool you, love. I'm still a pirate."

"You're a pirate," I acknowledged with a slight nod. "But you're also a good man."

He shifted uneasily under my words as he rose from his seat. "I've done questionable things, and I've made many mistakes," he continued to argue as he turned his back to me and poured another drink.

"Well, so has everyone else. Mistakes don't define who you are."

"They do when you consciously and consistently make them."

"I think...maybe you just do what needs to be done."

Demetri placed the bottle down thoughtfully before turning to meet my gaze again. "That's what I try to tell myself."

His stare was almost too intense to behold. He had a funny way of intimidating me when we locked eyes like that, and it made me wonder what kind of thoughts were hidden behind the storms that swirled in his. I broke the bond for my own sake, peering down at the table where my attention landed back on the map. Demetri wordlessly bypassed his seat and came to stand at my side.

"We're right here." He brushed against me as he leaned down to point to a spot in the middle of the ocean.

"And there's Shadow Ridge," I muttered, scanning over the drawing of a narrow waterway. My stomach twisted as I came across another word I recognized. "...and Castleberry...wait," I pointed at an area near the middle. "Does that say Neverland Lagoon?"

"Aye," he took a swig. "Trust me, love, you don't want to go there."

"Neverland, as in where Peter Pan lives?" I exclaimed in disbelief as though I hadn't just spent a whole ass day with Little Red Riding Hood and her grandmother.

Demetri responded by offering a confused expression. "I'm afraid I don't know who that is; I was referring to the vile inhabitants of the land who call themselves 'the lost boys.'"

My mouth gaped open at the confirmation. "Lost boys exist?"

"You just better hope you never see one; they're almost as bad as the sirens...who, by the way, also inhabit the lagoon."

"What else is on this map?" I asked, enthusiastically pulling it closer to analyze it. "Isles of Dragons!" I shrieked as I stared up at him. "There are dragons here?"

A smile tugged at his lips as he slid the map away from my view. "I think perhaps you've looked at this long enough. I'd hate to cause you any additional unwarranted distress."

"But the dragons—"

"Are of no concern to us." He fought back an amused expression as he took in my alarmed one. "They don't leave the Isles."

He walked to the window, pulled the curtain back, and gazed out for a moment before unlatching the hook. "The sunset is quite breathtaking tonight. Care to join me on the ledge?"

The last hazy glow of dusk rendered subtle hues of twilight across the low-hanging blanket of puffy clouds. I sat next to Demetri on the small, perched balcony, taking in the striking scene and watched as the light faded away and nightfall gradually drifted in on the waves.

He leaned forward, propping his arms against his knees as he stared out across the water. It was the most peaceful I'd seen him look in the short amount of time that I'd known him.

Water splashed against the ship from down below, and a glimmer of something recognizable caught my eye. "Demetri! Look!" The command came out as more of a squeal as I pointed at the three dolphins swimming alongside the ship.

"Those are called dolphins, love."

"I know what they are!"

"Oh," he chuckled. "I wasn't sure if you had those in your world."

"Yes, but you don't typically see them, not in the wild anyway." I stared in awe as they leaped over one another in a playful manner. "It's like they don't have a care in the world." That thought alone brought me a strange sense of comfort. "Aren't they beautiful?"

"Aye." He gleamed at me. "I like seeing you like this."

"Like what?"

"Less guarded. Dare I say, happy?"

I extended a sad smile at the observation. "I haven't exactly been allowed enough time to be happy here. I've just been trying to stay alive."

"So far, that does seem to be the case."

"How do you stand it?" I asked. "How do you live like this all the time?"

Demetri shifted his body into a more relaxed position, leaning against the ship as he stared out into the darkening abyss. "It isn't always so eventful. Quite the contrary on most days."

Sparkling constellations emerged across the fresh sapphire sky as the outline of a heavy crescent moon woke to take its place on the horizon. I couldn't help but compare the scene to the ones locked away in my memories.

"This might sound strange, but everything looks more beautiful here...more vibrant."

"Maybe you're just taking more notice," Demetri responded.

"Maybe," I admitted. "In my real life, I was always preoccupied with something...work, friends, family issues..." I trailed off.

"Or your fiancé?" Demetri finished the thought as he took another swig from his glass.

"Yes." I mirrored the move, taking a sip from mine. "Or Jacob."

"Tell me more about your life."

"I wouldn't want to bore you." I smiled, tapping my fingers absentmindedly against the rim of my glass.

"So make it sound exciting," he teased.

"Okay, Captain, I'll try my best..." I conceded, making sure he saw my eyes as I rolled them in his direction. "I'm a copywriter. Basically, what that means is I write blogs and marketing content for different companies to help them sell their products. But I get to stay home and do it, so it's not so bad."

He yawned and let his eyes fall shut as if my explanation had lured him to sleep.

"Stop it," I laughed, smacking his shoulder. "I warned you in advance it was boring."

"You did indeed," he jested. "Is that truly all that you do? Sit inside all day and write stories on paper?"

"First of all, it's on a computer," I asserted. "And there aren't as many swashbuckling career opportunities in my world, you know."

"That sounds dreadful...and mind-numbing." He extended his hand out in front of us in a theatrical manner, sloshing his drink around as he did. "Now I understand why you're so fascinated by the sky...because you never see it." He shook his head mockingly. "Such a pity."

"You are the worst," I laughed.

"And what about your family?" He probed.

"My family...well, that's kind of a touchy subject." I stared out across the water, hoping he'd get the hint and choose to interrogate me about something a little less personal. He didn't.

"I had a... different sort of childhood." I sighed, giving in to his request. "My mother, my real mother, had me at a young age. That's what I was told anyway. She gave me up for adoption right after I was born. My adoptive parents were wealthy. My father was a lawyer, and my mother was a nurse. They already had a daughter, Juliette. She's three years older than me."

"That doesn't sound so complicated," he interjected.

"It wasn't. Not back then. Things changed as I got older. I was at odds with them...a lot. They were loving enough but often absent. Juliette and I were always fighting, and my parents were always in her corner when we did." I swished my glass around as the memories I'd managed to suppress over the years began to bubble back up.

"She went off to college when I was 15. A year later my parents retired and decided that it was an ideal time to move and uproot our entire lives in my last two years of school. It was a nightmare, and I was mad about it for a long time...so, I got out of the house as soon as I could. I moved four hours away and learned the hard way how to live on my own. And that's what I've been doing for the past ten years."

"So, you no longer speak to any of them?"

"Not much. They'll call every now and then to check on me...to make sure I'm still alive, I guess." I kept my eyes fixated on the swirling liquid in my cup. "My sister got married, moved closer to them, and had some kids. So, they stay pretty busy."

Jacob had only met my parents once before, and that was only because he insisted on traveling with me to see them after Juliette had her third child. Leading up to that trip, I'd had false hopes that it would be a turning point with my family, but they could have cared less that we had even come. Afterward, Jacob tried to pressure me into reaching out to them again. God, I don't even remember what I'd said to him that night during the explosive argument that suggestion had led to, but he never dared to bring up the subject again, so it must have been pretty bad.

In the heat of that moment, I just knew I'd already made up my mind. The rifts I had forged with my family over the years had long been weaved together, constantly chipping away until they created one giant canyon that was far too wide and deep to try to cross now.

Demetri disrupted my silent memories. "You're still angry at them, then?"

I mulled over the question for a moment before answering, mentally wavering across the range of emotions it had struck. "No, not anymore." I finally determined. "I was for a while, but being angry for so long is exhausting. I don't hate them; I never did. I just don't have anything in common with them...not even blood."

He waited silently as I sucked in a shaky breath.

"I must admit, though, after everything that's happened recently, my old problems don't seem quite so problematic anymore. I don't even know if they know that I'm gone." I laughed unevenly. "...or if they'd care."

"Of course they'd care," he said softly. "And I'm sure they harbor no ill feelings toward you, love."

Something in my chest tightened at his words. Something I couldn't quite pinpoint. There was a sudden, heavy sense of sorrow for the time that had been lost and the time that may never be obtainable again. I loved my family; that was never a question. I just wish I hadn't spent so much of my life desiring the same level of affection back.

"I wish I could believe that," I confessed. "Looking back on it now, I can better understand the reasons why a lot of things played out the way they did. I think I felt inadequate in a lot of ways." I sighed as I said the words out loud for the first time. The weight of them was heavier than I'd expected. "I still do, I guess. But that doesn't mean I never wanted to not make amends. Now I don't know if I'll ever get the chance."

"You will." Demetri placed his hand over mine and squeezed before letting go. "I promise you, Gwen. I will find a way to get you home." He smiled down at me, and I instinctively laid my head against his shoulder before realizing what I'd done.

"Sorry," I whispered, gently sliding away several inches.

"You know I don't mind."

I glanced back up at him. "I just don't want to make you think something else."

"Don't worry, love," he said, increasing the space between us. "You've made it abundantly clear to me that you're not available. I intend to respect your wishes."

"I just...I don't want to make you uncomfortable."

"Thank you for sparing me," he jabbed, the tone of his voice cutting much harder than the words it accompanied.

"Don't get me wrong," I blurted. "It's not that I don't find you attractive...I do." Wait. Oh God. Did I just...I did. My soul was damn near snatched from my body as the realization that I'd let my thoughts escape settled in.

I cleared my throat in a failed attempt to create a distraction. "I'm sorry, wow, no, I mean...." My head was spinning too fast to even formulate a coherent sentence. Every inch of my skin heated as I momentarily considered jumping off the perch into the ocean.

"And the truth comes out," he spoke as he finished off his drink.

"I...um...I'm sorry. I did not mean to say that." I finally managed to voice.

"Yet, you did."

"Dammit, Demetri." I lowered my head into my hands, wondering if anyone had ever actually died of embarrassment before or if I'd be the first to accomplish such an achievement.

"No need to act shy now, love," he purred.

"Okay, fine." I lifted my head and stared back at him defiantly. "Clearly, you're attractive. You're incredibly fucking hot. I mean, look at you..." I huffed, raking my eyes over him. "For Christ's sake. You're all dark and dangerous and essentially the exact fucking prototype of what women find universally attractive. Is that what you wanted to hear?" I divulged with rapid breaths.

He smirked at my undoing. "It certainly doesn't hurt."

"You're infuriating." I took another sip from my glass. It wasn't quite so strong anymore.

"When you finish that one, I'll get you another. I rather like where this is going."

"In your dreams." I scoffed.

"For now." He smiled wickedly, launching an icy shiver down my spine.

"We're not doing this. Next topic!" I exclaimed.

"Jacob," Demetri demanded, his eyes practically danced with amusement.

I shot a harsh glance at him. "I don't think that's a good idea."

"Would you prefer to continue telling me how dashingly handsome you think I am?" He stroked his stubbled chin in an arrogant fashion.

"I met Jacob through mutual friends..." I blurted. "He'd just gotten out of a relationship, and so had I. We just started...hanging out. That's it, really."

"Are you trying to spare my feelings again, or is your relationship truly as bleak as you make it sound?"

"It isn't bleak," I stammered, glaring up at him. "It's just awkward to discuss with you."

"Why is that?"

"I don't know. I just feel like there's some tension here."

"There's tension, love, but it has nothing to do with your boyfriend." He leaned back as though he were inviting me in closer.

"He's my fiancé." I corrected, clenching my jaw. "And what you're doing here is not going to work."

"I haven't even tried yet." He arched his brow, and the corner of his mouth ticked up. "It'd be unfair to you if I had, and I'd hate to put you in a precarious position."

"You sure do think highly of yourself." Granted, he had good reason, but I wasn't going to admit to that...again.

He laughed melodically and shook his head. "I can read people very well, love." His gaze burned into mine. "It's something I pride myself on." My head felt dizzy, but I was sure it was from the rum.

"You might want to reread me, *love*," I mocked.

He bit his lip. "See, I knew you'd get defensive."

"I'm not defensive."

"Aren't you?" He narrowed his eyes in skepticism.

"Why don't we talk about you now?"

Demetri shifted his body away from mine with a movement so slight I almost didn't catch it. "There's not much to tell."

"Uh...you're a freaking captain of a pirate ship in some sort of magic fairytale land. That sentence alone is already way more exciting than all of the stuff I told you combined."

He smiled faintly, mindlessly spinning his empty glass between his hands. "You talk a lot of storybooks and fairytales."

"Because that seems to be what I'm stuck in. These things, these people, they don't exist where I'm from. My world is not magical."

"Did you ever consider there were more worlds other than your own?"

"Not really," I admitted. "Did you?"

He smiled thoughtfully. "I suppose I've never had a reason to until now."

"Are you trying to change the subject?" I interrogated. "I answered your questions. It's your turn."

"What exactly is it that you want to know?"

"Oh, I don't know; tell me about your parents, your childhood...or you could start by telling me how the hell one becomes a pirate."

He seemed to ponder for a moment. "Perhaps another time. It's getting late and we need to rest before our imminent battle." He stretched out his arms and stood to go back inside.

"Demetri! Come on, give me something!"

A sly smile flickered across his face. "I'd love to, but I doubt you'd let me, even with all that liquor running through your veins."

"You don't have to give a perverted response to everything, you know."

He offered his hand to help me up. "You truly do walk right into them, though."

CHAPTER THIRTEEN

fter helping me climb back through the window, Demetri turned to pull the curtains shut.

I cursed as I took a step toward the bed and toppled forward, catching myself against the wall. I didn't think I'd had that much to drink, but my numb, wobbly legs begged to differ.

"Whoa. Careful there." His hands wrapped around me as I moved again and nearly collided with the floor.

Demetri pulled me back into a vertical position. His face was inches away from mine, close enough to feel the warmth of his breath as it drifted across my lips. The scent of rum mixed with that infuriating and invigorating woodsy aroma twisted around me in a dreamlike haze.

"Why do you always smell like Christmas trees?" I blurted out angrily. "You're a damn pirate on a ship in the middle of the ocean."

"I don't always spend my time on a ship, love." He attempted to conceal his laughter. "And I think perhaps you've had a bit too much to drink."

He moved his arm around my waist and guided me over to the bed while I focused all my attention on trying not to stumble over my traitorous feet.

"Thanks," I whispered, sitting on the edge of the mattress as embarrassment settled in.

He kneeled in front of me, examining my face intently. "How do you feel, love?"

"Fine," I mumbled. If I wasn't so out of it, I'd be more concerned about what he saw to even make him ask that.

"Do you feel sick?"

I scrunched my face in resentment. "Do I look sick?"

His laugh echoed through the room. "No. My apologies. I was merely asking."

"I can't feel my feet."

"Ah." he smiled. "Allow me to help you then." Before I could refuse, I felt his hand brush down my leg.

"Demetri!" I gasped, startled by my own body's response to his touch.

He lifted my foot into his lap and slid my shoe off before placing it on the floor by the bed. I didn't bother to object when he reached for the other.

"There now," he finally spoke before gazing back up at me. The beats in my chest thudded wildly, and I wasn't sure if it was from the alcohol or the way that he was looking at me right now. I reached out to touch the side of his face, unable to fixate on anything but his mouth and the way his lips had slightly parted. I tried not to let myself linger there, but I couldn't help it. I'd never say so out loud, but he truly was the most handsome man I'd ever laid eyes on.

"You should go before..." I started.

"Before what?" The question rode on a deeper tone of his voice, making my head spin even more.

"Before I change my mind," I admitted.

He rose from the floor, scooping me up easily into his arms, and carried me around the side of the bed. The coolness of the quilt enveloped my body like a cloud, and the weight of my eyelids felt much too heavy.

"Demetri?"

"I'm here, love." His voice already sounded farther away. "Get some rest."

My head pounded as I cracked my eyes open. Immediately, the blurry events of last night flooded back into my mind.

"Oh no." I groaned to myself as I pulled the covers up over my head.

Demetri's voice broke through the incriminating memories, "Good morning."

I peeked over the covers to meet his sprightly stare. Demetri sat with his legs propped up on the surface of the table, leaning back in his chair with his hands placed comfortably behind his head.

"Hi," I replied meekly, hoping he'd been drunk enough to not remember how much of a fool I had made of myself last night.

"Enlightening night, eh?"

Well, fuck.

I sat up, shifting out from under the covers in my shame. A draft rushed over my shoulders, and I looked down to see my dress balled up between the sheets. Panic set in as I tried to remember the events of the night and if any of them explained why I was currently naked in this bed.

"About that…" I said, quickly yanking the quilt back up to my neck. "I guess I can't hold alcohol as well as I thought."

"No need for apologies." He held his finger up before grabbing a bottle from the edge of the table and taking a gulp. "I've a feeling this is a bit more potent than what you're used to."

"You're seriously drinking again?"

"Don't worry, love. I've got much more of a tolerance for it than you do." He smirked.

"I see. I don't really know if I remember everything…Um, weird question, but did we…?"

His face fell as he immediately understood what I was asking. He shifted forward in his chair, planting his feet firmly back down on the floor.

"Are you asking if I took advantage of you?" His voice carried an unfamiliar threat that made my breath catch in my throat.

"No! No, I didn't mean it like that."

"Do you truly think so little of me, Gwen?"

"No…I'm sorry, Demetri. It's just, I don't remember anything after you put me in bed. And, well, I'm sort of naked."

His eyes grew wide as he inspected the covers I tightly clenched.

"Well, that is indeed an interesting development." His brow ticked up in confusion.

"So, you're saying nothing happened?"

"I may be a pirate, Gwen, but I've never had to get a woman drunk to sleep with her, nor would I have ever considered doing that to you." He stood from his chair and grabbed the trunk of women's clothes before nearly slamming it on the floor beside the bed.

"Demetri, I truly didn't mean it like that." I rubbed my temple in exasperation. "I didn't know if I acted like I, um, wanted to…" I trailed off.

"You did," he replied indifferently, crossing his arms as he propped himself against the bookshelf.

"Excuse me?"

He glared down at me as I held the sheet against my body and fumbled with the lock on the trunk using my one free hand.

"I could have taken you last night, right then and there if I wanted, if I had no honor. Remember how I told you it'd be unfair for you if I'd tried."

"What?" I scowled at him. "You were just trying to see what I'd do?"

"Not originally. Nevertheless, you enlightened me."

"I don't really know how to take that," I said crossly, finally popping the latch open.

"Take it as you will, love." He bent down beside me until his eyes met mine, holding me in place with the force of his stare. "Just know that if you ever do succumb to your desires, I promise you this, it would not be something you'd forget about by morning's first light."

"Demetri!" I shrieked, instantly flustered at the thoughts he had planted in my head.

"Until then, we've got other things to worry about." He turned away. "We'll be approaching Shadow Ridge today. I'll need to get the crew prepared."

"Okay." I nodded. "What do you want me to do?"

"Stay in the cabin. You needn't worry about trying to help. I'll leave you to get dressed."

"What? No! I can't just stay in here the whole time!"

"You can, and you will. It'll be more dangerous if you're out there putting yourself at risk."

"But what if I—"

"No." He raised his hand to stop me. "You will stay here. That's my final word." He shot me a fierce look that would rightfully scare the living hell out of anybody, the same look that he'd given half his crew the night when we boarded the ship on the shores of Castleberry. My breath stalled at the sight. That wasn't the same man he had been to me, but I understood it was the man he had to be today.

I sighed in defeat as he let the cabin door fall shut behind him. I hated this feeling...being locked away inside this room, forced to do nothing while things went to shit on the other side of the door. I may not be able to fight, but I could do *something* besides sit here and hope for the best.

I rose from the bed, pulling the sheet along with me as I searched through the trunk of elaborate clothes. If only there were something more practical in here...I gasped at the wild thought that abruptly materialized. Perhaps if I had something inconspicuous to wear, I could sneak out onto the deck and blend in just long enough to make it through Shadow Ridge to try to help the crew.

I hurriedly tore through all the clothes in the trunk, deciding that none of these would serve my purpose. They were too colorful, too frilly. There had to be something else around here. I glanced around the room until my attention landed on Demetri's closet.

Remembering the look that he'd given as he ordered me to stay in the cabin made me hesitant to carry out my newfound plan, but the indecision only existed for a moment. He'd be mad, of course, but he'd eventually get over it. Perhaps, if I played my cards right, he wouldn't even realize it.

Thumbing through the clothes, I pulled out a pair of black pants, a white shirt, and a gray vest. Demetri clearly wasn't a fan of colors.

After assembling the vest, I decided it would still be evident to a ship full of men that I was indeed a woman. I shifted back through the closet and found a long, black coat that did a much better job of hiding my curves. I then grabbed one of the hats from the top shelf and stuffed my hair into it the best I could manage. If I kept the brim down and popped the coat collar up, it would be hard to see my face at all unless someone was actively trying to.

I approached the door slowly, second-guessing the decision as Demetri's furious face flashed through my mind once again. But I'd already made it this far, and the anticipation outweighed the apprehension. With a crack of the door, I followed the sounds of the crew's faint voices up to the top deck.

"...Captain will seize them...Turner on lookout..." The anxious mumbling was hard to decipher as I held my breath and passed by three of the men.

"When we first see the rocks on the horizon, everyone will need to get into place," Alistair shouted the order on the wind.

"We'll need to steer the ship left toward the furthermost sea cave," Demetri added from beside him. "Remember, that's the only entryway to Mystic Grove. The sirens will try to throw us off course."

"Are they in the sea cave too, Captain?" a voice asked.

"Once we get the entire ship past the entryway, they can't touch us."

"How many will there be?" another asked.

"Dozens, probably."

"How are we gonna fight off dozens of 'em all at once? Why, there's only fifteen of us!"

Alistair whistled through the noise of questions, and everyone quieted. "We will have to stick to the plan. Everyone's got their weapons. Be prepared that we'll each have to face at least two or three of 'em at a time."

"Ahoy!" a voice called from above the men. I glanced up to see a man looking through a telescope in the crow's nest. "I can see the ridge, Captain!"

"Alright, men, it's nearly time. Assume your positions." The pirates quickly scattered around Demetri and Alistair.

"You there!" a man called out nearby.

I turned, then realized he was addressing me. "Aye," I said as deeply as I could muster.

"Captain said it's time to get in place. We'll be approaching the ridge soon," he said hurriedly.

"Aye," I grunted and nodded before walking away quickly.

Keeping my head down, I avoided eye contact and tried to distance myself from the frantic men buzzing around me as they lined the sides of the deck. I squeezed into an open spot and watched as the jagged peaks of Shadow Ridge slowly came into view. The sky was strangely ominous as wispy dark green clouds hovered over the horizon, stretching out in our direction as though they were waiting to claim the ship.

"Captain!" Felix shrieked, running up the deck toward Demetri.

"Yes, Felix?"

"I don't mean to alarm you, but I just went to check on Miss Gwendolyn to tell her we were approaching the ridge, and she's not in your room!"

My stomach dropped to the floor. Dammit, Felix.

"Are you certain?" Demetri furrowed his brow. "I told her to stay in the captain's quarters."

I looked away, quickly hiding my face from the exchange.

"I'll go check again. Perhaps she ventured under-deck."

"Find her," Demetri ordered. "Before we get there." A look of unbridled urgency flashed across his features.

"Yes, Captain!" Felix ran back toward the cabin.

I glanced back at Demetri, who had propped himself against the ship's railing and was staring blankly before us at the oncoming rocks. He lowered his head, furiously rubbing the space between his brows. This was not going to go over well for me.

As we sailed under the darkening skies, angry claps of thunder sounded, rattling the floorboards under my feet. Tensions on board were growing heavier by the second, along with my regret for thinking it was ever a good idea to come out here.

"There, Captain Hawkins! I can see them!" Alistair pointed to the far-off figures waiting in the water.

"There's no turning back now, men." Demetri faced the crew. "They've seen us; they'll be coming soon," he said, drawing the sword from his side.

The sound of scraping metal followed as the other men drew their own weapons.

"Felix!" Demetri roared over the thunder.

"No sign yet, Captain!" Felix yelled from under the deck.

Demetri turned and paced angrily near the helm. I felt guilty for being a source of stress right before the battle, but it was too late to try to fix it now. He was going to be mad regardless.

"Captain..." Wiley's voice called curiously from across the ship.

"Block it out, Wiley!" Alistair yelled as he covered his own ears.

"I hear it too!" A slender, darker-skinned man standing near Wiley exclaimed.

"Ignore their songs! Block it out!" Demetri ordered as another clap of thunder rumbled overhead.

The ridge was nearly upon us, and the waves crashed violently around the base of the ship.

A few silent and unnerving moments fell between the roars of thunder. Then I heard it—a soft melodic hum coming from underneath the water, much like an echo. I approached the rail cautiously, peering down at where the sound resonated. A radiant mermaid with pearls tangled in her yellow hair broke through the surface. She emitted a saccharine smile before opening her mouth.

"Follow me into the sea where all your wildest dreams run free...deep blue waves will lead you here...come with me...we'll disappear..." She sank back into the water, revealing her luminescent green tail as she submerged.

A few moments later, she reappeared with an equally beautiful mermaid whose long raven hair was adorned with small seashells and starfish. They both smiled up at me as they hummed the tune in unison. It wasn't exactly an enticing sound. If anything, it was just plain creepy.

"Cover your ears!" Demetri ordered.

The men on the ship were trying to drown out the sounds of the sirens by yelling at each other.

I stared back at the singing mermaids who impishly splashed below. Was I immune to their song? It wasn't affecting me nearly as much as it was the rest of the crew.

I ran to the other side of the ship where Wiley and the others were. They sang louder now, but it was more of an annoyance than anything else.

"Captain Hawkins! Alistair!" a man called out. "They're climbing the walls!"

Demetri and Alistair ran over with their swords drawn to join the men.

I leaned over the rail. Dashes of color blurred across my vision as the mermaids rapidly clawed their way up the side of the ship.

Their faces came into focus as they neared the top, twisting into crooked, hungry smiles as their nails screeched and clanked against the wood. This was horror movie worthy. I spun around...my thoughts running rampant as I tried to find something to help the crew fight them off. Then I whirled right into Felix.

"Miss...!" His eyes looked as though they would pop right out of his head.

I covered his mouth quickly. "No-no! Shhh! Please, Felix!"

"If Captain Hawkins knew!" he exclaimed.

"There's no time for that. I can help! Please, Felix, they don't affect me. Let me help," I pleaded with him.

He contemplated for a fleeting moment before quickly handing me his own sword.

"Thank you, Felix!" I rushed back toward the crew.

The men were trying to fight off the demented half-fish creatures by stabbing them as they tried crawling over the railing. Their voices were so loud now they reverberated through the caves ahead.

A man standing nearby shouted.

"Hold on, Thomas!" Wiley yelled as a purple-tailed mermaid with crazed eyes grabbed ahold of his shirt, pulling him over the edge.

Wiley grabbed Thomas by the legs and pulled against her. I raced over to them with my sword, not even sure if I was capable of doing anything productive with it.

"Let me go, Wiley!" Thomas yelled back, hypnotized, as he reached for the creature.

"No! I will not! Don't look into her eyes!" Wiley grunted, struggling to keep his grip.

"Leave him alone!" I rushed closer with the sword, waving it near her face as I yelled, breaking her predatory trance.

She dropped back into the water and swam away.

"Thank you!" Thomas sputtered breathlessly as he and Wiley lay sprawled out on the deck.

"Felix!" Alistair yelled from behind us. "He's in the water!" he exclaimed, stripping out of his coat.

Alistair didn't hesitate. He leapt off the side of the boat and disappeared into the misty gray waters. Demetri raced to the edge, his eyes darting across the waves where Alistair had submerged, only moving long enough to slash his sword across the neck of a siren who'd made her way to the top and was trying to pull another man overboard.

She shrieked a horrible noise as she fell from the boat, crashing back into the water.

The rain beat down on top of us, blurring my vision as I frantically prayed for the men to emerge.

"Thomas, Wiley, help Hayes and Jackson!" Demetri ordered as he stripped his coat off and peered back over the side for any sign of Alistair and Felix, looking as though he were about to dive in himself. Oh God, no…

"I got em'!" I heard Alistair yell from below, and a surge of relief engulfed me.

Demetri threw down a rope for them to grab onto. "Griff, help me pull them up!"

"Yes, Captain!" The burly, dark-skinned man complied, abandoning his spot at the helm to extend aid.

"Thank you, Alistair," Felix said, still spitting out water once they were safely back on the ship. Alistair patted his back before running off again with his sword.

"Felix, oh my gosh, Felix! Are you all right?" I exclaimed, grabbing hold of him.

"I'm fine, Miss Gwen." He shuddered.

"Hayes! Look out!" Thomas yelled as a mermaid snatched him from behind off the side of the ship.

Hayes plummeted into the water, and Wiley jumped in after him. They resurfaced moments later, grabbing the rope as Alistair and two other men pulled them back up.

"I've got to start steering this thing to the cave!" Demetri exclaimed.

The boat began to rock violently from side to side as more mermaids clung to the boards. I couldn't do anything but hold onto a mast and watch in horror as the men ran aimlessly, trying to stab the ones who reached the top.

"They're trying to tip us over!" Griff bellowed.

"Hold steady, mates. Here they come again!" Wiley yelled beside me, readying his sword as the other men lined up near him and prepared for the defense.

The yellow-haired mermaid from before had climbed to the rails and had her sights set on Wiley. Her voice rang high as she fixated her unnatural, teal-colored eyes on him. I watched his posture go limp as he gave in to her. She grabbed ahold of his shirt collar, slowly luring him over the edge.

"Let him go!" I drew my sword again, and she stared quizzically at me, breaking the trance long enough for him to fall out of her grasp. She locked her eyes with mine as she crawled closer to me, humming a lower tune.

"That's not gonna work, bitch." I jabbed my sword at her, unable to force myself to make contact.

She reached for me with her long, sharp nails before she let out a blood-curdling squall and fell back into the water. Beside me stood Felix with a bloody-tipped sword.

"Thank you," I whispered, fighting to tame my racing heartbeat.

"Captain, look out!" Thomas yelled.

My head spun in his direction. He was pulling someone back onto the ship when a blue-haired mermaid latched onto him.

"You can live your wildest dreams...if you follow me into the sea..." Her voice cut into me like shards of glass.

I watched in horror as he surrendered himself to her...as his face softened to her song...as he reached for her while she pulled him closer to death.

All of the other men were too busy fighting their own battles to help. "Demetri!" I yelled, his name pounding through my head as I raced over to him as fast as I could.

The siren had nearly pulled him over the rail. "No!" I shrieked, wrapping my arms around him as I pulled him back to the safety of the ship. The mermaid hissed at me as she tugged him harder.

"Let go of him!" I screamed.

Demetri shook his head, trying to regain his composure.

She placed her hand on his face, luring him back into a stupor and spoke in an echo as he reached out for her. *"Join me, Captain."*

My blood boiled beneath my skin as I drew my sword and climbed onto the side of the railing, stabbing her viciously in the side. Her face distorted as she screamed, the horrible noise scraping against my very bones. She reached for me, slashing her hand across my shoulder. The blistering pain was immediate. I pulled out the sword and plunged it through her shimmering skin again as she shrieked.

"You...will...die," she weakly promised, clinging to the side of the ship as the blood poured from her side.

"Not before you do." I declared, withdrawing the blade once more before thrusting it into her chest this time. Her body writhed as she fell into the raging sea.

When I turned, Demetri was staring back in complete and utter shock.

"Gwen!" His composure nearly broke. "What the bloody hell are you—"

"There's no time for that," I interrupted, too stunned to accept the fact that I'd just killed someone...something. "Go steer the ship."

He didn't argue. He rushed back over to the helm and started pushing it with all his might as the thunder rolled through the caves. They weren't too far now.

Griff quickly joined him while several of the other men were trying to reposition the sails.

"Miss! Are you alright? You're bleeding!" Felix exclaimed as he reached for my neck.

"I'm fine. Let's worry about it later!" I yelled under the intensifying storm.

"Someone, help me!" An older man was trying to pull someone back to the safety of the ship. Felix and I glanced at each other before we both ran in his direction.

"I can't hold on much longer," the man yelled.

I automatically dropped my sword and started pulling him as hard as I could.

"Look out, Felix!" The man beside me exclaimed, loosening his grip long enough to extend the warning. That was all it took for the siren to overpower us, pulling her victim over the railing while I was still clinging to his waist.

"Felix!" I yelled, barely hanging on to the bars.

"Miss Gwendolyn!" Felix shouted in a panic as he ran over to me in what seemed like slow motion. I saw Demetri's face vaguely from my peripheral as I lost my grip and plunged into the tumultuous water.

I opened my eyes, wincing as the salt burned them, but what I saw when I did made it impossible to close them again. The ocean was illuminated by the frantic mermaids. Their tails glowed; their wild, flowing hair glowed. Like rainbow prisms, they darted around uncontrollably, too focused on overthrowing the ship to exert their attention on me. I kicked fervently, somehow managing to break through the surface of the water to allow my lungs a breath of air before the waves overtook me once more.

I sank lower despite my best efforts. *Stay calm, stay calm*, I forced myself to think as the panic was starting to set in. I struggled to swim up but fell further from the shadow of the ship. I turned in a panic, finding myself face to face with a dazzling auburn-haired mermaid. My stinging eyes grew wide as she stared back at me in wonder. Her face was youthful and devastatingly beautiful, but she looked different from the others. Her eyes weren't lifeless voids like theirs, and she didn't look wicked at all. No, she looked...curious.

She reached for my hair, running her fingers through it as it floated around me. Her attention shifted to my wound as the blood clouded the water around us. She darted away to a nearby coral rock, her bright green tail fluttering behind her.

I tried to swim back up before she came to her senses and attacked me...before she sought retribution for me killing one of her kind. I couldn't hold my breath much longer, but every kick I made seemed to weigh me down more. This was it. I would surely die here. Hopefully, it would be quick. Hopefully, it wouldn't hurt too much. The light from the surface was fading fast when I felt something wrap around me. Pressure beat against my face as the water rushed around my body and the flashes of red and green were gone as fast as they appeared. I broke through the waves again, gasping wildly for breath as my lungs seized.

"Help!" I managed to yell through my burning throat.

Again, I went under, but the curious mermaid was there, waiting for me. She looked around conspicuously before grabbing my hand and placing a small sparkling cylinder into my palm. Then she motioned to her own shoulder. She was...trying to help me. I didn't know why, but I could conclude that much. I clutched the jar and nodded. She smiled before grabbing my arm and pulling me back to the surface of the water.

"Gwen!" I heard as I reappeared.

I gasped, trying to find the frantic voice as the mermaid disappeared under the water. The waves knocked me in the face, blurring my vision.

"Gwen!" Demetri roared. I turned to see him swimming in my direction as I struggled to stay afloat. He grabbed me tightly as a rope dropped into the water and pulled us back up onto the deck.

"This is precisely why I told you to stay in the cabin," he scolded, leaning over me with his drenched hair as he'd done once before.

"Good thing I didn't," I challenged. "Otherwise, you'd be too busy lying at the bottom of the ocean to argue about it."

His glowering face gave way to a grin. "Good to see your sass is still intact."

"Captain, we're approaching the sea cave!" Griff yelled from the helm.

Demetri rose from above me, helping me to my feet as we all stood and watched as the mouth of the sea cave slowly engulfed us.

"What dangers await us in here?" I whispered the question as though the shadows that settled in would overhear me.

"No bloody mermaids," Demetri replied.

I wanted to tell him about the one who'd helped me, but it'd have to wait until we were alone again. Maybe he would know what the container was.

The ship plunged into silent darkness as we glided inside.

"Is this the right cave, Captain?" a voice asked from somewhere in the darkness.

"Aye." Demetri swiped a match, illuminating the dirty, victorious faces of the crew.

"We've made it past the hardest part of the journey, men." Alistair joined him, giving him a celebratory pat on the back.

"And we've all lived to tell the tale," Alistair hooted, striking a match of his own before passing them around to the other pirates.

"Indeed. But we must still exert caution. Our journey is not yet over," Demetri warned. "We should reach the shores of Mystic Grove within about a day's time."

The men cheered happily, their celebratory shouts bouncing against the walls of the cave.

"But be warned, Mystic Grove has its own set of threats. We mustn't let our guard down."

"What kind o' threats, Captain?" Hayes interjected.

"It's the most magical land in our realm. It's also the home of some of the most dangerous witches and wizards."

"What else, Captain?" Someone asked.

"Giants, trolls, fairies, centaurs—"Demetri started rolling creature names off his tongue like he was reciting a grocery list.

"Those all seem to be highly problematic creatures," I exclaimed, ignoring the surprised reactions from the crew.

"Yes." he nodded. "They certainly can be. Which is why we'll need to stay on guard."

"What is it exactly that we're looking for?" another man asked.

"Not what, but who," Demetri answered. "We are in search of a certain dark witch. Now, here's where you need to listen up. When we get there and dock the ship, most of you will be staying on board. It's far too risky to have more than a handful of men gallivanting about the island."

"Won't they see our ship as a threat?" the same man asked.

A tall, younger man standing next to Demetri spoke up. "No, there are no enemies on the shoreline. It's a guise, you see. All the threats lie inside the forest on the other side of the barrier."

"Aye, Dalton's right. You'll be safe on the ship. Just don't venture off into the forest unless you're looking to get killed," Demetri warned.

Well, that was a decent enough-sounding plan for everyone else, but Demetri and I would inevitably have to venture into the forest, so it didn't seem too promising for us.

"And...how exactly are *we* going to make it through there without getting killed?" I inquired.

Demetri responded by pulling out a small item from the inside of his coat.

"Captain Hawkins! Is that a..." Felix sprang closer to get a better look at the object, the quick movement forcing his hat to bob enthusiastically on top of his head.

"Aye, Felix." Demetri held up the thin vial and the dark, shimmery liquid trapped inside splashed around.

I scanned the faces of the astonished men before turning my focus back to Demetri. "Am I missing something here?"

"This is Evenfall Elixir," he answered. "When we get to our destination and dock the ship, this will aid us on our journey. Should we need it, the contents of this bottle will allow us to discreetly travel through the land by providing us with a protective shield," Demetri responded.

"Okay..." I nodded as I processed that information. "Hey, weird question here, but why didn't we use it to shield ourselves from the mermaids who just tried to drown everybody?"

The pirates stood silent with half-gaped mouths as they stared back and forth between me and Demetri. My eyes darted to his in confusion, and it was only then that I realized that questioning him like that in front of his men was probably a problematic thing to do.

"Captain?" A scruffy-faced man broke the silent tension. "Are ye just gonna let that lass talk to ye like that?"

Demetri cocked his head as he huffed out an unnerving laugh. His untamed gaze flickered straight to mine, and the men standing near me backed away like they were expecting a sword to fly through the air in my direction any moment now.

I forced a stare back, praying that the increasingly loud thump of my heartbeat couldn't be heard pulsing against the walls of this cave as loudly as I heard it pulsing in my chest. Praying that no one noticed the way my hands started to shake or that the quiver in my clenched jaw wouldn't expose the escalating terror that surged through me.

"Yes," Demetri finally spoke through gritted teeth. "She meant no harm by asking." His unrelenting gaze pinned me to the floor where I stood as though he was warning me never to do it again. "As for you, Garrett," he said, shifting his tone as he turned his head to the man. "It seems you don't place much value on your life."

Garrett stammered as he took a step back. "No, I...I do, sir. Very much."

"Well fucking act like it then," Demetri retorted.

"Yes, Captain." Garrett nodded, then peered at me with a dash of remorse in his eyes.

I looked away immediately, hoping that would be enough to subdue the urge to send a vulgar gesture his way.

Demetri turned from the man and took three painfully slow steps toward me. "It was a valid question." He threw an icy stare in my direction, smirking as I took a step back. I barely recognized the man he was portraying right now. The spectrum of his unpredictable and contradictory behavior was enough to give me whiplash. *I'm a pirate, Gwen.* He had said last night. I guess this is what he meant by it.

"Water is everchanging," he explained. "It's always moving...always shifting. That's why the elixir won't work on it. It must take root, in a sense, which is why it can only be used on solid ground."

"Makes sense," I whispered breathlessly.

"Where on earth did you get it, sir?" Felix asked, as though he were oblivious to what had just transpired. Then again, maybe he was.

Demetri smiled deviously, instantly melting the tension away. "It would seem that the malevolent prince likes to leave his treasures on display for his house guests. It's almost as though he wants them to be taken."

"Who will accompany you in Mystic Grove, Captain?" Hayes asked.

"The smaller the group, the better. I'll only be bringing three along: Griff, Alistair, and Miss Winters."

Thomas scoffed from somewhere close by. "No offense Captain, but she's not familiar with the area. Don't you think taking her would be a liability?"

What the fuck? My skin heated in anger at the unwarranted outburst as I turned and shot him the dirtiest look I could construct on my face. How he could even summon the courage to question Demetri after what had just happened was an entity on its own.

Hayes quickly sidestepped Thomas, leaving him to fend for himself in Demetri's warpath. "What I think, Thomas, is that she saved several of our asses out there today against those demon fish," Demetri snapped as he narrowed the gap between their bodies.

"Aye, Captain, she certainly did." Felix nodded, smiling at me.

"But she did disobey your orders," Thomas pressed, his dark eyes widening as Demetri's tall frame towered over him. "And that could be a matter of life and death out there, 'specially with all the creatures you were just talking about."

"I'd advise you to watch your tongue with me if you want to keep it, lad." Demetri's voice came out as a low growl as he placed his hand on his sword. "You may be young and new to the crew, and you may not understand my reasons. Nevertheless, you'll heed my orders. If you can't adhere to that, then there's no use for you here, and there's only one way off this ship."

"Step down, Thomas." another man chirped.

"My apologies, Captain," Thomas sighed in defeat, lowering his head.

"Don't apologize to me." He released his grip on his blade and motioned a hand in my direction.

"I'm sorry, Miss," Thomas muttered.

Demetri's footsteps were the only hollow sound following the awkward exchange as he returned to the head of the ship.

"The reason I'm taking Gwen"—his voice soared across the emptiness of the cave—"is because she's familiar with the witch I'm searching for. Therefore, her assistance is quite vital." He waited as he analyzed the scarcely lit faces that stared back at him. The small flames they held in their hands reflected in his eyes, dancing ruthlessly across the contours of his face. God, he looked terrifying right now. "Are there any other concerns I can address for anyone?"

"No, Captain!" several men exclaimed.

"Excellent. Now that that's settled, this would be an ideal time to retreat to your beds. For those of you who haven't taken this journey with us before, we'll be traveling smoothly for a while. I'm sure you're all ready to rest after today's events."

The men shuffled by, conversing incoherently as they went to settle in for the night.

<hr>

"I think you scared Thomas and Garrett half to death out there," I declared back inside his room.

"I think the faster Thomas and Garrett learn their place, the better off they'll be." Demetri struck another match and illuminated the lantern on the table as I claimed a seat nearby.

"Don't you worry they'll resent you?"

"No," he huffed in amusement. "They knew what they signed up for."

"I know but—"

Demetri cut me off, "The only thing you should be concerned about right now is explaining yourself." He stared at me, and I watched as the fury ignited in his eyes again.

My breath ceased momentarily at the sight. "...I'm sorry I didn't stay in here. It's just that—"

"It's just that you deliberately disobeyed my orders."

"I just wanted to help," I blurted, observing him cautiously.

Demetri closed his eyes and pinched the bridge of his nose as though he were trying to keep his composure. "You put on my clothes. You impersonated a member of my crew, and you put yourself in mortal danger against an enemy you knew absolutely nothing about."

"Demetri, I..."

"What the hell were you thinking, Gwen!" he exploded.

I stared back, too stunned to answer.

His head tilted back as he groaned in frustration.

"I'm sorry I left," I conceded. "I know you were just trying to keep me safe."

"Gwen, how the bloody hell do you expect my men not to question my authority the way they did tonight if I can't even get a woman to obey me?"

His words hit their mark as I narrowed my eyes on him. "Excuse me?"

"I don't know how your world works. Clearly, not like mine. In my world, you obey a captain's orders." He paused to take in my infuriated reaction, but it had no visible effect on his outrage. "I do not say these things to be offensive; I'm only telling you that's the way it is. In my world, not following orders can lead to dire consequences."

Fury flared inside my chest, threatening to burn me from the inside out. "Well, in your world, need I remind you that I am not a part of your crew?" I spat back. "I get that you're in charge around here and that people are supposed to be afraid of you, but you can save your threats for your men. You don't frighten me, Demetri."

"Is that so?" He lurked toward me.

I stared up at him defiantly.

"You've not seen the worst side of me yet, love." He growled, looming over me in the chair. "That's why you harbor no fear."

"Dammit Demetri, how many times do I have to apologize? What else do you want me to say?"

He brushed his hand against my face, letting his fingers fall around my neck before tilting my head up to face him. "Apologies hold no bearing. Sometimes there must be consequences."

"Stop acting like you're going to hurt me. Because we both know that you won't," I said through shallow breaths. The expression he let slip made me silently wonder if I was right about that.

Storms raged behind his eyes as he glared down at me and loosened his grip, visibly morphing back into the man I'd come to know before today. "No," he whispered in return. "I won't." He released his hand and turned away, leaving me reeling from the tense proximity.

"Forgive me," he uttered, pulling in a deep breath as some of his volatility appeared to melt away. "Sometimes my temper tends to get the best of me." He stroked the defiant strands of his dark hair back into place before clenching his fingers together...the fingers that were just clasped around my neck.

"I suppose I shouldn't be so unforgiving. You did save me after all," he acknowledged, crossing his arms as he put distance between us. "And you helped the other men, too."

"I tried."

"I must say it's impressive, especially for someone with no prior experience. I'm still quite angry at you, though, for putting your life at risk."

"I'll take what I can get." I fought back a smile, sliding his coat off my shoulders.

His eyes went wide as I did. "What happened?" He demanded.

I trailed his gaze, noticing for the first time the bloodstain on my shoulder.

"Oh. I almost forgot about this." I pulled the fabric down to inspect the scratch. "The mermaid that tried to pull you off the boat scratched me. I'm...really sorry about your shirt." I winced apologetically.

He rushed over to me, stripping it off in one quick tear.

"Demetri!" I screamed, desperately grasping at the remnants to cover myself.

He raced to the door and called for Alistair.

"Demetri, what's wrong?"

"Your wound," he responded as he waited impatiently.

"It's not as bad as it looks." I assured him. "It doesn't even hurt anymore," I said, attempting to reexamine the area.

Alistair's footsteps entered into the room. "Captain?"

"Come in." Demetri shut the door behind him. "Show him," he commanded, and I slid the tattered shirt away from my shoulder.

"Oh no." It was all Alistair could say as he stared at me, but the way his face fell as he glanced back at Demetri suggested this was more serious than I wanted to accept.

Fear trickled across the length of my spine as I examined the worry lines etched on their faces. "Can someone tell me what's going on?" I exclaimed.

"Sirens are poisonous creatures. While their main weapon is their voice, their scratches can be lethal if enough of the poison is injected into your body," Alistair responded much too calmly.

"Oh...okay..." I replied frantically as the realization took hold.

"How do you feel?" Alistair asked.

"I was fine until you told me I was poisoned by a mermaid. Now I'm kind of freaking out."

"No headaches? Dizziness?"

"Maybe some dizziness. I don't think it was from poison, though."

"Why don't you come lie down?" Demetri said, guiding me to his bed.

Through the newfound information spiraling through my head, I heard Demetri ask Alistair, "Do we have anything?"

"No, just the Evenfall, but that won't do anything for poison. Our best bet will be to try to find some help when we dock at Mystic Grove. There are natural remedies for this sort of thing. We'll just need to find them."

Even their pacing shadows seemed troubled as they moved through the room, trying to come up with another viable option. Tears prodded at the corners of my eyes. "Am I gonna die?"

"No. You're not," Demetri asserted.

"Oh God, I'm gonna die," I whispered.

"Let me check the stash again; maybe there'll be something in there to help." Alistair suggested.

"Yes. Go now," Demetri ordered, and Alistair hurried off.

"Demetri?" I sat up, swiping my tears away. The blue mermaid's warning flashed through my mind. *"You...will...die..."* she had told me after she split my skin open.

"You are not going to die," Demetri declared. "We didn't get this far for you to die from a little scratch." He inspected it again, actively trying to not seem as concerned as I knew he really was.

"I should have listened to you," I cried.

He brought his hands to my face, tilting my chin up to him, only much gentler this time. "Perhaps if you had, several men would be lying at the bottom of the sea right now, including myself."

"Maybe..." I whispered. "But I still made it hard. I got pulled into the water, and you risked your life for me unnecessarily."

"And I'd do it again if need be."

"Wait...Demetri. I got pulled into the water," I murmured, recalling the auburn-haired mermaid.

"Aye..." he said quizzically. "Are you still feeling well?"

"Demetri!" I dismissed his question. "When I was underwater, one of the mermaids...she helped me. She had just pulled me back to the surface when you found me."

His brows drew together in confusion. "That's rather uncharacteristic behavior from a siren."

I darted off the bed, grabbed his coat, and fervently dug through his pockets. "She also gave me this." I pulled out the tiny container and handed it to him. "I meant to tell you earlier, but with you being so mad and all...what is this stuff? Do you know?"

"Aye." He smiled, lifting his eyes back to mine. "It's fairy dust."

He pulled the lantern closer as he further inspected the specs of golden glitter inside.

"Will it help?" I asked.

"It will depend on how much poison is inside your body, but fairy dust has immense healing powers. I think it could do the trick." Relief glistened in his voice.

"Well, let's try it and see." I jumped up onto the edge of the table where the light seemed to shine the best.

He approached, carefully opening the jar. "You'll have to move that." He motioned at the decimated shirt I held against me.

"Can't you work around it?"

"No, the wound goes from your neck to your shoulder, and I can't tell how far down. We aren't chancing this, love."

I pulled it down slightly, ensuring no eye contact was made. The air that chilled my skin was quickly replaced with the heat of awareness.

"That's enough." He stopped me just before I completely exposed myself.

"Well, aren't you the perfect gentleman?"

He smirked as he moved my hair behind my shoulder. "Hold still," he whispered as he poured some of the contents out into his hand, and a heavy scent of lavender filled the room.

He sprinkled the dust over the scratch, enough to fully cover it, and poured the rest back into the jar. Then he stepped back, examining me for any physical changes. "Do you feel anything?"

"No... but I didn't feel anything beforehand either."

A knock sounded at the door. "Captain?" Alistair yelled from the other side.

"Come in," Demetri said despite my half-exposed state.

"Oh, I'm sorry, miss." Alistair attempted to avert his eyes upon finding me half-naked and glittery on the table.

"She had fairy dust," Demetri tried to explain between Alistair's uncomfortable glances.

"Oh!" Alistair exclaimed, rushing over.

"It's not doing anything yet," Demetri added.

Alistair leaned in closer, squinting as he tried to get a better look before Demetri held out his arm and stopped his advance.

"Close enough," Demetri ordered.

Alistair chuckled. "It takes a few minutes sometimes, but look." He pointed.

The glitter was slowly shifting colors before our eyes.

"What's it doing?" I asked.

"It's sucking the poison right out of you! See, it's turning white." Alistair exclaimed. "Here, try to wipe it off now."

I swiped at my shoulder, clearing away the specks that remained. The scratch had already healed. Taking its place was a slightly visible scar.

"It worked!" Demetri confirmed.

"Oh my gosh!" I squealed as a wave of relief surged through me. "It worked!" I echoed, flinging myself forward and wrapping my arms around Demetri.

"Er...I'll be leaving you two alone then," Alistair interjected, a slight smile taking shape on his face. "I'm glad you're alright, Miss Gwendolyn."

"I'm sorry." I laughed at his reaction, pulling the shirt up higher. "I'm just so relieved."

"Aye, lucky thing you came across some fairy dust."

"Lucky indeed," Demetri agreed. "And Alistair, not a word of this to anyone else," he added.

"Of course, Captain."

"Why can't he tell anyone?" I asked as he left the room.

"If the men knew we had fairy dust...they'd have suspicions," Demetri explained. "Something such as this"—he held up the vial—"is extremely hard to come by. I simply don't want the unnecessary pressures of answering the questions they would undoubtedly have."

"I guess I can't blame you for that."

"Alistair is one of my most trusted advisors. He and Felix...they've been with me the longest. Our secret will be safe with him."

I smiled at the way his face lit up when he spoke of them. "That's good to know. Sometimes it's hard to distinguish the trustworthy pirates from the regular pirates around here."

"Yes, it can be quite difficult at times. I suppose it's a good thing you have me here to enlighten you every step of the way." He winked. "How lucky you are."

CHAPTER FOURTEEN

"No one will ever believe me when I tell them about this," I said to Demetri, who stood beside me on the ship as we watched a flock of mermaids splashing below. "Jacob, Bree...my parents...they'll all think I've gone mad."

"You mustn't tell them. They wouldn't understand," he responded.

Thunder crashed around us as the sky grew dark. I struggled to grasp onto something to keep from falling overboard as the boat began to tilt sideways. Demetri stood silently as though nothing were happening. The screeching sound of the mermaids' nails stung my ears as they began to climb up the walls of the boat.

"Demetri, I'm scared!" I yelled as I reached out for him.

"You should be," he said as he began to help the mermaids onto the ship.

"No! What are you doing?" I cried out as they bypassed him, crawling manically in my direction. Their beautiful faces contorted right before my eyes into a blur of terrifying, exaggerated expressions.

"Help!" I screamed. But Demetri only stood back, smiling absurdly as he watched.

The blue-haired mermaid latched onto my leg. *"You...will...die..."* she yelled, pulling me closer to her bloody body. I kicked frantically, trying to aim for her face, but realized I was tangled up in a web of strings. She dug her nails into my skin, dragging them down as they cut into me like razor blades. The scream that followed was just as piercing as the pain. I twisted my body away from her next swipe, landing hard on my back in the process. Facing the sky, I saw the tangled strings weaving over me. The storm clouds faded away, and to my absolute horror, the face of the old witch took form in their place.

"Demetri, it's her! It's Cosmina!" I yelled, but he was no longer there.

The mermaids morphed into wooden ventriloquist puppets, their mouths bobbing open as Cosmina laughed, tugging at their strings. "Hurry, child," she croaked against the thunder. "The Snow Moon draws near," Cosmina warned. She released a chaotic cackle, dragging the puppets closer to me until the darkness finally took hold.

I woke up in a frenzy, kicking the covers away violently. My heart felt like it would surely explode through my chest. *It was only a dream*, I reassured myself, taking purposeful deep breaths until the frenzied beats slowed to a semi-normal pace.

A warm breeze blew across me, drawing my attention to the open window where the moonlight flooded in.

"Demetri?" I leaned through the window.

"Gwendolyn." He acknowledged me with a halfhearted smile.

"What are you doing out here?" I asked, ignoring the flutter brought on by the sound of hearing him use my whole name.

"I couldn't sleep."

"I know the feeling...mind if I join you?"

"You needn't ask," he said, offering me his hand as I climbed up to settle in beside him.

I wasn't sure how long ago we'd made it out of the sea cave, but the ocean was peaceful as we sailed under a sky of glittering stars.

"I had a dream about mermaids and puppets..." I confessed. "And, well, it doesn't sound quite as scary when I say it out loud."

He laughed softly. "Sounds rather horrifying, actually."

"The worst part was Cosmina." I shuddered. "I almost don't even want to find her."

"I suspect she probably doesn't want you to find her either." Demetri countered with a grin that chased away the haunting memory of her cryptic green eyes.

"You know, it's weird," I mused. "You and I, we haven't even known each other for very long, yet it feels like a lifetime with everything we've been through. It still seems surreal to me, though...like this is just a dream that I'm going to wake up from at any given moment."

"Aye, strange indeed." He rested the back of his head against the ship, bathing in the glow of the silver beams. "It feels like a lifetime, yet not long enough."

"And while I enjoy your company, I cannot say the same when it comes to the absurd amount of death-defying quests."

Demetri's mouth pulled up at the corners. "I must admit, I've had more death-defying quests with you recently than I've had in quite some time."

"How special for us." I threw him a sarcastic smile.

"I fear we will soon have more of them to look forward to."

"Read the room, Demetri," I joked. "This world is stressful enough without your less-than-optimistic observations."

He suppressed a laugh, and I couldn't help but compare how different he was right now to the person he had been earlier today. I knew both variations existed in him, balancing him out to who he was at the core, but I'd seen enough of both sides to conclude I liked him a lot better when the burden of everyone else's expectations wasn't weighing him down.

"Very well," he teased. "Then tell me about your world. Is it not stressful there?"

"I would have answered that question very differently before I came here...but now I'll just say that there isn't always something trying to kill me in my world. And there also aren't very many journeys across lands and seas to find time-traveling witches. Oh, and there definitely aren't venomous mermaids."

He leaned up, propping his arms on his knees. "I am rather curious about your world. Are there kingdoms and villages like the ones here?"

"Not really. There are some old castles in other places around the world, but we don't have kings or queens, not where I live anyway. We don't have mystical creatures. We don't have magic at all."

"No magic," Demetri repeated with noticeable astonishment, as though that were something he had a hard time processing. "...And the place where you live? What's it like there?"

"My home is in a city, but not like the ones here. There are tall buildings and loud cars everywhere...restaurants on each corner with any type of food you could possibly imagine. There are stores where you can buy anything and everything...clothes, furniture, televisions..." God, I missed home.

"What are televisions?" Confusion etched Demetri's tone.

"It's...uhh, like a box that you watch things on...movies and shows." A glance at his foggy expression confirmed he had no earthly idea what I was talking about. Of course not; he had never heard of movies or shows before.

"It's kind of like a theater play..." I continued, "But you can watch the people in the box anytime you want to." I looked over at him again. Nope, still no clue. "It's like a little magic box, with a screen and people in it," I said, laughing as his posture stiffened and his face crumpled with uncertainty.

"You said there was no magic in your world," he countered.

"There isn't..." I giggled. "Sorry, I've never had to explain what a television is to someone before. It's surprisingly a lot harder than I thought it would be. Basically, you can watch things on it...moving pictures."

"Is that where you watch the fairytales you always speak of?"

"Yes...but there's also so much more. You'd probably be pleased to know there are tons of movies about pirates."

"Are they all as dashing as I am?" he joked, leaning closer as he flashed a smile that would surely make my knees wobbly if I were standing right now.

"Not even close," I muttered.

Demetri's stare lingered on me for several moments before he spoke again. "What does your home look like?"

Visions of the city flashed vibrantly through my mind. I'd once taken it for granted...assumed I'd never have to fight to have a comfortable life. Thinking of it now, wondering if I'd ever see the welcoming lights of the skyline again, it was almost physically painful.

"Well, I live in an apartment, which is basically just a big building where a lot of people live."

"So, you live with many other people?" He stroked his chin while considering the thought. "How does that operate? Do you have to share beds?"

"No!" I couldn't contain the laugh that erupted. "Not like that! A lot of people live in the building, but they each get their own room...and their own bed."

He laughed at my response. I wasn't sure if it was because of the misunderstanding or the fact that I was still snickering about it.

"I did have a roommate, though. My best friend, Bree." My smile faded away slightly. "She's gone now. She just got married and moved out." I reached for her necklace as I spoke. The chain was just long enough that the pendant frequently fell behind the fabric of the dresses I wore. I ran my finger over the jagged edge of the moon, pulling it back out into view.

Demetri's eyes flickered down to it. "Did she give you that?"

"Yes. On the same day that I was sent here, funnily enough," I said, squeezing my palm around it. Having a part of my world here, a part of Bree, brought me a strange sense of comfort. It grounded me and made me feel less alone somehow. "It used to be hers. She said she thought it brought her good luck." I laughed at the thought. "Although, I'm not so sure how true that is considering what happened right after I put it on."

"I'd say she was right." Demetri cracked a satirical smile. "It brought you to me, did it not?"

"Yes, I suppose it did." I laughed as a rush of heat flashed across my cheeks. "Also, I feel like I should clarify that when we were roommates, we had separate bedrooms and did not have to fight over who got to sleep in the bed."

"What a relief."

"Yes. I imagine it is incredibly hard having to share your bed after all," I taunted, gently jabbing him with my elbow.

"That it is. But sometimes, sacrifices must be made." Demetri glanced at me again, and I half expected him to add some sort of perverse comment based on the subject matter. But he didn't. Instead, a soft and almost sad smile inched across his face as his gaze lingered over me.

Several moments of silence fell between us before he spoke again. "You frightened me today."

"Which time, exactly?"

"Numerous times, but I was mainly referring to when I realized you'd been wounded."

"I was scared, too," I quietly confessed.

"If you didn't have that dust, then who knows what would have..." His voice trailed off.

"Yeah. I've been trying not to think about it." My body trembled involuntarily. I'd been so close to death and hadn't even realized it at the time. I didn't even want to ponder over the moment when things would have inevitably taken a turn for the worst...I couldn't. "Why do you think that mermaid helped me?"

Demetri looked out across the endless moonlit sea. "Truth be told, we'll probably never know."

I crawled back into his bed as he latched the window and surrendered himself to the armchair for the night. Every attempt made to drift back to sleep was foiled as soon as I closed my eyes...when the mermaid faces from my nightmare came back to haunt me.

"Demetri?" I whispered against the silence.

"Yes, love?"

I held my breath as I debated. "Could you...maybe, come lie down with me? Just for tonight?"

The soft noise of his footsteps approached as the edge of the bed sank down beside me. I rolled over to face him, barely able to see anything beyond the shroud of night. Not a word was uttered as he pulled the blanket over us and pressed his body against mine.

I curled into him instinctively, taking pleasure in the warmth he provided and the lulling sound of his steady heartbeat. It was an all too real reminder of just how much I missed having close contact with another person.

He wrapped his arm around me like he knew exactly what I needed. I settled into his embrace and closed my eyes again, no longer worried about the visions in my dreams.

Demetri's arm was still draped around me when I woke. The light of a new day intruded as golden-flecked hues broke through the cracks of the dark curtains. I shifted carefully under his weight, analyzing his face to ensure I hadn't accidentally stirred him into consciousness. How someone could look so flawless as they slept was beyond my comprehension. Even his sleep-tousled hair seemed intentional in the subtle way that it framed his face.

In the time that I'd known him, his stubbled jaw had grown a little darker, further accentuating his sharp features. He was ruggedly beautiful, and the longer I gazed, the more entrancing he became.

"Captain!" I heard on the other side of the room, followed by several meddlesome knocks.

The door shot open before anyone had the chance to respond.

"What is it, Felix?" Demetri asked groggily as he sat up in the bed.

"Oh," Felix's face grew red as he gawked at us. "Terribly sorry to interrupt."

Demetri glanced down at me as though he just remembered I was there. "Is there something I can do for you, Felix?"

"No, Captain. I just wanted to inform you that we'll be making landfall at Mystic Grove within the hour. I've already gathered the supplies for your journey."

"Yes. Very well. Thank you, Felix. Everything is well on track. You'll oversee the ship while we're gone."

"Of course, Captain. I'll leave you to it then." Felix nodded before rushing out.

Demetri drug a lazy hand through his hair before lying back down.

"Did you sleep well?" he asked, his voice still raspy from sleep.

"I did," I admitted. "Did you?"

"Aye, it was nice to be back in my own bed. It's much more comfortable than that bloody stiff chair."

I attempted to stifle a laugh, but the endeavor was unsuccessful. "You know, I think Felix thinks we're having sex."

Demetri's eyes flared in surprise, abandoning all traces of the fatigue that had just resided there. "Yes, but to be fair, he probably already thought that."

"You're probably right." I bit my lip to keep from laughing again.

"If you feel regretful for deceiving him, we could resolve the issue rather easily." He casually suggested.

I tapped my finger on my chin and pretended to think about it. "Hmm. What a dilemma."

His eyes flickered to my mouth and up again. "You are an evil...evil woman. I just want you to know that."

"How dare you." I gripped my chest, pretending to be wounded by the remark. "I'm just trying to keep you on your toes."

"I've other things in mind I'd rather be on."

"Mmm, tempting." I laughed. "But it seems we've got another busy day ahead of us, so we should probably get out of bed."

"Tempting, you say?" He arched a daring brow. "Am I starting to sway you, Winters?"

"I'm not easily swayed, Captain."

He propped himself up with his arm and unleashed the full power of his gaze on me. "Hmm..." He pondered. "That's not quite what I asked, though."

Desire swelled in the pools of his eyes, threatening to pull me under if I ventured too close to the edge. It was impossible to look away, but even if I could, it was safe to say that, in this moment, I would still risk drowning.

I wasn't quite sure what he saw in my expression, but whatever it was persuaded him to make his move. Lifting his free hand, he ran the back of his fingers across my cheek with a touch so soft it sent chills dripping down my spine.

I reached for him with trembling fingers, stroking a rogue piece of hair away from his brow. He intercepted my hand, pulling it to his mouth as he pressed his lips against the underside of my wrist. There was something so purposefully intimate about the gesture that made my body heat with an inexplicable ache of longing.

The insatiable hunger surged violently through my veins, igniting in all the places where I craved his touch. There was no refusing him. In a matter of seconds, I'd become a willing victim to the desire that had easily encompassed me.

His sea-storm eyes locked with mine again, an unbridled and chaotic urgency blazing in them. The sight alone was nearly enough to send me spiraling. But then he pulled back, visibly hesitating, almost as if he were waiting for me to give him some type of permission.

"Tell me what you want." His voice deepened as his composure threatened to unravel.

I tangled a hand in his hair, gently tugging through the dark strands as I slid it down to clutch the back of his neck. "Don't stop," I whispered.

That was all the confirmation he needed. Demetri was on top of me in an instant. I tightened my grip on him, pulling his face down feverishly to mine, relishing the rush of our lips colliding. I didn't want to overthink this or consider all the reasons why it was wrong. I didn't care about any of that. In this moment, I just wanted him.

He ran his hands across my body, expertly exploring all the dips and curves as I dug my nails into the tight muscles of his arms and arched closer into him. I needed more, and I needed it now.

Time stood still here underneath him. His lips crashed into mine over and over again like waves that were desperate to meet the shore. His hands set every single inch of my skin ablaze, each touch sparking something in me that I'd never felt before. God. It was too much but not enough all at once. This whole damn ship could go up in flames around us and I don't think I'd notice or care.

Demetri drew back breathlessly, but I gave him no time to recover. The ache was too strong, and the distance between our lips felt like a slow suffocation.

"Kiss me," I begged.

His eyes flared with desire as he obliged, pressing his lips back to mine in a forceful manner as though he, too, relied on the air between us to survive. He lingered there for several moments, then trailed his mouth down the edge of my collarbone and across the white scar that now existed there.

"Captain Hawkins!" Another knock sounded at the door.

"Not now!" Demetri roared.

I pulled his face back to mine, starving for the taste of him again. He unleashed his tongue, intertwining it with mine as he ran his hand under my gown and firmly gripped my thigh. My legs wrapped around him desperately, feeling the pulse of his own need as he cursed under his breath.

Demetri lifted his body away long enough to tear off his shirt. His slender, lean muscled frame flexed above me as he raised his arms over his head. I traced the contours of his hard-planed chest with my hands, taking in the immaculate sight of him as quickly as I could before he lowered himself back down to meet my lips again.

"Captain!" Another voice yelled as the beating on the door grew louder. "Land ho!" The door swung open as Alistair, Thomas, and Wiley stood bewildered in the entryway.

"For fuck's sake," Demetri muttered.

We changed clothes quickly and joined the other men out on the deck. It was evident by their dirty sneers they'd already been informed of our morning activities.

"Mornin', Captain!" One of the newer crew members laughed as he enthusiastically slapped Demetri on the back as we walked by. "Beautiful day, eh?"

Demetri shot a confused glance at him.

"Captain. Miss." A stocky man with a short brown beard greeted us, tipping his hat as he approached. His dark, knowing eyes fell across my body so quickly that I almost didn't catch the movement.

"Feeling better today, Jonah?" Demetri acknowledged him.

"Aye, Captain." He smiled, baring a row of perfect teeth. "Good as new."

"Glad to hear it, lad."

"I was wondering if I might ask a favor of ye?"

"We'll be making landfall soon. There's not much time to be granting favors," Demetri responded coolly.

"That's the thing, actually. Me and Dalton was wonderin' if we could join you and the others when we dock." Jonah motioned over to the lean blonde-haired man standing several feet away. I recognized him from yesterday. He had been the one talking about the magic barriers when Demetri told the men that much of the crew would remain on the docked ship.

"I think the fewer men out there, the better. Any extra commotion would only draw unwanted attention," Demetri responded.

"That's a good point, and normally I'd agree with you, but..." Jonah stepped closer and lowered his voice to barely a whisper. "I've seen the witch before, too, and I think I can help you find her."

I glanced over at Demetri as he deliberated the request.

"Cap, I grew up in an area not too far from Mystic Grove," Dalton interjected. "I know what kind of creatures we are up against out there. I've seen some of 'em before with my own eyes. Having a few extra men to help you fight ain't such a bad idea."

"Perhaps you're right," Demetri appeared to contemplate. "We would just need to try to stay as inconspicuous as possible."

"Aye, we'll go pack some supplies before we dock," Jonah said as they both turned away and disappeared under the deck.

Demetri leaned against the rail, appearing to be deep in thought.

"Is something wrong?" I asked.

He crossed his arms. "I didn't exactly want a whole fleet of men along for the journey," he said quietly. "The fewer people who know about the situation, the better."

"We don't have to tell them everything. I think having them could be helpful, though."

"Aye, especially if Dalton knows the area so well."

"And they could help you fight...if it comes to that." I tried to push the panic of that possibility away from my mind.

"I don't anticipate a fight. There should be no need for one."

"How can you be so sure? What about all the random creatures out there?"

Demetri took note of my anxious tone, softening his features as he attempted to settle my nerves. "Giants can generally be avoided. It's easy to hide from them. Centaurs are typically peaceful unless they're provoked, and I don't intend on provoking them. Trolls can be stealthy, but like centaurs, they don't often go looking for fights."

"And the witch?"

"I imagine we will likely encounter a witch or wizard. It's hard to say if it will be the particular one we seek, but there's simply no way of knowing until we start our search. And, if we do come across another witch, it's possible they could still offer their assistance in the matter."

I tried to focus on the structure of his sentences but instead found myself fixated on the way that his lips moved as his words eloquently tumbled out. My mind wandered back to his bed and the way his body felt on top of me...the way his fingers had entangled with mine as he'd licked my skin, and the feral need that had raged behind his eyes not even thirty minutes ago.

"Are you okay, love?" he asked, dragging me back down to reality as I realized I'd been blankly staring at him.

"Sorry, yes. I'm fine." I smiled weakly. "Just thinking about...the creatures," I added.

"You needn't worry, love, but if you're just not feeling up to it, I suppose you can stay on the boat. I could try to find the witch myself and—"

"What? No, absolutely not. I'm fine, Demetri. I promise," I assured.

How could he stand here so nonchalantly and act like we hadn't just been on the verge of completely ravaging each other in his bed? Had we not been interrupted...

"Gwen?" He met my distant gaze.

"Hm? Sorry, what?"

"Are you certain you're all right?" he pressed.

"I'm great." My voice betrayed me as it squeaked.

"So, you're ready then?"

I peered over his shoulder as the trees shifted closer into view. The men were already readying the anchor.

"Let's go." I smiled.

I sat in the rowboat between Demetri and Alistair. Griff, Jonah, and Dalton squeezed in uncomfortably together across from us, each of them carrying bags of supplies on their backs.

"What's in there?" I whispered.

"Some food, water, tents..." Demetri called off.

"Tents?" I glanced nervously at the dense jungle we sailed toward.

"And rum." Alistair leaned over to add, snickering at my worried expression.

"Can't forget the rum!" Dalton snorted.

Once we had made it ashore, we pushed our way through the hanging vines and lush tropical greenery. Demetri and Alistair headed the line, slicing through with their swords to make the path more accessible where they could.

Vibrant-colored birds chirped and sang cheerfully in the canopies above us. The humidity was nearly unbearable, and I imagined this was probably what being in the middle of the Amazon rainforest would feel like.

"So, you used to live around here?" I turned to Dalton, who was following close behind me.

"Not here exactly, but I am a bit more familiar with the area than most. I grew up near a place called Starlight Stream…it's between here and the kingdom of Winterhaven."

"Seems odd." I laughed. "A land called Winterhaven so close to a tropical jungle."

"It's not so different when you actually get into Mystic Grove. The jungle here just surrounds it. Think of it as more like a protection spell that helps conceal the location."

"That's…interesting…" I swiped my hand across my forehead as the sweat beaded up.

"Gotta throw off the invaders from knowing where all the magic is," Jonah added as he caught up to us.

"That makes sense, I guess," I replied. Jonah swiftly grabbed me by the arm as I stumbled over a ground root.

"Be careful, miss. There's a lot of dangerous stuff out here," he said, glaring around as though he heard something off in the distance.

"Enough, Jonah," Demetri commanded from the front.

"Did you live nearby too?" I grabbed onto Jonah's shoulder as I stepped over a web of vines.

"No, but I have been here before. That's where I encountered the old witch."

"What happened?"

"I went to her, seeking help, but she wanted me to do something for her first…retrieve an item that I'd never even heard of. It was an impossible task. I looked for it, o' course, exactly where she told me to, but the old bat just spoke in riddles."

My stomach twisted as he spoke of Cosmina. I couldn't help but picture her abnormally green eyes glaring from behind her gaunt, wrinkled face.

"What did she want you to find?" I finally gathered the courage to ask.

"She called it the turning stone. Said that was the only way she'd help me get back to my home."

"Where is your home?"

Jonah's face fell. "I wish I could remember. You see, I'd been with my old crew on the ship for weeks when we sailed straight into a monster storm. The waves were so high they overtook the boat. The last thing I remember was falling into the water. I woke up sometime later washed up on the shore of Mystic Village, which is just north of where we're headed."

"Oh my gosh, how horrible," I said softly.

"I journeyed through the town, not even knowing who I was, for days. Finally, I started regaining some of my memories, but I still don't know if the rest of the crew even made it."

"And you never remembered where your home was?"

"Maybe I never even had one." He shrugged. "All I remember is being on that boat."

"Jonah, that's awful," I placed my hand on his arm, trying to provide some sort of comfort. "I'm sorry. I hope one day you can get your memories back. You deserve to know about your past. If you have a family..."

"Don't worry about me, miss." Jonah placed his hand over mine. "My crew is my family now. Perhaps, one day, I'll remember more, but I've had time to accept what's happened."

"I'm not sure I could ever say the same in your shoes," I admitted. "Your outlook is truly inspiring."

"Well, your outlook is all you have sometimes, isn't it?" Jonah sighed through a strained smile.

"I suppose it is."

"What about you?" he inquired. "Whereabouts are you from?"

"Oh, um..." I cleared my throat, hoping Demetri wasn't too far ahead to hear the question and would intercept it. No such luck.

I tried to recall the name of the land that Demetri had told me he was from, but my memories abruptly evaded me.

"It's an island south of here. You probably haven't heard of it before, though. It's a bit of a long way."

"Oh, I know of a couple places south of here. Is it around Storm Haven?"

"Yes," I smiled. "I'm from Storm Haven." Desperate to change the subject, I asked, "I'm curious though, how'd you know to seek the witch out for help?"

"Word of mouth. While I was making my way through Mystic Village, I met an old couple. They took me in and kept me fed for several days as I battled with the amnesia. When I could finally make sense of a little more than what my name was, they told me to seek her out for help. I didn't even really know who I was looking for. I just kept going. Then, one day, there she was...it was almost like she was looking for me too."

His story conjured a coursing chill throughout my entire body.

"So, you think she let you find her because she wanted to be found?"

"Yeah...it was the strangest thing. When I found her, it almost seemed like she was expecting me. Like someone told her I'd be coming before I even knew I would be."

"That's kind of creepy," I cringed.

"Aye. It still unnerves me to this day when I think about it."

"So, why'd you want to come with us then?"

"I don't know," he confessed. "I do believe I can help you find her. And while I've mostly accepted my fate, I think part of me still wants to see if she'd be willing to help me. If not to go home, then maybe to at least regain my memories."

"I can understand that."

"Did you get to the best part of the story yet?" Dalton interjected, severing the tension.

Jonah let out a hearty laugh, slapping his hand across his friend's back. "I think Dalton's referring to the part where I gave up my senseless quest and trekked down to Starlight Stream, where I met him."

"I was on my way to sign up for Captain Hawkin's crew and convinced this goon to join me," Dalton boasted proudly.

"Figured I might as well. Didn't really have anything else to lose at that point." Jonah snickered.

"What are you three chattering about back there?" Demetri threw a glance back over his shoulder.

Jonah's back straightened and he cleared his throat. "I was just telling Miss Gwen some old stories about how I came to join the crew, Captain."

"Well, keep it down. We're getting closer to the threshold. Remember, we all need to exert discretion."

"Yes sir, Captain," Jonah complied.

Demetri slashed his way through a thick wall of vines, revealing the mouth of a narrow cave. As he ushered us through, the air around us shifted. A sudden burst of white, blinding light came rushing past us like a gust of gale-forced wind.

I latched onto Demetri's arm and pressed my face into his shoulder until the light on the other side of my eyelids had seemingly receded. "What the hell was that?"

"That was us passing through the boundary of the protection spell," Jonah answered. "Welcome to Mystic Grove."

We stepped out of the other side of the cave to an entirely different type of forest. This one wasn't tropical; it was chilly and foggy. The tall black trees twisted and towered menacingly over us, blocking out the color of the sky. I stared past the men, silently watching as the unusual hues of pink and purple leaves floated down from the treetops, littering the ground all around us.

"This way then. Be on the lookout for anything unusual." Demetri's warning rang low.

"This is the trail I saw the witch on," Jonah whispered, and the hair on my arms stood in response.

"I think I prefer the jungle," I muttered.

We trudged underneath the swaying trees in silence for a while, stopping every now and then when the force of the wind would crack the tree limbs overhead. It was hard to tell how late it was getting, but the sporadic light that bounced through the cracks of the canopy leaves was noticeably dimmer than before.

I walked beside Demetri now, who'd had his sword drawn and ready to strike from the first moment we'd crossed through the portal barrier.

"What if we don't find her?" I dared to ask, afraid to extensively dwell on the outcome of that question myself.

"Then we'll expand the search."

"Jonah said that when he found her before, it seemed like she knew he was looking for her. Like she wanted to be found."

Demetri smirked, briefly allowing his gaze to settle on me. "Jonah is a bit of an embellisher when it comes to the details, love."

"You think he'd lie about something like that?"

"I don't know, I just know I wouldn't put much faith into his stories."

"The way you did when you agreed to let him join us on the trip to look for her?" I jeered.

"I do not doubt that he's seen the witch before. He's not foolish enough to lie to my face about that."

"We'll need to set up camp soon, Captain." Alistair appeared beside us, keeping his voice at a volume lower than what I was accustomed to. "Night falls faster here in the forest."

"Right," Demetri agreed. "Let's be on the lookout for a spot to set up."

"There should be a place up just ahead," Dalton chimed in from behind us. "The locals call it Cavern's Creek. It's the midway point between the shore and Mystic Village. We can probably make it there before night sets in. It'd be one of the safer places to set up camp."

"Very well." Demetri nodded. "We'll rest tonight and get an early start in the morning. If we haven't found the witch by tomorrow night, we'll head north to the village and start asking around. We're bound to find something sooner or later."

When we'd finally reached the creek Dalton had told us about, and the men had decided where the campsite would be best suited, Demetri retrieved the vial of Evenfall Elixir from his coat pocket.

"How does it work?" I asked, eyeing the dark liquid.

"We'll need at least four drops," he responded. "One for each corner of the campsite. They'll connect to form a barrier wall. Anything inside that barrier—like the campsite—will be hidden from view of anything on the outside."

Alistair and Griff assisted Demetri in deciding where to let the droplets fall. I watched as the first one hit the ground. It vanished almost as fast as it hit the dirt, but not before emitting a bright purple light that spread across the ground like a spiderweb.

"You can't go past these points," Demetri warned. "It will shock you if you touch it, and believe me, it's quite painful."

I grimaced at the thought. "What if I don't remember where all the barriers are?"

He drew out his sword and slashed it along the ground beside us. "Just don't pass this line. I'll draw more marks for the other walls as well."

"But how are we supposed to get out of here if we can't pass through?"

"Evenfall is temporary," Demetri assured. "It gets progressively weaker as the time passes. It will wear off enough by morning to not inflict any injuries."

Once the entire perimeter was secured and the ground was distinctly marked, the crew got to work setting up the campsite. Griff got a fire going faster than I'd ever seen anyone be able to, then insisted that I sit near it to keep myself warm as the temperatures dropped. I was plenty warm in the long, fur-lined coat from the trunk of clothes that I'd packed, but I politely complied anyway.

As the men finished setting up the tents, I wandered down to the edge of the small creekbank that was included inside the barrier lines. Demetri had insisted when he and Alistair created this side of the wall earlier that the water wouldn't nullify the shield here because the drops had firmly rooted into the ground. I really didn't understand the specifics of it all; I just hoped he was right about that.

My feet were aching more than they ever had before. My body was not used to all the physical activity it had endured lately, and it was finally letting me know that it was angry about its unwilling participation.

"What are you doing over here all alone?" Demetri's approaching voice was so smooth it almost made me forget about the persistent pain.

"My feet are killing me." I groaned, dipping them into the edge of the stream and squinting as the frigid water splashed up onto my legs. "And now I'll just have frostbite instead."

He squatted beside me, laughing at the discomfort I displayed before I slid my shoes back on.

"I'm going to assume you don't do much hiking in your world?"

"You'd be correct. My body is in a state of shock right now." I winced.

I felt the heat of his gaze linger over me, and he emitted that familiar halfhearted smile when I met his eyes.

"Are you okay?" I asked.

"I'm fine, love." His words were reassuring, but the tone behind them didn't match.

"Sorry." I forced a smile, silently regretting even bringing up the subject. "I know we've been on the move a lot today, and there hasn't been much time to talk. You just seem a little...off. And distant. Are you sure you're okay?" I pressed, unable to shake the feeling that something wasn't right.

He glanced away quickly and seemed to contemplate his thoughts for a moment. "I've been thinking about what occurred between us this morning."

"Oh...I see." My cheeks heated instantly, and I looked down at my lap to shield them from his line of sight.

"I needn't get distracted from our mission, but you keep inhabiting my thoughts."

My eyes flickered back up at the admission. His face was laced with some sort of confusion—or intrigue—I wasn't entirely sure which. Flashbacks of his body pressed against me invaded my mind for the thousandth time today. I'd tried my damnedest to push them down, but the way his cosmic-colored eyes morphed into a raging sea of overwhelming desire was not something I could easily or ever forget...nor was the way he bit my bottom lip between his ragged breaths. And the feeling of coming alive when his skin touched mine, lighting me up as the fire inside blazed violently; it was unlike anything I'd ever felt before...even with Jacob.

My face fell instantly, and I struggled to catch my fleeting breath. Oh God. Jacob. What the hell was wrong with me? A colossal wave of guilt rushed through my core, consuming me effortlessly. I fought against the nauseous feeling forming in the pit of my stomach. What would he say when he found out what I'd done? How would I ever even begin to explain the way I'd been so willing to compromise everything?

"What is it, love?" Demetri must have noticed my altered expression.

"How will I tell..." I started to whisper.

Demetri's eyes went cold, the constellations behind them burning out faster than I could even finish forming the question.

"I'm sorry, I didn't mean to..." I started.

"The blame is mine," he uttered blandly, angling his body away from mine. "I knew your situation and still pursued it."

"I'm sorry, Demetri. I should have never let it get that far. I don't know what came over me."

His icy stare made my hands tremble as I clasped them together against my body. "Are you...mad at me?" I asked, afraid to hear his answer.

"As I said, the blame is mine." He stood and turned back toward the campsite.

"Wait!" I exclaimed. "So that's it then?"

"We did something regrettable. It won't happen again. Once we find a way to get you home, you can explain your indiscretion. I'm sure all will be forgiven, considering the circumstances." He rambled as he dusted off his coat.

"Demetri..." I whispered.

"What else did you expect?" he blurted before storming away.

"I...I don't know." My words tumbled out in his absence.

CHAPTER FIFTEEN

Several hours had passed. Demetri had successfully avoided my existence ever since our uncomfortable exchange. I still wasn't quite sure whether to be angry or sympathetic regarding the way he'd reacted, but right now, I was leaning more toward the angry option.

I'd taken up a spot under a pink-leaved willow tree that resided near the edge of the barrier line. I needed some distance, but this was the best I could do given the constraints of the elixir.

Several yards away, the group of men sat in a circle, drinking and singing sea shanties around the dancing flames. Apparently, shrouding spells not only blocked out the visuals but also the voices of loud, drunken pirates.

Alistair and Griff had both approached me on separate occasions to ask if I wanted anything to eat or drink. While I appreciated their concern, I wasn't exactly in the mood or headspace for doing either of those things.

My body was beginning to throb back to life now that it had time to adequately rest. Alistair's voice boomed in the background as he reminisced about something that happened on the ship long ago, followed by the voices of the other men adding in the forgotten details.

I stole a glance just as Demetri threw his head back freely and laughed at whatever contribution Griff had just made, and I couldn't help but smile at the sight. I hadn't heard him laugh that way before, and the sound was damn near delectable.

No. I'm mad at you. I reminded myself.

Making the conscious decision to ignore him, I began to let my mind wander into darker thoughts...the ones I had been too scared to previously let myself consider.

What if we didn't find the witch? Or maybe even worse, what if we did? What if she couldn't or she *wouldn't* send me home? What if Demetri didn't want to help me anymore? There was nothing tying him to me, and he was liable to change his mind at any given moment. Despite that, he was the closest thing I had to a friend here, and I'd be lying to myself if I said his resentment didn't sting...lying if I said I wasn't worried he'd hold a grudge and decide that none of this was worth it. I couldn't help but wonder if he'd be mad at me, even after I left.

The anxiety of it all made my head spin. I tried to block it all out, if only for a moment. I allowed my body to sink down to rest against the back of the narrow tree trunk. Forcing myself to take a few deep breaths, I attempted to devise a plan to bridge the gap I'd forged between us.

A slight breeze rustled through the branches of the tree as pink leaves broke free and danced in the air around me. A flicker of light caught my eye from somewhere near the creek. It bounced into the top of the tree, darting around irregularly as though it were trying to hide from view.

I crawled out from under the swaying branches on all fours, trying to keep my sight set on the glowing object. It flitted back to the water's edge, exposing its wings as it raced across the rocks on the surface.

"A fairy?" I whispered in disbelief.

Demetri had mentioned them, of course, but never in my wildest dreams did I ever think I'd actually see one.

It hopped closer, as if it were trying to figure me out as well, before disappearing again. The tree branches swished once more as it settled safely near the top.

"I won't hurt you," I said softly.

The figure seemed to hesitate before drifting down closer to me. Still resting on my knees, I held my hands out in good faith and tried to keep my wits intact when it finally decided to land there.

"Oh my...hello," I whispered in bewilderment to the little fairy who I could see clearly now.

Her translucent wings shimmered and shed sunny specks of gold into my hands as they flapped behind her. The glitter wove through her honey-colored hair and clung to her flower-petal dress like drops of morning dew.

She leaped out of my hands, flying closer to my face quizzically as though she had never seen a human up close before. She tugged at my hair, inspecting the strands, then compared them to her own.

"Miss Gwendolyn? What in the world are you doing down there?" I heard Alistair call out.

I looked back at him, meeting the glances of five very confused men.

"I found a fairy!" I exclaimed as softly as my excitement would allow.

"That's impossible. They never approach humans!" Dalton called out.

I stood from the ground, dusting my coat off as the fairy leaped from my hand and encircled me.

"She's got a fairy!" Dalton shrieked.

As the wide-eyed men rose to rush down to the creek, the fairy flew away as quickly as she'd appeared.

"You scared her off!" I scowled.

"How'd you catch it?" Jonah asked, his eyes bulging in astonishment.

"I didn't catch her. She came to me."

Jonah reached for me. "Let me see your hands."

I held them out, showcasing the glitter in my palms. Alistair pulled out an empty bottle and carefully shook my hands off over it.

"Fairy dust is very hard to come by," he said. Something he knew I was already all too aware of.

"That's amazing, Gwen, how she just came up to you like that! Why, in all my years I've never seen anything like it," Dalton exclaimed.

Demetri stood unimpressed behind them as they collected all the dust she had left behind.

"You feeling okay, Captain?" Jonah questioned.

"Aye, just dreadfully tired from today's excursion. I think I'll turn in soon."

"That's a good idea." Griff yawned in agreeance. "Which tent will you and Miss Gwendolyn be taking?"

"I don't think..." I started.

"The one on the end will do just fine. Our belongings are already in there," Demetri interrupted.

"What was that about?" Demetri asked once we had settled in.

I knelt to spread the blanket out on the ground. "What was what about?"

"For God's sake. The blasted fairy, Gwen." He swiped the unruly strands of his hair back in an agitated manner, then tugged at the corner of the blanket closest to him to lay it flat.

I shrugged, unsure of what other information he was trying to gather. "I told you what happened."

"It's a bit hard to believe."

"What reason would I have to lie?" I glared up at him. "You saw it, didn't you?"

His eyes burned into me as though I were the person he hated most in this world...in any world.

"Look, is it going to be too uncomfortable for you to share a tent? You're clearly still upset with me. If you want, I can switch spots with someone else. In fact, that might be preferable."

"Like hell you will," he growled. "Don't be foolish, Gwen."

I narrowed my eyes. "What's that supposed to mean?"

"It means I don't trust another man around you to be able to control himself."

I scoffed at his candor. "You don't trust your own men? That's reassuring."

"I trust Alistair, perhaps even Griff. Regardless, I don't underestimate the power that a woman can have over men. Especially men who haven't so much as laid their eyes on a female in several months."

He was being so absurd right now. "Goodnight, Demetri." I rolled over hastily, grabbing the blanket in a manner that purposefully wrinkled his side.

When he didn't respond, I turned my head again to peer at him. He sat in the same spot, glowering at me.

"Are you going to do that all night?" I asked.

"Do what?"

"Glare at me angrily. It kind of makes it hard to sleep when you're burning holes through my head."

"I am not glaring," he said through gritted teeth. "And I am not angry."

"Well, shit. You could have fooled me."

"Fine. I am angry!" he exploded. "Is that what you want to hear?"

"Wow. What a breakthrough. Are you going to tell me why exactly, or do you want to play twenty questions about it?"

An angry smirk twisted the edges of his mouth. It inadvertently contorted the rest of the features on his striking face, and I found myself fighting the overwhelming urge to shrink back from the cruel expression. "You know, you may be an astonishing woman, but dare not forget your place, love. You're still a woman, and women of this world typically show a little more restraint and respect for the men."

What the fuck? A blinding rage instantaneously shot through my core. "Oh, believe me, Demetri"—I sat up to confront him head on—"I am showing a lot of restraint. Restraint to not leave a permanent hand mark across your arrogant face."

His eyes darkened and he huffed a threatening laugh. "I've done nothing..." he said. "Nothing but try to help you since the first moment that I met you. I've put my crew's life...my own life at risk. All for the sake of helping you." His words were low, but they cut deep all the same.

My stomach twisted. I had been so ready to combat whatever words he chose to weaponize next, but those were not the ones I had expected. "You're right," I whispered after several moments. "You've helped me more than I deserve, and I don't take that lightly. And even if you don't believe it, I am grateful for everything you've done, more than you could ever know."

The hard lines of his face appeared to smooth as I spoke.

"If I've hurt your feelings, I'm sorry," I added. "I never intended to."

He shifted his stance, reclaiming part of the mask he'd let slip. "You've not hurt my feelings. You've only reminded me not to get distracted from the mission."

I winced at the statement, for some reason it was painful to hear. Regardless, it was an improvement over the ones that had just come before it. "So, are we okay now? Can we put this feud behind us?" I pleaded.

He sighed in return. "Aye."

"I don't like it when you're angry with me," I admitted.

"It's hard to stay that way, no matter how much I'd like to." He leaned over to extinguish the flame in the lantern before lying down a few feet away from me.

"Why would you want to stay angry though?" I whispered through the darkness that separated us.

"It makes things easier. Wouldn't you agree?"

Demetri had no trouble falling asleep. He was clearly more experienced with taking camping trips in magical lands that were inhabited by menacing creatures than I was. I tried to stifle my nerves but shifted uneasily under the sound of every noise.

While the knowledge of the shrouding potion was comforting, I couldn't shake the nagging fear that something might break through. The fairy had managed to make it through...what was stopping something more sinister from doing the same?

"Watch it, will you?" A muffled voice sounded outside.

I froze as I heard footsteps shuffle past our tent.

"Do you have to be so loud?" Another whisper faintly responded.

I sat up, peeking through the crack of the curtained door. Two silhouettes that I recognized to be Jonah and Dalton were making their way down to the creek.

"Demetri," I muttered, nudging his leg, but he barely stirred. He probably wouldn't care much about what they were up to anyway.

I peered out again, watching their figures fade into the night.

My curiosity got the best of me, and I found myself sneaking out quietly to avoid waking Demetri. The last thing I wanted was to start another argument with him.

I tiptoed closer to the bank until their voices grew louder, watching them from behind a nearby tree.

"I don't see anything." Dalton moved closer to the water.

"I wonder how the lass caught the one earlier," Jonah replied.

"She said it hopped right into her hand."

"Well, she's lying, obviously. Fairies don't just go around hopping into people's hands."

"Thomas said he heard she was a witch." Dalton snorted in amusement. "That he thinks she's got the captain under some sort of enchantment spell to take her somewhere...remember how the sirens didn't affect her? Maybe she put that fairy in a trance, too."

A wave of anger rolled through me. *Why in the hell does everyone around here always assume I'm a witch?* It was becoming a challenge not to get a complex at this point.

"Makes sense, eh? Why else would she still be tagging along with us? Captain never keeps anybody around for this long. No snatch is that good." Jonah laughed. "I wonder what it is she's plotting."

If I actually were a witch, I'd strike him down right now.

"Nothing good. Why else would she want us to bring her here to meet up with another witch? Something fishy is going on," Dalton declared. "And we ought to be ready for whatever it is."

"Shhh... Dalton. Look there," Jonah whispered.

"It's the fairy!" Dalton exclaimed.

"Be quiet! You'll scare it off and wake the whole damn crew up."

The fairy landed nimbly near the edge of the water and pranced across the rocks.

"Go that way. I'll distract it, and you grab it from behind," Jonah commanded.

I watched as Dalton disappeared and Jonah approached the fairy like some sort of wild animal sneaking up on its prey.

"There there, little lady." Jonah held his hands out.

Just as she was about to dart off, Dalton sprang and cupped her in his hands.

"I got it!" he exclaimed, laughing in absent-minded disbelief. His hands illuminated as they clenched around her.

Jonah ran over to them. "Hold her still. I'm gonna pull her wings off," he instructed.

The fairy fought against Dalton's grasp as she struggled to get away.

"She'll die then, won't she?" Dalton asked.

"Aye, but the wings will have enough dust to sell our weight in gold. Now, hold her still," Jonah commanded, inching closer.

I emerged from behind the tree before they had a chance to defile her. "Let her go!" I demanded.

"Miss Gwen, what in the blue blazes are you doing out here?" Dalton's voice was shaky as he watched me approach.

I cautiously held my palm out in front of me, keeping my eyes locked with his. "Let her go, Dalton."

"Why don't you go on back up there to the campsite now, lass? This don't concern you," Jonah spat.

"I think it does. And I'm sure Captain Hawkins will be interested to know that you two think I have him under a spell."

"Shit," Dalton said, throwing his arms up and allowing the fairy to make her getaway.

Jonah charged at Dalton in a rage. "Look what you did, you damn idiot!"

"Good! I can't believe you were just going to kill her! What's wrong with you?" I exclaimed.

"That dust would have made us rich for the rest of our lives. Now, call her back here like you did before." Jonah glared.

"I can't call her back. But even if I could, you're crazy to think that I would."

"Call her back, witch," Jonah demanded, his voice lowering an octave with the threat.

My face tightened as he examined my reaction. "I'm not a witch," I replied sternly.

"Is that so..." He stepped toward me as a wicked smile crept across his face. "Cause that's not what I heard. In fact, you'd be surprised to hear what everyone thinks."

I inconspicuously took a step back. "I seem to have already heard, and it's not that surprising. People often criticize the things that they don't fully comprehend."

"I believe you, lass." He inched closer. "Just cause the other men think you're a witch doesn't mean I share their sentiment." Jonah raked his gaze over my body. "I do think you're hiding something, though."

Every instinct I had was screaming, warning me to put distance between us. "I'm not hiding anything."

"Don't lie to me, Gwen, not again. We should be past all that by now."

"I haven't lied to you," I stammered.

He nodded, circling me like a predator. "Oh, but you have."

I stared at him, trying to read the odd expression coated on his face. Then he lunged.

Jonah grunted as he grabbed a fistful of my hair and dragged me to the ground. I clawed at his arm, but he refused to release his grip and pushed his weight down on top of me.

"What are you doing, Jonah?" Dalton exclaimed as he jumped back in horror.

"Where are you from?" He ignored Dalton entirely and grabbed my face with painful force. "What are we really doing out here?"

I struggled under him, trying to scream, but his grip made it impossible to speak at all.

"Tell me what the hell we're doing out here." He loosened his hold just enough to allow my breathing to stabilize. "And if you even try to scream, I swear to God I'll slit your throat."

"Why are you doing this?" I managed to ask between gasping breaths. "The witch...you said you wanted to find her too."

"Oh, I do. So that I can kill her," Jonah snarled.

I searched his face for some type of clarity but found only unbridled fury. "Why?"

"Because she ruined my fucking life!" he exclaimed, glancing over at the tents to ensure he hadn't woken the others.

"I don't understand..."

He pressed his weight down on me. "Why are we here, Gwen?" he taunted.

"To...find the...witch," I mumbled through shallow breaths.

"And why would we want to do that?" He eased his arm enough to let me speak.

"Because she's the only one who can help me," I confessed.

Jonah's frustration was growing stronger by the second. "Spit it out, Gwen. We don't have all night."

"I can't go home without her. She sent me here."

A chilling smile curved his lips. "Now we're getting somewhere. Tell me where you're really from because we both know it isn't Storm Haven."

"Please, Jonah," I begged. "Please stop."

He wrapped his hand firmly around my throat. "And do you want to know how I know you're not from Storm Haven?"

Tears stung the corners of my eyes as he tightened his grip. "Because Storm Haven doesn't even exist," he growled.

"Jonah…" I gasped for air, grabbing at his hand.

He released his grip slightly. "Don't make me ask you again. I promise I won't be as nice next time."

"North Carolina," I whispered in defeat, feeling the stinging marks of his hand throb across my neck as I spoke. "I'm from North Carolina."

A look of smug satisfaction swept over his face. "Ah, there it is. We finally have the truth. I must say I had my suspicions, but it's always nice to be validated."

He shifted his weight off me, but the glare in his eyes threatened me against attempting to make any sudden movements.

"And because you were finally truthful with me, I suppose it's only fair to offer you a little bit of honesty in return."

Dalton stood silently behind Jonah, wearing an anxious look on his face.

"Would you believe that I've worked on ships all my life? Not in the same manner as I do now, of course." Jonah laughed to himself. "I used to be a fisherman. But that all changed one late August night when a storm capsized our boat."

"You were sent here too," I mumbled, feeling the blood drain from my face as I stared up and said the words aloud. "During the shipwreck."

Jonah huffed out a laugh. "Nice work, Nancy Drew."

"You said you lost your memories."

"Well, I couldn't just run around here telling everyone I was from fucking Rockport, Massachusetts, could I?"

"You just told Dalton."

"Dalton is the only one here who already knows." Jonah shot me a cunning smile.

"Of course he is." I coughed, the lingering sting of his handprint on my throat flaring with pain. "So, what's your big plan here?"

"Well, lass, my big plan was to tag along on this little group mission and kill the witch. Then you had to go and lie to me about where you were from. I gotta say it kind of piqued my interest...made me wonder what you were hiding. But I knew there could have been a lot of reasons why someone would wanna lie about something like that. So, I was gonna just let it go."

Jonah stroked the side of his face as though he were pondering his next move before he reached for something in his coat pocket. "But then you had to go and eavesdrop on me and Dalton here tonight. Not only that, but you also robbed us of our fairy dust." He tsked sarcastically. "Bad form, Gwen."

"You were going to kill her."

"A small price to pay."

"Taking a life is never a small price, Jonah."

"Tell me, Gwen, do you believe some lives are worth more than others?" Jonah pretended to wait for an answer. "You yourself killed a mermaid. What's the difference?" He finally pulled his hand out of his pocket. The blade of his knife reflected the moonlight as he twirled it in his hand.

"Are you planning to kill me with that?" I asked, hoping he couldn't hear the way my heartbeat sped as my quivering voice betrayed me.

"That wasn't part of my big plan." He smiled down at me. "Of course, as we both know, things don't always go as planned."

"Demetri would slaughter you," I threatened.

"He would. If he knew I was involved. But as luck would have it, we are in the middle of a magical forest. There are...so many things that could go wrong."

"There's literally a protective spell around us, Jonah. He's not stupid. He would know."

"A shield that is already only half as strong as it was hours ago." He lifted the knife and edged the tip of the blade across my cheek. "It wouldn't take much to convince the others that a creature had gotten through the wall...that it attacked you as you walked along the edge of the creek...that I heard the commotion, but when I came out to help, it was already too late."

"You're disgusting," I spat.

Jonah laughed at the insult. "No, Gwen, I'm just a better liar than you are."

Jonah ran his knife under my chin, resting it at the base of my throat. Every ounce of me was trying not to fall apart underneath the sting of the cold, steel edge.

"Jonah, you don't have to do that." Dalton finally made his presence known.

"Unfortunately, I do. Because if I don't, Gwen here will run right back to that little tent and tell the captain everything. And while I could hold my own against him, it'd be an unfair fight with the other two lackeys."

A laugh escaped my lips.

"What's so damn funny?" Jonah pressed the flat side of the knife hard under my chin to tilt my face to his.

"Do you honestly think you'd win in a fight against Demetri?" Another laugh materialized. "Because I can't think of any scenario in any world where you would or ever could."

Jonah drew his hand back and slapped me across the face. The taste of blood formed in my mouth, and I leaned over to spit it out. He grabbed hold of my hair, forcing me to face him once more.

"I'm going to enjoy killing you," He mused. "To put an end to all those incessant things coming out of your mouth..."

I glared back at him, floods of anger and fear mixing together. "Well, quit talking about it, and just fucking do it then," I challenged, glaring at him through the mist in my eyes.

"With pleasure." Jonah lifted the knife up over me, seeming to take in the moment before committing to his decision. I squeezed my lids tightly together and waited for the end to come.

A swift whipping noise echoed through my head, followed by an instant release of pressure as Jonah's weight fell off me.

I froze for a moment, waiting for the pain to kick in, but I didn't feel any different. Had Jonah changed his mind?

I cracked my eyes open and turned my head to see Jonah's knife lying on the ground several feet away from me.

"What the bloody hell is going on out here?" A vehement voice echoed from somewhere behind me.

I stared toward the sky to see Demetri's figure standing over me, but his focus was elsewhere.

"Captain," I heard Dalton respond. His apprehensive tone was unmistakable. "Jonah and I were just trying to collect some fairy dust, and she stopped us."

I turned my head again at the sound of a groan. Jonah was clenching his side on the ground and trying to sit up.

"Is that so?" Demetri asked. "It wouldn't by chance have been from this fairy, would it?" A shimmer of gold encircled Demetri before flying away again.

"Aye," Dalton responded nervously.

"You know, I gotta be honest, lad. It didn't look to me as though you were trying to collect fairy dust." He stepped around me, positioning himself closer to Jonah. "It looked to me as though your friend was trying to stab Miss Winters here."

"No sir, I..." Dalton began.

"Enough." Demetri roared as he stood over Jonah and pointed his sword toward Dalton. "Don't lie to me, boy."

"Captain Hawkins, Jonah was just mad that she ran the fairy off. I told him to stop, but he just kept on."

Demetri ignored him, taking several steps my way and kneeling beside me. "Are you all right, love?" His eyes glistened just as brightly as the stars dangling over us.

"Yes." Was all I could manage to whisper.

He lifted my face and gently wiped the blood away from my mouth. I silently stared up at him, detecting the exact moment that his concerned expression transformed into one of undiluted rage.

He stood, zoning in on Jonah, who continued to wallow on the ground in pain.

"Just so we're clear"—Demetri's voice dripped with danger—"you will die for this." The whipping noise struck again, silencing the pained groans. I snapped my eyes shut, trying to block out what I could.

Dalton reeled at whatever sight he saw. "Captain, please...I didn't have nothing to do with it. I told him to stop."

"I think you lacked conviction, lad," Demetri responded distantly.

Alistair's voice rang out as his and Griff's heavy footsteps scuffled by. "Captain, take Miss Gwen back to the tent. We'll take care of it." I wasn't sure how long they'd been standing there or how much they knew of the situation.

Demetri hesitated before returning his sword to its sheath, a consolatory sound I'd come to know. "Very well," he complied, appearing beside me once again before lifting me into his arms.

We had barely made it back inside the tent when the tears erupted from my eyes. I gripped onto him and let the waves of emotion consume me.

"It's alright. You're safe." Demetri whispered, rocking me against his body, allowing the tears to stain his shirt.

"I'm sorry," I said, attempting to regain a sense of self-control.

"Don't apologize." He raked his fingers through my tangled hair. "You've done nothing wrong."

"He almost killed me," I acknowledged, mainly to myself, as the tears overwhelmed me again.

He pressed his lips to my forehead. "They'll never hurt you again."

I wrapped my arms around him, burying my face in his neck. "Thank you," I finally managed to whisper.

"Don't speak of it, love."

CHAPTER SIXTEEN

The next morning, Alistair and Griff were the first ones to start packing up the supplies. Demetri remained by my side, only excusing himself from the tent long enough for me to change clothes. I slipped out of the dress I'd worn all night, mindlessly balling it up before throwing it to the ground. I had no desire to ever wear it again. It reeked of Jonah, and I didn't need any reminders of what had almost happened.

"Where are they then?" I heard Demetri ask quietly on the other side of the door as I pulled a new dress over my head.

"We dumped 'em in the creek," Alistair replied nonchalantly.

"Thank you for tending to the matter."

"You had more pressing obligations to tend to."

"Aye," Demetri agreed.

"How is Miss Gwendolyn feeling this morning?" Griff's voice joined in on the conversation.

"Still a bit shaken, but she's faring well, considering everything that happened," Demetri responded.

"That's good," Alistair said. "What in the hell were they thinking?"

"I don't know. I never fully trusted Jonah, but I never expected him to pull something like that." Demetri's tone grew angrier by the second.

"Aye, nor Dalton." A trace of something that sounded like disappointment knotted in Alistair's words. "No doubt it'll be harder to find our way around here without the two of 'em, though."

"We'll manage," Demetri responded coolly.

I finished fastening my coat and tugged open the door of the tent, meeting the eyes of the three men who were blissfully unaware I had just heard their whole conversation. "I'm ready whenever you are."

We walked between the lavender-topped trees for several hours. Demetri had mentioned he'd traveled through Mystic Grove once before, years ago, when he had visited the area just north of here called Mystic Village with some of his crew. While his directions weren't as reliable as Dalton's, he was the most equipped remaining member of our group to lead the way.

"How are you feeling, miss?" Alistair appeared by my side.

"I'm okay." I mustered a weak smile. "Thank you."

"I'm awfully sorry for what you went through last night," he added.

"I haven't really had a chance to process it yet, not fully," I admitted, swallowing down the feeling of nausea that the memory evoked. "I'm sorry you were forced to deal with the aftermath."

"Oh, don't you worry about me. Killing men doesn't bother me much anymore, 'specially not when they deserve it."

I couldn't help but glance up at the front of the line. Demetri strolled with his sword at his side, ready and willing to slay anything that stood in his way. We hadn't talked about it; the events were still too fresh, but he had killed Jonah right in front of me. I didn't see it happen. I was far too dazed at the time to even fully realize what was about to unfold. But the sound of the sword slicing into him was something I wished I could forget.

I turned to look at Alistair again. "I'd be lying if I said it didn't bother me a little, whether they deserved it or not."

"Well, that's to be expected from a dignified lass such as yourself. I don't suppose you've done much killing before?"

Momentary images of the bleeding, blue-haired mermaid that Jonah had tried to taunt me with last night filled my head. While I had technically taken her life...she was trying to take Demetri's. She had left me no other option that day. Truth be told, I'd kill her a hundred more times with no hesitation or regret if I had to just to spare his life again.

"No, not much anyway."

Alistair chuckled. "Well, lass, at least you have us now in case more matters need resolving."

"Thank you," I returned the smile, laughing to myself at his shameless offer. It was kind of sweet in a weird, violent sort of way. "While I hope that's not necessary, it is...strangely comforting."

"As long as you're with us, miss, you'll be protected."

"What will you tell the crew?" I inquired. "Won't they be upset?"

Alistair shook his head indifferently. "We'll tell 'em the truth, that Jonah tried to kill you and had to be dealt with."

"And Dalton? He didn't technically do anything, I guess."

"If he didn't, he shoulda," Alistair huffed angrily. "He shoulda killed Jonah himself, but instead, he let it happen. He proved himself untrustworthy and paid the price for it."

Jonah's confession rang through my head again. He was from my world, and Dalton had known it the entire time. I still wasn't sure what they assumed they were going to accomplish by killing Cosmina. To be fair, they weren't very reasonable people. Any additional amount of thought I could give to the situation would still probably never help me understand the reason behind their lack of logic.

Several hours had passed when we finally stopped to rest. Alistair and Griff not-so-subtly excused themselves as they ventured off to find a secluded enough spot off the trail to relieve their bladders.

"How are you doing, love?" Demetri asked, moving to stand by my side as we waited.

I knew he wasn't referring to my throbbing feet as I rested against a large nearby rock and began to take my shoes off.

"I'm okay," I said, rubbing my soles to relieve some of the ache. "How about you?"

A hint of a smile flashed across his face. "You know you don't have to do that. Not with me."

"Do what?"

"Deflect." He arched a knowing brow.

"I'm not deflecting. I'm genuinely concerned about your well-being."

"As am I," he retorted with a smirk.

"I'm fine, Demetri," I declared, grimacing as I slid my shoes back on. "I'm not at all traumatized by almost being murdered by your crew members if that's what you're worried about."

The humor deserted his eyes. "I want to know what happened, but I understand if you aren't quite ready to tell me."

"I've actually been wanting to talk to you about it," I confessed, scanning the area to make sure Alistair and Griff weren't yet approaching. "Jonah told me something...you know, before things got all crazy and he tried to stab me in the chest."

Demetri flinched at the visual.

"He knew that I wasn't from this world, and he kept demanding that I tell him the truth...that he would kill me if I didn't. So, I told him. And once I did, he said he was from my world, too. That he was sent here when the ship that he worked on wrecked in a storm."

"He was from your world..." Demetri repeated, his voice dwindling away as he tried to piece the missing parts of the puzzle together. "That's why he wanted to find the witch too."

"Yes, but not so she could send him back. He said he wanted to kill her for ruining his life. But, from what I gather, she wasn't the one who sent him here. He said he only met her after he arrived, and she refused to help him."

"Yes, love. But we must bear in mind his affinity to lie and manipulate."

I propped myself against the rock again, trying not to shudder as I recounted the events. "And Dalton knew everything. I don't know all the details as to why or how..." I pondered out loud. "But he knew."

"The details don't much matter anymore. If anything, we now have a better idea why the witch refused to help him when he sought her assistance."

"You're probably right." I agreed. I didn't know Cosmina very well, but I got the feeling she didn't do anything unless she wanted to or it benefited her in some way. "There's no telling what really happened when they stumbled upon each other."

"I need to ask you something." Demetri blurted, taking hold of my hands. "It's been bothering me since last night when everything happened."

"What is it?"

There was something indistinguishable in the way he looked at me. "Why didn't you call for me, Gwen? Why were you so willing to let him end your life?"

"He said he'd kill me if I screamed."

"He was going to do that anyway. You should have called for me. I would have come."

I wrapped my fingers around his, trying to ignore the anguish reflecting in his eyes. "Honestly, it all just happened so fast. By the time I realized what he was trying to do, it would have been too late anyway."

"Had I been even a moment later..." Demetri's voice dropped. "I don't know what I would have walked out there to find. The mere thought of it makes me sick to my stomach."

"How...how did you know...to come outside?" The question hadn't occurred to me until this instant.

"The fairy," Demetri answered. "She flew into the tent and all but terrorized me until I opened my eyes. As soon as I woke and realized you were gone, she flew straight for Alistair and Griff's tent."

"She was trying to save me?" I asked in disbelief.

"Aye. And was damn persistent about it too." He lowered his gaze as he laughed. "Turns out, she was trapped inside the barrier the whole time. She flew through what was left of the wall this morning right before we finished packing up."

Our conversation halted as Alistair and Griff emerged from the tree line in a peculiar hurry.

"Demetri, what are they—"

"Go, go, go!" Alistair exclaimed as they both rushed by us to grab their bags from the ground.

Demetri ignored the command to flee, seizing his sword instead as he turned to face the trees. He pushed me in line behind him as Alistair and Griff reluctantly followed his lead, bounding around me as they held up their own blades.

At the same place where they'd appeared, something loudly shuffled out into view. I latched onto Demetri's arm, attempting to peer over his shoulder to see what in the world had terrified the two strapping pirates badly enough to elicit such a reaction.

"Who are you?" A deep voice roared. "Why have you come here?"

"I'm Captain Hawkins," Demetri replied, his voice cool and steady. "My crew and I are only passing through; we do not wish to cause you any trouble."

The sound of heavy footsteps crunched over the forest floor leaves as they drew closer. I felt Demetri's arm tighten underneath my grip as he repositioned his sword.

"Your men were lurking near my home."

A shadow fell over us as I shifted to the other side of Demetri, finally able to find a big enough opening between him and Griff to peek through. Once I glimpsed the monster standing on the other side, I regretted being so eager.

The mythological creature, half man and half horse, stood several yards away. He glared furiously at Demetri with his dark-colored eyes as strands of his black hair whipped in the breeze. His brawny, gray colored body loomed over our group, and there was no questioning the fact that he could easily break us all in half...including Griff. To make matters even worse, he wasn't alone.

Not far behind him stood three other centaurs whose colors ranged in various neutral tones. They weren't quite as large as the one who stood before us, but they were still big enough to cause extensive bodily harm, if I had to guess.

I clenched my jaw as tight as possible, fighting the scream that was desperate to escape. Demetri glanced down to find me staring at the creature, then moved his body to shield me from its view.

"My men had no knowledge that your home was in this vicinity. We are regretful of the misunderstanding," Demetri purred persuasively. "As I said, we are not looking for any trouble."

"I so rarely see people in the forest," the centaur huffed dismissively as he took another step forward. "Tell me human, are you lost?"

The trees swayed around us nervously as though they were trying to pull up their roots from the ground and escape the monster themselves. I shifted behind Demetri, trying to hide as he came closer.

"What is it that you're hiding behind you?" The creature asked.

My heart dropped to my feet.

Demetri glanced at Griff as though he were exchanging silent orders.

"Bring it forward," he commanded.

To my utter horror, Demetri pulled me to his side in full view of the monsters as his sword-free hand stayed tightly latched around my arm.

"Do as he says," he whispered lowly.

The centaur stepped closer, and I tried to lock my knees in place to prevent my legs from collapsing underneath me.

"A woman?" The centaur seemed baffled as he stared down at me. "On your crew?"

"My wife," Demetri answered automatically. "She is with child."

I tried to keep my composure as I glanced back quickly at the men, but my eyes grew so wide from the remark that I worried they might pop straight out of my head and roll across the ground. Alistair and Griff appeared to be unfazed, as if this hypothetical situation was old news to them.

"Why are you here?" the intruding creature asked once more. "These woods are unsafe for humans."

"Which is precisely why we are trying to find our way out." Demetri gently pushed me back behind him. "We were passing through on our way to Mystic Village to find a healer for my wife. She fell ill on our voyage, and we want to ensure the health of our child."

It was kind of unnerving, the way he lied. His composure never cracked, and his voice was so smooth...I almost believed him myself.

The centaur shifted the weight of his attention back to me, and I instinctively touched my stomach.

"Cyro," the only female centaur in the group called. "The woman is with child; I do not suspect they had ill intentions."

The fearsome-looking being mulled over her words for several moments before nodding. "Very well, Erwina."

A slight smile of approval emerged across her sepia-colored face before she stepped away from her group and looked straight at Demetri. "The village is not very far from here. Just a couple hours north."

He nodded in return. "Thank you."

"Do try to keep your men from lurking about, though." Cyro sharpened his glare at us once more. "My clan is not the only one living in this area. If the others see you, they might not be so forgiving."

"Of course," Demetri said, carefully gathering a supply bag from the ground. "We will be sure to stay on the main trail."

"There's one more thing you should know before you go," Erwina added. "When you get close to the village, do be careful of the silver mist."

"The silver mist?" Demetri asked suspiciously. "What is that?"

"Remnants of a spell once cast to keep the inhabitants of the forest from entering the village," Cyro said.

"I've been there once before but do not recall such a spell." Demetri countered, pulling the bag over his shoulder.

Erwina stepped closer. "It was created several years ago by a witch who resides in the village."

"So, we're to be trapped?" Demetri asked the approaching female.

Erwina's dark hair flowed freely around her slender neck as she stopped several feet away and shook her head. "No, the spell was broken by another, but traces of it still exist. It lingers between the edge of the forest and the village," she explained. "It is very painful if it touches you."

Her penetrating indigo eyes conveyed the weight of the warning. "In your wife's condition, I felt that you should know."

"Thank you for telling us." Demetri lowered his head out of respect. "We will be on the lookout."

The centaurs bowed their heads in return and proceeded to disappear into the trees again.

"Let's get the hell out of here," Alistair finally said when they were out of earshot.

"Leave it to you to go pissing about on a centaur camp." Demetri jeered as he snatched up the last bag and threw it to Alistair.

"I wasn't the only one pissing about. Griff's big head was the one they saw first." Alistair smacked Griff on the shoulder as they both exploded into laughter.

"Just be thankful they were feeling lenient today," Demetri said.

"Yes, very fortunate indeed that your pregnant wife was accompanying us," Alistair said as he and Griff roared in amusement again.

Demetri rolled his eyes and joined in on their laughter. I couldn't yet bring myself to find the humor in the situation...at least, not until we were far enough away from here and the possibility of the centaurs changing their minds.

As we traveled north, Demetri's hand stayed tightly wound around his sword in case we had another unfortunate encounter.

"Are we actually headed to the village now?" I asked.

"Aye, we need to get out of the forest. Word of our journey has likely already spread among the centaur community. I'd hate to press our luck."

"How will we get back to the ship?"

"That will depend," he pondered, "on whom or what we come across. If we don't find anything in the village, we'll need to figure something else out. Until then, we will concentrate on the mission."

I appreciated his focus. His lack of planning, though, not so much.

"Captain," Griff huffed from behind us. "I see the mist."

We followed his gaze to the cloudy mist hovering along the border ahead. It appeared to be heavier in some spots than others. As we drew closer, I noticed that it moved constantly, materializing erratically between the blackened tree trunks.

"The village is just on the other side," Demetri announced. "We'll need to try to make it through when it diminishes."

"There's so much," I observed.

"Aye. Remember what the female centaur said. Try not to touch it if you can help it."

"I'll go first, Captain," Griff volunteered. "To see how bad it is."

"Very well." Demetri nodded.

Once the fog before us had thinned out into a faint haze, Griff barreled through, groaning as he collapsed on the other side.

"Did it hurt?" Alistair asked as the clearly pained Griff rolled over on the grass before us.

Griff tried to pick himself up several times before finally succeeding. "Would I be on the ground if it didn't?" he finally grunted, shooting Alistair an infuriated look.

Alistair's eyes grew five sizes as he looked back at us, and I knew what he was thinking. Griff was a beast of a man. If the fog had pained *him* that much, what would it do to the rest of us?

"We've nowhere else to go but through," Demetri persuaded as though he were listening to our thoughts.

Alistair winced just before taking off into another layer of the mist. He screamed as it hit his skin and I found myself holding my breath until he stumbled over to the safety of the other side.

"Alistair?" I yelled.

"I'm okay, Miss Gwen," he said weakly, bracing himself against Griff's body.

"I don't know if I can do this," I admitted.

"We've no choice," Demetri said. "Together? Just like we did on the cliff?"

I nodded reluctantly as he locked his arm with mine.

We watched and waited until the mist began to dissipate in front of us, clouding up heavily in front of another tree several feet away.

"Now," Demetri said as he pulled me toward Alistair and Griff.

My skin erupted in fire as we broke through. The barrier of clothing did nothing to relieve the blast of searing pain that rendered me unable to move as it encircled us.

Demetri's face twisted in agony, and I screamed as he fell to his knees. The mist had returned, thicker than before and flaring around us like flames as though it were trying to catch us before we escaped. It materialized around Demetri as he attempted to stand. I tried to pull him closer, to get him out of the heaviest part of the cloud, but he shoved me away forcefully.

Unfamiliar hands took hold of my waist. Alistair gripped onto me tightly as I fell over on top of him. The pain diminished some, but my skin still stung as though it were trying to recover from a severe sunburn.

"Demetri!" I yelled, unable to find him in the midst of all the chaos.

"Griff's got him," Alistair said as he rose from the ground and helped me to my feet.

Demetri was hunched over as Griff helped steady him.

"Jesus, are you okay?" I scrambled over to him as fast as I could.

Demetri struggled for a few moments to answer but finally nodded.

"The worst of it came back just as you were coming through," Alistair said to Demetri. "You got hit with more of it than all of us."

"I'll be okay," Demetri said, groaning as he raised his flushed face to meet my eyes. "Are you sure you're all right?"

"Yes, I think so."

"Oh, that bloody hurt." He straightened his back, carefully trying to reclaim his normal posture.

"It doesn't last too long," Griff assured.

"Good to know." Demetri managed a weak laugh. "I do believe that a centaur beating would have been more enjoyable than that."

CHAPTER SEVENTEEN

The village reminded me of the one where Rowan lived. It was noticeably bigger, but many of the buildings looked similar with their sandstone walls and pointed brown roofs.

The people standing in the streets pretended to ignore us as we walked by, but their wandering eyes stung almost as much as the mist had. Perhaps if I were alone, it would be easier to believe I belonged here. The dark fur-lined coat I wore was relatively modest and looked like something that the people in this town were probably used to seeing. But I was with three pirates, and there was *absolutely nothing* modest about the way they looked.

"What is this place?" I asked, staring up at the entrancing Tudor-style home that Demetri led us to. A crisp wind cut through the air, scattering leaves across the sloped, shingled roof. They tumbled down, splitting around the tall stone chimneys and settled along the edge of the protruding arched windows. "Is it the witch's house?"

"No." Demetri laughed. "I'm afraid she's not going to be that easy to find. This isn't a house at all, love. It's a tavern."

"A tavern?" I felt my face crinkle at the word. "Do you really have to indulge in a drink right now?"

"A tavern is one of the best places to find out information," he responded.

"He's right," Alistair intruded. "A drunk man will tell you anything you wanna know."

"All right, fine," I finally complied.

"And considering recent events, I must say that a drink sounds well-deserved." Demetri pushed open the wooden door and ushered me inside.

An uncomfortable hush fell over the crowd gathered inside as we entered the room. These people didn't bother pretending not to look at us, but as I stared around the room, meeting dozens of mystified eyes, I wished they would.

"Well-well-well," a hefty voice finally said. "If it isn't the captain himself."

"Rhett," Demetri acknowledged the bald, husky man with tawny skin standing behind the bar. "It's been a while."

"What brings ye and yer men in here today?" The man asked, crossing his tattoo-covered arms in displeasure.

"We're just passing through." Demetri leaned over the bar top and smiled at the man. "Thought we might as well drop by and say hello to our old friends."

"If ye came back in here looking for more trouble…" He narrowed his eyes angrily, causing creases to form along the top of his shiny head.

"Rest assured, Rhett, we've had enough trouble to last a lifetime. We're just here for the drinks."

"What's he talking about?" I whispered.

"Very well," the man submitted, turning to grab glass mugs from the counter behind him as the crowded room slowly resumed their conversations. "What'll it be? Rums?"

"Aye, but give us the bottles," Alistair demanded as he and Griff took their seats at the bar.

"What did he mean by starting trouble?" I asked again as Demetri helped me settle into the tall chair beside his.

"Nothing to concern yourself with. It was just a rather inconsequential mishap that resulted in a few minor injuries." Demetri took his seat and glanced away as he reached for one of the glasses that Rhett placed in front of us.

"Care to elaborate?" I asked, pulling the other one closer to me.

"Not particularly."

"Captain Hawkins?" A shrill voice rang from the back of the tavern. "Is that really you?"

"Marlena," Demetri smiled politely at the bouncing, robust woman who was quickly running down the stairs and making her way over to us.

"Well, I declare, I never thought I'd see you again!" She shuffled her hands through her dark blonde curls as she eyed him enthusiastically.

"Aye, lass. How have you been?"

"Well, I sure can't complain, Rhett's been keeping me busy here. She bit her bright red bottom lip as he shifted in his chair and raised his glass to his mouth. "So tell me darlin', what in the world are you doing back in town?"

He downed a gulp before flashing his eyes up to hers. "I'm rather glad you asked. As it happens, I am trying to find someone. Perhaps you can help me."

"Sure, I'll do what I can, sweetie." She brushed against his shoulder before propping herself in between us at the bar, purposely pushing her cleavage closer to his face. I stared in disbelief, swallowing down my liquor as he appeared to fight off a smile.

Giggling at something that he said, the woman stood to flip her hair. I moved quickly, accidentally kicking her in the back of the knee as her long curls nearly slapped me in the face. She turned to face me with much less enthusiasm than she was showering Demetri with.

"Do you work here?" I asked.

"Why yes, I do, shug," she replied. "Care for another drink?"

I looked down, noticing my glass was already empty. "That would be lovely," I said, forcing a cold smile.

"Of course," she replied, as she painstakingly peeled herself away from Demetri's side long enough to walk around the bar and fetch another bottle.

"Here you go, shug." She filled up the glass before leaning over the counter to slide it back to me, her chest nearly toppling out of her too-small dress when she did. Before I could say anything, she was rushing back over to reclaim her position beside Demetri.

Their conversation picked up right where it left off. "I'm looking for a witch named Cosmina," Demetri quietly explained.

"Oh, sweetie, you know good and well as I do there are a lot of witches and wizards that reside around these parts. Of course, most of 'em don't ever socialize with us regular folks."

"Any information you can give me, Marlena"—he smiled that heart-stopping smile when he spoke her name— "would be so helpful."

"Well, you know I hate to get involved in other's affairs..." she started.

"Oh, I know you do, darling, but you'd really be helping out an old friend." He placed his hand over her arm and lightly stroked his fingers across her skin. "It's imperative that I locate her."

"Oh Demetri! You know I never could say no to you." She gushed, squirming underneath his touch.

My body had a visceral reaction to this woman. The heat flooding my cheeks was all the proof I needed to realize that. Perhaps it was because she seemed so desperate for his approval. Perhaps it was because I was an unwilling victim being subjected to the pure idiocy of the way they were interacting. I stole a glance at Demetri, who was clearly enjoying the attention.

Of course this was why he had wanted to come here. Well-deserved drinks, my ass. I took several deep breaths and tried to center myself. I did not want to cause a scene right now, but I could already feel my nostrils flaring. I turned away from them, meeting Alistair and Griff's stunned faces as I did so. It was clear from their expressions that they found the whole situation highly amusing.

"That's what I was counting on," I heard Demetri say suggestively.

"Oh you! You haven't changed a bit!" She squealed.

I threw a threatening glare at the two pirates as they tried to repress their laughter. Then Marlena moved again, nearly knocking me out of the chair when she bumped into me with her backside. I narrowed my eyes her way, but she was not even remotely aware of my existence. She was far too focused on trying to crawl into Demetri's lap, cackling at everything he was saying. Her laugh made my skin crawl. It was far too loud and high-pitched, and every screech she let out made my eardrums throb. I don't know what she found so humorous over there. Demetri wasn't *that* damn funny.

"So, what do you think?" I heard him say. I threw another glance in his direction, immediately noticing the way his eyes danced around her face. "Can you help me out, love?"

I slammed my glass down onto the bar as soon as the word left his mouth. Did he seriously just run around calling everyone "love" to get what he wanted? He met my livid stare momentarily before forcing his attention back to Marlena. I chugged what was left of my liquor as I searched the depths of my soul for the willpower to not throw the empty glass against his hollow head.

"Well, darlin,' I don't know anything about this Cosmina that you're looking for, but if it's magic that you're after, I do know someone who could probably help you out. Her name is Isadora, and she doesn't live too far from here."

"Thank you, Marlena. If she is unable to help us, perhaps she knows the witch we are seeking," Demetri suggested.

"Maybe so." Marlena nodded, leaning into him. "They tend to be a tight-knit group, but I'm sure Isadora will help you if she can. She's always been very kind. Just tell her I sent you her way."

"And her house is nearby, you say?"

Marlena nodded. "It's a few miles east on the outskirts of town. You'll know it when you see it...all that dreadful overgrown ivy." She chuckled to herself. "For the life of me, I can't imagine why she'd wanna live in such a place."

"Thank you, love. Your help has been quite invaluable," Demetri said.

"Captain, before you go"—she lowered her face to his ear and wound her arm around his neck— "why don't you follow me upstairs? I'll be glad to help you out again...for old times' sake?"

A bolt of anger exploded through my core as I rose from my chair. "Thanks for all your help, *shug*, but we really need to get going," I announced, shoving the seat back underneath the bar until I heard it collide with the wood.

Demetri stared tensely as the desperate woman still clung to his body.

"I'm sorry, are you two...together?" She asked, pointing between us.

"Yes. We are. So please get off of his lap," I declared, not entirely sure why I just lied to this exasperating woman.

"Oh, my stars," She muttered as she stood, straightening her dress as she backed away from us. "I'm terribly sorry. I had no idea."

"No, of course not, we only came in here together and sat down beside each other. How could you have possibly known?" I countered as I spun to leave. Demetri's footsteps sounded behind mine as I marched furiously toward the exit.

I'd only made it about ten feet outside when I heard the door slam.

"What in the bloody hell was that all about?" Demetri exclaimed. "The drinks weren't even that strong."

"Oh, shut up," I commanded, storming away from him.

Alistair and Griff emerged through the door in a much calmer fashion with bottles in hand.

"So, you're not going to tell me where that outburst came from?" Demetri asked again, following closely on my heels. "Are we just pretending that it didn't happen?"

"What outburst?"

"Gwen!" he shouted after me in a forceful tone.

I stopped in my tracks and turned to face him. "There was no outburst. We simply do not have the time to waste for you to run upstairs and fuck some random bar floozy right now, Captain. In case you forgot, you used a similar excuse when the centaurs found us."

"Woohoohoo!" Alistair cackled behind us before taking a swig from his bottle. "I've never seen anyone talk to the captain the way you do, miss!"

"Because anyone else who would dare to address me as such would be swiftly executed," Demetri growled angrily. "And I only told the centaurs what I did so that we could all avoid a preventable and painful death."

I tried to restrain my smile at his noticeable attempt to redeem himself in front of his men.

"And I only told the woman at the bar what I did so we could all avoid our breakfast from making a sudden reappearance on the floor."

Griff's mouth dropped and he pulled Alistair back several feet as Demetri's face contorted into an expression of disbelief.

"I had to entertain her a bit to get the information that we needed," he said through his teeth.

"Sounds like you've entertained her before."

"Aye. I won't deny that."

"You know, what gets me the most is the way you try to pretend like I'm something special to you when you clearly have no standards and will just fuck anything that gives you attention," I snapped, utterly repulsed at the thought of them together.

Demetri's baffled gaze altered into one of utter fury as Griff and Alistair erupted into laughter behind him.

"Why does it even bother you?" he spat, glaring back at me with darkening eyes.

"Trust me. It doesn't."

"It seems as though it does. As you've made glaringly obvious, my dear, you're the one with a preexisting relationship. The company I keep shouldn't matter to you."

"I'm done talking about this." I scowled back at him, matching the fire in his eyes. I knew the other two men were listening far too closely for me to say anything else on the matter. At this rate, I would accidentally incriminate myself if I kept engaging.

He parted his lips to speak.

"It's done," I reiterated, walking away from the group.

Demetri's ardent admirer was right. There was no mistaking this house. When she mentioned there was ivy, I had envisioned a quaint cottage wrapped with delicate, picturesque green vines...I was not prepared for this visual assault. The dwelling before us had long been devoured by the large, twisted plants that stretched across the walls and reached out toward the yard as though they wanted to drag us inside.

"What the shit happened here?" Alistair muttered with a disgusted face.

"Watch your step, Miss Gwen," Griff added, kicking a tumbleweed of thorns away from where we stood.

Demetri brushed by, mindlessly crushing the vines in his path on his way to the front door. He hadn't bothered saying anything to anyone since our argument earlier, which made the several-mile-long trek to the house more uncomfortable than I was willing to admit right now.

"Isadora!" Demetri called out, beating his knuckles against the door.

A moment later, it squeaked open, and the face of a young woman with brown hair and unusual violet eyes emerged through the crack.

"She's not here," she said, staring up at Demetri.

"When will she be back?" he questioned.

"Not for a while." She studied us suspiciously. "She's gone up to Winterhaven for the annual celebrations."

"Annual celebrations?" I asked.

"Perhaps you can help us instead," Demetri interjected. "We are attempting to locate someone. We were told Isadora might know how to find her."

The door shut in his face before the noise of the clicking latch could be heard. When it opened again, the fresh-faced woman took a cautious step into the entryway, clasping her hands together at her waist. "Who do you seek?"

"A witch named Cosmina," I answered.

She stiffened where she stood. "I know of the woman you speak of. I'm afraid I cannot help you."

"We have come a very long way to find her. I need her help," I pleaded, taking a step closer. "We were sent here by a lady at the tavern."

"Marlena," Demetri's grating voice sounded from somewhere behind me.

It took an honest effort not to roll my eyes at his needless input. "Is there any way we can get in touch with Isadora? If Cosmina isn't an option, she may be the only other person who can help me."

She shook her head. "My mother left several days ago. You'll have to wait for her to come back from her trip." She retreated through the door and tried to shut it.

Demetri shoved his foot into the threshold before she succeeded.

"You're Isadora's daughter?" he inquired.

She nodded a confirmation. "I'm Charlotte."

"What a lovely name." He flashed his stupid smile.

Oh lord, here we go again. I swallowed down the disgust that threatened to bubble up.

"Charlotte," I whispered, locking eyes with her. I was all too aware that Griff and Alistair were standing close enough to prevent me from revealing the vital information she'd need to know to help us. "Please. I don't know what else to do."

Her face softened as she sighed in defeat. "Come inside," she said, glancing around quickly before allowing us access.

Late afternoon sun flooded in through the kitchen window, scattering a kaleidoscope of rainbow light across the floor as it filtered through the glass-blown wind chimes hanging from the ceiling. They clattered together loudly as Charlotte pulled the door closed, the movement ushering in a strong gust of air behind us. Griff grunted as he moved around us in the cramped space to create more room, smacking his head against several of the low-hanging pendants. Demetri was clearly not a fan of the whimsical décor and could barely hide his horrified expression.

"My mother has had dealings with the woman you speak of. Questionable dealings." Charlotte crossed her arms as she leaned against the counter. "She's not one to be trusted, and I don't think it would be in your best interest to find her, nor would I even know how to go about doing so."

"How far away is Winterhaven?" I probed. "We can go there to meet your mother if we have to."

"A few days' journey on foot," she replied. "But the conditions are much too harsh to walk this time of year. Especially if you're unfamiliar with the territory."

"Well, it's a good thing you got a flying horse out there then, eh? How fast would that thing get us there?" Alistair pressed as he stared out the window.

"Flying horse?" I squinted past him in an effort to see for myself.

"That *thing* is Zola...and don't even think about it," Charlotte scolded. "She doesn't fly. She can't."

"She's got wings, don't she?" he huffed.

I gravitated to Alistair's side, gazing at the white mythical creature standing on the other side of the glass. Her massive wings were folded down by her sides as she grazed in the yard. How unusual it looked for something so majestic to be doing something so...normal.

"Her wings were broken as a foal. The bones were crushed to the point they would have never healed naturally. My mother tried to mend her." Charlotte paused to take in our expressions. "It's an excruciating thing, you see, a broken wing for a Pegasus. In any typical circumstance, the humane thing to do would be to put it out of its misery."

"That's horrible," I whispered.

"It was an act only a heart of pure evil could commit." Her face tightened. "Luckily for Zola, Mother was with her when it happened. She tried to mend her bones as quickly as possible, but the injury was so bad. They never healed quite right." She turned to Alistair as if she were only addressing him. "So, no, she cannot fly."

"Why would anyone do that on purpose?" I asked.

"Evil comes in many forms." Charlotte sighed. "As for motives, though, that usually comes down to one thing—power."

I stared back at the animal. She held her head high as she walked across the sunlit yard, her wings shimmering beneath the golden beams.

"She stays here now. She doesn't have to, but she does." Charlotte smiled out at the horse. "We are quite fond of her."

"Is she tame?" I asked.

"Relatively. She doesn't frighten easily like most Pegasus tend to. She's more used to having people around." Charlotte swept a mousy strand of hair from her face before drawing in a deep breath. "I really am sorry I cannot help you any further. You seem like nice people. My mother should be back in a few weeks if you'd like to come back then."

"Is there no other way to reach her sooner, then?" Demetri asked.

"I'm afraid not."

"Are you a witch too?" Alistair squinted at her.

Charlotte chuckled at the unexpected question. "No. I was born with no extraordinary powers. Mother has taught me to do a few things over the years to help with chores...simple incantations that anyone can do with a little practice. However, my domestic abilities are nothing compared to the magic she can wield."

"Very well then. I suppose there's nothing more we can do now but wait. Thank you, Charlotte, for all your help," Demetri said as he turned to leave.

My head was spinning as I watched Alistair and Griff eagerly walk out of the house ahead of us. This was in no way an ideal situation. We couldn't just wait around here for weeks on end...where would we even stay? The tavern? Jesus...there was no viable way I could deal with Demetri and Marlena for that long.

"Charlotte?" I asked, turning just before I reached the doorway. "I know this will probably sound strange, but do you happen to know anything about the breaking sky?"

Confusion filled her eyes. "The breaking sky?"

"Yeah, I don't know." I shrugged. "It was something Cosmina had said to me. I was hoping you could make some sense out of it."

Charlotte shook her head. "I'm sorry. I don't know what she would have meant by that."

"Wasn't there something else too?" Demetri asked, acknowledging me directly for the first time since our blow-up. "About a snow moon?"

Charlotte did me the favor of answering him before I had to. "I believe there is an approaching snow moon," she revealed.

Demetri froze beside me, and both of our gazes shot to hers.

"What does that mean?" I asked.

"It doesn't really mean anything, not that I know of," she replied with a small shrug. "It's just a full moon."

"When will it happen?" Demetri questioned.

Charlotte appeared to contemplate. "A couple of months, I believe."

"So, why would she even bring that up?" I asked, looking toward Demetri.

"If the date itself bears no importance, then perhaps it is a deadline," Demetri suggested. "To complete the task that she wanted you to do."

My eyes went wide at the realization, and I was suddenly too aware of the sound of my pulse throbbing through my head. Fuck. That actually did make sense. I don't know why I hadn't considered it before, but if there was a deadline, that inevitably meant there would be repercussions to missing it. That meant that if I didn't figure out what the hell I was supposed to be doing here within the next two months...oh God.

"Thank you again, Charlotte," Demetri blurted, grabbing hold of my hand as he pulled me outside.

"Now what?" I asked, my voice breaking around my shallow breaths as we walked toward the tree line where Griff and Alistair waited.

"Now we go find Isadora."

"What? You heard Charlotte." I stared at him incredulously. "She won't be back for several more weeks."

"I did hear Charlotte, and what I heard was that Isadora's at Winterhaven. So, that's where we shall go." He held out his hand as we reached the men.

Alistair reached into his vest, pulled out the vial of fairy dust, and placed it in Demetri's palm.

"It'll have to be quick," Alistair said.

"Well, let's not keep wasting time then, mates." Demetri strode off as the other men fell in line behind him.

Zola stood several meters from us, just on the other side of the trees. Panic immediately set in as I realized what they were planning.

"No! Absolutely not," I exclaimed. "You all heard Charlotte. You all heard what happened to the horse."

"Her wings never healed properly," Demetri confirmed. "This could fix it. It could solve all our problems, including Zola's."

"And if it doesn't?" I asked.

"It healed you, did it not? And what's the harm in trying?"

"We can't steal their flying horse, Demetri! She's essentially their pet. Charlotte, Isadora...they'd both be furious."

Demetri turned his back to the men and lowered his voice for just me to hear. "And we both know something bad will likely happen to you if you don't find her in time. Are you willing to risk your future—your life—on whether someone you don't even know will be angry with you? Because I'm not." He raised his brow, but it might as well have been his sword.

I glanced over at Alistair and Griff, hoping to find some sort of support.

"We'll be out of daylight soon, Miss Gwen. If we're doing this, we need to do it now," Griff said.

"What about you two? We can't all four fit up there," I stalled.

"Griff and Alistair can head back to the tavern in the meantime. We'll fetch them when we come back this way," Demetri answered. "When we bring Zola back. And we *will* bring her back."

"It's a great plan, Cap." Alistair nodded in agreement. "I am out of rum, after all."

I glanced at Zola once more. What if the dust actually did restore her ability to fly? She'd be able to spend her days soaring through the clouds, living the life she was meant to live. She wouldn't have to settle for a stagnant existence, grazing on grass all day under the weight of her damaged wings like some glorified racehorse put out to pasture.

"Okay," I finally consented. "We can try it. For Zola."

Griff whistled out to the creature. To my surprise, she lifted her head and began to trot in our direction.

"He used to have horses," Demetri explained as he glanced down at me. "Go stand with him. He'll get you on her back."

"What about you?"

Demetri held up the vial. "I'll throw the dust on her."

"Aren't you coming too?"

His lips curved up into a faint smile as Zola approached. "Do you want me to go with you, Winters?" The sarcasm of his tone danced in the air between us. It infuriated me, but I didn't want him to pick up on that.

"Well, someone will need to. I don't think I'd fare too well on my own."

"Hey there, ol' girl," Griff murmured as he ran his hand down the bridge of Zola's nose.

Alistair guided me closer to them, mumbling something incoherent about pirate horse whisperers as we waited for Demetri to silently slide behind Zola's line of view. He threw his hand up over her back and let the glittery specks fall like snow across her wings, soaking into them as soon as they made contact.

Zola reared back in a panic and fell to the ground. I broke out of Alistair's grasp and ran over to her.

"Get out of her way, Gwen!" Demetri yelled.

Kneeling before her, I placed my hands on either side of her face, stroking the white strands of hair out of her speckled sapphire eyes.

The mere sight of her nearly brought me to tears. How many people in this world, or any other world for that matter, could ever know what it felt like to behold something so rare and so mystical?

Her eyes were mesmerizing. They glistened like stardust from distant galaxies, as though she herself had been created from ancient constellations and was brought to this world to show people what the heavens looked like.

As I held onto her, shimmery golden flecks glistened through her mane and her coat began to glow. Then her body began to lift away from me.

"What's happening?" I turned my head just as Demetri snatched me off the ground.

Zola's entire body radiated as she levitated over us. The glow expanded to her wings as they stretched so far out that they covered the view of the sunset-colored sky.

As the luminosity wore off, she gently glided back down. No sooner than the moment that her hooves hit the dirt, Zola flapped her wings. Griff grabbed me, throwing me forcefully onto her back. Her wings whooshed again, harder this time, cracking the unlucky tree branches that hung nearby.

Before I could assess the situation, we were off the ground and flying over the trees. I gripped onto Zola's neck for dear life.

"Demetri!" I yelled down below, searching frantically for his figure.

"I'm here, love," I heard from behind me as I recognized the pressure of his grip around my waist.

"She did it!" I laughed as the wind lapped the tears away from my cheeks. "Oh my God! Look at her! Zola's flying!"

We soared swiftly over the treetops, through the misty clouds, and past the outskirts of the village. Zola flew wild like she had been pinned up for years and now had something to prove.

"Tell me, Gwen," Demetri exclaimed, "did you ever in your wildest dreams think you'd be riding on the back of a Pegasus?"

"Never," I laughed, relaxing my hold on the animal as I leaned back against him.

"I wonder if Charlotte even realizes that she's gone yet?" I mused out loud.

"I would imagine she heard the commotion when we took off," he said.

I smiled, taking in the view of the bewitching creature. "I don't even care if they're mad. It was worth it."

The sky grew dark and hazy against the outline of the mountaintops emerging on the horizon.

"Is that a storm up ahead?" I asked.

"It's hard to say," Demetri said. "Night will soon fall, but perhaps we should venture farther south to be on the safe side. Try to steer her away from the mountains."

"I've never steered a flying horse before, Demetri."

"I don't suppose many people have."

"Demetri!" I shrieked, frustrated with his utter lack of assistance.

"Try placing your hand on her neck and applying pressure to the left. And shift your body to the side."

I did as he said, but Zola didn't budge. She was barreling straight for the mountains.

"She's not turning," I exclaimed.

"Hold on tight to her," he commanded, wrapping his own arms tightly around my body as he grabbed hold of her mane. I leaned into Zola's neck, burying my face down as we flew by the first mountain.

A chilly surge of air crashed into us as rumbles of thunder boomed in the distance.

"Zola! Slow down," I pleaded. But the impending storm only seemed to energize her. She weaved through the mountain range, emboldened by her new capabilities.

In and out of blinding clouds we flew, narrowly missing the concealed mountain peaks.

Darkness quickly settled in around us as the last vivid bursts of sunlight dissipated behind the wall of rocks.

"Gwen, look." Demetri pointed to somewhere down below. "It's not thunder, it's rock giants! They're moving through the mountain range."

I glanced down just as another explosion shattered through the sky and witnessed the snow-covered stones slowly moving underneath us. It looked like the entire crust of the planet was shifting.

Another boom sounded, closer and louder than the ones before, startling Zola. She plunged down, clipping the edge of her wing against the mountainside. I didn't hear my scream, just the sound of the crunching snow as we plummeted into it.

There wasn't a single spot on my body that didn't ache. Not one single spot. I cracked my eyes open and groaned as I rolled over onto my side. The reflection of the moon was painfully bright against the snow. I sat up shakily, pushing through the agony that radiated through my bones.

"Demetri?" I called out. There was no answer.

I forced my legs to stand. Taking note that the rumble of the giants sounded more distant now.

"Demetri?" I called out again, squinting at the sight of the fluorescent snow.

A huffing sound near the base of the mountain caught my attention. "Zola!"

Her white body blended in with the winter scene, but she lifted her head long enough for me to locate her. I raced over as fast as I could manage, and Zola lifted her intact wing to reveal Demetri lying unconscious underneath.

"Demetri!" I screamed, noticing the deep red blood that stained the snow around him.

"No...no-no-no!" I cried, dropping to my knees beside him. "Wake up, Demetri. Dammit, wake up!" I grabbed his arm to check for a pulse, sobbing even harder when I finally found it. "Demetri, come on. Please. You've got to wake up," I begged as I tried to pull him up from the snow.

We couldn't stay here. Demetri's condition was already dire, and we would surely freeze to death soon enough if we didn't find shelter.

Zola stood, shaking off the frozen flakes. I inspected her quickly, noticing the way she winced when she took a step, and the limp wing that was dragging on the ground beside her. Wait...the fairy dust. Where was it? I dropped down again, vehemently grabbing at all the pockets in Demetri's coat...hoping, cussing, and praying that he hadn't given the vial back to Alistair.

Relief engulfed me when I felt the outline of the small cylinder. There wasn't a lot left, but it was potent. I didn't need much.

I poured the remaining contents into my palm before splitting it in half. I carefully scattered the first handful over Demetri and waited for him to stir. Then I turned to pour what was left on Zola's newly injured wing.

Another rumble sounded; this one was unnervingly close.

"Are you okay, love?" Demetri's voice was weak. "Where are we?"

I collapsed onto him, clinging tightly to his battered body. "I'm fine. You're fine. We crashed, but we're gonna be fine."

He lifted up slowly. "Where's Zola?"

I snapped my head around to the place where she had stood moments ago.

"She was right here..." I surveyed the area. "I just saw her."

I helped him stand, silently wondering if I'd given him enough of the dust to accurately recover.

"Her wing was broken. I used the rest of the dust on you both," I explained.

"It appears she may have taken off. Probably back to Isadora's house if I had to guess."

"Well, that's..." I huffed in annoyance. "That's fucking fantastic. How in the hell are we supposed to find our way out of here?" I turned to take in our surroundings. The snowy mountain range seemed to stretch for more miles than I was willing to consider at this moment.

Demetri limped away several feet as he tried to assess the area. Another rumble exploded nearby.

"We need to find some shelter for the remainder of the night," he finally determined. "I've never encountered a rock giant before, and I personally have no desire to tonight," he professed.

I helped lead him past the base of three mountains. It took hours, and I was exhausted, but I knew from the way he was limping that he was far worse off than I was.

"I thought the fairy dust was supposed to heal you?" I observed as we slowed to catch our breath.

"It does." He exhaled deeply, leaning his body against the rocks. "But there are a few things to take into consideration; the amount given must equal the severity of the injury."

"I would have given you more had I known."

"Then you would not have been able to save Zola."

I laughed to myself. "And the irony of that statement is that Zola left us out here to die anyway."

"It would seem so." He managed a weak smirk.

We continued the treacherous expedition until we stumbled across a tiny cave inside the wall of the fourth mountain. Demetri assured me we would be safe from the rock giants for the night once we were inside. He did his best to conceal how much pain he truly was in, but in the scarce moments when he would accidentally drop his guard, it was abundantly evident on his face.

We sat close together. Bracing our backs against the wall and huddling in front of a fire that Demetri had almost not been able to start.

"I'm scared," I finally admitted after a long stretch of silence.

"I know." He didn't look away from the fire. "We're going to be all right."

"You don't know that," I countered.

"Yes, I do." He broke his trance. "Do not let your doubts get the best of you."

I turned my head to dab my sleeve at the traitorous tears pooling in my eyes.

"I'm sorry," I whispered when I realized that he noticed.

"Never apologize for your emotions, love," he said.

I leaned into him, resting my head against his shoulder. "How do you do that?"

"Do what?"

"Say exactly what I need to hear."

"It's a gift."

"It almost makes me forget how infuriating you can be." I smiled as he chuckled at the jest.

"I want to tell you something." Apprehension tinged his tone as though he were still contemplating that statement. "But it's not something that's easy for me to talk about."

"You can tell me anything," I whispered, raising my face to meet his

"You once asked me about my past," he started, "...on the boat one night after you told me about your family."

"I remember."

"I didn't tell you then, partly because I cannot remember much of my childhood, but also because I don't like to talk about it." He drew in a deep breath, wincing as he did. "You see, Gwen, I was an orphan. I still don't know exactly what happened to my parents. No one ever told me. I lived with three different families until I became old enough to care for myself." His expression was pained, and I wasn't entirely sure if it was due to his injuries or the memories that he was reliving.

"Demetri, you don't have to tell me about—"

"Gwen, please." He beseechingly whispered as I nodded for him to continue. "I took refuge in another land when I was fourteen. That's where I met Alistair. He was many years older than me and helped me get back on my feet. His methods weren't always noble. Nevertheless, they were effective. That's when my perspective on the world changed. I started to realize that I could have a better life; I just needed to do what was necessary to obtain it."

He studied my face, waiting for any type of reaction.

"So, you became a pirate."

"So, I became a pirate," he echoed. "It wasn't necessarily anything I had planned, but in order to navigate through the world, I did what I needed to survive. Sometimes, that meant doing things that were immoral. Things that still keep me up at night. Things that I'll never be able to unsee in my mind's eye."

I placed my hand over his. I knew he needed to get this off his chest, if only for his benefit.

"You asked how I became a pirate..." he scoffed as he reminisced. "I killed the captain of my ship. The original captain. And with the help of Alistair, we hijacked the ship and the crew, disposing of the disloyal men along the way.

"That's...intense."

He smirked. "I don't necessarily regret that one, though."

"I'm glad you told me," I admitted.

"Are you?" He sounded surprised. "You're glad to know I'm the type of man to kill for what I want?"

"I see you, Demetri." I held his gaze. "You've done bad things, but you're not a bad person. No matter how dark your past might be, the fact that you trust me enough to let me in means a lot."

"I've killed people, Gwen. In cold blood." He lowered his head to face the ground. "For my ship and for things worth far less."

"Look at me, Demetri," I demanded. He lifted his eyes, once again locking them with mine. The despair I saw swimming inside them nearly crushed my heart. "That's not who you are to me. It's not who you've ever been. You helped me when no one else would, when you didn't owe me anything. I'll always be grateful for you. No matter what you've done."

He was silent for several moments.

"I've never met anyone like you," he said quietly.

"I'm not sure if that was meant to be a compliment or not," I teased.

"It was intended as one."

An isolated rumble sounded through the cave, and I buried my face into his shoulder as the walls trembled around us. He didn't flinch.

"How are you not scared?" I asked when the silence resumed.

"I've been through worse things."

"But it's freezing. We're lost, we're alone…"

"We have a fire," he interrupted. "We have shelter. Most importantly, we have tomorrow. As for tonight, we must at least try to get some rest."

Demetri drifted off quickly. I wasn't quite as fortunate. The thunders of the giants sporadically continued throughout the night, but they weren't the only things that contributed to me staring at the ceiling of the cave.

I wasn't sure if I could handle much more of this. I wasn't mentally, emotionally, or physically built for it.

I wasn't brave. I wasn't resilient. I wasn't like Demetri.

I missed my home. I missed my friends…my bed…my security. I even missed my family. Being displaced in another realm against your will sure had a funny way of adjusting your perspective.

Demetri shifted in his sleep and a slight groan escaped from his lips as he repositioned his leg.

I wished I had given him more of the dust. It was my fault he was still in pain. He'd never say that, of course. I watched as he moved again, holding my breath until his had eased back out. I couldn't deny how appreciative I was of him. He had risked life and limb to help me, and I still wasn't entirely sure why. He had put not only his life but the lives of his crew in harm's way to get us here.

I wasn't proud of that. It made me feel guilty. My life was not worth more than any of theirs. But...I had been desperate, so I let him do it. Tears stung the corners of my eyes as I allowed a wave of remorse to overtake me. I didn't want to be a burden, but sitting here now, watching him wince in his sleep, I realized that was all I'd been for Demetri since the moment he met me.

We left the cave as soon as the first golden light of dawn broke through the clouds. Demetri's injured leg resulted in a slower pace than what we would have normally traveled. While his limp wasn't as severe as it had been yesterday, it was still an obstruction. He apologized a few times during the more physically grueling parts of the hike, but we carried on.

By the time twilight fell, we were utterly exhausted. I wasn't sure how far we'd traveled today. Everything looked the same, minus the occasional car-sized footprints left by the rock giants. Luckily, we hadn't run into any of them despite hearing the thunderous booms throughout the day.

"Give me a moment, love," Demetri panted, doubling over as he placed both hands on his legs for support.

"Are you okay?" I leaned down to analyze his face, trying to search for the answers I knew he wouldn't verbally volunteer.

"Fine," he grumbled just before collapsing into the snow.

"Jesus!" I tried to catch him to no avail.

His face had gone unnaturally pale. I pulled him into my lap and wrapped my arms around him, hoping to provide a little extra warmth.

"We can stop for the night," I said, frantically inspecting the nearby mountains for somewhere to take refuge. But there was nowhere around us that appeared to offer a feasible place to sleep.

"I'm sorry, love." He flinched in pain. "My injury is holding us both back."

"It's okay." I stroked my fingers through his hair. I hated seeing him like this, especially knowing that I couldn't make the situation any easier for him. "You just need rest," I reassured him. "Like you said last night, we have tomorrow."

"Gwen, leave me here," he commanded. "Go find help."

I glowered down at him in disbelief. "What? How could you say that, Demetri? I'm not leaving you here."

"You'll have a better chance without me slowing you down."

"I said I'm not leaving you here." The vicious tone of my voice surprised me as I doubled down.

Demetri painfully pulled himself up from my lap to sit upright and face me, grimacing as he did. "I'll be fine. Don't be foolish, love. We've made it this far. You can still make it to Winterhaven. You can still go home."

I took his face in between my hands and stared him directly into his pleading, stormy eyes.

"Don't ask me to leave you again. If you care about me in the slightest, then don't ask me to do that..." I shook my head as he parted his lips to speak. "...Because we both know what that means, and whether you believe it or not, I care about you. So, I will not...I cannot leave you here. If that means that we die here, then so be it. But if we die, we will die together."

Demetri's face shifted into an expression that I'd never seen him make before.

"You'd risk your life for me?" he finally asked.

"I think it's only fair at this point." I smiled sadly.

A loud huff echoed through the darkening sky. The sound was immediately followed by a rush of snow blowing past us. I leaned over Demetri in an effort to shield our faces as Zola, looking magnificent as ever, landed nearby.

As soon as her hooves hit the ground, she raced toward us. She was at our side before I was ever able to move. Her frantic behavior prompted me to look around for any signs of a hidden danger. There was nothing.

"Zola, thank God," I breathed. "What is it?" I looked her over quickly to ensure she hadn't been hurt again.

"I think she wants us to go with her," Demetri said as he struggled to stand.

I grabbed onto him, carefully helping him rise, and wrapped my arm around his waist.

Zola galloped around us as though she were in a hurry to leave.

"Come on, you've got to get on her back," I said, leading him closer to her.

He scowled at the thought, no doubt imagining how painful that would be.

Zola steadied as I placed my hand on the side of her neck. Then, she mercifully bowed down to allow Demetri easier access. He positioned his intact leg over her back and pulled himself up. Once he was secure, I climbed up behind him, wrapping my arms tightly around his body as Zola took to the sky without a moment of hesitation.

Demetri did a better job at steering her away from the mountains, even in his injured state. Zola seemed to be a bit more cautious this time as she soared farther away from the peaks. Her rushing wings amplified the sting of the icy air. After what seemed like an unbearable amount of time, she finally swooped down at the edge of the mountain line. Sunlight broke over the horizon as Zola landed on a slush-covered trail laced with massive evergreen trees.

She bowed down and silently waited for us to descend. I slid off easily, then helped Demetri dismount as painlessly as possible. As soon as we were both safely on the ground, Zola lifted into the air again and was gone as quickly as she had returned.

A brief glance at Demetri's face told me he had no idea where we were either. As he opened his mouth to speak, we both froze under an indistinct noise.

"It sounds like...horses," I whispered, peering toward the nearby hill where the steady clicks grew louder.

He pulled me off the trail onto the snow-splattered grass and we watched wordlessly as a gilded carriage came into view.

CHAPTER EIGHTEEN

The carriage door swung open, and an exquisite young woman stood mystified on the threshold. "My goodness! Are the two of you alright?"

Her wide blue eyes studied us as she tugged her white velvet cloak closer to her body. A bitter breeze shifted through the wispy strands of her long golden hair. She looked like a snow goddess, one gifted with immeasurable beauty and grace. Despite those things, I noticed something very obvious and very disturbing about her—the ornate crown that sat atop her head.

Demetri and I stared in silence, unsure of what sort of response was warranted here. We'd had our share of unfortunate run-ins with royalty before, and now, with Demetri's injury, we weren't exactly capable of escaping this time.

"Surely, this is no place to be wandering about," she admonished, dismissing our wary expressions. "We're miles from town, and you'll freeze to death in those wet clothes!" She stepped down to our level, unhooked her cloak, and gently draped it over my shoulders. "There now." She smiled.

"Thank you." I shuddered under the warmth.

"We've been lost in the mountains for a couple of days," Demetri finally said. "We were trying to make it to Winterhaven with our Pegasus, but she crashed and flew off when the giants spooked her."

"Oh no, you poor dears! Those giants can be quite loud and quite territorial. Are you injured?" She shifted her attention to Demetri and the arm I had clasped around him.

"Only my leg," he responded.

"Well, it's a good thing we found you." She leaned back into the carriage and retrieved a blanket to hand to Demetri. "We were just on the way back to the castle. We can get you the help you require there."

"The castle?" I mumbled; flashbacks of Phillip invaded my thoughts.

"Yes, I insist. There's someone there who can tend to your injury. And you'll both need warm baths and a new set of clothes so you don't catch colds."

"That's very kind of you," Demetri replied.

"Of course. Do come inside." She stepped aside, gesturing for us to get into the stagecoach.

<hr>

"What business do you seek in Winterhaven?" The woman asked as the carriage bounced along the scenic trail.

"We are looking for someone named Isadora." I shivered, huddling closer to Demetri under the blanket.

The radiant beauty smiled. "Isadora is a dear friend of mine. She just arrived at the castle a few days ago, in fact. I'd be happy to arrange a meeting as soon as you are feeling up to it."

"Really?" I exclaimed. "That would be wonderful!"

"Of course. In the meantime, you are both distinguished guests of my kingdom and will be welcomed by all and treated as such." She positioned her gloved hands neatly across her lap. "Do let me know if there is anything that we can help you with."

"Thank you..." I began to say, "I'm sorry, I don't believe I got your name earlier. I'm Gwen, and this is Demetri."

"It's such a pleasure to meet you both." She smiled, and her crystal eyes sparkled with wistful sincerity. "I am Cinderella."

My body tensed as the weight of her revelation hit me like a ton of bricks. What even was my life right now? I'm sitting in a carriage with...Cinderella? Of course, she's fucking Cinderella. She's refined and compassionate, and she looks exactly like Cinderella would look if she were real. I mean, she is real. She's really here, sitting right in front of me anyway...

My chest tightened, and the breaths I drew were quick and shallow. God, I'm going to hyperventilate right in front of Cinderella. I tilted my head back, trying to allow more air down my throat.

Demetri's hand fell across my knee, and the slight squeeze that followed tugged me back down to reality. Or whatever this was.

"Oh, are you all right?" she asked.

"Yes," I muttered, clearing my throat. "I'm sorry. I'm just...so tired." I couldn't even look at her, so I threw my focus to Demetri instead. He didn't seem nearly as fazed by the discovery as I was. But why would he be? He'd never heard of her before, at least not in the same capacity.

"I can only imagine," she responded.

"We are incredibly thankful for your generosity, Cinderella," Demetri acknowledged, already seeming to be in better spirits than he was moments ago.

"After you get settled in and catch up on your rest, Prince Andrew and I would love for you to join us for dinner tonight. We've several family members visiting us this week, and it's sure to be a joyous occasion."

"Thank you for the invitation, that sounds wonderful." Demetri nodded before nudging his arm into mine, "Doesn't it, love?"

"Yes. Wonderful," I managed to whisper, desperately trying to appear as normal as possible as I rode off to a wintery castle in a gold-plated carriage with Princess-Freaking-Cinderella.

"Oh, how delightful!" She gleamed. "I can't wait to tell Andrew the news."

As we came to a stop, Cinderella gracefully departed the carriage with the help of her footman. I gawked at him, secretly wondering if he used to be a mouse.

"Is something wrong, love?" Demetri whispered as he leaned against the doorframe and offered his hand to help me down.

"No. Nothing." I tore my stare away from the confused footman and stepped out.

The towers of the pearl-colored castle stretched so high they nearly disappeared into the pastel-colored clouds. This was the castle of all castles, the one that storybooks were based on. It was whimsical and dreamlike and far more majestic than anything I could have ever imagined.

"Are you sure you're all right?" Demetri whispered with a visibly concerned expression.

"Mhm." I nodded quickly, tearing my eyes away from the enchanting palace. "It's fine. I am fine," I lied. "I'm not going to freak out about this at all."

Demetri arched his brow quizzically.

"It's just freaking Cinderella out here inviting us inside her freaking fairytale castle. No big deal," I muttered.

"Ah," He nodded as the realization set in. "So, you've heard stories of Cinderella in your land?"

"Stories, films, theme park replicas…"

"I'll not pretend that I know what most of that means," he replied. "But, with a castle like this, I'm not surprised to hear there are stories."

"Just…try not to let me act too weird," I pleaded.

His mouth curved into a smile as he linked his arm through mine. "I am but a simple man, Gwen," he said as we trailed behind Cinderella to the main entrance. "I'm afraid such extreme requests are completely out of my control."

"Hello darling," Cinderella said, greeting her husband with a swift kiss at the stairwell as we entered the elegant sunlit foyer. "I'd like to introduce you to my friends Demetri and Gwen. I've invited them to stay with us."

The prince bowed his head in greeting. "It's nice to meet you both. Welcome to our home."

"It's an honor to meet you." Demetri bowed back. "We are very grateful for your hospitality."

"Will you be staying for the ball?" Andrew inquired.

"Oh, um. A ball? No, I don't think so. We weren't aware," I replied.

"Oh heavens. I do believe I forgot to mention that." Cinderella chuckled. "Our annual winter ball will be held this weekend. You are both welcome to come if you'd like."

"I've never been to a ball."

"Oh, well then, you simply must come!" she insisted. "There's just something so magical about them. Andrew and I even met at a ball."

"I know…" I blurted. "I mean, wow, that's incredible." The heat of Demetri's gaze fell over me.

"It was the most magical night of my life." She smiled lovingly at her husband.

"Mine too, darling," Andrew replied, taking her into his arms. "You were a vision. One I'll never forget for as long as I live."

I fought back a laugh at the irony of that statement, picturing all the girls who had to try on a shoe to determine who he'd danced with. Perhaps, though, that wasn't what actually happened.

"I'd love to hear the story." I declared.

"Perhaps another time, love." Demetri smiled convincingly as he spoke. "Maybe after we get out of these snow-covered clothes." The statement sounded innocent enough, but his rapid warning glance wasn't lost on me.

"Of course. We'll have plenty of time to talk about the details over dinner tonight," Cinderella agreed. "Your husband is right; you'll both feel much better after a change of clothes. Please feel free to help yourselves to any of the garments and commodities located in your room."

"My hus-—" I started to say.

"Violet will draw you a bath and help you get ready, Gwen. Demetri, you can follow Gustav. We look forward to seeing you again later tonight at dinner."

After taking the longest bath of my life, I searched through the gown options that my assigned maid, Violet, had laid out across the bed. They were all pretty, but I ultimately settled on a timeless black one with a cutout that dipped to the bottom of my back. It was long and sparkly and almost looked like something I would wear back home. I finished off the look with Bree's necklace, then took a seat at the vanity stationed in the corner of the bedroom. I hadn't seen my reflection since the night in Phillip's castle when Cecilia had prepared me to meet with the monster. The wear of the excursions I'd experienced since then weighed heavily on my face. My cheeks looked slimmer—sharper somehow. Exhaustion lingered in my eyes, pooling below into the dark circles that now existed.

"You have such beautiful hair, dear." Violet walked to my side, running her slender fingers over the damp brown strands before brushing through it.

"Thank you," I smiled back at her in the mirror. "But you don't have to do all of this."

"You are very kind." She returned the expression, wrinkles forming at the corners of her soft, dark eyes. "And so lovely. You quite remind me of our princess."

That statement was almost laughable as I took in my depleted appearance. I hardly even recognized the girl who stared back. The fact that anyone would dare to compare me to Cinderella, especially in this state, was unbelievable.

"Thank you, Violet," I suppressed a laugh. "That is truly a compliment, whether it is true or not."

"Oh, indeed it is," she said as she placed down the brush and gently dabbed my cheeks with a hint of rouge. "I wouldn't say so if it wasn't true."

"Cinderella and Andrew seem very kind," I responded.

"Truly they are. Many kingdoms aren't fortunate enough to have such fair and kind rulers. Our Prince and Princess have hearts of gold."

"Lucky for us that she was the one who picked us up on the side of the road then."

"Yes, indeed," Violet agreed, pressing her thin, mauve lips together as she examined her work. She shifted her hands through the soft, wavy locks one more time before leaning back and smiling in satisfaction. "You're a vision, my dear. I'll show you down to the dining hall and will start preparing the guest bedroom for you and your husband tonight."

"Um, thank you, Violet. That is very thoughtful, but he's, uh, not my husband."

"Oh, my apologies, dear!" she exclaimed, bringing a hand to her face. "I just assumed since you were together..."

"I know, it's fine. No need to apologize," I reassured her.

"So, you'll be needing separate bedrooms for the night then?" The tone of her voice nearly made me wonder if there was a hidden meaning in her question.

"Yes..." I nodded. "Of course."

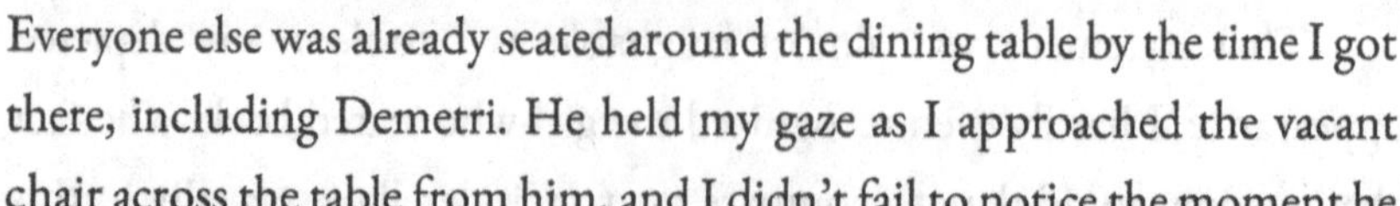

Everyone else was already seated around the dining table by the time I got there, including Demetri. He held my gaze as I approached the vacant chair across the table from him, and I didn't fail to notice the moment he raked his eyes down my body before I took my seat.

The dining room was luxurious. It didn't feel cold, the way Phillip's had. The diamond chandelier hanging over us emitted flecks of shimmering light across the warm-toned room that burst with lively laughter. It was a far cry from the empty, solemn, stone-walled room that I wished I could forget.

"Hello, darling. What's your name?" the sharp-nosed, raven-haired woman to my right asked casually.

"Oh, hello. I'm Gwen."

"I'm Odessa, and that's Rosalind." She pointed to the chatty strawberry-blonde woman on the other side of me.

"Nice to meet you."

"Likewise." Her bright pink smile was oddly pleasant. "How do you know our sister?"

"Who's your sister?"

"Oh, darling!" She emitted a lively chuckle. "What a funny one you are. Why, Cinderella, of course!"

"Oh, really?" I exclaimed, nearly choking on my food. "I'm sorry, I didn't know she had any sisters. I've only just met her today."

Demetri stared at me from across the table as though he were reminding me not to say anything incriminating.

"Well, it's lovely to meet you, dear!" The other sister chimed in.

"Thank you. You both seem very...nice," I noted, internally comparing them to their fictional counterparts.

"Well, we'd like to think so!" Odessa laughed loudly, earning her some looks from a few others at the table.

"How long will you be staying here at the castle with us?" Rosalind said, sweeping her long hair behind her shoulder.

"I'm not sure, to be honest."

"Well, the more the merrier, I always say. I do hope you'll be joining us for the winter ball. Did our sister tell you about it?"

"Yes, she did, but I don't know. I've never been to a ball and-—"

"You've never been to a ball!" Odessa shrieked, pulling her hand up to her chest dramatically.

Rosalind raised her voice as the rest of the table fell quiet. "Cinderella! Did you hear that?"

"No, it's not a big deal. Please don't..." I whispered at her as I tried to inconspicuously shield my face from the confused eyes of the other guests.

"Our newest guest has never been to a ball before!" Rosalind continued as she blatantly ignored my pleas. Perhaps they weren't so nice after all.

"Oh Rosalind. Now, there's no need to make a scene. Our new guests aren't from around here. It really isn't so strange that they've never been to a ball," Cinderella sweetly reassured.

"Well, they simply must come to ours then!" Odessa interjected. "Why, it'll be the talk of the town for months to come!"

"Of course, they are invited to come if they'd like." Cinderella shifted her gaze to me and smiled apologetically.

"Thank you for the invitation." Demetri's voice eased my nerves. "We will certainly consider the offer." He glanced back at me, appearing slightly amused.

"Indeed," I forced out before shoveling a spoonful of mashed potatoes into my mouth.

The rest of the dinner was spent saying as little as possible to the two sisters. I couldn't risk another embarrassing public announcement. Cinderella and Andrew delightfully engaged with each person around the table. The princess was graceful and effortless in everything she did, even when she thought no one was watching her.

Through their conversations, I concluded that two of the other guests were Andrew's brother Eli and his wife, Vanessa. They had arrived a few days prior from a place not too far from here called Starlight Stream; it was the same place where Dalton had said he was from. I tried not to think about that for too long.

Accompanying them was another couple. The woman, Morgana, was Andrew and Eli's cousin. She reeked of wealth and had a timeless sort of beauty. She looked to be younger than both Andrew and Eli. The same could not be said for her husband, Royce.

Noticeably not in attendance, however, was Isadora.

"Can I get you anything else, madam?" The butler leaned down to whisper.

"Oh, no, thank you. I'm fine." I smiled up at him.

"Don't be silly; you haven't even tried the wine yet. It'll change your life," Rosalind declared. "Bring us two glasses, Jaq."

"Of course, madam." He disappeared from the table and was back before I could decline the offer.

"How is everything?" Cinderella asked.

"Simply amazing," Morgana chimed in. "As always."

"Wonderful. It's such a pleasure having everyone here tonight. It doesn't happen as often as I would like." Cinderella's eyes fell to me. "And we are always happy to make new friends. Are you enjoying your dinner, Gwen?"

"Everything is fantastic," I confirmed. "Will, um, Isadora be joining us tonight?" I forced myself not to look in Demetri's direction after voicing the question. I already knew the disagreeable look I'd see there if I did.

"Oh, no. I'm afraid not.," Cinderella replied. "Isadora is helping the staff prepare for the ball. There is much work to be done between now and then."

"Of course." I nodded.

"I will make a point to introduce you to her tomorrow," Cinderella added. "I am to meet with her in the morning to discuss the floral arrangements and a few last-minute details."

"Jaq, more wine!" Rosalind called out as she held up her glass.

"Here we go," Odessa cackled at her sister's drunken outburst.

"Oh, Rosalind." Cinderella chuckled. "Do go easy on Jaq. At this rate, he'll be all tired out before dessert."

To my surprise, Demetri fit in well with the regal group. He charmed them with fascinating tales from the lands that he'd once ventured to, careful to leave out certain incriminating details, such as him being the captain of a pirate ship and a prior prisoner of another royal figure. As far as they all knew, he was simply a well-versed traveler.

"Are you to tell me that you actually saw sirens on your journey here?" Odessa gasped in disbelief.

"Aye, and I'd be content to never lay eyes on one again," he retorted.

"We've always heard the myths." Vanessa leaned in. Her deep hazel eyes grew wide as she zoned in on Demetri. "But I suppose it's one of those things you never really believe until you see it."

"What did they look like?" Odessa mirrored Vanessa's actions, leaning in to hang onto Demetri's every word. "I've heard they're the most hideous creatures."

"They're not," I let slip out. Everyone's eyes turned to rest on me as they waited for me to reveal more details about the vehement monsters. "They're very beautiful, not in the way you would imagine – not classically but in a haunting sort of way. And you can only feel the full extent of how dangerous they are when they lock eyes with you. It's like they don't have souls, so they try to compensate by taking yours."

My thoughts settled on the one mermaid that had saved my life. At first glance, she had looked like the others – senselessly beautiful and mystical solely because of the creature that she was – but different in the way that her eyes conveyed compassion that the others had lacked. Different in the way that she was visibly wary of her own kind before making the conscious decision to save my life.

I pushed the thought away. I wasn't willing to divulge that much information to these strangers.

"When my father was just a boy, my grandfather sent a fleet of ships to Willowbrook as part of a trade deal," Andrew began. "It was in the dead of winter, so the crews were instructed to sail south of Cloudbay Canyon to avoid wrecking the ships on icebergs. They were told to stay away from Shadow Ridge because of the sirens that inhabited the area, but they deviated. No one knows why to this day. The instructed route would have taken a few days longer, so perhaps they were trying to save time. Or perhaps a storm blew them off course. Whatever the reason was, they never reached Willowbrook. My grandfather believed the entire crew was killed that day and that our kingdom's ships still lie at the bottom of the ocean."

"Aye," Demetri nodded, meeting Andrew's tortured gaze. "He was right. I've seen the ships." Demetri's face paled as he recalled the memories. "And the remains of some of the men lying near them."

"My word," Cinderella gasped, grabbing hold of Andrew's hand.

"If it wasn't for Alistair...my friend," Demetri said, careful to contain the details, "I'd be down there now as well."

"Alistair sounds like quite the blessing," Cinderella responded.

"Indeed," Demetri said, a thoughtful smile forming across his face.

"I'll drink to that!" Rosalind shouted, evoking some much-needed laughter from the solemn table.

"Needless to say, we actively avoid that area during our travels," Andrew added.

"A wise decision." Demetri seemed to have already shaken off the recollection as he pressed a wine glass to his lips.

"Tell us, Demetri, where else have you traveled?" Eli asked.

"It might take less time to tell you all the places where I haven't been yet." Demetri laughed.

"Do indulge Eli, dear," Morgana quipped, her voice dripping with sarcasm. "He and Vanessa never travel anymore. They're essentially hermits. The fact that they're here tonight is a feat in itself."

Eli narrowed his eyes at her playfully. "Oh, sweet Morgana, you're young yet, but you'll soon realize it's quite difficult to live a life of luxury when you have children to tend to."

"That's exactly why we're putting it off, cousin," she laughed deeply. "I'm not done being selfish yet."

"At least you're honest," Eli quipped.

"Children are certainly life-changing." Cinderella gazed over at Andrew. "Aren't they, darling?"

"Indeed," Andrew nodded with a luminous smile.

"You have a child?" The words rushed out before I could even think them through.

"Why, yes," Cinderella beamed, "Two children, actually. Our little Lily and Theodor. They're up in the nursery now with the nanny."

"That's incredible." I smiled. "How old are they?"

"Lily just turned three last month, and Theodor is one." Her face softened as she spoke of them. "They are the joys of my life."

"And they sure know how to keep us busy!" Andrew added with a laugh.

"Indeed," Cinderella giggled. "What about you? Do you have any children, Gwen?"

"No." I smiled politely. The weight of the question hit me a little heavier than I expected. "But maybe someday."

Her eyes softened. "I know that if you two decide to have them, you and Demetri would make such wonderful parents. Just imagine all the worldly stories he would share with them at bedtime!" she exclaimed as the others began to chime in in agreement.

It immediately occurred to me that the only person I'd informed of my relationship status was Violet when she'd brought it up earlier. I hadn't thought it necessary to announce to everyone else at the table that Demetri was not, in fact, my husband...not until now anyway.

"Yes, I keep trying to convince her," Demetri laughed from across the table.

If my eyes could shoot daggers, he'd be in excruciating pain on the floor right now.

"Demetri, you must tell me more about what you've encountered on your travels," Morgana exclaimed. Clearly, she had tired of the previous conversation.

Hours had passed. The food had long since been eaten, but the conversation was still very much alive. We'd left the table and transitioned into the drawing room across the hallway, where we picked out our lounging spots.

Demetri took his place beside me on what was quite possibly the most elegant sofa I'd ever seen in my life.

Odessa and Rosalind had already decided to retire to their room, much to Rosalind's dismay.

Demetri's stories continued to enthrall everyone, including myself. I'd have to ask him just how truthful they were later...especially the last one he had shared about a grim encounter he'd had with a sea beast.

"Were you near Juniper Jungle when you saw it?" Cinderella asked; the color had long been drained from her face as she listened to him describe the massive creature he'd seen that had at least a dozen tentacles.

"Not far from it. I was leaving Seaspire Port and on my way back to the western hemisphere," Demetri responded.

"Was this recently?" She set her glass down and focused all of her attention on him.

"No, it was back at the beginning...before word of the horrors really got out. I haven't been back that way since then."

The horrors? What the hell was he talking about?

"You're very fortunate to have made it through the channel unscathed. Ever since the curse, it's been so dangerous to travel through the Summer Sea."

"Aye," Demetri agreed as though the topic were common knowledge.

I didn't know what curse they were referring to, but asking questions right now only had the potential to expose me. I'd have to remember all of this and ask Demetri about it later when we were alone again.

"Seaspire has certainly changed over the last few years," Andrew chimed in. "And what a shame, truly. A vibrant, colorful city that once flourished, now dammed by dark magic."

"I always did love visiting with the people in the marketplace when we were on our way to The Golden Empire," Cinderella reminisced.

"And now, no one will risk crossing the beast-infested waters to go help them." Andrew sighed. "It's very unfortunate."

"When's the last time you saw Xavier and Farah anyway, brother?" Eli chimed in. "It's been ages since Vanessa and I have heard from them."

"We haven't been down there since the curse befell. Cinderella was with child at the time, so almost two years now. We briefly considered it after Theo was born but decided that the risk was far too great. Even so, that was before we knew the extent of everything that was going on down there."

"The last we heard, Xavier was training troops from across the land," Royce added.

"That won't do them any good," scoffed Eli. "What can the troops possibly do against dark magic?"

I glanced quizzically at Demetri, hoping to gain some sense of clarity in the conversation, but he simply shook his head and looked away.

CHAPTER NINETEEN

I found Violet cleaning in my room when I returned.

"How was dinner, dear?" she inquired cheerfully.

"The food was incredible." I sprawled out across the bed, rubbing my stomach. "I'm afraid I might have eaten too much, though."

"Well, we do have the best chefs in all the land. So, I can understand your discomfort." She laughed. "Is there anything else I can do for you before I settle in for the night?"

"No, I'm okay, Violet. Thank you." I smiled.

She shut the door behind her as I stared up at the sophisticated fabric draped across the top of the absurdly large canopy bed. I sat up, trying to take in all the intricate details of the room. Everything about this place was immaculate, from the lavish furniture right down to the lesser-known distinctive designs carved into the molding and mantle over the dimly lit fireplace.

I rose from my spot to pull the bed sheets back, but the enchanting view outside the window commanded my attention instead. The iridescent glow of the other castle towers shining from the lower level stole my breath. God, this place was stunning. It was nearly impossible for me to even begin to fathom the things that had happened to lead me here.

A soft knock sounded at the door.

"Come in," I responded.

Demetri entered, softly shutting the door behind him before he began to cross the room. His limp was still evident, but it was nowhere near as bad as it had been when we were stranded in the mountains...when he'd told me to go on without him. I shook the thought from my head. I couldn't stand to think about him like that.

"I thought they were giving us separate rooms."

"They did," he replied. "But I didn't know if that's what you wanted."

"So, you thought you'd mosey on down here and share a room, did you?" I smirked, making sure he saw it.

"An opportunity not taken is a missed one." He smiled deviously in return.

"You're impossible."

"Does that mean you want me to stay or leave? It's a bit difficult to tell with all the eye-rolling you're doing."

"Violet knows we're not married despite the confusion at dinner tonight. I'm sure she's enlightened them by now, and they might think it's improper if we stay together."

Demetri smiled that devastating smile that only he could construct. The one that always managed to make me go weak in the knees. "I'm more surprised you think I give a damn what they think," he growled, and the seductive look on his face nearly made me come undone.

"Yes, I suppose I should know better by now." I laughed, shaking off the nervous feeling that I suddenly had. "Speaking of dinner...I didn't want to say anything in front of everybody, but what's up with this curse everyone was talking about?"

Demetri leaned against the bedpost and crossed his arms. "I was hoping you wouldn't ask," he admitted. "I wanted to spare you from needlessly worrying about it."

I narrowed my eyes at him. "Well, now I'm even more curious. So, spill it."

"Has anyone ever told you how alluring you are when you make that face?" His brow ticked up suggestively behind the dark strands of his disobedient hair.

I glowered back. "Demetri."

"And that dress..." He stroked his jaw, allowing his eyes to fall freely across my body. "I could barely control myself at dinner tonight."

"Stop stalling," I demanded. "Tell me what's going on."

He reluctantly tore his gaze away from my chest. "It's something that happened years ago."

"Okay...but how?"

"There's a lot of specifics that I still don't know," he said with a small sigh of defeat. "What I do know is my crew was near the area when we got word that a curse had been enacted. That's when we went to make our escape, unaware at the time that the curse was not just limited to the land we were visiting."

"So, the story of the sea beast...that was real?"

"Aye." He nodded ruefully, uncrossing his arms to roll up his sleeves. "And there's more than one from what I've heard since our initial encounter."

"And they don't let people leave the land?"

"Or enter into it."

"But why? What was the reason?"

"As I said, there's much I don't know. Rumors suggest that the rulers of The Golden Empire, Xavier and Farah, angered the mad queen, so she enacted a curse on their land to punish them."

I felt my face contort. "Who the hell is the mad queen?"

Demetri shifted away from the bed frame and joined me near the window.

"Sometimes I forget there's still so much you don't know about this world," he confessed as he peered beyond the glass. "Remember when I told you about the four kingdoms?"

"Yes."

"There's one north of the Castleberry territory. It's called Willowbrook."

"I remember. It's the one Andrew was just telling us about."

"Right. And it's also the land where the lost princess once reigned."

I thought back to Phillip's deranged story about how he wanted to exact his revenge on the girl who publicly humiliated him. "The one who ran away so she wouldn't have to marry Phillip," I confirmed.

"Aye."

"After she disappeared, someone else had to take her place as ruler of the kingdom. You see, her father, King Edward, was murdered mere days before she vanished," Demetri explained.

"What?" Phillip had left out that little detail during his rant.

"Some suspected Barrington did it to take over both kingdoms, which is what I would assume. And if I had to guess, it's probably what the princess thought."

"Which is why she ran off...so he wouldn't murder her too after they got married?"

"It's a theory, anyway."

"So, then what happened?"

"The king was unmarried at the time of his death. So, without his daughter there to take his place, the duty fell on the next closest blood relative—his only sister, Evannah."

"The mad queen?" I speculated.

"Precisely."

"And she's mad because...she didn't want to be queen?" I asked.

Demetri chuckled as he glanced down at me. "Oh no, she wanted to be the queen. Just as there are many people who believe that Barrington killed the king, there are just as many who believe his sister did it."

"And either way, the lost princess probably figured that whoever killed her father was coming after her next."

Demetri nodded. "Once they realized she was gone, they both went looking for her."

"Jeez."

"She's somehow managed to keep a low profile all these years, despite the substantial efforts to locate her."

I crossed my arms, musing over the theories. "I think Phillip's just looking to settle the score, but why would the queen still want her dead? She already got what she wanted."

"I don't know." Demetri shrugged. "Pirates typically don't get told such sensitive information. Perhaps she just wanted to ensure that the princess wouldn't decide to come back one day to reclaim her throne."

"That still doesn't answer the question of why the queen would go through the trouble of cursing an entirely different land that had nothing to do with any of it?"

"Ah, but it does. You see, several months later, the queen received word that the princess had taken refuge there. So, she went to see for herself. She found nothing, of course, but it wasn't for lack of trying. She tormented many people there who she thought had information. When

Xavier and Farah discovered what she had done to their people, they had no choice but to banish her from their land."

"I see."

"What they didn't know at the time was that the queen was highly skilled in the field of charms and incantations."

I stared up at him as the pieces started falling into place.

"Where is she now? The queen?"

"I assume she's back in Willowbrook, but she's rarely seen or heard from now. Wielding that sort of power takes a toll, and some have suggested that enacting the curse weakened her. No one wants to know badly enough to find out firsthand, though."

"So, she cursed an entire land and just disappeared into the night?"

"Essentially."

"Maybe she's dead?" I said, the suggestion came out a little more optimistic than I'd intended.

Demetri shook his head. "I don't think so. If she were, word would have gotten around by now. And Barrington would have probably already overtaken Willowbrook."

"Why hasn't he tried? It's what he wanted to begin with; it was the whole reason he was going to get married. If this so-called mad queen is weak, you'd think he would make his move and take what he could."

"While Barrington is an imbecile, he wouldn't be foolish enough to risk a similar curse on his own land. And if he tried something that brazen, she would probably kill him herself before taking it out on the people in his territory."

"He doesn't care about them." I scoffed.

"No, he doesn't." Demetri agreed. "His motives are purely self-serving."

"This is a lot to take in," I admitted.

"Aye. I try to stay out of kingdom politics as much as possible, but you tend to find out a lot of useful information when you travel around as much as I do."

"I guess I see why you like living on the water."

"It's not only that," he replied thoughtfully. "I've spent the better part of my life mapping out the stars and chasing horizons, not always knowing what lay beyond them." His shadow eclipsed the soft light streaming in from the window as he stepped closer to me. "It's an intriguing thought, wouldn't you agree?"

"Chasing the horizon?" I laughed, arching a confused brow at him.

"Aye." He smiled back affectionately. "Knowing there's a new adventure waiting for you just on the other side of it."

"Spoken like a true pirate," I teased.

His smile faded slowly as he seemed to reflect on the remark. "I suppose I simply wasn't meant to live a stagnant life."

I leaned against the wall and took him in for a few silent moments. "You've never thought about settling down somewhere, though? You could pick anywhere, after all."

"I've never given it serious consideration," he confessed, tearing his eyes away from mine as he turned back toward the window. The pastel glow from the other side fell across his dark features, reminding me just how sharp the contrast between the two entities truly was. "A castle such as this would be a tempting option, though." He grinned.

"I guess you'll have to find yourself a good princess to marry then."

He laughed. "I'm rather content with where I am right now. If I ever do get tired of sailing the seas, I'll consider where to plant roots at that time."

"Just not Castleberry." I smiled.

"That would be the last bloody place in this world. If I never see it again, it would be too soon."

His downright aversion evoked a laugh from me. "I can't really picture it though..." I confessed. "You planting down roots. I don't know if a stationary life would ever truly satisfy you."

"I would have to have some damn good motivation." He glanced back at me in a way that made my breath catch. God, he was beautiful.

"I hope you find it," I whispered, feeling my throat tremble as the words escaped. "You deserve a life full of happiness."

He lowered his head as though he didn't share those thoughts. "Thank you for saying that, love."

"I mean it."

"And you deserve to have everything you've ever wanted," he replied.

I pulled him closer to me and wrapped my arms around his shoulders. "I'm really going to miss you, Demetri," I admitted, inhaling deeply as his crisp, woodsy scent consumed me. He tightened his grip around my waist, and I was surprised at how heavy the thought of not having him in my life suddenly was. "Honestly, I don't even know how I'm going to be able to carry on with my normal life when I go home after all of this."

He pulled away from me in an instant, averting his apprehensive gaze as he pinched the bridge of his nose. "I'm sorry Gwen, but if I don't say this now, I fear I will regret not doing so," he uttered before lowering his hand and turning to face me with a wild look.

"What is it, Demetri?"

"Perhaps you weren't meant to carry on a normal life."

"What do you mean?"

"You were sent here for a reason, were you not?"

"So I was told, but I still haven't figured out why." I laughed unevenly. "I've just been fighting to stay alive, and I haven't even been very good at—"

"What if you stayed?" he blurted, the weight of his imploring eyes crashed into me like a violent wave, nearly pulling me under a tumultuous sea of uncharted uncertainty.

"What?" I stammered. The outlandish suggestion was not on my radar of things I had expected him to say. "I can't stay here." I shook my head defiantly. "I don't belong here, Demetri. I had a life before this...a good life."

"I think you're meant for more, Gwen."

"Do you really believe in all that stuff, Demetri? Fate...destiny? That we're all just part of some big cosmic plan?" I huffed at the thought.

"I can't be certain of anything," he admitted. "I used to believe we were responsible for creating our own destinies." He extended his hands out to grasp mine. "But how else would you explain this? You being here? You didn't choose that path. There has to be a reason that this happened to you."

I stared back at him woefully, unsure of the reaction he was expecting from me. "The reason is simply this: an old magical crazy lady, Demetri. No, it doesn't make any sense, but I'm not sure that even makes a difference." I pulled my hands away from his, crossing my arms as I refuted the idea. "I have no ties here...to this land. I have no powers, I'm not special. I'm just an ordinary person. There's no big cosmic reason to this...no twist of fate. It's just something that happened."

"People have questioned fate since the dawn of time," he pressed. "And maybe it's simply not meant for you to know all of the answers right now." He brushed a strand of hair behind my ear. "And don't ever say you're not special in my presence again."

"I can't stay," I repeated softly.

A fleeting glimpse of pain flashed across his face, but he composed himself quickly and took a step away from me.

The sight of it made my chest feel like it would surely cave in. "Demetri?"

"It's getting rather late, love," he answered, dragging his hand through his dark hair as he retreated. "I'll let you get some rest."

"Hey, don't leave," I said as he made his way to the door.

"My room is just at the end of the hall," he responded, ignoring my plea. "In case you need me."

"Demetri, stop," I demanded, the words coming out harsher than I meant for them to.

He paused reluctantly in the threshold.

"I'm sorry. I wasn't trying to..." my voice trailed off.

"Don't apologize." He turned to face me again. "In regard to fate, I must admit I have been questioning it." He lowered his head and laughed softly to himself. "Not only questioning it...but trying to bend it to my will, trying to change its trajectory." He hesitated as he tried to find the words to say, then lifted his face back to mine. "But I finally understand, love, that no matter what I do, I'll eventually have to accept the fact that it will always end the same way. With you gone."

I froze where I stood, unable to respond. Unable to offer any gesture of comfort. Demetri's confession gutted me to the point of physical pain. The last thing I ever wanted to do was hurt him. Unfortunately, it was the one thing I seemed to excel at.

"Goodnight, love," Demetri whispered, letting the door fall shut behind him.

CHAPTER TWENTY

"Are you awake, madam?"

I rolled over, pulling the quilt over my head.

"Rise and shine, Miss Gwendolyn!" The curtains jerked open, filling the entire room with unnaturally bright sunlight. "Breakfast will be soon, and I promise you, you'll not want to miss that." Violet swiftly pulled the quilt off my body.

"I'm exhausted." I groaned.

"Did you not get a good night's rest, dear? Was the bed not comfortable enough for you?" She patted the mattress as if she were testing it out for herself.

"No. The bed was fine. I just had a lot on my mind." Like the look on Demetri's dejected face when he left my room last night.

"Ah, I see. Trouble in paradise, is it?" She pressed her lips together and arched her thin black brows.

I climbed out of bed and crossed the room to pull the curtains closed again. It was too early for this much sunlight.

"Well, no. We aren't together," I reminded her, assuming she must have forgotten that tidbit of information.

Violet fetched a silky rose-colored dress from the wardrobe and held it out for me to take. "I know you say that, dear, and I'd hate to impose my opinion when it hasn't been asked for, but it's quite obvious there are some feelings involved."

"What? No...there are no feelings, Violet," I combatted, sliding the dress over my head. "It's...it's just complicated." She led me to the vanity and examined my face in the mirror as she grabbed a brush lying nearby.

"It always is, isn't it?" She huffed. "Men! Am I right?" she exclaimed, throwing her hands up in an amusing fashion.

After I was deemed appropriate, Violet led me downstairs to an airy morning room. Windows serving as walls all the way around offered stunning views of the distant mountain range and the snow-spattered gardens surrounding the castle. Cinderella, her sisters, and Vanessa were already sitting around the table, laughing as they sipped on mimosas.

"Gwen! There you are!" Cinderella exclaimed. "Please come and join us! How did you sleep?"

I sat down in the chair beside her in front of an empty plate.

"Very well, thank you." I smiled.

Andrew walked into the room and headed straight for Cinderella to plant a kiss on the top of her head.

It was then I noticed there were no other openings at the table.

"Is Demetri coming?"

"Oh, no." Cinderella took a quick sip from her glass. "Typically, the men don't join us for breakfast. Andrew and I were just going to quickly go over some last-minute details for the ball."

"Oh, right. The ball." I smiled.

"I do hope you and Demetri decide to come," Andrew interjected.

"I suppose I should check it out while I'm here. I don't have any other dresses, though. Could I just wear this?" I pulled at the slinky pink gown.

Cinderella giggled. "Oh, Gwen! Don't be silly. We have so many beautiful formal dresses for you to choose from."

"You can always get Isadora to make her one. I'm sure she could whip up something special in no time!" Andrew suggested.

"That reminds me, I am to meet with Isadora in a few hours. You're welcome to join me, Gwen," Cinderella offered.

"Of course, I'd love to," I replied, trying not to seem overly enthusiastic.

"Until then, please feel free to explore the castle. We have the most beautiful library on the second floor."

"It truly is exquisite," Vanessa chimed in.

"Or, if you'd like to take a stroll through the gardens, we have some beautiful landscapes you might enjoy. The snow is nearly melted, so you'd probably be able to see some of the flowers."

"Of course," I nodded. Thank you. I would absolutely love to see as much as I can of your beautiful home."

"Oh, wonderful. Take your time; I'll be sure to come fetch you before I go see Isadora."

The hours dragged by slowly. All anyone at the palace could seem to talk about was the upcoming ball. I still hadn't seen Demetri and was beginning to wonder if that was the way he preferred it after the way we'd left things last night.

I took Cinderella up on her offer and explored as much as I could of the castle. The library really was a sight to behold, with sunlit spiral staircases and books stacked so high against the walls they faded away from view from the bottom floor. The gardens were also exceptionally beautiful, but despite the melting snow, it was still too chilly to spend too much time out there.

I secluded myself in my bedroom all day with a book that I'd picked out of the library. It had been an overwhelming task to pick a book out of the thousand others, but the shimmery pearlescent cover of this one had caught my eye as I was about to give up entirely and leave. Every knock on the door elicited a rush of hope that on the other side stood Demetri with that halfhearted, crooked smirk that I'd grown so fond of. But it was always Violet.

"Are you sure there's nothing I can get you, my dear?" she'd ask.

"I'm fine." I'd smile back.

On her fourth check-in, Violet informed me that Cinderella had requested my presence. It was finally time to meet Isadora.

"Did you get a chance to explore the castle?" Cinderella asked as Violet dropped me off at the drawing room.

"I did," I responded. "The gardens were amazing, and I even picked up a book in the library."

"Oh, which one?" she squealed.

"Songs of Winter Fables. It's a collection of short stories." It had been too intriguing to ignore; there was just something about a fairytale land having a book of unheard-of fables that I couldn't pass up.

"I adore that one." She took a seat on a long lounging chair. "We sometimes read the stories to the children, the age-appropriate ones anyway. That's only about as long as they manage to sit still for," she laughed.

I settled into the armchair beside her. "I'm up to the one about the three deer who cross into other realms every night to bring dreams to the children."

"That's one of Lily's bedtime favorites," Cinderella smiled. "When she wakes sometimes, she will tell us that the deer brought her new dreams."

"It's very imaginative. I can see why it's her favorite."

"I feel I must caution you, though, Gwen, some of the stories near the end of the book aren't quite as lovely." She grimaced.

Before I could respond, Morgana and Vanessa entered the room and took their seats.

"Isadora will be joining us shortly," Morgana said, kicking off her shoes before throwing her feet up across the couch. "Apparently, she got held up with the chefs, deciding which hors d'oeuvres we'd be serving."

"Don't wait on us, dears," I heard a voice yell from down the corridor. "Go ahead with the meeting. We're coming!"

I turned to see a small, plump woman hurrying toward us as Rosalind and Odessa followed swiftly behind her.

"Oh, don't be silly, Isadora!" Cinderella exclaimed. "Of course we will wait for everyone."

"Here we are then," Isadora exclaimed as she breezed by in her light blue dress and claimed the other chair sitting beside mine. Wispy strands of white wavy hair escaped from the ribbon holding together her untidy bun.

"So sorry, sister. Odessa couldn't make up her mind on anything the chefs prepared," Rosalind snorted.

"Pardon me?" Odessa retorted. "You were the one who couldn't decide between the oysters and the finger sandwiches."

"All right, all right." Cinderella laughed. "I'm sure whatever was decided on will be perfect."

"Yes, it's all taken care of now," Isadora assured as she readjusted her glasses.

"Splendid. Now, before we start to go over all the details…Isadora, I'd like to introduce you to Gwen. She's staying here at the castle for a few days and is planning to attend the ball tomorrow."

"Hello, my dear!" Isadora greeted me with a friendly smile, the lines of time crinkling her bright, rosy face as she did. "It's lovely to meet you."

"It's so good to meet you too," I smiled, fighting the urge to divulge everything to her, desperate to see if she was the one who could finally help me get home…but I couldn't right now, not with so many other people sitting here listening. It would have to wait until later.

A piece of hair fell across Isadora's face. "Oh heavens, all that running about has done a number on me," she chuckled before pulling out a small wand from her sleeve and tapping it against her head.

Faster than I could blink, Isadora's bun was restored to mint condition.

I realized my jaw had dropped when she looked in my direction and began to laugh. "Terribly sorry, dear; I usually don't forget to warn new people about that before I pull out my wand. I'm rather frazzled today with all the planning."

I sat in on the whole meeting as the women discussed every aspect of the ball, from the food to the music, and even down to which chandeliers would be lit during which songs. No stone had been left unturned by the end of the meeting, and I was left drained by the whole production schedule by the time they'd finally decided to adjourn.

Isadora had rushed out as quickly as she came earlier, and I had been unable to find an ideal moment to pull her aside privately. I figured it could wait until a little later. I needed to find Demetri first anyway…and maybe even squeeze in a nap.

<hr>

A knock sounded at the door. "Miss Gwen?" I heard Violet ask on the other side.

"Come in." My voice came out groggier than I had anticipated.

"I figured I'd bring you up some soup when you didn't come down for dinner tonight."

"What time is it?" I rubbed my eyes.

"Eight-thirty p.m."

"Oh no," I muttered. "I slept for five hours?"

"Are you feeling all right? I can fetch the nurse if you'd like," Violet suggested.

I sat up quickly, shaking my head as I stretched. "That's not necessary, Violet. I'm fine; I was just very tired. I feel much better now, though."

"The prince and princess were very concerned about you when you didn't come down." Violet gently sat down the food tray beside me on the bed. "I told them not to worry, that you were resting comfortably, and that I'd just bring you up some dinner."

"Thank you, Violet. It really smells amazing." I hadn't realized how hungry I was until the appetizing aroma filled the room.

I shoved a spoonful in my mouth, nodding in approval as Violet smiled. "I wanted to speak with Isadora again tonight, but I suppose it's too late now."

"Yes, she has already retired to her room. I'm sure you will have ample opportunity tomorrow before the ball, though."

"Violet, was Demetri at dinner tonight?" I asked, gulping down another helping. "I haven't seen him all day, and I'm starting to worry that he's actively avoiding me."

She seemed to reflect on the question for a moment. "I don't remember seeing him while I was down there, dear. But he could have just been running late."

I tried to calm the uneasy feeling that formed in the pit of my stomach, but focusing on it only made it worse. "Thanks, Violet."

"Do you need anything else before I go to my room?"

"No, thank you." I smiled. "I think I might just stay here and read my book tonight."

"Very well," she nodded. "Goodnight, Miss Gwen. I'll bring you some ball gowns in the morning for you to sort through."

CHAPTER TWENTY-ONE

I awoke to Violet and two other maids hanging up dresses in the wardrobe, automatically clenching my eyes together tightly as one of them pulled back the curtains to let the sun rush in.

"Good morning, dear!" Violet exclaimed, yanking down the covers when I tried to pull them over my head. "Today's the big day!"

I somehow wasn't as excited as everyone else, but pretended the best I could, "Yay..." I yawned.

"The ball doesn't officially start until eight o'clock, but some of our guests will be arriving in a few hours."

"I don't know if I want to go, Violet," I admitted, grudgingly climbing out of the bed. "I still haven't heard anything out of Demetri. I have a feeling he isn't going to be feeling up to going tonight, and I wouldn't want to go alone."

"Nonsense!" she exclaimed, throwing the dresses she held onto the bed. "You'll go to the ball, and you'll have a lovely time. You'll not let the actions of a man dictate your happiness, not tonight, not on my watch!" she declared.

"Well, when you put it that way..." I laughed, rubbing the sleep from my eyes. "I suppose you're right."

"Of course I am, dear. I may be older, but with that extra age comes extra wisdom." She winked lightheartedly, then turned to grab several dresses to display across the bed. Some were slim, some frilly, and some were unpleasant colors that made me squint when I looked at them.

"I didn't know your style, so I just brought a few of each," she said proudly.

"These are...something," I voiced, flipping through the mountain of ruffles.

I picked up an olive-green dress and placed it to the side as I tried to formulate a nice way to tell Violet that I hated them all. That was when the one lying underneath it caught my eye.

I held up the long, sparkling princess gown to inspect it closer. It was black at the top with elegant notes of laced ivy that trickled down its length. The ombre-tinted fabric seamlessly faded until turning completely white at the bottom.

"Oh, I don't remember seeing that one," Violet said quizzically. "Marie must have brought that one in this morning."

"It's gorgeous."

"Try it on," she insisted.

She helped me slide it over my head and laced up the back for me. The off-shoulder straps were just delicate enough to balance out the sweetheart neckline, which was low enough to show off Bree's necklace perfectly.

"Oh, darling. That one looks like it was made just for you!" Violet exclaimed, standing back to observe the way it glimmered. "Spin around! Let me see it in action."

"I love it," I said, obeying her request. "This is definitely the one I want to wear."

A few hours later, I had finished reading the book from the library. Cinderella's warning about the last couple stories had rung true. I'd been too immersed to skip over them, but the cursed land storylines had hit a little too close to home with everything that I'd recently learned. I was still trying to banish thoughts of the fictional fallen kingdom and the people who had been brutally conquered by deranged royal assailants when Violet hastily entered the room and instructed me to move to the vanity so she could finish getting me ready. She chatted leisurely about the guests who had already arrived as she weaved two small braids in my hair, pinning them in place like a crown before shuffling the rest of the waves over my shoulders.

"You look beautiful, darling." She stepped back when she finished to admire her work. "Absolutely stunning."

A few nights in this castle had done wonders for the girl who stared back at me in the mirror. Eating three generous meals a day had brought some roundness back to my face. Even the pesky dark circles had diminished to a reasonable extent. I had to admit I had never felt prettier than I did right now.

"Do you think I could pass as a princess tonight?" I asked, laughing as I met Violet's gaze in the mirror.

"I think you'll have the whole damn room fooled." Violet smiled back.

The lights were dim in the corridor as I followed the distant sound of chatter toward the grand staircase. Truth be told, I still wasn't feeling up for this. I wasn't in the mood for forcing smiles and making small talk with strangers.

My mind was already too hazy, consumed with worry over Demetri. I'd stopped outside his room on the way to the party, hoping he'd finally decide to grace me with his presence. It was no use because he never answered the door. I was beginning to wonder if he'd left altogether...if the conversation in my bedroom had been the last straw, and if he'd finally decided to give up on me.

No matter how much I tried to distract myself, I couldn't shake the look on his face the other night. I just wanted to see him...to fix this. I needed to thank him for risking so much to help me when he never even owed me anything. I needed to apologize for the things I'd said and done in my moments of frustration. I needed to tell him how sorry I was that I'd taken his help for granted. I only hoped now I could get the chance.

"Oh, Gwen, you look absolutely stunning!" Cinderella greeted me at the base of the stairs, embracing me warmly.

"Thank you." I smiled back. "So do you." Her blush pink gown made her stand out even more against the crowd.

"Darling, you look radiant." Andrew rapidly approached, kissing her softly on the cheek.

"I was wondering when you were going to show up," she said, giving him a playful look.

"I know. I'm sorry, dear. We got back as soon as we could. Thankfully, we made it before the introductions." His eyes wandered past us. "Is that Baxter over there that your sisters have cornered near the balcony?"

"Oh my, yes. He looks as though he's in need of a rescue." She chuckled. "Gwen, you're welcome to join us."

"That's okay, go ahead." I smiled. "I'll just...go mingle."

Shuffling through the crowd of people, I tried not to appear as uncomfortable as I felt. This was a mistake. They all seemed worldly and sophisticated. Even their laughs sounded eloquent as I politely pushed my way through.

I wondered how many other prominent storybook characters were gathered in this room tonight. It was hard to tell just by looking, especially considering the lavish dress code.

I made my way outside to the balcony after Cinderella and Andrew had managed to wrangle her sisters away from that poor man, who I assumed had gone to hide immediately. The chatter melted away as I peered over the kingdom. Lights twinkled across the village below for as far as I could see. The snow had finally melted, and the air wasn't quite as harsh tonight. I took a deep breath in, taking in the stillness of the moment. Then I heard the glass doors softly open behind me.

"Good evening, love." His voice sent shockwaves through my body.

My breath caught in my throat as I turned to face him. He took a slow step forward in return, and I couldn't help but notice how devastatingly handsome he was in this very moment. He was always handsome, of course, but seeing him standing there in his royal, blue-fitted embroidered coat...God, it was almost heartbreaking.

"You look beautiful." His eyes went soft.

"Where in the hell have you been?" I whispered.

"Out with Andrew. He had us all up at the crack of dawn. We've been hunting, fencing, and even sitting in on his meetings. The royals don't seem to place much value on having spare time. I don't know why the bloody hell he'd think we'd want to go to those excruciating things..."

I ran to him, throwing my arms around his neck as I buried my face in his shoulder. "I thought you left me," I divulged.

His arms instinctively wrapped around me. "You know me better than that, love."

"I'm sorry, Demetri. For everything that I've done. Everything that I've said." The confession poured out. "I know I took you for granted.

You didn't have to help me, but you did. I just wanted you to know I'm sorry."

He ran his hand down my back. "There is no need for apologies, love. If anything, I feel as though I should be the one saying sorry. I got a bit caught up in the moment the other night and said some things that I shouldn't have said."

"You've risked your life so many times for me..." I shook my head. "And I haven't been..."

Demetri grazed his fingers down the side of my face, stopping only when he reached my lips. "Aye, and I'd do it a hundred times more."

"I never wanted to hurt you or make you feel the way I did the other night." The words were strained as I spoke them out loud.

His eyes searched mine as his hand found its way under my chin. He lifted my face to his and pulled me closer.

"Gwen! There you are!" A musical voice sounded over all the others as the doors swung open. "And you found Demetri! How wonderful." Cinderella beamed, oblivious to her accidental intrusion.

He dropped his arm and stepped back tentatively.

"Hurry, they're about to do the introductions!" She eagerly motioned us inside.

We piled into a line outside the main ballroom with some of the familiar faces I'd seen over the last couple of days.

"How's your leg?" I asked, noticing the absence of the slight limp he'd been carrying.

"Good as new," he smiled. "Thanks to Isadora."

I peered around at the people standing around us. "Why are they introducing Cinderella and Andrew? It's their castle; doesn't everyone already know who they are?" I whispered to Demetri, careful not to be overheard.

"Formalities," he replied as he slipped his arm around mine.

"What's with the line? Shouldn't we be inside to see them announced?"

"We'll be there in time to see that after they introduce us."

"I'm sorry, what was that?" I stammered.

The line moved forward as I realized there was only one more couple in front of us now.

"We're guests of the royals, so they'll introduce us also."

My eyes went wide with fear. "Isn't everyone here considered a guest? I don't want to be announced in front of all those people!"

The doors opened dramatically as the couple in front of us was announced. They promptly descended the ballroom staircase. Once they'd cleared the way, the doors snapped shut again in front of us.

"Demetri, I know I never told you this, but I don't do well in front of big crowds. It stems back to my public speaking class in college. Come on. Let's leave before the doors open again."

"Luckily for you, love, there is no public speaking required."

"I have to admit that does not make me feel any better."

"Just focus on me. Don't look at anyone else." He smiled down at me, and for an instant, my nerves fell silent. Then, the doors swung open.

"Mr. Demetri Alexander Hawkins and Ms. Gwendolyn Elizabeth Winters." The voice rang out.

"How the hell do they know my middle name?" My voice cracked.

Demetri stifled a laugh as he led me down the staircase. I clung to him tightly, trying to ignore the sea of eyes fixated on us as we entered the crowd.

"Gwen," Demetri whispered, sensing my oncoming panic attack. "Look at me."

I obeyed, melting as his smile washed over me. It wasn't the devastating smile that would have surely sent me tumbling down the stairs. No, this was the one he wore in the moments when I'd catch him staring at me from across the room. This was the soft and familiar one that warmed the coldest, darkest parts of my heart like rays of morning sunlight. I found myself trying to memorize the way his lips curved and the way his dark blue eyes twinkled like shooting stars under the flickering lights of the chandeliers. I knew what he was doing, effortlessly distracting me from the terror of everyone else staring at us. It worked. His eyes were now the only ones in this room that I was remotely concerned with.

"There, it's over," he whispered as we took our spot with the other couples.

"That was...the worst," I lied.

We watched as everyone else's name was announced. The roll call ended with applause as Cinderella and Andrew finally made their appearance last.

"I'm not sure how or why you're such an expert at how things are done at royal functions, but I'm glad that one of us at least knows what we're doing."

"How fortunate you are to have me here to show you the way." Demetri laughed to himself. It was admittedly cute how he found himself so funny sometimes.

"It would seem so," I reciprocated.

"Perhaps you'll allow me to help you blend in even more."

"How do you propose to do that?"

He turned to face me before extending out his hand. "Dance with me."

"Demetri, I can't dance..." I felt my cheeks growing hot under his penetrating gaze. "Not like this anyway." I watched as the couples swirled around us gracefully and envisioned the looks of horror that would surely ensue if they witnessed any similar attempts from me.

"You needn't do anything but take my hand."

"But..."

"Take my hand, love," he instructed. "Or else I'll have to drag you out here and make a scene. And you know I'll have no qualms about doing so."

The look on his face indicated that the threat wasn't a bluff. I swallowed nervously, glancing around at the crowd once more.

"Gwendolyn." His voice lowered an octave, the sound of it humming through my bones. "I want to dance with you. Please allow me the immense honor."

My reservations dissipated at the sound of my name, and I placed my hand into his. He pulled me closer, expertly wrapping his other arm around my waist.

"Just follow my lead," he reassured me as he intuitively stepped in time to the music.

A surprised smile spread across my face as he twirled me around. He was just as graceful as everyone else in attendance, if not more so. I wasn't sure what I was expecting when it came to his dancing skillset, but this certainly wasn't it.

"Is ballroom dancing a requirement to living in this realm? You're a pirate, for God's sake," I blushed as he pulled me in close again. "How do you even know how to do this? Do you practice with Felix?"

His head tilted back as he let out an exuberant laugh, much like the one I'd heard that night in Mystic Grove as he sat around the fire. "I like that I can still surprise you."

"I don't normally like surprises." I smiled again. "But, this is a pleasant one."

He pulled my hand up higher, spinning me around again before wrapping his arm around my waist and lowering me into a dip.

The music faded away instantaneously, and I found myself swimming in the shadows of his stormy gaze. The people brushing by us morphed into slow-motion blurs as my feet sought to find solid ground again. I searched his torn expression as we stood still in the middle of all the indistinctive figures silently swooping past. He lifted his hand to my face and tilted my chin up once more, just as he'd done on the balcony earlier tonight. Then he pressed his lips to mine.

It wasn't like the first time. It wasn't frenzied or forceful. It was slow and all-consuming. Demetri took his time, letting his fingers wind through the back of my hair. Melting into his frame as he pulled me closer, I opened my mouth to allow him deeper access. I had no fight left in me when it came to this man. He drew me to him like the tide, and right here, right now, I was more than willing to be swept away. I'd resisted this urge for too long, but I no longer had the strength or desire to do that anymore. I didn't care who saw us. No one else mattered. There was only him.

He pulled away slowly, bringing his lips to my neck, and I struggled to keep my composure as the rush of voices soared back to life around us.

"Perhaps...we should go somewhere more private," he uttered lowly against my ear.

His words electrified every sensation in my body. I simply nodded, completely aware that I was in no position to refuse him.

He took my hand and led me through the crowd of blurred faces. Our impatient footsteps echoed as I followed him up the staircase and down a desolate hallway. Unable to control himself for another moment, he pushed me up against the wall, a gasp escaping my mouth as his lips found mine again.

I needed all of him, and I needed it now. I dug my fingers into his chest as I tried to tear off his coat. He stepped back, snatching it off in haste before tossing it to the floor.

My body trembled underneath his ravenous gaze. He took a step forward, rolling up the sleeves of his shirt as he did, and dragged a hand through his disheveled hair.

My heart felt like it might just explode. I had never wanted someone this much...never felt such a desperate desire. Nothing I had ever experienced in my twenty-eight years of life compared to the way Demetri was staring at me right now.

"I am yours, Gwen." His voice hummed deep and low for only me to hear. The reverberation sent waves of adrenaline rolling through my core. "Tell me that you're mine."

I was physically incapable of looking away from him. "Yes." It was all I could manage to whisper before he cupped my face in his hand and leaned down to steal another deep kiss. My head was spinning irrepressibly as I braced myself against the wall.

He swooped his arm underneath me, lifting me up as he pressed his body against mine, and I impulsively wrapped my legs around him.

"Fuck," he uttered under his breath. "What are you doing to me?" He moved his other hand to my hair, tugging my head back as he trailed his lips down my throat and across my chest.

"Demetri..." I breathed. "Oh my God." I couldn't even think straight with his hands on me like this.

My words fueled him even further, and he growled as he pushed me harder against the wall. I ran my hands over his body, feeling the way his muscles tensed under the thin fabric of his shirt. He pressed his hips into me, and I could tell he was just as ready as I was.

"Wait..." I whispered, pulling away from his lips.

"Don't make me wait any longer, love," He groaned, gripping my legs harder.

"No...listen." I hushed him. "Do you hear that?"

He froze as the distant murmur of voices grew louder.

"It is truly an honor to have you here this evening," a voice echoed from down the hallway, followed by the sound of a creaking door.

Demetri drew back, glancing around as he let my legs fall back to the floor.

"I'd like to extend my apologies for arriving late. We had some unexpected occurrences on our journey," another man responded, a bit louder now.

"Dammit. Quickly...in here." Demetri grabbed his coat from the floor and pulled me inside the nearest doorway.

"Cinderella will be delighted to see you," the first voice—that I now recognized to be Prince Andrew's—replied. "It has been far too long, Phillip."

"Phillip?" I whispered in a panic. My eyes grew wide at the realization. I stared up at Demetri as he raised a finger to his lips.

"Indeed. The blame is mine. Kingdom affairs have been keeping me quite busy, but it's wonderful to be here now," Phillip responded.

Demetri pushed me deeper into the shadows of the room. My shallow breaths nearly ceased altogether as the footsteps neared the door and grew louder. I closed my eyes as they passed by the threshold, then allowed myself a moment of relief as they faded from earshot.

"What are we going to do?" My words came out soft and shaky.

"We're getting the bloody hell out of here," Demetri whispered back.

"We can't do that!" I said, a little louder than I intended.

"Shh!" He pressed his finger against my lips. "Are you mad? If he finds us here, he will undoubtedly have us killed."

"We haven't accomplished anything here. We can't just leave now. We might not get another chance to talk to Isadora."

"We'll find another way. It's far too risky to stay here another night."

"Aren't you tired of running, Demetri? It's all we seem to do."

"I'm a pirate, love," he said, brushing his hand down my arm. "I've been running all my life. It's typically in my best interest."

"Maybe you're right..." I whispered, defeated. There was no telling what Phillip would do if he knew his escaped prisoners were right here under his nose.

"Right, well, let's get on with it then. I'll fetch a few things from my room, and as much as I enjoy you in that dress, perhaps a more practical set of clothes would be better suited." He extended a regretful gaze across my body.

I silently fought against my better judgment. I knew Demetri was right about fleeing from Phillip. I wasn't sure what jurisdiction he'd have in this land, if any, but it was far too risky to tempt it. On the other hand, we *had* come all this way. To leave now would undermine everything, and I wasn't even sure how long I had until Cosmina's potentially destructive deadline.

"We could hide out in my room for the night...just lock the doors. No one would find us." I whispered, attempting to sway him the best way I knew how. "We could...finish what we started in the hallway," I suggested, still swirling from the euphoria of it all.

"And in the morning?" He snapped. "We'll just join our old friend for breakfast and catch up in the drawing room? Perhaps he'll even join the men on their mandatory hunting trip. It's sure to be a rousing good time."

"Okay...okay. I hadn't planned that far ahead."

"Listen, love. It's better to get a head start, especially while everyone is distracted. By the time they realize we're missing, he won't even know where to start looking."

"Fine," I ultimately conceded. "I suppose you're right. Let's go get our things."

We snuck through the hollow hallways cautiously, peering around every corner and freezing under every audible sound until we reached my room.

"Go on, pack only what you need," Demetri commanded as he shut the door behind us to my room. "I'll go gather my things and meet you right back here. Don't let anyone else into your room."

"Where will we go?"

"We could head south." His eyes searched my face for validation. "Perhaps we can make our way back to Mystic Village and just wait there for Isadora to come back home."

"Through the snowy mountain range where all the giant rock monsters live, and we almost died? Yeah. Great idea." I blurted.

He rolled his eyes before grabbing the doorknob a little too aggressively. "We'll figure it out. Don't open this until I get back."

I allowed a few moments to pass before I ventured back into the hallway. Perhaps it was Demetri's condescending tone, or perhaps it was the thought of leaving here without any resolution, but I had to try to find Isadora, and I had to do it now. We had come too far to just give up. Demetri would be angry, of course, when he came back to find me gone. But it wasn't anything I couldn't handle.

I peeked around the corner of the hall before making my way back toward the ballroom. As the music grew louder with each step, my sense of terror equally intensified.

This was a bad idea. I should turn around. Maybe we *could* just try to make it back to Mystic Grove as Demetri had suggested. But who's to say we would be lucky enough to survive the journey through the snowy mountain range again? No...I shook off the uncertainty. It had to be tonight.

I wandered onto one of the several balconies that overlooked the ballroom. It was secluded enough to spy on the guests without worrying too much about who might be watching me.

Odessa and Rosalind had cornered the same poor man who had managed to escape them earlier, and now they looked as though they were trying to drag him out onto the dance floor.

Morgana and Royce were in the middle of the floor with a circle of onlookers, and Eli and Vanessa were chatting with a large group in the corner of the room.

There was no sign of Cinderella, Andrew, or Phillip.

"There you are," a furious growl rumbled as a hand latched onto my arm and snatched me out of view.

"What the bloody hell do you think you're doing?" Demetri pushed me up against the wall, but it wasn't as enjoyable this time as I witnessed the rage boiling behind his hardened stare.

"I know. I'm sorry, I just can't leave, Demetri. Not yet."

He closed his eyes and stepped away as though he were trying to collect himself.

"We almost died in those mountains. Do you really want to press our luck again?" I asked, reaching for him. "I, for one, don't."

"We can head south and go around them," he started. "It would take longer, but-—"

"No, Demetri. I'm not going." I announced. "I understand your reasoning, but please...try to understand mine."

He swung his gaze away from me, and I watched as his jaw flexed in response to my defiance.

"Demetri...." I whispered, reaching for his hand and pulling him closer.

He sighed in defeat as he tightened his fingers around mine. "Fine. We'll try it your way. Let's go find Isadora, shall we?"

CHAPTER TWENTY-TWO

Demetri insisted on walking ahead of me to be the first line of defense. We slipped past the noise of the ballroom, finding a door in the nearby study that led outside.

"Where are we going?" I whispered, silently wondering if Demetri was only trying to lead me far away from the castle and the dangers that lurked within.

"The gardens," he responded. "We'll be able to see into the ballroom without exposing ourselves."

That was a good idea. The windows on this side of the castle were enormous and provided us with an ideal place to lie in wait. All we needed to do was place our eyes on Isadora and make our move.

"Do you see her?" I asked, squinting past the vibrant, revolving dancers.

"Not yet."

We took cover behind a tall row of hedges as he peered around the side.

"I see Cinderella and Andrew..." He paused; his voice twisted into a raspy rage. "Phillip is with them."

"Well, at least he's occupied." I stole a glance around the corner to see for myself.

Phillip stood laughing with the royal couple. His hand rested on his chest as he threw his head back in amusement. If I didn't know any better, I might have accidentally assumed he was an amicable person. Cinderella and Andrew certainly seemed to think so.

Demetri's fury felt palpable as it settled in the air. "I could kill him."

"Yeah, I know what you mean." I fought down the memory of that night. Of the way he'd pushed me to the table and the unspeakable things that had almost followed.

My heart raced as the repulsive thoughts of what he wanted to do consumed me. I tore my eyes away from his laughing figure; I couldn't bear to look at it anymore.

When I did, my focus settled on another familiar form. "Demetri, there's Isadora." I grabbed his arm. "She's going up the stairs."

"Stay here," he commanded. "I'll go find her and bring her to you."

"No! What if you get caught?"

"Your utter lack of faith in me is painful, love."

"Fine," I complied. "Be careful."

"Don't move." His tone conveyed a warning that I had no intention of defying this time.

"I won't."

And with that agreement, he was gone. I watched the windows anxiously, despite knowing Demetri would keep his distance from the ballroom...and from Phillip.

The minutes that followed were excruciatingly long. I tried to fill them by rehearsing the words that I'd soon have to tell Isadora. What would she say? Would she even believe me? I'd have to tell her about Zola. The thought of that alone terrified me.

I took a deep breath and peered around the hedge again. There was still no sight of either one of them. My stomach twisted in knots. Would Isadora even be able to help me? And if she could...*would* she?

My thoughts settled on Jacob and Bree. I wasn't even sure how long I'd been away anymore; in some ways, it felt like a lifetime. I had no clue what I was going to tell them when I got back home.

Home. The thought washed over me, providing an air of comfort as the memories of a life once lived wrapped its arms around me like an old friend. But there was something else, too—an increasing sense of trepidation. But how could there not be? After everything that had happened here, I always knew there was a chance this wouldn't work...a very considerable chance.

I couldn't let those doubts creep in now. They'd eat me alive if I allowed them to.

The approaching footsteps silenced my screaming thoughts.

"Finally," I breathed, turning toward him as he stepped around the corner. "Did you have any luck?"

But the man who stood before me wasn't Demetri.

Phillip laughed to himself as he took me in. My heartbeat stuttered under his watch as I instinctively took a step backward.

"It's been a while, Gwendolyn," Phillip taunted. "You know, I didn't think much of it when Cinderella said she was hosting several new guests in town for the ball." He flashed a threatening smile, one that didn't reach his wicked eyes. "But imagine my surprise when I walked out onto the balcony and saw your face peering back at me from the garden."

"I wasn't looking at you," I said through gritted teeth.

"I sense you still have hard feelings about the way we left things." He inched closer.

"You could say that." I glared.

His egotistic laugh made my insides coil.

"Did you follow me here?"

"Follow *you*? Across the whole world?" He huffed in amusement as he cornered me against the ivy wall. "Darling, you are hardly that significant. Seeing you here tonight was purely coincidental."

"What do you want, Phillip?" I scowled.

He smirked at the disrespect. "I wonder how surprised Andrew and Cinderella would be to know they've been hosting an escaped prisoner of my kingdom."

"I wonder how surprised they'd be to know you tried to have me killed after I wouldn't let you rape me on your dining room table," I retorted.

He sprung forward, pushing me into the prickly hedge as his hand latched around my throat. "Tsk Tsk." He sneered as he stared down at me with darkening eyes. "Honestly, darling. Who do you think they would believe?"

I struggled under his grasp, forced to relive the moments when I was last put in the same precarious position. I raised my knee up to strike, a move that he was clearly expecting. Before I could make contact, he repositioned his stance and let his free fist fly up at me. It slammed into my side, knocking the breath out of me.

He dropped his hand from my throat as I doubled over, catching myself with my hands as my knees hit the ground.

Phillip's laugh echoed around me as the pain blasted through my ribs.

He kneeled in front of me, meeting my hardened gaze. "How does it feel to get what you deserve?"

"I don't know," I muttered, inhaling as deeply as I could manage through the sting. "You tell me." I thrust up, slamming my head against his face as hard as I could. I heard his body collapse on the ground as I regained my footing and raced back toward the castle.

"Whoa, whoa, whoa!" Demetri caught me in an embrace as I turned the corner of the garden wall. "Where are you going?" he exclaimed.

Isadora appeared beside him. "Oh, my word! You're bleeding, dear!"

"Phillip found me," I said through an explosion of ferocious tears.

"Where is he?" Demetri's eyes darted around wildly behind me.

"Come here, my dear." Isadora displayed her wand and touched it to my head. A flash of blue light beamed from the tip, and the pain substantially subsided by the time she pulled it away.

"How's that?" She inspected the gash from which my blood had just been streaming.

"Better," I responded, wiping the tears away.

"Sometimes it takes a few moments for the pain to fully dissolve."

"We need to get out of here," I asserted.

Demetri's furious expression revealed that he had other thoughts in mind, but he inevitably complied with my request.

Once we were back inside the castle, we followed Isadora to a secluded room on the second floor.

"What did he do to you?" Demetri demanded once the door had been secured.

Isadora lit the lanterns in the room with the flick of her wrist.

"He saw me in the garden..." I began, not wanting to share more details than necessary in front of Isadora just yet. "When I was waiting for you."

Another beam of blue light flickered from her direction, followed by the sound of two armchairs sliding across the floor.

"Sit down, dears," she instructed as the chairs came to a halt behind us. "What is going on?"

"I'm sorry that you had to see that," I started, still trying to shake off the feeling of Phillip's fingers wrapped around my neck. "The truth is, I've been wanting to talk with you since we arrived in Winterhaven, but seeing Phillip tonight was not exactly part of the plan."

"Tell me everything," she insisted.

"I don't really know where to begin," I admitted. "Your daughter, Charlotte, said maybe you could help me."

"You know my daughter?"

"No, not exactly. We met her back at your home when we were trying to find you. She told us you were here in Winterhaven but that you wouldn't be back for several weeks. We couldn't really wait that long. You see, we had already traveled so far...and we had left Demetri's crew at Mystic Grove...and there may or may not be some sort of deadline..." I began to ramble.

"We were initially looking for a witch named Cosmina," Demetri interjected. "Charlotte suggested we seek you out instead."

"Cosmina?" Isadora asked suspiciously, her eyes shooting suspiciously between ours. "Why were you looking for her?"

"Because she sent me here, to this world," I confessed. "And I know how insane this all sounds," I stifled a nervous laugh. "I know you might not believe it. But Cosmina sent me here, and we've been looking for her ever since...so I can go back home."

Isadora fell silent for several moments.

"Is there anything you can do? To help me?" I pleaded.

Isadora looked down at her lap before responding, as though she were weighing her unspoken words. "Cosmina is my sister," she finally confessed.

"What?" I whispered, scrutinizing her face in an effort to see the similarities that weren't there.

"I haven't seen her in years, not since the queen's curse befell." Her face was solemn.

"She and I forged very different paths in life," Isadora began. "We were both born with incredible capabilities, ones that our mother passed on to us. However, such gifts never come without heavy burdens to bear." Isadora's wistful gaze hinted at stories I would never know the full extent of.

"What do you mean by burdens?" I pressed.

Isadora's eyes settled over me. "It's the decisions we make over the course of time that shape the journeys we walk in this life." She hesitated uneasily. "Cosmina and I made different decisions. Her power was magnificent, and she could have used it to do great things...to help so many people. But she chose wrong. She didn't care what it cost her, and it proved to be her biggest downfall."

Demetri and I sat silently, waiting for whatever additional details Isadora was willing to provide us with.

"Her decisions quite literally changed her," she continued. "Every choice she made, every horrible thing she did...it slowly tainted her power—her soul—with darkness. I saw it happening. I realized she was slipping away, day by day, from what she could have become. It consumed her." Isadora's lips tightened into a thin line. "She grew to resent me when it was too late to change her fate's design...when she realized how miserable she would be for the rest of her life and that there was no one else to blame."

"Is she more powerful than you?" Demetri inquired.

"More powerful?" Isadora contemplated for several moments. "I suppose that is subjective. There are differences in our capabilities. The abilities Cosmina lacks compose my strongest powers and vice versa," she explained. "Light and dark magic so rarely overlap, you see. Cosmina is capable of great and terrible things, and she has no conscience to stop her from doing either of them."

"Like sending me here," I muttered.

"Yes." Isadora nodded. "I rarely know the reasons for the things that she does, and I'm afraid that still rings true in this case." Isadora clasped her hands together. "Is there anything you can think of that would have made her single you out?"

"I wish I knew," I said, shaking my head as the events of that fateful night played through my head. "I was at my friend's wedding, and Cosmina was there. She was pretending to be a fortune teller, and she lured me into her tent. That's when everything happened."

"My sister wasn't pretending about that," Isadora acknowledged. "She can indeed see glimpses of the future, but they do tend to be subjective."

"She showed me...myself. She had a crystal ball. I saw myself running through the woods, wearing the dress I had on that night."

"Cosmina can pass her visions onto others through various means. Do you remember, dear, if she told you anything when she showed you the premonition?"

"She only said there was something that I needed to do here, but she never elaborated on what that was. She said something about the sky and a snow moon and that 'great evils' existed...and that I was somehow relevant to all of it."

Isadora considered me as I spoke, her face twisting with confusion as she waited for more information. "That's all she said?"

"That was the gist of it anyway," I confirmed. "But I have no connections to this world. She basically threw me here and left me to fend for myself."

Demetri stared blankly as I recounted the more extensive details of the events that had occurred. I told Isadora about Phillip and the reasons behind why he had attacked me earlier tonight. I told her about Demetri saving my life back in Castleberry. I told her about our journey across the sea, the sirens we encountered along the way, and of our journey through Mystic Grove.

Isadora listened carefully to everything and only spoke after I recounted our conversation with Charlotte.

"What Charlotte told you was correct," she said. "If you were able to find Cosmina, she probably wouldn't send you home, not until you've completed whatever immoral task it is she wants you to do." Isadora rubbed her temple as though she were trying to piece the deluded puzzle pieces together.

"There's something else I need to tell you..." I stammered, glancing over at Demetri for moral support.

"What's that, dear?" she asked.

"When Cinderella found us, we had been stranded in the mountains for several days," I began. "...And the reason we were stranded was because the rock giants spooked Zola."

"Zola?" Isadora's eyes lifted at the mention of her name.

"Yes..." I muttered.

Isadora glanced between me and Demetri. "She can fly now," I revealed.

Isadora scoffed in disbelief. "Zola has never been able to fly."

Demetri cleared his throat, signaling that he was about to take the reins of the uncomfortable conversation. "I'd first like to clarify that Zola is fine. But Gwen is correct. She now possesses the ability to fly."

"How is that possible?"

"Charlotte told us the story about what happened to her, how her wings were broken," Demetri replied. "The vial of fairy dust we were gifted on our journey, the one that helped save Gwen's life after she was scratched by the siren, we thought it might help Zola as well."

"And it worked?" Isadora's expression was one of astonishment. "Zola can fly?"

"She can indeed," he confirmed. "She took us halfway across the mountain range. When the noise of the giants scared her, we crashed. Gwen used what was left of the dust to save my life and heal Zola's newly injured wing."

"Where is she now?" Isadora asked.

"She flew off after that, but she came back. She brought us here to Winterhaven...to you. I imagine she flew back home after that."

A tear slid down Isadora's cheek.

"I'm so sorry, Isadora," I said, waiting for the repercussions of what we had done. "While we did need her wings to get here, it wasn't the only reason we did it...we wanted to help her too."

"In your conversation with Charlotte, did she ever tell you who injured Zola?" she asked, disregarding my apology.

"No..." I responded.

"My sister." Another tear fell at her admission. "It's the reason I couldn't restore Zola completely. Because the same blood that runs through my veins runs through Cosmina's. And no spell, curse, or incantation can fully be expelled if it was committed by the same bloodline. It's the same reason she cannot fatally harm me or Charlotte."

"Cosmina did that?" I whispered in disbelief.

"Yes. Because she knew how much Zola meant to me. And how much Zola's mother, Pheresa, meant to me."

"Isadora, I..." my voice trailed off. "I had no idea."

"Thank you." Her eyes glistened as she took hold of mine and Demetri's hands. "For helping Zola. For doing what I never could for her. I cannot tell you what it means to me."

"Why didn't anyone else ever help her?" Demetri asked. "There are other witches and wizards. Surely, they could have tried."

"Cosmina is very powerful," Isadora answered, her voice still quaking. "More powerful than most. The darkness that corrupted her feeds into her magic, making it stronger. Beyond that, there are no limits to the crimes she would commit. No one crosses her because they are afraid of what she might do to them or their loved ones."

"Will she come back...to hurt Zola again?" I asked.

Isadora shook her head. "Certain measures were put into place after what Cosmina did. I placed a protection spell over Zola that would shield her from dark magic. Because she has already been touched by it once, it would counteract anything Cosmina could ever try," she hesitated, seeming to reflect on the situation. "After that, I banished her to Mystic Grove, trapping her behind a wall that was intended to negate her powers."

"That was you?" I asked, reflecting on the centaur's story and the sting of the mist that was left behind. "You cast the spell between the lands?"

"Yes. I couldn't risk her hurting anyone else in my village. She was too dangerous, too vengeful. She needed to be contained. It worked for a while, but she eventually managed to escape."

"That's what the centaurs said when we encountered them," Demetri added.

"I still don't know how she escaped, but I imagine the extensive effort it took for her to break through the wall weakened her magic. It was a strong barrier." Isadora took in our stunned expressions. "Despite that, she is still undoubtedly dangerous."

"Do you even know where she is?" I asked.

"I suspect she's been staying somewhere secluded, somewhere no one can find her as she tries to regain some of her strength. While I have no way of truly knowing, I have a feeling she's taken refuge in Seaspire."

My thoughts filtered back to Demetri's revelation that night in the castle bedroom. "But the curse?" I asked. "Does it not affect her?"

Isadora shook her head. "Because the curse was created with dark magic, Cosmina could essentially use it in her favor to rebuild her strength...by stealing it from the land. Such practices are frowned upon, but kingdom decrees have never stopped her before."

"So, if finding Cosmina is out of the question, what am I supposed to do?" I asked. "Please tell me there's some way you can help me, Isadora."

She gazed at me as sorrow gradually etched the lines on her face. "I'm sorry, dear," she began. "If I could, I would. I don't have my sister's ability to open portals or to see into the future. I can't begin to know what Cosmina saw that drew you to her, or the reasons why she sent you here. I'm afraid that I alone am unable to send you back to your home."

I sat frozen as Isadora's chilling words swirled around me. Demetri's hand found its way to mine. The warmth radiated up my arm and through my core, but it was still not enough to bring me any peace of mind...still not enough to recover from the crushing weight of this agonizing emptiness. I'd never see my home again. Jacob, Bree, my family...they were no longer a part of my life.

I exhaled deeply, too aware of the hollow heartbeat barely thumping in my chest...too aware of the way my grip tightened around Demetri's hand as my nails dug into his palm...too aware of Isadora's eyes regretfully resting on me. Her mouth still moved, but none of the words coming out mattered anymore. I couldn't even hear them. I didn't want to. There was nothing left to say. There was no hope left here.

CHAPTER TWENTY-THREE

A knock sounded at the door.

"Isadora?" Cinderella's voice shook on the other side. "Are you in there?"

"Yes, dear," Isadora got up and stepped toward the door. "Is everything alright?"

"Can I come in?"

Isadora glanced at us before responding, "Certainly, dear."

The door creaked open as Cinderella and Andrew stood waiting. Standing behind them was an angry and bloodied-up Phillip.

For a moment, everyone stood silently as we waited to see who dared to start the war first.

"I've told them everything," Phillip said as he barged past the couple. His eyes burned with vengeance, and they were solely fixated on me.

"Is it true, Gwen?" Cinderella asked warily. "Were you a prisoner of Castleberry?"

"Yes," I admitted. "But there's much more to the story that you don't know."

Demetri slid his chair out and stood and Phillip's wrathful attention shifted to him.

"Why, Mr. Hawkins. What a pleasure it is to see you again," Phillip declared with a sarcastic laugh.

"You have no jurisdiction in this land," Demetri spat. Rage radiated from his body as he took a defensive step closer to the sadistic prince.

"Smart words coming from a thieving pirate."

Cinderella's and Andrew's eyes went wide at the accusation.

Demetri's jaw tensed as he visibly tried to restrain himself.

Phillip sneered in satisfaction as he watched. "We have already settled our quarrel, Mr. Hawkins. I suggest you don't try to create a new one."

"That's enough," Demetri snapped.

I stared back and forth between the two men, unsure of what was transpiring right before me.

"What's he talking about?" I asked Demetri.

A twisted, repulsive smile took form on Phillip's face as he glared between us, but Demetri said nothing.

"Demetri, what's going on?" I asked again as I rose from my chair.

"You should know this by now, darling." Phillip taunted, reaching into his coat. "You can never truly trust a pirate." He pulled out a small black bag and tossed it at Demetri's feet as the gold coins inside spilled out onto the floor. "For your trouble."

My eyes darted up to Demetri, waiting for his response. Waiting for a reaction, a repercussion. Waiting for him to do something besides just fucking stand there...God, Demetri, *do something*.

But something never came.

Isadora now stood at Cinderella's side with her wand drawn, eyeing every move that Phillip made.

"Now, if Andrew and Cinderella see fit, I shall take my prisoner back to Castleberry where a suitable punishment will be carried out."

"Phillip, we agreed to hear Gwen's side of the story," Andrew interjected.

"Of course," Phillip nodded before glaring back at me. "Go on then, tell them what happened. Tell them about the ways you have physically assaulted me and endangered my life on numerous occasions...a crime that is punishable by death, might I add."

"This wasn't what we agreed on," Demetri finally said through gritted teeth.

"Refresh my memory, pirate. What was it exactly that we agreed on?"

I stared in disbelief as Demetri's face silently shifted from rage to agony.

"Are you having a hard time recalling the details?" Phillip's voice intruded. "Think hard, pirate."

Demetri turned to me. His eyes held an intangible pain that I had never seen there before. A pain he'd never revealed, not even when he was injured or recounting the trauma of his childhood.

"I think you remember the details just fine," Phillip boomed through the silence. "I think the problem here is that you just don't want to admit them out loud."

"I never intended for this to happen," Demetri confessed. His conquered gaze broke away from mine.

My heart felt as though it might explode through my chest. "I still don't understand."

"You see Gwendolyn, Mr. Hawkins here made a deal that fateful night when the two of you met in the castle dungeon," Phillip said. "His life for yours."

"That was never the deal!" Demetri roared.

Phillip ignored the outburst. "When the guards brought him to me, I wanted nothing more than to pierce my sword through his heart. We have a bit of a distressing history, you see. But then he made me an offer I just couldn't refuse."

Phillip stepped closer to us, "He assured me, if I let him go that night, if I didn't end his life, he'd help me find the one thing that I've been desperately searching for."

"The princess," I whispered.

Phillip smiled in response. "Mr. Hawkins revealed to me that you had arrived to this world in a rather precarious manner. That you were sent from another realm," He hesitated. "…Which I'll admit sounded very curious. Nevertheless, stranger things have happened."

He paced in front of us, the smeared blood on his face melting into the color of his ugly cape.

"And then he said that you were in search of a witch who sent you through a portal. He suggested you may even be a sorceress yourself. But as I'm sure you remember, we determined that not to be true." Phillip smiled to himself as though he were reliving fond memories.

My chest caved in as Phillip relayed the news of Demetri's betrayal to me. I couldn't breathe. Phillip had known all along I was lying to him that night. Demetri had told him everything I had confessed to him in the dungeon cell, even after he had told me not to say anything to anyone…all just to save his own skin. All just to use it against me when it benefited him the most.

Isadora's stance remained unchanged. She already knew most of these truths. Andrew and Cinderella were another story. Their expressions of shock became more striking by the second.

"And a witch who has the capability to open portals to other lands would certainly allow me to find Gabriella rather quickly. There'd be no place left for her to hide."

"And what makes you think the witch would even help you?" I spat.

"Power is persuasive, darling. Just ask your pirate."

It was all I could do to keep my head straight, to force myself not to turn and face Demetri. I wanted to face him. I wanted to see his reaction to the truth being spilled like fresh blood on the floor. But what I wasn't going to do was give him the satisfaction of seeing how absolutely gutted I was.

"After all, he's the one who proposed the idea that he would find her under the guise that he was helping you. It was an impressive plan, truly. I would let you escape the dungeon...or let you think that you had, anyway. Then, you and the pirate would sail off on your adventurous little journey to Mystic Grove, where you'd lead him straight to the witch for me."

"No..." I whispered. It was too much to process all at once.

"Foolish brat," Phillip taunted. "Who do you think gave him the keys to the cell? Who do you think told him the way out?"

"But the guards..." I tried to rationalize.

"The guards weren't aware of the deal," Phillip dismissed.

I felt Demetri's eyes burning holes through the side of my head as though he were pleading with me to look at him, but everything inside me was screaming. He never cared. He never wanted to help me. Everything he had done...he only did to save himself. Tears pooled together in my eyes, blurring my vision.

"That's when things got a bit more difficult, though," Phillip mused. "I already had plans to come to Winterhaven this year for the celebrations. So, my crew followed several miles behind your ship...up until they realized you were headed straight for the sirens. That's when we turned north and headed for the Frozen Sea."

He grinned at Demetri. "I was planning to resume our mission after I left Winterhaven. To meet you back in the village just as we initially agreed." He laughed to himself. "I suppose now I don't have to."

"Oh my," Cinderella's distressed whisper broke the silence that followed.

Phillip turned to her, his expression shifting to one of artificial sympathy. "I do profoundly apologize for how this has impacted the festivities."

She didn't even look at him.

"Gwen," she finally said, "is all of this true?"

I looked to where she stood, to where everyone's gazes were fixed on me as they waited for a response.

"It would seem so," I managed to voice.

Phillip laughed to himself, turning his attention back to Demetri. "So, tell me, Hawkins, were you ever able to find that witch?"

"No," Demetri muttered.

Phillip sighed. "I must admit I expected more from you, especially considering there was so much on the line. You assured me you'd find her."

"No one will find her if she doesn't want to be found," Isadora interrupted, gripping her wand tighter as she glared at Phillip.

"All right...all right...everyone, let's calm down," Cinderella demanded, looking to her husband for some sort of guidance.

"It's a shame, though," Phillip said to Demetri, "that you didn't uphold your side of the bargain. You knew the price that would have to be paid."

"No," Demetri retorted, his voice shaded with fury. "We can still find her."

"I'm afraid your time is up, and frankly, you've proven yourself to be quite worthless to me. I must now employ other options...but not before I collect my payment."

Phillip held out his hand to me, motioning me forward. "We can do this the easy way or the hard way, darling."

"Take me," Demetri demanded. "I'm the one who ruined the deal. She knew nothing of it."

"While that may be true, the conditions were clear and were meant to serve as your motivation: bring me the witch, or the girl returns to my custody."

"Now, Phillip, I'm not sure if that's even lawful." Andrew entered the conversation. "Not when she did nothing to warrant an arrest."

"Oh, but she did." Phillip pointed to his face. "She assaulted a royal figure. More than once at that."

"You tried to rape me," I whispered.

Cinderella's brows furrowed as she analyzed Phillip.

"Hearsay," was his response. "Of course, you would make those disturbing accusations to condone your reckless behavior. You could never prove those false claims. However, I can stand here before everyone and prove your violent tendencies. They only need to look upon my face to see the truth."

"Gwen, did you do that to Phillip?" Cinderella asked. Something in her tone told me to lie. But I didn't have it in me anymore.

I wasn't sure what had broken me more – the confirmation that I'd never see home again or the revelation of Demetri's treachery. I was just so tired. So tired of running. So tired of trying.

"Yes," I confessed, lifting my eyes to meet Phillip's. "And I'd do it again if given the opportunity."

A wicked smile spread across Phillip's face. It was all the damming evidence that he needed to prove his case.

"Gwen!" Demetri exclaimed as he tried to reach for me. "What the bloody hell are you doing?"

I didn't acknowledge him. "I assaulted Prince Phillip," I said again, louder this time. "And I'm ready to accept whatever punishment comes with it."

Astonishment illuminated the faces of everyone standing in the room.

"Gwen!" Demetri called out again, his voice cracking with disbelief.

Within an instant, guards from Phillip's court marched in from the hallway where they had been waiting and grabbed hold of my arms.

I gathered enough courage to glance at Demetri once last time as they approached.

"Goodbye, Demetri," I whispered as he stared in horror.

It was all I had time to say before the guards led me out of the room, down the staircase, and past the ballroom full of bewildered guests.

CHAPTER TWENTY-FOUR

I'd been here before, but it felt different now. I had been scared of dying back then. Scared of never getting the chance to return home.

And now...now I sat alone in the dark. Now I waited, but not to be rescued. Now I didn't recognize the person who had been here once before. The person who had held on so tightly to the notion of hope. The person who had trusted so blindly and had an unrelenting belief that things would find a way to work out.

That person was a fool. And she didn't exist anymore.

It had been days since I had been brought back to Phillip's dungeon. I wasn't sure exactly what he was waiting on. He had seemed so eager to end my life before we left Winterhaven. He even made sure to visit me several times in his ship's holding cell to tell me all the various ways he had dreamed of doing it.

I wished he'd just get on with it.

Sitting here was torture. Maybe that was what he wanted, to torture me slowly before killing me by making me rot in this same jail cell and reflect on everything that had happened...to force me to relive the way Demetri had crashed into my life just on the other side of those bars. The way it had felt when he came back for me. The way he had risked everything. And most importantly, the way it had all been a lie.

I still couldn't wrap my brain around it, and I didn't want to. Thinking about it only reminded me of the pain...the unbearable, agonizing pain that would spread and consume me completely if I gave it the chance to. And I had no use for that pain here. This prison was temporary. Soon enough, I'd be free.

Voices echoed down the hallway, and I cracked my eyes open as the light of the torches filtered in.

"Gwendolyn Winters," a guard declared, "by the order of Prince Phillip Barrington, you are set to be executed for your crimes."

"In what manner?" I asked.

"Public hanging."

"Very well." I began to stand.

"The execution will take place tomorrow evening when Prince Barrington returns from his travels."

He'd left me here to deteriorate for days, all so he could go off gallivanting? I rolled my eyes. "Fine," I huffed. "It's a date."

CHAPTER TWENTY-FIVE

The dull noise of footsteps shuffled in front of my cell. Was it tomorrow already? I hadn't heard anyone come in through the door, but I'd also spent the last few hours drifting in and out of consciousness.

"Who's there?" I asked, narrowing my eyes to take in the tiny silhouette standing on the other side of the cell door.

"It has been a while since I saw you last." A dry voice answered, disregarding my question. I watched the shadow as it struck a match and illuminated the lantern in its hand. The light of the responding flames danced wildly across a pair of glowing green eyes.

"Cosmina," I acknowledged with a slight laugh. If this were any other scenario, her face would have struck fear in me.

"My, you've gotten yourself into quite a situation," she observed.

"No shit."

The gravelly sound of her chuckle made me cringe. "Come closer, child."

"I'd rather not," I answered harshly, leaning my head back against the stone wall.

"I want to show you something."

"Is it my impending and excruciating death? I'd prefer not to see it, but thanks for your kind offer."

"I know you met with my sister."

I glared up at her. "What do you want, Cosmina?"

"I have come to help you."

Fury sparked to life in the shattered fragments of my soul. The blood coursing under my skin heated, boiling even hotter as she motioned me toward her. I rose from the floor in a haste, letting the unbridled rage take over as I charged toward the wall of bars that separated us. "You're a little too late, I'm afraid!"

"It's never too late, child." It was the most infuriating thing she could have said.

"Where were you?" I shouted. "This whole time?" I struck the bars between us, imagining it was her face. "I've been looking for you ever since you sent me to this god-forsaken place!"

"I was waiting for you to complete the mission." Her voice was too calm. God, I hated her with every fucking fiber of my being.

"Well, lucky me. Here you are," I spat. "What was it that you needed me to do exactly? Was it fighting off a monster wolf? Was it to nearly die in an ocean full of venomous, bloodthirsty mermaids? Or maybe it was to crash into a snowy mountain range and risk getting crushed to death by the fucking rock giants that live there. Am I getting close?"

"No," she muttered thoughtfully. "I saw none of those things in my visions, but it is impressive that you survived them."

"I'm glad to hear it's impressive, Cosmina." I scolded, striking the bars again. "What was it then? What exactly did you need me for? Did you need me to encounter Demetri in this prison? To believe his lies from the very first moment that we spoke? Hmm? Was that it?" My eyes stung as I said the words out loud. "Did you need me to put every ounce of faith that I had in him, just for him to crush it in his hands like it never even meant anything? Or was it that maybe, just maybe...you needed me to believe that he was the entire reason I was sent here in the first place."

Her response was dismissive. "The pirate was not the reason, child."

"Then why, Cosmina?" I yelled. "Why did you ruin my life? You at least owe me that much."

"What I saw was that of which I showed you on that first night...you in the Emerald Forest...this castle that we're in now. I saw you with the prince. I saw flashes of a great battle for this world on the horizon, and you were there. That is what I saw. That is why I placed you here."

I took a long, deep breath to try to calm my nerves. "Isadora said your visions were subjective."

"Yes. They can indeed be altered if something shifts in the timeline. They don't always make sense right away; they sometimes even vanish altogether," she said, an unusual expression taking shape on her face. "But sometimes, they grow stronger as the time for them to occur draws nearer. I still see these things, child, and they're only growing stronger."

I clenched my jaw so hard it felt like my teeth would crush under the pressure. "So, what you're saying is that you yourself don't even fully know why I'm here—other than to fight in some battle that I most definitely will not be partaking in?"

"It's not over yet. Everything that you've done, everything that has happened...it has all led you back here. To the place where I first envisioned you. Can't you see, child?" A crazed laugh erupted from Cosmina's tiny frame. "There are no coincidences in this life! There was a reason why your spirit called to me. A reason that perhaps you never even considered. I believe that reason is that you're meant to break the curse that was placed on these lands, to restore this world to what it once was."

I stared back at her, completely dumbfounded. Unable to repress my annihilated emotions any longer, I let them take hold of my body. An irrational laugh escaped from my mouth. The disjointed noises that followed soon after quickly transformed into something far more unsteady and hysterical.

"Jesus Christ, Cosmina," I finally exclaimed when I had regained the lung capacity. "You have got to be kidding me right now." I slid back down to the floor and rested my head in my hands. "I don't even know what to say to that, honestly."

"Say that you will try again."

"Are you clinically insane?" I snapped. "I can't break a fucking curse. You do it. You're the all-powerful dark witch, after all."

"I cannot break it because my powers were used to enact it."

"What? Why would you do that?" I glared up at her. "I thought the queen did it."

"She did, with my magic," Cosmina revealed, her words were stained with something unidentifiable. If I didn't know her any better, I might assume it was shame. "We struck a deal," she continued. "But that was before I knew what she was planning. She stole a great deal of my powers, and I cannot break the curse when my own magic is being used against me to sustain it."

"Sorry." I shrugged callously. "It sounds like a personal problem. Ask Isadora. Maybe she will feel inclined to help."

"She cannot undo the curse because our blood..."

"Yeah, yeah, bloodlines, curses, can't be broken, yada-yada. She told me all of that already…and while we're on the subject of Isadora, what you did to Zola was really fucked up."

"That was a long time ago." Cosmina scowled as though I was the problem here.

"It was still fucked up. You're not a good person," I spat. "You hurt people, innocent people. And for what? I don't trust anything that comes out of your mouth."

"You may not trust me, but trust this, child. The curse will spread. By the rise of the Snow Moon, it will slowly extend to cover all the lands of this world. It must be stopped. And I believe you have the power to do so."

"Cosmina…" I started. "I…honestly don't care."

Her cryptic eyes narrowed; I wasn't sure if it was from anger or confusion.

"I wish I cared. But I just don't. I don't have it in me anymore." I sighed. "There's just… nothing left."

"I thought you wanted to go home," she retorted. "Have you changed your mind, child?"

The notion sent a surge of pain shooting through me. "Don't do that to me," I demanded. "Don't dangle false hope over my head."

Cosmina rotated the lantern in a circular motion, creating moving swirls of golden sun inside the cell. A flurry of voices sounded all around me as they floated closer.

"Gwen!" Jacob's voice rang out loudly over the others as mirages of him at the Renaissance Faire flashed before my eyes.

"Have you seen Gwen?" He appeared worried as he frantically approached the wedding party. The crowd behind him rapidly dwindled away as he stood alone.

Another golden vision blasted across my line of sight. Bree stood crying with her face buried into Jacob's shoulder as he relayed the news of my disappearance.

"Stop it!" I yelled, clenching my eyes together tightly to block out the images.

"Any news yet?" I heard my father's voice say.

"No," my mother sobbed. "Where could she be? My sweet baby..."

"This just doesn't make any sense. How could she just disappear off the face of the earth?" His voice broke as he began to weep.

I covered my ears and screamed to block out the sound. Until this moment, I didn't think there was any way I could possibly feel worse.

A rush of unfamiliar voices rang in my head. "Oh my gosh, you're that girl. The one who's been missing! Are you hurt? Come on, come with me. We'll get you some help..."

"What is wrong with you!" I yelled at Cosmina.

"They're still looking for you, child," she replied. "They haven't given up their hope so easily." Another round of images swirled outward from her hands.

A vision of Isadora appearing to comfort a distressed Cinderella materialized. "We shouldn't have allowed him to take her back," Cinderella said. "It all feels so very wrong."

"It will all be alright, dear. The boy has a plan," Isadora replied.

A brighter burst of golden light blasted through the cell, flooding my senses as they exploded into fragments all around me. Demetri's voice called from them, echoing against the stone walls and demolishing whatever composure I thought I had left. The sight of his face brought me physical pain. I clenched my arms around my body in an effort to keep myself from unraveling.

"Tell me exactly where I can find her," he pleaded with Isadora.

Another image raced by of him flying on the back of Zola over a place I didn't recognize.

"Cosmina?" I heard him say in the next golden glimpse. "I'm prepared to make any deal; I just need your help."

"Are you sure, boy?" her bitter warning rattled around me, raising the hair on the back of my neck.

"Yes," Demetri echoed. "We must fetch my crew. We haven't much time."

"Stop it!" I screamed, and I didn't stop. I screamed so loud that it jolted through my bones. A scream fueled by every ounce of hurt and rage that I'd been holding onto for as long as I could remember. I couldn't take this anymore. I was so fucking tired. The noise shuddered against the stone walls and shattered all the luminous visions Cosmina insisted on tormenting me with. Only when my voice gave out and there was no breath left in my lungs to utilize did I stop screaming at her.

Cosmina's silhouette shook as she laughed to herself. "Yes, child. There it is. The rage you'll need."

I raised my head from the floor to face her...to tell her to go to hell...to offer to send her there myself. Then I noticed another figure was standing in the room.

"Cosmina?" I whispered against my burning throat.

"We're here, child."

"Who?"

"It's me, love."

My heart splintered into a million pieces all over again the moment that he spoke.

Demetri's voice had once brought me immeasurable comfort, even during the times when nothing else could. Now it rained down over me like sharp-pointed daggers.

"Gwen?" he called out to the responding silence. "I'm...so sorry, love. I truly never intended for any of this to happen."

"Please leave me alone," I whispered through the treacherous tears that had resurfaced.

Cosmina struck another match for her lantern, and I buried my head in my knees. I didn't want to see either one of them.

"Gwen, please. I swear to you," he said unsteadily.

"Why are you doing this to me?" I cried. "Please just...go away. I don't want you here."

"We're trying to save you, love. You must believe me."

I stood carefully, trying to focus on stabilizing my breaths. My legs trembled weakly underneath me as I took slow, small steps to the bars where he waited. His face was more heartbreaking than I anticipated.

"The way you saved me before?"

"I hate seeing you like this," he said.

"I'm not sure exactly what you expected to find here."

"Can we have a minute?" He turned to ask Cosmina before taking the lantern that she offered.

She nodded silently before quickly vanishing into the darkness.

"I know you are upset with me. And I don't blame you, love..." he said, placing his hands on the bars between us. "...I don't blame you one bit."

"How could you do that to me?" I whispered the words so he couldn't hear the pain etched in my voice.

"I didn't know you then...not truly. And it was the only way I could think of at the time to try to save us both."

"You told him *everything*. After you told me not to tell anyone...you put me at risk to save yourself."

"I'll be the first to admit I made an unbearable mistake, Gwen. I had a sword pointed at my throat and said the first thing that came to mind."

"You broke my heart," I cried.

"I know, love." He reached for my hand, but I pulled it away. "I've been trying to make up for it ever since. I'll try forever if I must. Seeing you like this, knowing I caused you to feel this pain, it makes me feel like the worst person to ever exist. You must know that I never wanted to hurt you. And I never intended on having you anywhere near Barrington again, so I didn't think it mattered if you knew."

"I don't really know what else to say," I inhaled, wiping the tears from my face.

"Say you'll come with me."

"I can't, Demetri." I shook my head, watching him as he eyed me intensely. "I can't."

"Gwen, please. You'll die if you stay here. You mustn't stay here."

"I'm just so tired. And I feel so...broken." My voice cracked at the admission. "I tried...I really tried. But no matter how much I did, everything just went so wrong. I'm tired of hurting, Demetri. I can't take any more pain."

"Come with me. We can figure it out together. We only need to get you out of here first."

"It hurts so bad to even see you right now," I confessed, forcing myself to not lock my gaze with his. "...to know that everything was always a lie."

"It wasn't a lie," he declared. "The last thing I'd ever want to do is hurt you, love. You have to know how much I care about you. Despite all of this."

"I thought you did," I laughed. "I really thought you did. That's what's so damn sad about it."

"I did. I still do, Gwen!" he exclaimed, reaching through the bars to touch my face. "Gwen, I..." his eyes found mine, drawing me back into him the way he always did. "I just need to..."

"Someone is coming," Cosmina warned as she appeared again and pulled Demetri away from view. They disappeared again into the shadows as though they were never even there.

CHAPTER TWENTY-SIX

I kept my head down as I followed the guards down the desolate hallway. I had been waiting for this for days...an end to this unbearable pain. My heartbeat thudded contentedly, matching the stride of the footsteps that surrounded me.

I wasn't scared. Strangely enough, the thought of this moment had provided me with a sense of comfort over the last several days. *No more pain*, I would constantly remind myself.

But then...Demetri showed up. His words had sparked something inside me again, against my better judgment. Something that I thought had died back in Winterhaven. Something I knew I shouldn't hold onto too tightly because it could be snatched away again just as quickly.

He had come back for me. He wanted to save me, truly save me. And this time, his intentions were noble...I think.

The way he'd looked at me, like he was worried, or maybe even afraid. He had told me he cared. I didn't want to accept his words or forgive him so easily for the cataclysmic damage that he caused when I discovered the truth…but he had come back for me. And that had to mean something.

It was nearly dark out when we walked outside and passed by the castle's courtyard. The scent of jasmine transported me back to the time when I'd fled down to the forest with Demetri. Back to the night when we jumped off a cliff into the furious ocean below to escape the guards and locate Demetri's pirate ship. I laughed to myself. To think, those were much simpler times.

A massive crowd of spectators waited down by the gallows, gathered together tightly in an arena of sorts, one that was surrounded by tall stone walls. Phillip really was the worst kind of asshole. It wasn't enough to kill me. No, he had to invite every person in the kingdom to come watch like this was some sort of vile talent show.

He waited by the steps with that hideous smile of his.

"It's a glorious night, isn't it? Are you ready for your big moment?" he asked as the guards ushered me up the steps.

"Fuck you, Phillip." I spat.

"I, for one, will certainly enjoy witnessing today's events," he taunted.

I stared out at the sea of faces, trying to push down the evolving dizziness I felt as the guard beside me pulled down a rope from the wooden beam. Perhaps I wasn't as content with this idea as I imagined I'd be a few days ago.

The faces began to blur together, and the urge to vomit was rapidly increasing. The only breaths I managed to draw were short and shallow ones.

"Gwendolyn," Phillip called from below as the guard dropped the rope across my shoulders. "Do try to give the people a good show, won't you?"

I closed my eyes, refusing to let his face be the last thing I'd ever see.

That was when I heard the horrible, piercing screams coming from the back of the crowd. My eyes flew open, zoning in on where the sound came from. The blood in my veins ran cold as I stood helplessly, watching a lifeless body being tossed through the air.

The shrieks were immediately followed by yells of recognition. The faces of the onlookers who stood before me began to morph into panic as the spectators scrambled to run, but the surrounding walls prevented them from doing so. Realizing they were trapped, they began to trample on top of one another to try to climb out.

"What is the meaning of this?" Phillip exclaimed from the foot of the steps.

A recognizable and terrifying sound erupted through the screams. A vicious snarl snapped as the monster wolf leaped up from the back of the crowd and pounced on top of several people at once.

His face was wild and vicious, just the way it had been the night he pinned me down against the dirt and snapped his teeth at me.

"What the hell is going on here?" Phillip shouted to his guards. "Don't just stand there! Kill that fucking wolf!"

The beast attacked the approaching guards, biting, barking, and slashing uncontrollably as they yelled out in pain.

I couldn't move. I watched from the wooden platform in absolute horror as he swiftly claimed his victims. But there was something else simmering beneath the initial shock and terror of it all. As the wolf aimed all of his rage at Phillip's guards, a fleeting thrill of awe and admiration overwhelmed me.

A flaming arrow soared above my head, penetrating the top of the gallows. I shifted out from under the rope as fire exploded across the wooden beam, instinctively searching the skies out of fear that another might be coming. My focus landed on the hooded figure standing on top of the stone wall.

Still clenching the bow tightly in her hand, she reached for her hood to expose her identity, smiling warmly as my recognition set in.

"Rowan!" I cried, collapsing to my knees.

Her scarlet silhouette darted across the edge of the wall until she got as close to me as she could manage. The flames from her arrow trickled down to the platform where I stood, blasting me with plumes of heat.

"Hi, Gwen," she beamed. "It's good to see you again."

"It's good to see you too." I laughed through the tears and tremendous relief.

"Come on"—she motioned me over—"while there's still a distraction in our favor."

I raced down the stairs, passing Phillip on the way.

"Get back here!" he yelled vehemently, slinging me around by the arm. "You're not going anywhere!" His enraged face quivered as beads of sweat rolled down it.

An arrow whooshed by me, grazing the top of Phillip's shoulder and taking part of his ugly cape with it. He yelled out in pain as blood spilled from his wound. I scrambled away from him in the chaos and rushed over to where Rowan stood on the wall.

"You forgot to set that one on fire first!" I exclaimed.

"I didn't have enough time!"

The growls of the wolf echoed loudly from somewhere behind me as dozens more castle guards rushed into the arena.

"Can you climb the wall?" she asked, crouching down to extend her hand to me.

"No, it's too high!" I yelled in a panic as the wolf's roars intensified. "I can't get out!"

"It's okay!" She pursed her lips together, quickly scanning the area for the nearest way out. "Run to the back...to the archway. I'll meet you there."

"But the wolf—" I shrieked.

"Don't worry about him. He won't hurt you!"

"But I'm not wearing a cloak!"

Rowan had already bolted off toward the proposed meeting point, drawing her bow again as she aimed it down at the crowd and motioned for me to follow.

I pushed my way through the frenzy of frightened people, hiding my face from the view of the guards. The wolf pounced near the center of the crowd, shaking the ground as he landed a dozen yards ahead of me. Panic set in as I realized I would have to pass right by him to reach the archway.

Screaming faces blurred my vision as they fought to get around me...to get away from him.

And then, there he was. I ran right out into the only vacant space and froze in my tracks as he caught sight of me. He was even more terrifying than the first time I'd seen him. Standing there, snarling at everyone with bloodstained fur as fresh crimson drops leaked from the corners of his mouth.

I wanted to yell for Rowan, but doing so would only give him the perfect opportunity to strike. And if he was planning on attacking me, I at least wanted to know it was coming.

His feral face shifted into a far less threatening expression as he watched me, just as it had done the night I fled from Rowan's house after I'd wrapped her cloak around me.

The wolf whined and lowered his head as he waited for me to react.

"Go, Gwen!" I heard Rowan shout from above.

And so, I did. I was halfway there now. Turning from the wolf, I raced straight into another flock of panicked people, breaking through the wall of bodies more forcefully than I intended. Only once I had made it through did the snarls and screams resume.

The moving crowds encompassed me, shifting me like the waves in the ocean as I tried to wade through them. I wasn't even sure if I was going the right way anymore. There were too many people closing in. I felt as though I was going to suffocate. I searched for Rowan, but the sky was darker now, and it was getting harder to see.

A pair of bloody hands latched onto me from behind, and I fought against my teetering balance.

"You'll not get away that easily, you deceitful little bitch!" Phillip shouted as more guards materialized around us.

A flurry of arrows flew by me as Rowan tried to take them down one by one...but there were far too many, and they were much too fast.

"Rowan!" I yelled, thrashing away from their clutches.

I watched as her silhouette lifted another arrow, sparked a flame on the tip, and shot it straight out into the night sky.

The men around me boomed with laughter.

"You missed, little one," one of them heckled her.

"No...I didn't," she responded just as an enormous tree near the courtyard exploded into flames. The eruption of fire illuminated her face as a subtle smile spread across her lips. "Just figured I could use some backup."

The roar of hundreds of voices came to life as the embers began to blow over the crowd, and I tried to cover my ears as loud piercing noises screeched against the walls.

Phillip ignored it. He pulled me against him, so close that his blood soaked into my gown.

The noises screeched again as I desperately searched for Rowan's figure. What I found instead were several other silhouettes standing on the ledge. I couldn't determine which one was hers even as the glowing flicker of the fire lapped across their shadows.

"Rowan!" I called out.

Phillip grabbed me by the jaw. Using the strength of all his anger, he pressed his fingers into my face.

I screamed out in pain as he threw me to the ground. The crowd cleared around us as he withdrew his sword.

"This ends now!" He roared, bringing his sword down.

I barely managed to roll out of the way as the point of his blade speared through the bottom edge of my dress.

He let out another yell of fury. Several arrows flew by, narrowly missing him as he leaned down to pull up his weapon.

"Well now, that's no way for a prince to treat a lady," a familiar voice declared.

"Alistair!" I exclaimed, scrambling from the ground to run to him.

His enraged eyes were focused on Phillip as he held out his own sword. He looked fiercer than I'd ever seen him before; the jovial man I'd come to know was not the one standing before me now. He was a frightening glimpse of the Alistair that Demetri had told me about inside the cave, the one he had known as a boy.

"Get behind me, lass." He commanded. "Over here, boys!" he yelled, pointing his sword up at Phillip's face.

The figures from the wall quickly descended into the crowd, clashing and scraping their swords against the stone wall as they did.

Then, one by one, the familiar, dirty, glorious faces that I had come to know appeared around us, the faces that I never thought I'd see again. I felt as though I might explode from pure bliss at the sight of them.

"Miss Gwen, are ye hurt?" Wiley asked.

"No, I'm okay."

"But you're bleeding, miss!" Felix exclaimed.

I followed his gaze down to where Phillip had slashed my dress. I hadn't even felt the sword slice into my leg until now...until I saw the blood dripping down and pooling near my foot.

"Well, isn't this heartwarming," Phillip sneered. "How valiant of you all to put your wretched lives on the line to save your little pirate whore."

"It's comments like that that'll get you killed before you ever have a chance to convince some poor, foolish woman to birth you an heir," Demetri asserted as he appeared behind Phillip.

"I was wondering when you'd show up, pirate." Phillip sneered.

"I'm never too far. You should know that by now." Demetri stepped closer, his face flinching as he detected the blood that stained the bottom half of my dress.

It didn't go unnoticed by Phillip. "Pathetic." He huffed out a laugh. "Like a dog on a chain."

Castle guards were quickly filtering in around Demetri's crew.

"I'm going to kill you, once and for all," Demetri growled through his teeth. "As painfully as I can."

Phillip's responding smile was short-lived as a fleet of Rowan's arrows pierced through several of his men.

Griff let out a war cry, and the other pirates yelled in response, raising their weapons and charging straight for the guards.

But not Alistair. He scooped me up as the battle erupted around us, moving me out of the impact zone before heading straight back into the violent mob. I watched helplessly as the men smashed and struck their swords together, praying that none of the ones I knew would fall.

I didn't want to watch; I couldn't stand it, but I also couldn't tear my eyes away from Demetri. Afraid that if I did, he would falter. Phillip was skilled, even in his injured state. But Demetri was an unbreakable force.

I'd never seen him fighting, not truly. The only time I'd seen him actively engage in combat was against the sirens, but this was different. This was the release of long-held rage. This was more than a mutual dislike...it was pure hatred. This was life or death.

Rowan yelled for me. The archway wasn't far now, and the crowd had dissipated enough to create the space to flee. I could make it if I tried, even though my bleeding leg now throbbed with pain.

Phillip's guards fell as Demetri's crew took the upper hand. Griff was a beast, keeping the guards at bay from Demetri as he fought against Phillip.

Wiley and Hayes were quick on their feet. Every move they made seemed choreographed, as though they had mapped this routine out before they ever even got here.

Alistair and Thomas raced back and forth to cover the others, charging the guards who tried to push past them.

Even Felix was greatly skilled in combat, which was possibly the most surprising thing of all to witness.

As I stood, watching the battle between the pirates and the guards unfold, watching the wolf finally start to tire from claiming his victims, I felt dizzy. I wanted to flee, but I was too paralyzed with disbelief to even try as everything fell apart around me. There was so much chaos and carnage it was nearly unbearable to witness. And there was so much blood...my blood.

I tried to steady myself, but the spinning intensified. Then everything went dark.

CHAPTER TWENTY-SEVEN

The breeze whipped around me gently, carrying me away from the noise...away from the smell of death, smoke, and all the destruction.

"Are you awake, love?"

I smiled as his voice drifted over me. There was nothing else in the world that could elicit this feeling.

"Where are you?" I asked.

"Right here, I've got you."

"Are we going to the ball?"

Demetri's gentle laugh sent fire flooding through my body. "Not quite. I'm taking you someplace safe."

Coherent thoughts began to take hold as I opened my eyes. I stared up at the black, starless sky, surveying the shapes of the trees as they rushed by us. Demetri was carrying me through the woods.

"Where are we?" I asked. "Where is everyone else?"

"They're going to meet us back at the ship."

"Rowan?" I asked.

"Yes, Rowan, too. She had to collect her wolf first."

"That's...so weird."

Demetri laughed once more, "Aye, but he served us well tonight."

I leaned my head against his chest, closing my eyes again momentarily as I allowed myself to revel in the sound of his heartbeat. He was really here. "You came back for me," I acknowledged.

"That's what I do, love. It's what I'll always do."

"How'd you figure it out?"

"Figure what out?"

"All of it..." I looked up to his face. "Where Cosmina was...how to find Rowan...how to get everyone here..."

"Cosmina was right where Isadora suspected she would be," He glanced down, the light of the moon reflecting in his eyes.

"The cursed lands? She showed me a vision of you there."

"Yes." His face tightened at the mention of it. "I told her everything and asked for her help."

"You made a deal with her?"

"She told you that?"

"Well, she showed it to me...she showed me a lot of things." My heart dropped as I thought of the visions she'd shown me of my friends and family back home.

"I see," he said. "I had to make a deal. It was the only way to ensure she would help."

"What was it?"

He released an apprehensive laugh. "I don't even know that myself yet. The details were vague. She only said that if she ever required my assistance, I would oblige."

"That's mildly concerning."

"It's what had to happen. Whatever she decides, I will gladly do it."

"What about your ship? How'd everyone else get here so fast?"

"Cosmina carried us back to the ship through a portal. Then she sent us here to the shores of Castleberry. We then went to find Rowan, who agreed to help in any way that she could. It was Rowan who suggested bringing the wolf, but she said that she needed the cloak back to help coax him...so Cosmina stole it from the castle."

"I'm impressed." I laughed.

"Well, we were all quite impressive, so I'd expect nothing less," he said sarcastically, smiling down at me.

"And...Phillip?"

"When you collapsed, my only concern was getting you out of there. Griff and Alistair took over the fight. But don't worry; I got in a few good strikes."

"I'm sorry," I replied. "I know you wanted to be the one to do it."

"It would have given me great satisfaction to have been the one to end his life for everything that he's done," Demetri confessed. "Nevertheless, you were more important."

"My leg really does hurt," I admitted.

"Here, let me see it," he said, halting near a fallen log. He placed me down gently on top of it and kneeled before me to inspect the injury.

"Can you even see anything?" I asked, squinting in the moonlight, trying to assess the damage.

"Yes," he responded. "It's still bleeding some." He ripped a strip of fabric off my dress and made a tourniquet to tie around my leg. "That should help, at least until we get to the ship."

Demetri gazed up at me. "I'm sorry for all of this," he confessed.

I stroked a hand through his hair. "It's alright. It wasn't all your fault."

"Much of it was."

I closed my eyes, trying to block out the pain of the last several days.

"I'm sorry too," I said, "for overreacting."

Demetri arched his brow skeptically. "Overreacting?"

"I did kind of go with Phillip willingly when I found out. Looking back, I realize that was a pretty dumb thing to do." I laughed weakly.

He smiled back. "It did pose a bit of a problem; I'll not deny that."

"When I saw you in the dungeon again..." I bit my lip in hesitation. "To think that you didn't care...it devastated me. More than I ever expected it to. I had convinced myself I was ready to die. That there was nothing to live for anymore. But when I saw you again, it—I don't know—it ignited something in me."

"I thought I'd lost you forever," he spoke softly. "I wouldn't have been able to live with myself if..." He silently shook the thought from his head.

I leaned down, cupping his face between my hands, and touched my lips to his. "You make me feel things," I finally admitted out loud. "Things that I've never felt before."

"Murderous rage?"

"That too." I laughed.

Demetri smiled in return. "I've always loved you, Gwen," he professed. "I thought you knew that."

My soul nearly fled my body. "What?"

"Ever since the first moment I laid eyes on you in that wretched dungeon. It's something that I questioned at times. Partially because you drive me completely mad. Partially because I didn't think I was ever truly capable of experiencing love. But that night in Winterhaven, when you left with Phillip. When you told me goodbye...that's when I knew for certain. I knew then and there I had always loved you. And in knowing that, I knew I would never be able to live a life without you in it."

"I love you too," I whispered, the confession triggering my heart to pound wildly against the walls of my chest and my breath to catch in my throat. "I think I've been trying not to for so long...but I'm tired of pretending that I don't. I love you, Demetri."

He rose from the ground, pressing his lips gently to mine. I wrapped my arms around his shoulders as he pulled me against his body.

"I've chased countless horizons, but you were always the brightest one of all," he whispered, resting his forehead against mine. "And nothing in this world or the next would have stopped me from coming back for you."

I moved my hand to stroke his face. In a matter of minutes, he'd managed to heal every ounce of the intolerable pain that had plagued me since leaving Winterhaven. I didn't know what the distant future held or even what direction our lives would take following the fallout of tonight, but I knew Demetri loved me. And right now, the reality of that knowledge was the only thing I truly needed.

"I'll never let anyone hurt you again, love," he vowed, placing a hand under my chin to raise my face to his. "I'd burn this entire world down to keep you safe if it were what you wanted."

I pulled him back to my lips and smiled. "I just want you."

CHAPTER TWENTY-EIGHT

Phillip and two of his men emerged from the shadows. I didn't know how long they had been there or how much they'd seen or heard.

"I suppose there's nothing quite like destroying a kingdom to set the mood, is there, boys?" he viciously jeered.

Demetri stood, placing himself between us.

"I saw you two sneaking off in the middle of the fight...all alone." Phillip continued his rant. "Don't worry, my men are still keeping your crew very busy."

"Why do you refuse to die?" Demetri asked the bloody, battered prince.

"I have so often asked myself the same thing about you," Phillip retorted. "Every time I get close enough to kill you, you somehow always manage to get away. It's incredibly vexing."

Demetri reached for his sword.

"Looking for this?" Phillip swung the sword forward. "You left it on my premises. I suppose that makes it mine now."

Demetri fumed as Phillip approached.

"It seems to me, pirate, that your stroke of good luck is about to run its course." Phillip sauntered closer. "It's a bit poetic, isn't it, to be struck down by your own sword?"

I tried to stand, to do what...I wasn't sure. Pain seared down my leg as I collapsed again.

"Let's see, I'd really like to make the most of this. I feel as though I deserve that much." He paced. "I'm not sure if I should just kill you first and finally get it over with, or..." His eyes landed on me.

Demetri's fists clenched in response.

"...if I should make you suffer a little bit first," Phillip pretended to ponder. "I must say, I am a bit fond of that idea."

"You won't go near her," Demetri growled.

Phillip pressed his lips together. "See, when you say things like that, pirate, it tends to make me contemplate it even more."

Demetri's stance tightened as Phillip stepped closer.

"What if I didn't hurt her?" he laughed to himself. "What if I made her feel really good instead?"

I screamed as Demetri lunged and landed on top of Phillip, viciously pummeling his face with his fists. Phillip's guards rushed over, struggling to pull them apart.

As they did, Phillip rose from the ground and spit out a mouthful of blood. He approached Demetri, who was being held on his knees by the guards.

"That was a mistake," he growled as he pulled his fist back and let it fly across Demetri's face.

"Stop it!" I yelled, tumbling from the log as I tried to get up and crawl to Demetri.

"Look how weak she is, pirate," Phillip taunted, wiping more blood from his face. "I suppose I'll have to do most of the work…"

Demetri cursed and thrashed against the grip of the guards as Phillip walked over to me and crouched down to my level.

I backed away, and the recoil elicited a sinister smile from him. There was no way I'd be able to outrun him now, or even fight him off.

"Don't touch me," I warned, spitting in his face.

Phillip laughed as he stood, wiping his hand across his cheek. "Now, now, darling," he snarled. "Be a good girl." I held my breath as he reared his foot back and kicked me hard in the side.

"I'm going to fucking kill you for that!" Demetri thundered.

The impact knocked me over, and I instinctively pulled my knees up to my chest and lay in the fetal position to shield my body from another brutal attack.

Demetri slammed his body down, bringing the guards with him, managing to break free from their grasp amid the scuffle. He stood quickly, kicking one of them in the face as they tried to latch onto his leg.

Phillip swung the sword around as Demetri crashed into him and knocked him to the ground.

They struggled for several moments over the sword as I tried to stand. My ribs were throbbing, and it took all the strength I had left to push through the pain.

Phillip rolled on top of Demetri as the sword lay in the grass nearby.

The still-conscious guard was advancing toward it, but I was closer. Just as I started to reach for it, Demetri kicked Phillip off top of him, and he landed right beside the weapon.

Phillip jumped up, snatching the blade as he did. He spun towards Demetri and held it to his throat, pinning him close to the ground.

"No!" I screamed, crying as I watched the scene play out. "I'll give you anything you want!"

Phillip laughed as I approached. "What I want is to watch as the life drains from his eyes." He pushed the sword against Demetri's skin.

"Kill me!" I cried. "Please, kill me. Just not him, please…not him. I'll do whatever you want. Just don't kill him."

Phillip smiled dementedly as I stood there, pleading for Demetri's life to be spared.

"Please, Phillip," I breathed, limping as I took several slow steps closer to the men.

"Stay back, Gwen," Demetri said, his voice low and guttural as he shot me a warning glance.

Phillip pulled his sword away from Demetri's neck and smirked as he pointed it at me. "I do love the way you beg, Gwendolyn. It reminds me of our first night together."

Demetri's face twisted with rage as he tried to rise. Phillip swung the sword back toward him, but I was just a few feet away now. I screamed and lunged for him as he pulled back his arm, readying the strike against Demetri.

The blade cut into my shoulder as I knocked Phillip to the ground, tumbling over Demetri's body in the process. Phillip scrambled to reach me as I tried to crawl away.

"Gwen!" Demetri yelled, but I couldn't find him. Phillip appeared again, knocking my arms out from under me as my face hit the ground. I rolled over long enough to see Demetri fighting with the uninjured guard as Phillip hovered over me, pinning me down with the weight of his body and crushing whatever bones I had left that weren't already broken.

"Let's end this now, Gwen," he growled, clasping his hands tightly around my throat as he stared down at me with chaotic, hate-filled eyes.

A fierce gust of wind swept over us. The ground began to rumble as though it were about to open up right beneath our bodies.

Phillip's grip loosened as the intensity of the tremors shook us violently. Demetri's voice sounded somewhere in the distance, and Phillip yelled as he toppled off of me. As I tried to stand, Demetri appeared, pulling me up from the ground.

"What's happening?" I asked, latching onto him in a panic.

His electric eyes were wide as he desperately surveyed our surroundings. "I don't know," he answered.

The ground continued to shake underneath us as a purple-tinted haze seeped out from behind the swaying trees.

"Gwen," Demetri's breath was unsteady. "Hold onto me."

The flickering hue became more vibrant as it drifted closer to the place where we stood. It settled in over us like a lightning storm, propelling in a cold burst of air.

The wind roared as I clung to Demetri. I couldn't see anything else beyond the mist that surrounded us, just the swirling bursts of lavender as it flashed wildly around him.

"It's a portal," Demetri yelled over the noise, confirming the assumptions I'd been too afraid to voice.

I gripped his body tighter, resisting the traction of the pull that the haze was beginning to have.

"No!" I shouted. "I'm not leaving you!"

"This might be your only chance to go home," he said.

"I can't," I cried, the tears drying on my cheeks moments after they hit the open air. "I'm not ready...I thought I was, but I'm not."

"I'm not ready either, love." Demetri placed his hands on my face. "But even forever wouldn't have been long enough for me."

"Why does it sound like you're telling me goodbye?"

Demetri brushed his lips against mine. "You should go, Gwen," he said. "Back to your world, your home. It's where you belong. It's where you'll be safe." His face twisted in pain as he said the words.

"How could you say that to me, Demetri," I lashed out from the sting, "when earlier tonight you said you wouldn't be able to live a life without me in it?"

"It isn't safe here, love," he reiterated. "And you're already terribly injured. If you stay...if something happened to you because you stayed for me, I'd never be able to forgive myself for being so selfish."

"But I love you," I confessed.

"I love you too. I always will. That's why it kills me to tell you to go."

"Then don't!" I exclaimed. "I want to stay here...with you. We can figure out everything else later."

"You deserve so much more than this." His eyes glistened as tears formed in the corners. "So much more than what I could give you here."

"Come with me," I blurted before even considering the entire thought.

He stared down at me in disbelief. "What?"

"Please," I begged. "I don't care which world we're in as long as we're together."

Demetri smiled softly as the ground shuddered under our feet again. Phillip's voice boomed through the air as the haze began to dissipate around us and rapidly shift colors.

"What's going on?" I shouted.

Demetri didn't say anything, there was no time. He shoved me out of the way as Phillip rushed toward us with the sword.

"Demetri!"

"Go!" he yelled from behind me as he tried to fend off Phillip.

"Not without you!" I shouted back.

Phillip charged again. Demetri dodged the blade, but as Phillip raced by him, he grazed the edge of it across my back. A thunderous boom shook the earth as I cried out in pain. The haze thickened again, whipping around me vehemently as it morphed into a blood-red hue.

Demetri pulled me into his arms and raced through the billowing crimson clouds.

"Where are you going?" I yelled through the noise.

"Phillip disrupted the portal," he replied.

Lightning sparked overhead as we chased the retreating purple mist back toward the tree line. A bright light flared in front of us as he lowered me back to the ground.

"You have to think about where you want to go," he yelled as we squinted against the glow. "That's how it works."

I nodded, grabbing hold of his hand. "To new horizons," I said, smiling back at him as he looked over at me and tightened his grip. Before committing to the decision, I closed my eyes and took a deep breath, silently praying that this would actually work.

Demetri groaned as I did, releasing his grasp as the weight of his body fell against me.

The noise of the wind subsided as Phillip's laughter echoed through my head. I turned to face Demetri and found him clenching his side as his blood spilled out onto the ground.

"Demetri!" I shrieked, grabbing hold of him. "No...no-no- no, Demetri," I sobbed. "Look at me. Hey, you're okay. You'll be okay."

"At last!" Phillip held up the blood-tipped sword as he roared victoriously in the background.

Demetri lifted his hand to my face and tried to smile. His eyes were weak as he stared back at me as though he were seeing me for the very first time.

"We can get you help. Don't worry," I could barely get the words out through my rapid, painful breaths. "Come on...we have to hurry though."

"I love you," he fought to say.

"No, don't do this," I shook my head as the tears streamed. "Don't give up on me."

"I'm sorry, love," he whispered as he fell to his knees.

I collapsed to mine, holding his face in my hands as his eyes struggled to stay open. "Demetri," I cried. "Please don't leave me."

"I would have followed you anywhere," he whispered, sinking into me as he placed his hands on either side of my waist.

I gasped for air as my lungs constricted. Demetri's face blurred behind the barrage of water filling my eyes.

"Don't leave me," I begged, trying to support the weight of his body. "I love you, Demetri. Please..."

"I'll wait for you," he muttered. "On the other side of the horizon."

Phillip was still reveling in what he'd done when he appeared again. "Don't worry, dear. It won't hurt quite as bad once I kill you, too."

"Kiss me, love," Demetri breathed. "One last time."

I sobbed as I leaned over and pressed my tear-stained lips to his. As soon as they parted, Demetri used what was left of his strength to push me away from him, straight into the blinding light.

CHAPTER TWENTY-NINE

I was staring up at a gray sky when I came to. I laid there for a while, under the canopy of silent trees...allowing the drops of rain that fell from the angry clouds to hit my face and merge with the tears that hadn't stopped pouring.

The scene replayed in my head, over and over and over again. No matter how hard I clenched my eyes shut, no matter any other thoughts I tried to have, all I could see was the life leaving Demetri's face as he clutched his side and his hands turned red.

I would never be able to shake the images or the excruciating pain that they brought with them.

I didn't know how long I'd been lying here...in this spot. It felt like days, but perhaps it had only been minutes.

Fuck. Demetri was gone. He was... I couldn't even force myself to think the word. How could I have let this happen? It was my fault...I knew that. He had followed me back there, to that hell-sent castle. He'd still be alive if it wasn't for me.

My heart thumped painfully in my carved-out, hollow chest.

"Oh my gosh, you're that girl. The one who's been missing!" I heard a voice exclaim. "Are you hurt? Come on, come with me. We'll get you some help…"

I didn't move.

"How are you feeling, Gwen?" the doctor asked as two policemen filed into the hospital room behind her.

When I'd arrived by ambulance, the nurses stripped my bloody clothes off and insisted on doing a full evaluation.

Minus the gashes, and fractured ribs, they seemed surprised to report that I was in overall decent condition…at least physically.

"How's your leg feeling after those stitches?" The doctor asked.

I leaned my head back and began to count the ceiling tiles again. One…two…three…

"She hasn't said a word since she's gotten here," I heard her mutter to the officers. "I don't think you're going to get anything out of her today."

Eight…nine…ten…

They wrote down a few notes before agreeing to come back again later.

A knock sounded at the door. It creaked open a few moments later after I didn't respond.

"Gwen," Bree whispered as she exploded into tears.

She rushed over to me, falling onto the bed as she held me in a tight embrace. I wrapped my arms around her, unable to control the burst of emotions that took hold.

"Oh, Gwen!" She sat on the bed, rocking me back and forth as I cried.

"Hi, Bree," I whispered.

"Your parents are on the way. I couldn't believe it when they called and told me you were here. I came as fast as I could."

"I missed you," I said.

"I missed you too. We all did."

I leaned back onto the bed, wiping the tears from my eyes.

"What happened, Gwen?" She asked. "Where have you been all this time?"

I rubbed my hands over my face, unsure how to even respond to that.

"How long was I gone?" I stalled.

"Nearly four months." Her eyes darted over every inch of my face as if she were analyzing everything that looked different.

"It didn't feel like that long for me," I confessed, silently wondering if time moved differently in the other realm.

"Jacob said the last time he saw you was at the reception."

"Yeah..."

"I'm sorry, I don't mean to pry." Bree brushed the strands of hair away from my face. "It's just been so long, and no one had any idea where you were."

I averted my eyes from her concerned expression. "I know..." my voice faded out. "...but I can't."

Bree took hold of my hands. "I understand if you're not quite ready to talk about it yet."

"I'm not, Bree," I admitted. "I know everyone will want to know what happened, but I'm not ready yet. I don't know if I'll ever be ready."

"Okay," she nodded. "That's all right, Gwen. If you ever do feel ready, you know I'll be here for you." She leaned down to embrace me once more. "I'm just so glad that you're back."

The door swung open violently as Jacob barreled inside the room.

"Gwen! Oh my gosh, baby," he exclaimed through the tears running down his cheeks. "I was so worried about you."

Bree stood as Jacob raced over to me. He grabbed my face and kissed me hard as I struggled to pull away.

"Easy, Jacob!" Bree scowled. "You don't know what she might have been through!"

"I'm sorry, baby," he apologized; his pupils were so large they nearly blocked out the color of his eyes. "I've just missed you so much."

"I missed you too," I said through the pain that was aching where that hole in my chest now existed.

I hadn't lived with this agony for very long, but I knew it was something that no amount of time would alleviate. The hole was too big, too raw, and there would never be enough things in this world that I could fill it with to make it stop hurting so damn bad.

"What happened that night at the reception?" He asked. "It was like you just vanished into thin air."

"She said she isn't ready to talk about what happened yet," Bree interjected.

"Bree's right," I whispered. "I know you want answers. I want to give them to you, but I just don't think I can talk about it yet."

"Did someone hurt you?" Jacob demanded as he noticed the bandages wrapped around my leg.

I tugged the white hospital sheets over my body.

"Easy Jacob," Bree admonished, "I'm sure she'll tell us when she's ready. Until then, asking her to do so isn't going to help her."

"I'm sorry," he said again as he turned to me. "It's just been really hard here without you."

"I know." I nodded. "I'm really sorry to have put you through that. I never meant for any of it to happen." Tears streamed down my face as my mind relived those horrible images of Demetri again…the way he'd fought to keep his eyes on me for as long as he could. The way he'd asked for one last kiss before his final courageous act of sending me home…

"Oh, Gwen, baby. I'm sorry. I promise I won't ask you anything else. Not until you're ready to talk about it."

"Thank you, Jacob," I mumbled through the tears.

He leaned down to kiss my forehead before stretching out in the bed beside me and throwing his arm around my waist. I didn't have the heart to tell him I just wanted to be left alone.

CHAPTER THIRTY

Two months had passed since I'd returned home. Jacob had moved most of his things into my apartment after I was released from the hospital. He rarely let me out of his sight these days, and I knew it was because he was afraid I'd up and disappear again.

My parents were making an immense effort to be more present in my life since I'd been home. We'd had a breakthrough on the day they'd come to see me in the hospital. I apologized for all the things I'd been regretting for a long time, things I thought I'd never get the opportunity to say I was sorry for. In turn, they apologized for letting too much time slip by between visits and phone calls and promised to start prioritizing family before anything else.

If there was any other good thing to come out of what happened, it was that Bree and Jacob had set aside most of their disagreements in the months that I'd been gone. It made things a little more bearable when she and Ryan would come over to visit or when we'd go out to join them for dinner.

I still hadn't told anyone about the things that had happened. It wasn't that I didn't want to...I did. But I was well aware of how crazy it all sounded. I knew they would think it was some sort of cry for help and would potentially try to have me committed. And even if they didn't, I honestly had no desire to tell Jacob anything about Demetri. He didn't need to know about the moments we had shared.

He didn't need to know that I still thought about Demetri nearly every minute of every day. He didn't need to know that it was Demetri's voice I could sometimes still swear I heard calling out for me. He didn't need to know that sometimes, in our most intimate moments, I'd see Demetri's face and imagine he was there instead. He didn't need to know that when I excused myself from the room, it was because I could feel another surge of grief coming on for the life that I never got to live with the man I'd been willing to give up everything else for.

No, he definitely didn't need to know those things.

Most days, I tried to push it all down. I had to in order to function at a basic level. I was constantly looking for new ways to distract myself from my own thoughts, but they always seemed to have a way of creeping back in. Especially at night.

I would often dream of Demetri and wake up in a puddle of tears. Sometimes, they were good dreams...visions of us sitting on the balcony of his ship as we watched the sky change colors and talked of life as we drank from our liquor-filled cups. And sometimes, they were the worst kind of dreams, the ones that had already played out in real time before my eyes. It didn't really matter what dream it was...when it was over, there was always a puddle of tears.

Jacob would try his best to console me, but there was only so much he could do, and only so many times he could tell me everything was going to be okay. Deep down, I knew things were never going to be okay again. I just had to figure out how to learn to live with that.

CHAPTER THIRTY-ONE

"Gwen!" Bree squealed as she strolled through the front doors of the banquet hall, waving excitedly to get my attention.

I laughed at her eagerness, politely squeezing through the crowd of people to go over and greet her.

"Hi, Bree," I smiled. "I'm so glad you came."

"Of course, I came! I wasn't going to miss this." She pulled me in for an embrace. "I'm so sorry we're running late; Ryan's shift ran a little over tonight."

"Oh yeah, no, I get it. Don't worry about that. It's a floating time anyway."

"You look so beautiful!" Bree exclaimed, her eyes lighting up with excitement. "Just think, only three more weeks to go and you'll officially be Mrs. Gwendolyn Jenson!"

I smiled at her enthusiasm. "I'm not going to lie, that kind of freaks me out a little bit," I joked. "And if you tell Jacob that I said that, I'll definitely deny it."

Bree laughed as she nodded in agreement. "I'm still not used to it either. I wonder exactly how long it takes before it starts to feel normal?" she teased as Ryan rolled his eyes behind her and smirked.

"Where is Jacob at anyway?" Ryan asked, searching the room filled with our wedding shower guests.

"I don't know." I turned around. "He was just over there by the buffet a few minutes ago."

"Typical." Ryan laughed. "I'll go try to find him." He leaned down to give Bree a quick kiss before stalking off.

"So, how's the party going?" she asked, glancing around the busy room.

"I'm counting down the minutes until it's over." I joked, as we walked over to an empty table nearby.

"Oh, come on, it can't be that bad." Bree laughed, pulling out the seat beside mine. "It's so beautiful in here." She looked up, admiring the twinkling lights strewn across the rustic ceiling. "Very fancy."

"I've seen fancier," I muttered.

"What's that?" She asked.

"Nothing. You know me. I don't do well in crowds. And the funny thing about wedding events is that everyone always wants to talk to the bride-to-be." I pretended to scowl.

"I remember it all too well." She smiled. "Where's your mom? I don't see her anywhere."

"She was here. She just left a little while ago actually... said she wanted to get back on the road before it got too late."

"How's she taking all of this?" Bree asked curiously, even though she already knew the answer.

My mother had made sure to express her opinions on the wedding more than a handful of times since Jacob and I had announced that we were still planning on going through with it. It wasn't because she didn't like him. In fact, my whole family loved Jacob now. He'd gotten fairly close to them during the last nine months, but because I hadn't told anyone about what had happened when I went missing, my family drew their own conclusions. My mother's was that I was kidnapped and forced to endure unspeakable trauma that I still needed to heal from. In a sense, I guess that theory wasn't too far off.

"Umm..." I laughed. "Better than a few weeks ago. So, I guess that's a good thing."

"She'll come around," Bree assured.

"Yeah. I know." I sighed, cracking my knuckles in my lap. It was a nervous tendency I'd picked up recently. "She just...she thinks it's too soon since everything happened."

"Well, it's been what, six months, right?"

"Five." I winced.

Bree's eyes narrowed as she studied my expression. "Do *you* think it's too soon?"

"Three weeks before the wedding isn't exactly an ideal time for a question such as that, Bree."

"You're right. I'm sorry," she laughed. "I think whatever decision you make is the right one. You know more than anyone else what's best for you...and I know I've had my doubts about Jacob in the past, but he's a good guy. And he really loves you."

"Thanks, Bree." I smiled. "It's kind of hot in here. I think I'm gonna go get some air."

"All right, I'll be here."

I pushed open the doors of the balcony, shutting them behind me before anyone else could conclude where I'd gone. I had reached my small talk quota for the day an hour ago, and it was all I could do not to sneak out altogether and go home.

"Not in the mood for celebrations?"

I whipped my head around at the question and felt the blood run cold through my veins.

"Cosmina!" I exclaimed. "What the hell are you...?"

Her frail frame stepped out of the shadows as she smiled at my reaction.

"It's good to see you too, child."

"That's not exactly what I was thinking. What the hell are you doing here?" I demanded.

"Months ago, in the dungeon cell, I told you something about the cursed lands. Do you remember?"

I clenched my jaw tightly, forcing down the painful memories that her mere presence brought. "I try not to remember, Cosmina."

"Ah...yes." She stepped closer, nodding her head. "I do understand. I am sorry for your loss."

I felt the familiar sting return to my eyes.

"Thought you might want a drink, Gwen," Bree announced as she pushed through the door and stepped outside.

I wiped my eyes quickly. "Thank you. I could definitely use one now."

"What's going on out here?" Bree asked as she eyed Cosmina.

"Umm...nothing," I replied as nonchalantly as I could manage. "I was just talking to...this person." I took a sip of the drink Bree had brought out.

"Do you know this person?" Bree asked.

"Yes..."

"How?" Bree's gaze darted back to me, and she looked like she was about to be sick.

"Bree, are you okay?"

"How do you know her, Gwen?" She demanded once more. I then noticed the unmistakable terror that was building behind her eyes.

Cosmina laughed loudly to herself, throwing her hand across her chest. "Oh my. Even I didn't see this coming."

"What's going on?" I asked angrily. At this point, I didn't really care who provided the answer.

Cosmina stepped forward. "So, this is where you've been hiding all these years, Gabriella Chamberlain."

CHAPTER THIRTY-TWO

The glass slipped from my hand, shattering into dozens of pieces as it hit the floor. I braced myself against the railing of the balcony as I searched to find my breath and sense of balance. The bewildered expression Bree displayed provided me with no additional comfort.

"What..." I whispered.

"Yes, child," Cosmina responded. "The missing royal you've undoubtedly heard about." Her terrifying smile was all the confirmation that I needed.

"Bree?" I asked, frantically searching her face for some sort of clarity.

"That's where you were?" Her eyes filled with tears as she stared at me in disbelief. "All that time you were gone?"

"Yes," I admitted. "I wanted to tell you; I just didn't think anyone would believe me."

"Yeah." She laughed, choking down a sob as she nodded. "I get that."

"So, wait," I shook my head, trying to comprehend everything that had just transpired in the last few minutes. "You're the lost princess?" I exclaimed.

"I suppose so." She threw her hands up sarcastically. "Surprise?"

The revelation of it all was too much to take in. How could I not have known...but how could I ever have guessed? "What the fuck is happening?" I mumbled to myself, gripping the fabric of my dress as I held my arms across my waist. I felt like I was going to vomit.

Bree's focus landed back on Cosmina. Now that her secret was out in the open, she exposed a new defiance as she faced the old witch. "Why are you here?"

"The curse is spreading, just as I said it would," Cosmina revealed, looking back in my direction. "It will soon be in Winterhaven."

"No..." I thought of how frantic Cinderella and Andrew must be. How scared they were when they talked about it with Demetri that night after dinner.

The thought of him there, sharing stories with their family, made that hole in my chest ache again.

"Isadora and I, we've been trying to find a way to stop it," Cosmina added.

I stared back at her in disbelief. "Isadora? You're working together?"

"Much has changed since you've been gone, child," she replied. "The queen is now working with Phillip. They have plans to overthrow the other kingdoms."

Phillip's name provoked an unresolved rage inside me. "He's still alive?" I scowled.

"Yes, and he's more unhinged than ever before," Cosmina said.

"Debatable," Bree interjected.

"I need you to come back with me, child." Cosmina turned to face me. "My visions that I shared with you those many months ago, the ones that had not yet come to pass...they're growing stronger."

"No." I backed away from her, crossing my arms again. "I can never go back there."

"You suffered a great loss..." Cosmina acknowledged.

Bree's eyes flashed up at me.

"Your pirate, he wanted to keep you safe. He made an unbreakable vow, one that secured your protection. That's why the portal opened on the night that he was killed—because your life was in grave danger."

"Oh, Gwen..." Bree whispered, tears filling her eyes.

"But his vow was not fulfilled," Cosmina cut in.

"What do you mean?" I asked.

"I upheld my part of the deal. I opened a portal for you to escape. But when the prince stabbed him, he had not yet had the opportunity to carry out his end of the deal."

"Phillip killed him?" Bree fumed.

"Phillip did many unspeakable things," I confirmed before turning my focus back on Cosmina. "What are you trying to say?"

"What I mean to say is that there is much power that lives in an unbreakable vow."

I shook my head in confusion.

"What she's saying, Gwen, is that he can be brought back," Bree explained.

"How...how would that even be possible?" I stammered, struggling to keep my composure.

"There is a place in our world where such things are possible," Cosmina said. "...under certain circumstances."

"Like an unbreakable vow?" I asked.

"Like an unbreakable vow," Cosmina echoed.

I fought back the lump that was forming in my throat. "You could really bring him back?"

"Not me, child. But perhaps you could," Cosmina answered, her green gaze piercing straight through me.

I looked to Bree for some sort of signal...a warning against the thrill that was already building inside of me at the thought of seeing Demetri alive again.

"Cosmina's not lying," she confirmed, glancing back and forth between me and the witch. "It's not always possible, but it's been done before."

"What's the condition?" I asked Cosmina.

"Your help," she replied. "A small price to pay for the one you love."

"If you go, I'm going with you," Bree declared.

"No, Bree, it's too dangerous."

"I lived there most of my life, Gwen. I know it's dangerous, but I also know I could help you. You're not going through this alone again," she said, reaching for her phone.

"What about Ryan? You can't just leave him here." And Jacob...oh God, Jacob. Flashes of him and Demetri soared through my mind as I reeled with regret for a decision that I hadn't yet made.

"I'm taking care of that right now," she replied, holding the phone to her ear and quickly mumbling something to him as he picked up on the other end. Her eyes darted back and forth between me and Cosmina as though she didn't trust either one of us enough to leave us out here alone.

"Phillip will kill you," I argued once she hung up.

Bree placed her hand on my arm. "I know how to deal with Phillip," she assured, locking her tenacious gaze with mine. "I'm going with you."

"We must hurry. Someone is coming," Cosmina urged. "Do we have a deal, child?" She extended her hand in an offer as the familiar purple haze began to drift across the balcony.

Voices roared to life as the doors to the banquet hall behind us opened.

I needed to talk to Jacob, but there was no time left to think. It had to be now. I grabbed hold of her hand. "Yes." I nodded. "We have a deal."

A fierce wind howled, and Bree's grip tightened around my arm. I squeezed my eyes together as a blinding burst of light flashed and carried us away...back to the Isles of Everwood.

ABOUT THE AUTHOR

Arielle was born and raised in North Carolina, where she still resides when not exploring the imaginary worlds inside her head. As a wife, mother, and avid fairytale fan, Arielle enjoys spending time with her family, writing stories in the quiet moments (however few and far between they are), attempting to paint pretty pictures, and having Disney movie marathons.

Arielle has always been inspired by the magic that lives inside the timeless stories of her childhood and contributes her decision to write her debut novel, *Disenchanted*, to the dreamy nostalgia that those stories sparked.

To keep up with Arielle and all the latest news and updates regarding future releases, you can visit her website at: https://ariellesnowauthor.wixsite.com/asnow

A NOTE FROM THE AUTHOR

Dear reader,

First and foremost, thank you. Your support truly means the world to me. I hope you enjoyed reading *Disenchanted* as much as I enjoyed writing it. While we've reached the end of this book, it's certainly not the end of Gwen's story. New adventures are on the horizon, and if you'd like to come along for the ride, I invite you to visit my website for updates. If you did enjoy the read and you have a moment to spare, I hope you'll also consider dropping a quick review to help other readers decide if *Disenchanted* would be a magical fit for them. Thank you!

https://ariellesnowauthor.wixsite.com/asnow